A

By
Kim Holden

Published by Do Epic, LLC

ISBN: 978-0-9911402-1-3

Cover image photography by Andi Hando
Cover design by Brandon Hando
Editing by Monica Parpal

For
B., P., Mom and Dad
I love you

PART I

Chapter 1
Invariably my story begins as it ends

"Hi, my name's Veronica."

"Hi, I'm Dimitri." His voice is quiet, but confident.

There's something vaguely familiar about this moment. Almost like déjà vu, like I've dreamt it, or seen a similar scene in a movie once. Classic boy-meets-girl I suppose, only slightly watered down to merely perplexing familiarity. Strangely, it bothers me, but I try to let it go.

Shaking my head slightly, I push through, gathering my thoughts and my books. "So Dimitri, did you just move here?"

He's early. And if there's one thing I've learned about teenage boys, it's that they're never early. For anything. *Ever*. I'm already suspicious.

He waits politely for me to grab my notebook, books, and cell phone before he answers. "Yes," is all he says with a small smile that at first glance appears shy. Upon a return glance—that's right I take a second, confirmatory peek—I realize he looks cocky.

"Where are you from?" I ask, suddenly distracted by the amount of stuff I'm trying to put in my bag. Why do I have so much stuff?

He answers, "Texas," but I'm not looking at him. I'm still trying to retrieve my brain that I've apparently dropped in my messenger bag—somewhere near the abyss at the bottom.

Abandoning the brain retrieval mission I return for another glance and aim for eye contact this time. "Quite a change. Do you like it here, Dimitri from Texas?" I'm doing my best to show some interest now.

Eye contact is a success.

"I don't know yet," is all he says. His expression hard to read.

Eye contact just took an uncomfortable turn. He's staring at me.

5

Intently staring at me.

It's purposeful.

And a touch unsettling.

And is now officially a staring contest …

… that I promptly and voluntarily lose. My eyebrows rise as I look away and toward the door. "Okay then … " I need an escape. This is going to be excruciatingly awkward. He's barely speaking and now he's staring. And I'm paired up with this guy for the next two days? Wonderful.

I'm a member of National Honor Society. Not that I think of it as much of an honor, at least not the way others do. To me it's more like an obligation. You see I'm the type of person that puts a lot of pressure on herself. I have high expectations and expect a lot of myself. I follow the rules and try to do everything the "right" way. If I want to get into a good university, being in Honor Society is one of many "rights" on a long list. It's a thorn in my side. Sometimes— by which I really mean unfortunately all-too-often—when something turns into an obligation, it loses its appeal. This is the case with Honor Society. I'll do it, but it doesn't mean I'll like it.

As part of the Obligation Society gig, members are required to volunteer twenty hours each semester. Don't get me wrong—volunteering is awesome. I do it often and I enjoy it. But enjoyment is somewhat tainted when it's born out of requirement. Even more so when our options are so thoroughly limited: churches (I'm not atheist or anything, I just don't attend), school (I'm already here enough), animal shelters (this is the redeemer on the list), and two local businesses (that I suspect are somehow in bed with school administration). I mean, come on? What about homeless shelters, blood drives, nursing homes? Would it kill them to be a bit more civic minded? Clearly Honor Society needs an enema; a new sponsor wouldn't hurt either.

Anyway … I'll climb down off my soapbox now. Back to Dimitri.

Pairing up with a new kid for the first two days of school fit the volunteer criteria and hypothetically seemed easy enough, but this is showing all the signs of becoming a painful experience. I should've gone to the animal shelter like I did last semester.

So, for the next two days I'll dutifully act as Dimitri's seeing-eye dog. I'm required to give him a tour of the school and escort him to each class. Basically to make sure he doesn't get lost. It would be a stretch to call our school big and it's definitely not overwhelming. A half-day and I'm sure he'll want to be free of me. The old ball and chain doesn't have pleasant connotations even in the best of times. And so far this is not the best of times. It seems either I'm not making a very good first impression or he just isn't that friendly. For the sake of my sanity, and partially my ego, I'm leaning toward the latter. It's strange; usually I get along with people very well, especially guys.

He's already walking toward the door of the school office that leads out into the main hallway, so I quickly follow. Wait, I'm supposed to be the one leading, right?

He holds the door for me. "After you." He's looking down at his shoes. Though I'm thankful the staring has ceased, I note that this intentional avoidance does not appear to be out of shyness, but arrogance.

On the other hand, holding the door open for me is impressive, and hints that this boy may have some manners. Another thing I've learned about teenage boys is that most of them do not possess manners, let alone any actual working knowledge of them.

I decide to reserve judgment. For now, the jury remains out on Dimitri from Texas.

We enter the hallway and he walks slowly beside me. Beside me may not be entirely accurate. The hallway is wide, but he's so close his arm brushes mine several times. *Too close.* Have they not heard about personal space in Texas? Maybe I should clue him in? After all, the halls are almost empty due to the fact that he's arrived almost forty-five minutes early. Fifteen would have been acceptable, but forty-five? Forty-five is a tad excessive. And by a tad, I mean *beyond* excessive.

The grand tour is likewise a tad (see above) extensive, given the amount of time we have to work with … through

7

... around ... yes we manage to cover every angle. I point out all the essentials: the gym, art building, lunchroom, math, science and English wings, as well as the restrooms. He says nothing, just listens, though he seems preoccupied or distracted.

As we finish up the tour, the normal congestion and hum of the school is ramping up. I've always enjoyed school and the excitement that has thus far been absent from my much-anticipated first day of senior year emerges as I see familiar faces. I smile.

"We should find your locker," I tell him. I'm expecting another short answer and he doesn't disappoint. He just nods ever so slightly.

My smile vanishes as quickly as it appeared. Am I boring him? Because at this point, he's kind of pissing me off. I look at him, widening my eyes as if to say, "You've got to be kidding me."

The corner of his mouth twitches toward a smile. Is he mocking me? I'm officially pissed off.

His locker turns out to be three down from mine. Isn't that convenient? Not that he'll probably ever speak to me again after tomorrow. Hell, he technically isn't speaking to me now so what am I worried about?

I peel off my jacket and put some of the stuff from my over-burdened messenger bag in my locker. I planned to have time to decorate the inside of my locker door with some photos and decals before he arrived this morning, but I'm certainly not going to do it with him watching. Oddly, he makes me feel self-conscious. And that bothers me more than anything because I usually don't care what other people think about me. I like who I am. I always try to do the "right" thing, but that's more about not letting myself down than meeting someone else's expectations. I don't look for confirmation or validation from anyone—except maybe my parents.

"Ready?" I ask as I shut the door of my locker.

"Ready," he answers quietly.

"Let me see your schedule again. I really should've made a copy of it before we left the office this morning. I guess I can just write it down." I'm irritated with myself for overlooking the obvious and for letting him fluster me. I'm usually very organized.

"Keep it," he says as he hands it over.

His nonchalance is irritating. "You'll need this later, newbie." I hate the word newbie. It's condescending. But he's been making me feel anxious all morning and I suddenly don't mind coming off as rude.

"No, I'll remember," he says, tapping his finger to his temple. There's that odd, small smile again.

I reach out and take it. "Okay, I guess I can give it back to you tomorrow afternoon when you're on your own."

"I won't need it. *I* have a very good memory." He's still smiling.

God, he's smug. "We'll see. Let's go, Mr. Memory. I don't want to be held responsible for your first tardy." An authoritative tone has managed to weave its way through the sarcasm.

Again, before I realize it, he's walking ahead of me. To my surprise, we're actually heading in the right direction.

"Where do you think you're going?" I demand. I'm surprised at his willingness to take off on his own. Most people are completely overwhelmed by their first day at a new school, but he seems to be in complete control, relaxed even.

"To Chemistry, of course," he says with a wink.

Did he really just wink at me? It stops me in my tracks. Is he teasing? Is he flirting? Whatever he's doing my heart just skipped a beat. And I'm not sure I like it. It feels like betrayal of my better judgment.

"Come on," he says, motioning over his shoulder for me to catch up. "I don't want to be held responsible for *your* first tardy." He's ahead of me, but I swear I hear him smiling, taunting me, as he throws my own words back at me.

The science wing is just down the hall from our lockers, so it takes all of twenty seconds to get there. Confident I'm following, Dimitri never looks back to see if I'm even behind him. I intentionally trail at a distance.

"I'll be back when class is over," I call out. "I have math this period and it's just in the next wing. It will only take me a minute to get here after the bell." I'm almost daring him to wait for me. Why am I being so bossy? And what's with the extensive explanation?

"In a bit then, Veronica," he says just loud enough that I can hear, as he reaches for the door handle. He never turns around.

Math is a nice surprise, and a good distraction from the strange morning I've had. Mr. White is teaching calculus this year. I had him for Trigonometry last year and I liked him a lot. He's older, maybe 55, and has thinning gray hair. His demeanor's quiet and calm, but he really seems to care about us. He has kind eyes and wears a perpetual smile. He takes time to explain anything we don't understand and is obviously excited about math. Students lucky enough to take his class often become his fans for life.

I have a few friends in class, too—friends that I didn't see much this summer. John, who's painfully shy and a little nerdy ... okay, a lot nerdy (but who says that's a bad thing?), is super nice, and has the world's most innocent face hiding under a head full of curly black hair. John's innocent to the point of being naïve, but I can't fault him for it. It's a relief when compared to the majority of my other male friends. John's the type of person that you know would never laugh at you even if you shared your most embarrassing secret with him. John, unfortunately, is one of those kids who's never quite fit in. It's not that he's bullied. To bully someone you have to notice him first. John doesn't get noticed. He blends into the background and people look right past him. This is a shame, because they're missing out. John's awesome. And he bakes killer banana bread.

Monica's also in my calculus class. She's almost the exact opposite of John, aside from the fact that she's also unbelievably intelligent and kind. She's tall and thin with long brown hair and huge brown eyes. She's captain of the

10

basketball team and one of those rare people who is very beautiful, very popular, *and* very smart. (When the planets align perfectly during a leap year one is born). I met Monica sophomore year when we both endured a semester of American History wrought with many, many bad Hollywood movies (shown not as a supplement, but a substitute to actual teaching) coupled with daily fire-and-brimstone, highly editorialized, creative interpretations of actual events from our teacher, Mr. Ranier. Mr. Ranier didn't return the following semester. We heard he was on "sabbatical." We also heard the following year he moved to the Deep South and not only started his own new church, but a new religion. Anyway, after that bonding experience with Monica, I believe she and I will indeed be friends for life.

Let me be clear: Mr. White is no Mr. Ranier.

Mr. White talks a little bit about his summer vacation to the East Coast and then gets right into the first lesson. Math has never been my favorite subject, but it comes easily to me. I'm trying to focus on the lesson, but about fifteen minutes in he's lost my interest and my mind begins to drift. For some reason, I can't stop thinking about my morning with Dimitri. How on earth did he aggravate me so much? I'm generally pretty laid back, but I was so keyed up after five minutes with him I wanted to run from the building screaming. And then the wink—what was that about?

The bell rings and summons me back to reality. I quickly jot down the homework assignment and jam my book in my bag while making my way to the door. My daydreaming's delayed my departure and now I'm apparently the last person in line to exit.

"Hey Veronica!" John's waiting at the door for me, a big, sweet smile on his face.

I can't help but return his smile. "Hey Brother John, what's up?" Seeing him standing there smiling at me takes me back to kindergarten. I feel five years old again.

"So, what do you think? Is calculus going to be hard?" There's earnest excitement, or maybe it's panic, in his voice. With John it's hard to tell.

11

He's definitely looking for reassurance. "Hard for me? Yes. Hard for you? No." For his sake I'm trying to hide my amusement.

"You know if you ever need a tutor— " He's looking down at his scuffed white tennis shoes as if he's embarrassed to offer.

I interrupt him before he can finish, "Thank you, John, very kind of you to offer assistance to a damsel in distress. Always the gentleman. You really should have lived in medieval times; you would've made a damn fine knight." He's blushing. "You'll be the first person I call on, mon frère. By the way, how's your mom? I heard she was in the hospital."

"She's doing fine. Cholelothiasis."

"Cholelo-what-sis?" John's always been obsessed with the all things medical, especially the terminology. Medical school will be a breeze for him.

"Gallstones," he clarifies.

"Oh right, *that* cholelothiasis. I'm glad she's okay." I smile and pat him on the arm as I squeeze past. Turning the corner heading toward the science wing—and my obligation—I call back loudly over my shoulder, "Hasta la pasta, John."

"See ya, Veronica," he calls back. He's smiling. I can hear it.

It's been several minutes since the bell rang. Dimitri's probably already gone. As I approach, the crowd's thinning out and I see him standing with his back to me leaning against the wall across from his classroom. A few steps closer and I notice he isn't alone. Chloe Murphy is talking to him. I take that back. She isn't talking—she's shamelessly flirting. She's standing very close, though flashing back to the personal space issue I encountered with Dimitri earlier, I decide he probably doesn't mind.

Chloe's pretty. Stereotypically pretty: petite, blond hair, blue eyes, big boobs, blah, blah, blah. She works her looks

12

hard, probably because she's been blessed with the IQ of an avocado and has nothing else to offer. Turns out teenage boys are into dumb blonds. Who knew?

Boys can be so stupid.

Predictably, she always treats boys badly. She chews them up and spits them out. In her world, guys are disposable. She's never come remotely close to gaining my respect. I've always hated her. Not that I'm jealous, I'm not. I don't have time for jealousy. It's exhausting and pointless. Chloe is just … mean.

"Sorry to keep you waiting," I apologize quietly through gritted teeth. The good mood John blessed me with thirty seconds ago is long gone. I clear my throat and add, "Especially given the stellar choice of company." I'm not sure he even hears me.

But he does. Dimitri simultaneously steps back from Chloe and turns around to face me. He's clearly not annoyed by the interruption. This both surprises and relaxes me—a little. Chloe leans to the side to glare at me. If looks could kill I'd be struck dead where I stand.

"I was beginning to think you forgot about me," he says, relief evident in his voice.

"No such luck, Texas Ranger," I mutter.

"Bye, Dimitri," Chloe says in a pouty voice, batting her eyelashes. She brushes up against him like a goddamn cat as she walks by.

Head down, eyes focused on rifling through my bag looking for Dimitri's schedule, I shout at her in my head as she walks by. "Slut!" I want to scream. God, I'd love to punch her right in her pretty little face. Just once. I'd never do it of course; I don't have it in me. My body, though physically suited, is pacifistic. My mouth, on the other hand, though not prone to pre-emptive strikes, defends stupendously when provoked. Lucky for her the two don't work in concert.

"Just a bit of advice," I mutter. "That sort of physical contact with Chloe Murphy should require a full body condom, lest you contract something extremely difficult—if not impossible—to get rid of." I can see the corner of his mouth rise as I continue the mad search through my bag.

After several seconds of watching me aggressively attack my book bag's contents he says calmly, "Photography."

"I'm sorry, what?" I ask though I'm not looking at him and I'm not listening either … obviously. I'm still focused on the stupid whore. And it's distracting me from the task at hand, finding his schedule. I'm annoyed with myself at this point. I hate feeling unprepared and unorganized. "Oh, here it is," I say as I look up at him, pulling a folded paper out of my bag and waving it in the air.

He looks at me patiently, the small, amused smile on his face as he leans toward me and whispers, "My next class. It's photography."

I unfold the paper and scan my finger down the page. It's not until I see the words on the paper that his words finally register in my head.

"It's photography," I whisper. My face blisters red. "I'm sorry." I don't know if the words are even audible, but I catch his acknowledging, forgiving nod out of the corner of my eye. I can't look up at him. I can be such an ass sometimes.

I turn and he walks closely at my side. I don't mind as much this time. We don't say anything as we walk out the doors and across the courtyard. He opens the door for me and follows me into the art building.

"Thanks," I whisper. My face is still blazing and I can't look at him. "The photography studio is the third door on the left." I point down the hall and turn to exit.

I run all the way to French class. The bell rings just as I reach for the door.

"Excusez-moi, I'm sorry," I say quietly to Madame Lemieux. I seem to be saying that a lot this morning.

She smiles back. "Bonjour, Veronica. Take your seat." She gestures to the empty seat near the center of the room.

This is my third year of French with Madame Lemieux. A foreign language is required for college admission, which is the initial reason I signed up my sophomore year. I was inexplicably drawn to French. It seemed the most romantic of my three choices. What I didn't anticipate was that I would fall completely in love with France and the language. I constantly daydream of someday looking out at Paris from the top of the Eiffel Tower under a full moon in the arms of the love of my life, or walking with him along the Seine at twilight near the end of summer when the air is still warm. Someday …

Madame Lemieux spent the summer in the Lorraine region of France visiting extended family. She shares dozens of photos. Each one accompanied by a wonderful story. She's an animated storyteller and can make even the most mundane traditions sound exciting. I'm so engrossed in the lesson that I jump in my seat when the bell rings. It startles me. It seems as if I just sat down and it's already over.

"Merci. Au revoir." Madame Lemieux's singsong voice bids us farewell.

French class propelled me back into my usual happy mood. I take a few deep breaths and vow to keep it going as I head back to the art building to meet Dimitri. My embarrassment has subsided.

As I step outside into the courtyard the sun shines on my face and warms me. The clouds that masked the sky earlier as I drove to school this morning have passed. The gray's been replaced by brilliant blue. Looks like the weatherman was right; it is going to be a sunny day after all. It's going to be a good day.

I smile as I open the door to the art building. I look down the hall toward the photography lab, but he isn't there. Did I miss him waiting outside for me? I turn to walk back toward the door, but as I turn I see him standing near a photography display opposite me. He's leaning up against the wall, arms crossed, staring at me. A smile slowly lights up his eyes.

"French or English?" He's trying, for the most part unsuccessfully, to stifle a laugh as he walks to meet me.

"Pardon me?" I'm confused now, but still smiling. I remind myself that it's going to be a good day.

He doesn't speak again until he's standing within a foot of me. He pauses, smiles again like the cat that caught the canary, and repeats himself, "French or English? Which class have you just come from?"

I'm caught off guard, but answer without hesitating, "French."

He nods, a look of satisfaction painted across his face. The smile grows wider. Obviously he's the only one in on the joke. "We'd better get going. I don't want to be held responsible for your *second* tardy, too."

I stand there dumbfounded. He holds the door open, waiting patiently. "After you?" He poses it as a question, gesturing toward the courtyard.

I should ask him how he knew. I want to. But I can't find the words. My mind's racing a hundred miles an hour. Did I share my schedule with him this morning? No, we barely exchanged ten words. I'm sure I didn't.

"Veronica ... are you coming?" His voice is slow and deliberate, but light. It jolts me back and without thinking, my body moves out the door, though my mind slips out somewhere along the way. I'm fairly certain it's still back inside the building ... puzzled.

We walk silently to and from our next two classes. Psychology and English are a blur, which is too bad, because English is my other favorite subject. I mechanically take notes in both classes. I can always review them in study hall to find out what I've missed.

I look at Dimitri's schedule as I walk to the gym to retrieve him, tracing down the list with my finger: third period Spanish, fourth period P.E., fifth period lunch, sixth period study hall. I stop. No movement, unless you count my heart that's now relentlessly slamming against my ribcage. I stand there holding the paper securely with both hands now, looking at it in horror. My stomach somersaults. He and I have the next two periods together. How am I going to face him for the next two hours? Wait, it's not like we have to eat lunch together, right? Am I obligated as his guide for the day? It's the polite thing to do, but is it the "right" thing to do? Do I ask him to join me? I don't want to give him the wrong impression and I honestly don't want to suffer an extra hour of the embarrassment that's sure to come.

I suddenly realize I'm standing completely still in the middle of a very busy hallway carrying on an internal conversation with myself. Though the conversation is internal, at least I hope I haven't said anything out loud. The way this morning's been going, I very well may have. I'm sure the expressions on my face revealed every emotion that went along with the dialogue. My forehead pinches together, and as I begin to move my feet, I whisper to myself, "Calm down, it's going to be a good day." This I do say aloud, because reassurance is necessary. That and it's just easier to convince myself if I hear it.

I try to clear my mind as I step through the double doors into the sunlight and walk across the courtyard to the gym. The heat of the day is comforting. The sky remains clear, the same brilliant shade of blue it had been earlier. I walk slowly soaking it in as I breathe deeply and steadily. My eyes are closed and my heart rate returns to a semblance of normalcy. I've walked this path a thousand times and can literally do it with my eyes closed. Besides there's no one in the courtyard—it's always empty. Most people prefer to walk indoors.

Our school is made up of four buildings: the gym and athletic facilities, the art and performing arts studio, the cafeteria and auditorium, and the academic classrooms and staff offices. Corridors connect all the buildings so you don't actually have to go outside to get from one building to the next, a handy thing to have in the winter since we do live in Colorado. The buildings and corridors surround the courtyard on all sides. It's a long grassy area slightly larger than a tennis court. There's a tree and a flower garden. It's a sanctuary in the middle of the chaos. I take every advantage to be out in it when it's warm. It's kind of like my little secret.

I reach the gym and see Dimitri through the glass doors. He's talking to a guy I've never seen at school before, but he looks familiar. He's shorter than Dimitri, a full head shorter, 5'6", maybe 5' 7". His hair is fair, almost white, and hangs just past his shoulders. It's wavy and intentionally messy. It's way better than girl hair; it's model hair. Guys having better-than-girl hair is so unfair. His eyes appear dark from a distance. His chest is broad and he's definitely muscular, it shows through his fitted shirt. His clothes are the same type the other guys at school wear, but are obviously higher-end. He holds himself confidently and his stance reminds me of someone. He doesn't look arrogant, but unapproachable. He's definitely going to get a lot of attention from the girls around here, but I wonder who'll be brave enough to try? My money's on Chloe Murphy. The thought of it brings up a strange feeling inside me. Nothing like jealousy—I don't feel attracted to him in that way. He's nice looking, but he's not at all my type. I like tall, dark, and skinny. Always have, always will. The feeling I have is more protective. The same way I feel about my closest friends. Weird …

I watch them talk. They can't see me from where I stand, so I take advantage of being inconspicuous. And it finally dawns on me why the other boy looks so familiar. It's like he and Dimitri are looking in a mirror. Despite the extreme height difference they both stand tall, unquestionably confident. Physically they don't look alike at all, but their mannerisms and hand gestures are similar. They are obviously at ease with each other. These two know each other well.

I shift my eyes to Dimitri. I've been so focused on myself and my obligation that I haven't taken the time to fully size him up until this moment. He's tall, at least six feet. He's taken off the long sleeved, button-up shirt he was wearing earlier to reveal a fitted T-shirt that shows off his physique nicely. His face and arms are bronzed, like he's been out in the sun all summer. He's skinny—not scrawny skinny, just really lean and fit skinny. Just *right* skinny. I *love* just right skinny. His hair's the color of dark chocolate, not short or long, but somewhere in between. It's perfect. Not perfect because he spends a lot of time on it though, he just has an incredible head of hair. He wears dark burgundy glasses. They're rectangular and stylish, but not the type any of our classmates wear. His clothes are different, too, a mix of different styles, nothing expensive or flashy, but neat. He looks artsy or European. I get the impression he doesn't even have to put effort into looking this cool … and that somehow makes it *so much better*. The height, the hair, the build—he's tall, dark, and skinny …

I've come to the conclusion that he would look good in anything, or nothing, I imagine. Okay, time to rein in my imagination; I'm drifting.

Now that I've actually taken the time to notice him, I realize that he's quite possibly the prettiest guy I've ever seen. Guys are rarely pretty or beautiful. Handsome is an inadequate description in his case. He's definitely handsome, but he teeters over into the beautiful range—off-the-charts beautiful, but in a very manly way. How has this fact escaped me all morning? My god, he's lovely …

The blond boy looks toward me and grins slightly. It's the same small smile I've already seen on Dimitri's face this morning, but it's warm. I can't help but smile back, feeling the protective, motherly instinct rise up inside me again. He puts his fist out toward Dimitri. They tap knuckles and Dimitri turns around to come outside.

Watching the two of them has put me in some strange calm state. It was wrong to stand and watch them, like some sort of snoop, but it didn't feel intrusive. It wasn't like I was watching two strangers, but exactly the opposite. I felt like I was watching old friends. It's eerily familiar.

"How was P.E.?" My words come out sounding more like myself than anything else I've said to him all morning. The edge is gone. We talk as we walk back to our lockers in the main building.

"It was good. Mr. Cannon seems alright. It should be fun, I suppose," he says reflectively.

"Did Mr. Cannon start with soccer or flag football this semester?" Before he can answer, I continue, "I took his class my sophomore year. I remember playing basketball at the end of the semester because it was too cold to go outside, but I can't remember if we started with soccer or flag football." I love sports and I'm pretty athletic. I was quite a tomboy when I was younger. I preferred to play with boys and they accepted me, and me alone, as one of their own. I don't think I had a friend that was a girl until I was in sixth grade. I was always captain when we picked teams for recess in elementary school. I'm still friends with all of them, too. Guys, I learned early on, are much easier to relate to and be friends with. They aren't petty. They don't play games and they're always honest. They are the brothers I never had.

"Soccer. You like sports don't you? I bet you take P.E. every semester, even though it's not required." This should've come out as more of a question, but it didn't. He says it as a statement, just something he already knows to be true.

"Yeah, I do like sports." I stop and think about his last statement. I *have* taken P.E. every semester even though we are only required to take it for two. I've never really thought about it. I just automatically enroll, kind of like French or English. "And yeah, now that you mention it, I do take P.E. every semester." I laugh at myself as I say it, not because it's funny necessarily, but because a complete stranger has just pointed out the obvious. But how did he know? I don't look like the hard-core, sporty girls that live in sweats and running shoes. I always dress fairly nice and girly, thanks to my mom. She loves to shop. I wear a little make-up and spend too much time on my hair—hardly your typical jock.

He holds the door again for me as we enter the main building.

"Thank you. So, you have lunch this period?" I ask, not offering that I also have lunch.

"And you?" He's looking at me … at my eyes.

Ugh, I'm not going to get out of this one, am I? I can't lie; he'll see it written all over my face. Honestly (no pun intended), lying is too much work; that coupled with the fact that I'm utterly horrible at it, so I don't bother. Even if I did he'd just find out eventually, so I confess, "Yeah, I do," though it's not as painful saying it as I thought it would be.

"What are our options?" He's still looking at me.

"*Our* options?" Does he mean our as in the student body, our as in the two of us, or our as in just him (an "our" variation on the royal we)? I wait for his answer, for clarification, suddenly hoping he's referring to the two of us. This is crazy.

"I *mean* do I have to eat in the cafeteria? May I leave campus?" His expression changes though he's still smiling. He's looking at me like he can hear every word running through my mind.

"Oh, of course. Option one is eating in the cafeteria, though I have to warn you that you'd be taking your life into your own hands. And I don't think I could live with myself or the proverbial blood on my hands resulting from the recommendation of your last supper. So let's forget that's even an option. Option two is eating off campus. There are a couple of places within a mile or two." I'm still not sure what to think of this guy, but I wouldn't subject my worst enemy to cafeteria food. Besides, I have to admit he's kind of growing on me … and not just because he's good looking.

We stop in front of our lockers and the conversation ends. He opens his quickly, puts his books and P.E. clothes away, and shuts the door before I manage to find the small piece of paper my combination is written on. Man, my short-term memory sucks. I open my locker and empty my bag of books—everything except my notebook—and grab my lunch sack to stuff it in my bag. I haven't heard him leave, but assume he has. It's quiet. I rearrange a few more things and hang the mirror, a few photos, and a sticker with my favorite band's logo on it on the inside of the door. I shut the door and involuntarily jump back, my hand to my chest, when I see Dimitri still standing there, looking at me.

"Holy mother of—," I shout. "You scared the hell out of me. I thought you left five minutes ago." My heart's attempting to pound itself free of my chest.

He's standing with his back to his locker three down from mine. His arms are crossed against his chest. He's waiting patiently. He lets out a quiet laugh, making it clear he thinks it's funny that he's nearly given me a heart attack. "Easy there, I didn't mean to startle you."

"It's okay." My heart is beginning to slow down and I can't help but laugh. "Still weighing your options, huh?"

"Well, as tempting as the cafeteria sounds ... I think I'll pass. The thought of you left to mourn my death shrouded in all that guilt is far too much to bear." He mockingly clutches his heart.

"That would be tragic." I deadpan.

"Tragic," he agrees and then he shrugs, "And I don't have a car today, so it looks like I'm out of options. I think I'll just grab a soda and a bag of chips from the vending machine." The laughter's died away, but it lingers playfully in his voice.

"I'm just going outside to eat in the courtyard. You can come ... with me ... if you want to." My voice is noticeably quieter as the last few words escape. Did I actually just invite him to join me for lunch?

No need to ask twice apparently. "I'll meet you out there," he blurts and turns to jog down the hall toward the vending machines.

I head out and sit on the bench next to the flower garden. I usually sit under the maple tree, but I can't resist the sunshine today. The flowers smell amazing and won't be around much longer before they die off to cold temperatures. The courtyard is empty, as always. It's so peaceful and quiet here. I open my lunch sack and remember I made myself a tuna salad sandwich. It's one of my favorite sandwiches, though I don't usually have the time to make it. I was up extra early this morning though. I unwrap it and open my mouth to take a bite as he walks up.

"Is this seat taken?" He asks politely, though I get the feeling that he would sit down regardless of the answer.

"Wide open. You can sit with me if you don't mind answering a few questions." I'm beginning to feel much more comfortable with him than I ever imagined I would. If you'd have asked me at 7:30, or even 10:30 this morning, I would've bet money that he would've ditched his guide by now and probably wouldn't even acknowledge me if he passed me in the hall. And yet, here we are eating lunch together in the courtyard, seemingly enjoying ourselves.

"Me first: what are you eating?" His nose wrinkles up and his face wears an expression of disgust. "Because if that

22

has mayonnaise in it I'm going to have to excuse myself to the other side of the courtyard. I have a nose like a bloodhound and an unparalleled gag reflex."

"That's an unfortunate couple."

"You're telling me."

"It's tuna salad. Do you want half?" I offer, unable to tell if he's serious or not.

The near dry heave serves as confirmation. He scoots to the end of the bench. At what appears to be a safe distance he rejoins the conversation, "I'll pass. I never could figure out how you, I mean people, eat that stuff. It's disgusting." The words are harsh, but his tone isn't.

"You don't know what you're missing," I throw back at him, in the same mocking tone.

"Afraid I do. There was a time, and I shudder at the thought of it, that I used to eat," he swallows hard, "and enjoy mayonnaise. But after a fantastic and colorful episode of food poisoning a long time ago, I can't even stomach the thought of it."

I can see by the look on his face that he truly recalls something unpleasant. "I had no idea a simple, yet tasty, condiment could be so repelling. I'll eat quickly." The taunting subsides and my voice softens and becomes serious, apologetic, "And while I have your attention I want to apologize for my behavior this morning. I'm usually not so moody ... or bossy ... or whatever." I exhale, searching for the words, "What I mean is, though I can be an ass sometimes, I really am a pretty nice person. I'm sorry for the way I acted." Apologies are usually much more difficult for me. I don't like admitting when I'm wrong. I'm stubborn like my dad that way. Still, it's easy to talk to Dimitri now.

He nods and flashes a beautiful smile. "Apology accepted. Now what are your questions?"

"This has been bugging me all morning. When we were in the art building, why did you ask me if I'd just come from French or English class?" I'm brave at first but feel silly by the time I get around to the actual question.

Matter-of-factly, he answers, "Because you looked so happy." He has the same look on his face now that he had

23

earlier when he'd asked the question. Like it's some inside joke, though I have no idea what he's talking about. He can see his answer has thoroughly confused me.

"I'm not following you, so enlighten me oh-wise-one. How did you even know I took French?"

"I saw your book this morning in the office when you were putting it in your bag. I'm not psychic, Veronica." He rolls his eyes. "And everyone is required to take English." He's already anticipated my next question. He says it as though it's so obvious anyone could've figured it out.

"Okay, I forgot about that. I'm actually surprised you even remember what books I had." He's consistently, continually, perplexingly, always one step ahead of me.

"I have a very good memory," he interrupts, tapping his temple with his finger again.

"Yeah, I guess so. It's Olympian. You've proven that today. But, that still doesn't answer my question," I persist. "How did you know, based on my *mood,* that I'd just come from French or English?"

"They're your favorite subjects, aren't they?" He has this strange way of making questions sound more like statements.

And suddenly I don't want to answer. Where is this going? But I succumb to curiosity—which killed the cat, and will quite possibly kill Veronica as well—and I proceed, "Yeah, so ... " I sound like a defeated child who isn't getting her way.

He sits back against the bench, takes a long drink and begins looking around the courtyard, subtly, yet unquestionably, indicating the conversation is over.

Not so fast I think. Each word comes out softly, slowly, deliberately, and hopefully persuasively, "How did you know?" I'm pleading now. "Please tell me."

He looks at me and for the first time I notice his unusual eyes. I can't decide at first what color they are. They looked blue at first glance, but with the sun bouncing off them I realize they're gray. I don't think I've seen anyone with gray eyes before, at least not like this. They're dark and stormy, beautiful. Mesmerizing.

His smile and voice are gentle now. "That is my secret ... for now."

I wait a moment to absorb, or try to absorb, what he's just said. I look away from him at the art building in the distance. I can't decide whether I am posing the question to him or myself and it comes out sounding that way too, barely a whisper, "You really aren't going to tell me, are you?" The defeat is evident in my voice.

"No. You'll figure it out ... someday. I hope." The gentle smile remains. Maybe I'm imagining it, but it's as if he isn't talking to me, but trying to convince himself.

I give up and finish my sandwich slowly. We sit in what should be uncomfortable silence for a few minutes. It isn't uncomfortable though. Just the opposite—it's strangely comfortable sitting next this mysterious stranger who knows too much about me.

Dimitri finally breaks the silence after he's finished his chips, "So, what was your other question?" He looks over at me only after he completes the question, tilting his head, genuine curiosity in his expression.

It takes me a few seconds to remember that I even had another question. "Mmm ... oh yeah, who was that you were talking to after P.E.?"

"Muscly bugger, blond flowing locks, nice dresser ... ?" The taunting is thick; he's obviously stringing me along. The smile on his face gives him away.

"You know who I'm talking about." He's trying to embarrass me and to some degree it's working.

"He's a great guy, Veronica, but I really don't think he's your type. He's probably a little young for you, too." His tone is playful.

I smack his shoulder with my hand lightly. "No, that's not what I meant." I feel my cheeks blushing. "He looks so familiar, but I can't place him. I would swear I've seen him before somewhere."

He lets out a mock sigh of relief. "Oh, well in that case he's my brother, Sebastian."

This little fact does surprise me. "Your brother, really? You two don't even look alike."

"That's because he's adopted." His voice is earnest.

"Oh, that explains it." I'm suddenly embarrassed again.

"No, I'm just kidding. He got the looks and I got the brains." He's getting too good at messing with me. I'm not usually so gullible.

"I don't know if I'd say that." I flash my best flirting smile.

I'm rewarded; he looks shocked. "Thanks." He takes what he assumes to be a compliment graciously.

Too graciously, it turns out. Now it's my turn to dish it back. "He looked pretty smart, too." I wink and smile wickedly.

"Wow, you really know how to wound a guy's ego. Here I thought we were getting along so well."

"Seriously ... you don't give yourself enough credit." Did I just say that out loud? My face is instantly hot again. I quickly look away.

He's staring at me, like the Cheshire cat, a huge, satisfied grin on his face. "Shall we go? The bell's about to ring." He's definitely smug as we walk back to our lockers.

As we open our lockers, he calls down to me, "So, where's study hall? If you tell me I'm sure I can find it on my own. I don't want to make you late again." Though this could be interpreted as a way to escape me, his voice is filled with concern instead.

"No, I'll walk with you. I don't mind." I sound a little too eager, and he likes it. "I have study hall this period, too."

Study hall is held in the cafeteria, as real estate seems to be in short supply. There aren't any extra classrooms this semester. It seems staffing is also in short supply. Mrs. Campbell, the office assistant, comes in to take roll when we arrive and peeks in the door once or twice during the hour, I guess to make sure we're all still here. Dimitri and I have the table to ourselves. We sit quietly across from each other. I'm reviewing the notes I took earlier in Psych and English. I don't remember even writing half of it down, let alone hearing it. Wow, was I distracted or what? The frustrations of the morning are a distant memory now and seem so silly.

Of course, my close proximity to Dimitri means I'm still distracted and I'm not retaining anything that I'm reading … again. It didn't mean anything when I wrote it down this morning and it still doesn't mean anything now. He's proving detrimental to my education. I catch myself peeking up and stealing glances across the table, hoping he won't catch me. Though I never make eye contact, I notice a smile emerge on his face each time and I look back down at my book. I guess I'm not as sneaky as I think I am. He spends the entire hour reading a car magazine. Though it's incredibly hard to resist being bossy and telling him he should be studying, I do. I'm very pleased with myself when the bell rings.

"What's your last class, ma'am?" he sounds very official.

"Weightlifting."

"No, seriously. What's your next class?"

His disbelief should be insulting, but I laugh it off. "Weightlifting. In a month or two I'll have to start charging you admission to the gun show."

That brings on a snort of laughter. "I'd like to see that. Then again, I have no doubt you are tougher than half the guys in there." He's shaking his head.

"I had to be tough growing up. My best friends were all guys and they took no mercy on me."

He opens the door for me and we walk back out into the courtyard.

"Thank you. You know … you're kind of a gentleman." I compliment.

"I'm old-school." He winks and smiles warmly. He points toward the gym. "Now, off to weightlifting, Hercules."

"Ha. Ha," I deadpan. "I need to get you to class first … I'm obligated. What's your last class?" I've finally learned it's better to just ask Mr. Super Memory than go digging through my bag for his schedule.

"English, but I can find it." He tries out his best Veronica voice impersonation, "English wing is right next to the science wing." It's surprisingly not bad. "You provided a very informative and memorable tour this morning," a touch of sarcasm there at the end.

"That was *very* Veronica, I'm impressed. Do I really have that strange accent thing going on?"

He doesn't hesitate, "Yes."

And he's right. I don't know where it came from. It's almost as if I spent some of my childhood in England, which of course I didn't, and the residual accent peeks through every now and then with only certain words. Other people have pointed it out throughout my life, but it's usually when they've spent years around me. It's subtle. How'd he pick it up so quickly?

"And it's adorable," he says, boyishly smiling at me.

I blush. "Okay, well I guess I'll leave you to it then. I'm going home straight after P.E. unless you need anything else before I go. Do you have a ride home?" I'm surprised how disappointed I feel at the thought of leaving him here.

He laughs under his breath. "Sebastian drove today, and I'll ride home with him. Thanks for asking though, and thank you for everything today. You don't know how long I've looked forward to this day ... you did not disappoint, Veronica." He smiles, winks, nods goodbye, and turns toward the main building.

"See you tomorrow, Dimitri," I call after him. My knees grow weak as I watch him walk away. How has he reduced me to mush in the span of a half-day?

"You can count on it," he yells back without turning around.

Life is sometimes ... memorable.

Chapter 2
Long ago yesterday
Revisited

The clock on my nightstand reads 4:08am. Excellent, I know what time it is. But the real questions remain: Where am I? Am I awake or dreaming?

I blink a few times and my sleep-blurred eyes fumble their way around my room. I'm awake, I decide. I sit up and attempt to rub the haze from my eyes. My dream had been so vivid, so real. I can remember every detail: see it, hear it, smell it … feel it.

I saw myself as a young child. I couldn't have been more than eight or nine years old. I was walking down a dirt road alone. My chestnut brown hair was pulled back in a ponytail with a white ribbon. I wore a plain, pale yellow dress. It was clean, but definitely worn. My brown leather shoes had holes in them. The fields on either side of the road were a brilliant green. The sky was pale blue and the air felt thick and sticky on my skin. I could hear children laughing and playing in the distance. My heart felt content, yet anxious with excitement. I rounded a bend in the road and saw a small one-room schoolhouse in the near distance. There were six or seven children chasing each other under a huge oak tree. I started to run. I could feel the air rush in and out of my lungs. I slowed to a jog as I approached the friendly-looking woman standing at the edge of the road. She wore a simple, long, cotton dress that brushed the tops of her black laced-up boots. Her hair was pulled back in a bun beneath her white bonnet.

"Good morning, Veronica. It's good to see you," she said with a welcoming smile. She hugged me tightly.

"Good morning, Miss Little," I said shyly.

The boys and girls were still chasing each other under the oak. She turned toward them and yelled cheerfully, "Children, it's time to go inside."

All of the children immediately stopped and ran inside the tiny schoolhouse, all except one. He turned and started running toward us instead. A strange feeling of anticipation came over me. I could feel it in the pit of my stomach. He stopped just in front of me, but didn't say anything. He looked up tentatively at the woman, who smiled warmly at him.

"We have a new student joining us this year," she said in a kind, motherly voice to the young boy.

As if given permission, he looked at me. He was slightly taller than me and was dressed in dark pants and a shirt that had probably been white once, but was now light gray. His clothes were too big for him and even more worn than mine. He wore no shoes. His dark brown hair was combed neatly and his cheeks were rosy from playing, they matched the color of his lips. And he had the most beautiful gray eyes.

"Hi, my name's Veronica."

"Hi, I'm Dimitri." His voice was quiet, but confident.

And then I awoke …

I try to coax myself back to sleep, but the dream runs over and over in my mind on a maniacal, sleep-depriving loop. I look at the clock again. 5:12am. The effort is officially futile. I can't lie here any longer. It's become abundantly clear I'm not going to get any more rest.

I shower and return to my room to pick out something to wear. This isn't an easy decision considering the many choices I have. My mom's always claimed to hate shopping, but she's clearly in denial. She doesn't like it. She loves it. She gets very few chances to really apply herself to her craft, but school shopping is where she really shines. She has good taste though, and since I, myself, despise the sport at which my mother excels, I can't complain.

My family's not rich by any means, but the fact that I have enough outfits that I can go a week straight without doing laundry, or wearing the same outfit twice, lumps me in with a very small percentage of my classmates. The fact that I have a car, especially a decent car, lumps me in with even fewer. I would consider my family middle class; our neighborhood is what sociologists or politicians might refer to as "disadvantaged," but more accurately, it's poor. It's not that I, or any of my friends, put much emphasis on what we do or don't have, but I do feel guilty sometimes about some of the non-necessities, and frankly some of the necessities, my parents can afford that my friends' parents can't.

It's supposed to be warm again today, so I decide on a dark pink tank top, jeans, and flip flops. I take extra time putting on my make-up and trying something different with my hair. In the end, I decide to just pull it back in a ponytail.

I run upstairs to grab some breakfast and pack my lunch. My mom is in the kitchen cleaning up. She's always cleaning up. If cleanliness is next to godliness, then my mother is a saint. "Bonjour, Mom."

"Right back at ya, Ronnie," she says cheerfully. My mom, like me, is a morning person.

"So, did you talk to Dad last night?" This question is kind of a ritual we go through every morning that my dad is on the road. He drives a semi for a living and is gone about four or five days every week. He loves it. He says it gives him a lot of time to think. Personally, I think maybe it gives him *too much* time to think.

"He called late. He was just leaving Chicago. He said they gave him an extra stop on the way home, but he should be home Saturday." She never sounds sad when he's gone, but you can see something's missing when you look in her eyes. You can feel it. She's completely in love with him and him with her. They're like two halves of one person. They've been together since they were teenagers and married when they were just eighteen (much to my grandmother's dismay). I can't imagine one without the other. They've been married for twenty-one years and still act like newlyweds.

"Great, maybe he can help me change my oil this weekend. Don't tell him, but I think I'm about two hundred miles past due." My dad is a car fanatic. It isn't his hobby—it's his religion. His cars are like his children. The siblings I'll never have.

"Scandalous." My mom does not share my father's religion.

Widening my eyes, I tease her back. "I know, right?"

"It's our secret." She smiles and winks at me. "So, how's school going? Do you like calculus? Have you made

31

any new friends? How's John's mom doing, you know I heard she was in the hospital a few weeks ago?"

"Mom, one question at a time. John's mom had Cholelothiasis."

"Cholelo-what's-sis?"

"*Exactly*. Gallstones. She's fine."

"And school?" she presses.

"School's good ... interesting, but good." She can hear that I've struggled for the right word.

"Interesting. What does interesting mean? Is it a boy?" She's standing next to me and prods me with her elbow.

"Maybe ... sort of ... I don't know." I shake my head and try to shrug it off as no big deal, but the heat in my cheeks contradicts and betrays me. I suddenly don't want to talk about it anymore.

"Who is he?" She's put down the dishcloth she was wiping the counter with and stares at me.

"He's a new kid," I offer as if under interrogation.

She's still staring. "And?" And prying.

"His family just moved here from Texas. I was assigned as his guide the past two days since he's new. He seems pretty cool." I'm trying to keep this low-key, but she's getting herself all worked up.

"What's his name?" She looks like she is going to burst.

"Dimitri Glenn."

She squeaks with excitement and says something under her breath that I don't understand. She has to see that her display is clearly embarrassing me and should, more importantly, be embarrassing her. I *do not* squeal and giggle about boys. With anyone. *Ever*. She takes a deep breath and struggles with composure. "Dimitri, that's a very unusual name. Texas, huh?" There's a huge smile on her face.

"Yup, that's what he said. You'd better get going, Mom. You're going to be late for work."

She gasps as she looks at the clock. "Shit, I didn't realize it was so late." She throws the dishcloth in the sink and grabs her purse from the top of the refrigerator. She kisses me as she scoots by. "Don't forget to put your dishes in the dishwasher."

"Aye-aye, Captain."

"Have a great day at school, Ronnie. I love you."

"Love you too, Mom."

She pushes the button on the garage door opener and steps out the back door.

I sit down to my cereal and look at my calculus homework. I was having trouble with one of the problems last night and chose to skip it and take a look at it with a fresh pair of eyes this morning. After putting pencil to paper, it works its way out in a matter of minutes. What I stared at last night completely stumped makes perfect sense this morning. Satisfied, I put my book in my bag and my spoon and bowl in the dishwasher. The dishwasher is empty of course—my mom emptied it this morning. Just like every morning.

I grab a bottle of water, an apple, a jar of peanut butter, and some crackers and throw them in my bag too.

It's only 7:15 and I usually don't leave for school until 7:30, but I am too anxious to sit in this house another minute. My "obligation" ended yesterday. Dimitri is officially on his own today. That fact makes me both sad and nervous. Though Monday morning was a complete disaster, Monday afternoon and Tuesday were awesome. We've been unbelievably at ease with each other and conversation's come easily. It's as if we've known each other for years, not days.

Thoughts of Dimitri force me back downstairs to brush my teeth. Again. After all, his locker is only down three from mine. I'm bound to see him at some point this morning and I don't need Cheerios breath.

I take the stairs two at a time, grab my bag off the kitchen table, and run out the door. I only live a few blocks from the school but I drive every day anyway. Not very environmentally-friendly, I know, I know.

My dad's religion—cars—warranted a shrine of sorts. He built a four-stall garage in our backyard when I was very young, which, for a neighborhood like ours, is unheard of. The garage is literally bigger than our house. It dwarfs it. The garage is generally full of cars and tools and boyish gadgets. Mom and Dad's cars are gone at the moment, so all that remains are my car and my dad's pride and joy.

My car is bright red. Her name is Jezebel. My friend Teagan named her, because he says it's kind of "sexy," which made me laugh, so the name stuck. Jezebel is several years old but in very good shape for her age (maybe she is sexy after all) and in my opinion is way too nice for a seventeen year old like me, but my dad picked it out.

Jezebel is parked next to my "half-brother," a beautiful 1955 Porsche 550 Spyder. When my dad bought it many, many years ago, it was a wreck. He spent five years lovingly transforming it into one of the prettiest cars I've ever seen. I admire his talent very much. He's a car-building artist.

I jump in my car and start it before I even have the door shut. "Get a grip, Ronnie," I tell myself. "Slow down. Good god, before I know it I'll be squealing and giggling like my mom."

I back carefully down our long driveway and out onto the street. Within two minutes I'm pulling in the small, but long student parking lot. There aren't a lot of cars in the lot yet because I'm so early. I always park in the farthest parking spot from school. It's a habit I've picked up from my dad. The farther away you park from your destination, the less likely you are to get door dings. That's the theory anyway. I've deduced that the lack of door dings is in direct correlation to the fact that no one else is dumb enough to park so far away and make the hike. I shut the car off but let the stereo continue to play. It's one of my favorite songs and I have time to kill so I turn it up and listen to it play out. I pull my calculus book out of my bag to make sure I put my homework back in it this morning.

There's a knock on the driver's side window and it brings me up out of my seat. I feel stupid for being so jumpy and I can hear laughter coming from outside. Whoever it is meant to scare the bejesus out of me and thinks my reaction is hilarious. I can only see the midsection of the culprit. I open my door slightly and he steps back so I can get out.

"I'm so sorry, Ronnie, but I couldn't resist," Dimitri says fighting through the laughter.

34

"What did you just call me?" My embarrassment quickly turns to shock.

The laughter dies, but he's smiling at me. "What?" It comes out quite innocent.

My eyebrows are pinched together. "Did you just call me Ronnie?"

"Yeah, I guess I did." He's still smiling, but tentatively now. He's waiting for my reaction. "Is that okay?"

"I guess so. I don't know ... " I'm having trouble finding my words. "What I mean is that my parents are the only ones that have ever called me that."

"I'm sorry. I didn't mean to offend you." There's genuine concern in his eyes. He's struggling with this as if he's done something wrong—really wrong.

Okay Ronnie, this is the part where you make the poor guy feel better. A little comfort please—you just irrationally jumped all over the guy because of a stupid nickname.

I allow myself a second of reflective consolation. He just caught me off guard. None of my friends have ever called me Ronnie. I imagine that even if they did it would sound strange and unnatural.

"Veronica?" His eyes are pleading.

But when he said it, the name rolled off his tongue so innocently and effortlessly. It just sounded right.

"Veronica?" Still pleading.

He's waiting. This is the part where you comfort and offer apology. It's okay. I'm looking down at the ground talking more to myself than I am to him, "You know what? It's okay." I look up and take in his anxious face. He's truly pained. I smile reassuringly and nod. "I'm sorry, it's really okay. I don't mind if you call me Ronnie." And it is okay ... more than okay.

Relief pours in as a smile emerges. It's a smile I haven't seen yet. His lips are parted, a departure from his usual closed mouthed grin. His teeth are straight and porcelain white. He grabs my messenger bag from the driver's seat and throws it over his shoulder and then locks and shuts the door for me. He offers his hand. "Shall we, Miss Smith?"

I take it slowly and feel the warmth in his hand spread up my arm and throughout my entire body as we walk across the lot toward the main building. He's touching me! And his touch is heavenly. He's gently swinging our arms back and forth.

"You know you're on your own today," I say, taunting. "How do you think you'll fare without me?"

He responds without hesitating, "Oh, I think I'm going to need you for a few more days ... possibly even weeks or months." His smile makes me melt.

"I think I can handle that."

My hand is still in his as we approach the front doors of the school and I can feel every eye on us. At this moment, I feel like the luckiest girl in the world and I don't care. Let them stare I think. He drops my hand only to open the door.

"Thank you," I say quietly. I look at his face as I walk through the door, unable to take my eyes off him. His confidence is irresistible.

He puts his arm around my shoulder and we proceed to our lockers. Everything is moving in slow motion. I swear I even hear background music. Wait, when did this turn into a 1980's John Hughes film? *Because it's freaking awesome.*

He actually walks me to my classes all morning. It's his turn to play tour guide. He has my schedule memorized. Mr. Super Memory asked me once in passing yesterday and easily committed it to memory ... naturally.

The morning is a blur. I can't focus. It's fuzzy. I watch the clock during English class, waiting and waiting as the seconds tick by slowly—no, not slowly, but painfully. The bell sounds and I let out a sigh of relief. I can breathe again. It's lunchtime.

I hurry to my locker. I know I'll beat him there because he has to walk across campus from the gym. I put my books away and steal a look at myself in the small mirror hanging in my locker.

"You look beautiful." The whisper comes from behind me. I feel his warm breath on the back of my bare neck and a shiver runs down my spine. I take a deep breath and it takes my mind a second to catch up.

I turn to look at him and he doesn't move an inch. The hallway's crowded so we're almost touching. His smile is alluring and playful. "Are you *hungry*?"

Maybe it's my imagination, but the way he enunciates *hungry* seems to insinuate more than the obvious reference to lunch. It's almost dirty. It makes me blush. My heart begins to pound in my chest. And I seem to have lost the ability to string a few simple words together into this little thing referred to as speech. Instead I stare.

"Hey! Veronica! Tracking you down." I don't know how but I pry my eyes away from Dimitri. There's a small hand gripping my right arm and it turns me with a sudden jerk. "Need help. Homecoming. You in?"

I feel like I'm underwater. I hear sounds, but not words. The voice doesn't register until I look into her eyes. "Piper? Piper! What? I'm sorry ... homecoming?"

She's frantic, and the words are coming quickly, tumbling out helter-skelter, "Homecoming. *Damn.* Two weeks away. Shitloads to do. *Damn.* Meeting after school tomorrow. Damn meetings. You coming? No Chloe. Bitch. *Damn.* Monica's coming. Need you, too." She's never been a fan of complete, grammatically correct sentences.

Piper's always high strung; you can feel the electricity coming off her at any given moment. I suspect she runs on batteries. I asked her once and she didn't deny it, so my suspicions remain. She's a tiny bundle of energy, with bright red hair to match her intensity. She's a bit scatterbrained, the type of person whose mouth moves faster than her brain can formulate full thoughts. To be completely honest, there are multiple, severe, legitimate, diagnosed medical disorders dwelling within her, which wage war against the multiple, severe, legitimate, medications being pumped into her on daily basis. To say her mental health is no picnic is an understatement. It's unfair that one person should deal with so much. She struggles. Socially, this means she's usually very direct and blunt. She doesn't give herself a chance to edit anything before it escapes her mouth. The upside is you always know where you stand with Piper. Piper is Piper and I love her like a sister. I've learned how to deal with her directness, and lack of filter. I know she means well and she's completely harmless. I also know she's freaking out at the moment and it's just become my job to try to relieve her.

I place my hands on her shoulders and look into her eyes. It's like looking at a deer in headlights. I've seen this look countless times before in the years I've known her and I can't help but give in to her pleas. I cut her off mid-thought, "Piper, calm down. I'm in, whatever you need, I'm in. But, I have to work tomorrow after school. I'll come over to your house afterward and you can fill me in, okay? Just promise me you'll defend my honor and won't sign me up for all of the crap that nobody else wants to do, alright?"

She grips me in a bear hug around the waist. For a small girl, she's incredibly strong. It must be all of the adrenaline constantly coursing through her not quite 5' frame. "Thanks Mom! Always count on you."

"I'm at your service," I say with an exaggerated frown on my face. "And you know how that scares me." I can't hide the sarcasm or the smile any longer.

"Ha. Ha." I love that she gets my sense of humor. Piper understands that sarcasm is an art that begs to be practiced and is as much about tone as the words chosen. She's mastered it. It's the glue that binds us.

Her eyes fall on Dimitri, who's still standing behind me. His hand has moved to my waist. I'm frozen. I know I'm not going to escape humiliation—I see it in her eyes. It's coming. I hold my breath and brace myself for it, because it's like an actual physical force.

Five, four, three, two …

"Veronica! Holy shit! New guy! New hot guy!" She shakes her head. "No. Not hot. Sex personified. Jesus Christ, he's effing delicious!" She looks him up and down as she speaks, smiling in approval.

And there it is, just as I expected. But I can't help smiling because: (a) She threw in a full-fledged sentence, and (b) I love that on a daily basis she talks like a sailor and says things most people would be mortified to say aloud, but that she flat-out refuses to say the f-word because she says "it's not ladylike."

She does have a point. Though effective, the f-word is not particularly ladylike.

"This is Dimitri, Piper. Dimitri, this is Piper." I lean forward and offer in a very loud whisper, "Just a reminder that you are speaking aloud, my friend. That coupled with the fact that Dimitri is indeed not deaf, means he can hear you. Might want to hold back on the aggressively forward comments upon first introduction. That's merely a suggestion though—not a steadfast rule. In the end, it's up to you, Pied Piper."

Dimitri smiles and politely nods an acknowledgement, "It's nice to meet you, Piper."

"Indeed. *Very* nice. Son. Of. A. Bitch. Dimitri. *Sexy* name." There's no attempt to hide the giddy emotion in her voice. She stares at him a moment longer and then looks back at me still smiling like she's been hypnotized. "YOLO."

God, no one makes me laugh like Piper.

Still smiling, she says, "Tomorrow night."

I nod and salute. "Tomorrow night."

Quickly, she turns and runs down the hall. No doubt to corner her next victim/volunteer.

"A touch of Tourette's syndrome?" he asks curiously.

And because he asked in a kind, inquisitive tone that lacked condescension or a hint of meanness, I answer, "I don't think that one's on Miss Piper's resume."

"That was very nice of you. You can't resist, can you?" As is his habit, he's whispering in my ear again. And right on cue the butterflies in my stomach return.

I fumble with the books in my locker, trying to distract myself. "Can't resist? What do you mean?"

"Helping people," he says thoughtfully. "You're a sucker, altruistically-speaking. You can't resist." The words he chose, spoken in a different tone, could've been insulting, but he says them so matter-of-factly that I can't take offense.

I shut my locker door and turn to face him. "Everyone likes to help people, Dimitri. I'm no different than anyone else."

"Ah, but that's where you're wrong. I don't." He shrugs. "Sure, there are certain people I'd do anything for; others, not so much." He has that small, curious, knowing smile on his face and pokes a finger at my chest. "But you, you are quite unlike anyone I've ever known. You love to help people and make them happy—for their sake, not your own. Your friends, your family … " He raises his eyebrows and laughs to himself as if pondering on something private.

I interrupt, "I wouldn't help Chloe Murphy."

He nods. "No respectable person would. Bad example. Don't steer this conversation away from the real subject at hand. Aside from Chloe, you would help anyone. Am I wrong?" Again with a question posed as a statement. He does this a lot and it gives me the strangest feeling every time it happens. Not uncomfortable, but as if there's something right there in front of me that I can't see. Like a challenge or a puzzle I can't figure out.

"You've only known me for three days, Dimitri," I say with a sigh. "You're quite observant, I'll give you that, but you're wrong. I do love to help people, but you make me out to be some sort of a saint or something. I'm quite normal actually. Stick around awhile and you'll find out."

"I intend to. Now shall we eat lunch or would you like to spend the entire period debating your sainthood? I'm okay with either." His smile fills his eyes.

"I'm kind of bored with all the sainthood talk, so let's eat." I can't help but smile at him. "Did you bring something? Do you want to go out to the courtyard?"

He points to the window down the hall. I can see drops splattering against the glass.

"Rain? But it's not supposed to rain today," I say, as disappointment fills my voice. I love my time in the courtyard and the rain has just stolen it away from me.

"Well, apparently mother nature had different plans today. What's plan B?"

"Plan B?" I pause for a moment. "I guess plan B would be going home for lunch. I didn't bring any money with me today." I'm still focused on the window and the rain falling more heavily now.

"If you don't mind driving, I'd be happy to buy your lunch, Miss Smith."

The rain demands my focus. "No ... thank you, but I'd rather just go home." My voice is distant.

"Okay ... I guess I'll see you in study hall then?"

I hear the dejection in his voice, even though he's doing a good job trying to hide it. I shake my head to pull myself out of my momentary misery. "I'm so sorry, that was rude of me. You're welcome to come with me. I'm not offering up anything gourmet, but I won't force mayonnaise on you either." I smirk, remembering his disgust at my tuna salad sandwich on the first day of school.

He laughs loudly. "Well, if I have your word on the mayonnaise, then I would love to join you."

He puts his books in his locker quickly and grabs his jacket, which he promptly wraps around my shoulders. "Let's go."

It's now officially pouring. The rain's coming down in sheets and, of course, I'm the brilliant one who's parked Jezebel clear across the parking lot. He pulls the jacket up over my head. "You ready to run for it? I'd race you, but you'd probably win," he says knowingly.

I nod. "You're right, I probably would. Ready, set ..." and I'm out the door running before I have a chance to say "go."

By the time I reach my car, I'm soaked except for my head and back thanks to Dimitri's jacket. I unlock the doors with the remote as I approach and jump right in. A few seconds later he's sitting in the seat next to me, laughing as we appraise each other's appearance. He looks like he's just stepped out of the shower fully clothed.

"You're soaked." I'm laughing so hard it's difficult to speak. I reach over, without hesitation, and carefully remove his water-spotted glasses, wipe them off with a tissue from my glove box, and hand them back to him.

"Thanks, Mom," he says jokingly.

"Like I haven't heard that one before. How did you know about it?"

"What?" He's laughing, but confused.

41

"Mom. That's what half of my friends call me. Wait, I bet Piper said it, didn't she? I don't even notice anymore."

"Maybe she did, don't remember, she was a little hard to follow at first. I only seem to recall the 'sex personified' comment. Impeccable taste. Nice girl." The smirk spreads across his face. "Seriously, they call you Mom? I was only kidding, though I completely understand. *You. Can't. Resist.*" Each word stressed deliberately.

"Okay, okay, you've made your point. I just like to help." I concede as I turn the key and start the engine.

"You're much more mature than other girls your age, Ronnie. You're kind, considerate, intuitive, and you've got an excellent bullshit filter. It's no secret why you naturally attract others in need or looking for guidance." His voice is almost tense, like he's trying convince me.

I back out and drive slowly through the parking lot. The wipers are whipping back and forth across the windshield full blast and it's still hard to see. Good thing we don't have far to go.

"How did this conversation turn so serious? It sounds like you're talking about my mother," I say, trying to lighten the mood.

"Yes, I suppose that's a fair description," he says quietly to himself.

I ignore what I assume is an innocent jab. I'm only half-listening, concentrating intently on the road as I turn onto my street. The rain is coming so fast and hard that I'm thankful there's no one else on the road. The asphalt is merely an elusive blur beneath the rushing water. I can't tell which lane I'm driving in.

I turn slowly into the driveway. As we pass the house and pull in front of the garage Dimitri's eyes widen and he says something under his breath. I swear I hear my dad's name, but I let it go. It couldn't be. How would he know my dad's name?

"Yeah, people are always kind of shocked when they see the garage. The house is so small; you'd never expect something this huge was hiding back behind it." The excesses my parents can afford sometimes embarrass me. I

42

never know how people will take it, since our neighbors generally don't have a lot of money. My parents have always worked very hard for what they have, but I still feel self-conscious at times.

"This is unbelievable! How many cars can he get in there?" Childlike excitement lights up his face.

"Four, along with lots of tools and general man-stuff."

"Amazing. I'd like to see the inside sometime." There's true wonder in his voice.

"Sure. You can stop by this weekend if you want. Dad will be home Saturday. He can give you the grand tour. Jezebel needs an oil change, so he'll be out here supervising me."

He stops me. "Jezebel?"

"Yeah, my car, that's her name. Doesn't everyone name their car?"

"Umm … no."

"Well, they should."

"Give me some time to think about that one, I'm still on the fence. Did you say your dad will be *supervising* you? As in, you change your own oil?"

"Yeah. Who else is going to do it?"

"Why does that not surprise me?" He's shaking his head and chuckling.

"We better get inside and eat or we'll be late for study hall." I open my door and run for the back door of the house.

The rain has let up a little. We step into the small kitchen and take our wet shoes off. I turn to look at him and find myself laughing again. He's wet from head to toe. "You look pitiful." I remove his glasses carefully. "You really need to get out of that wet shirt." The words fall out as I pull, what I endearingly refer to as, a "Piper."

He smirks playfully. "Ronnie, you are speaking aloud. And we have established that I am indeed not deaf, which means I hear you *loud and clear*. So, I urge you *not* to hold back on any aggressively forward comments or requests you may wish to share. That's merely a selfish, *selfish* suggestion, not a steadfast rule. In the end, it's up to you." He's enjoying this.

I blush instantly. "God, you do have a great memory. Let me put your shirt in the dryer."

"You want my trousers, too? They're pretty wet," he adds quickly.

"Just the shirt."

"Remember, it's not a rule. Don't hold back … "

I focus on his mouth because I can no longer look him in the eye. His lips are the color of deep pink roses, the bottom slightly fuller than the top. They look so soft and smooth and they're wet from the rain. I wonder what they taste like. Just as I'm starting to feel dizzy, something happens that makes me forget his perfect lips for the moment. He pulls his shirt up slowly to reveal the tips of his hip bones and the little indention just inside them … then his stomach … and finally his chest. He's all lean muscle. His skin is golden-brown from a summer in the sun. I fight the urge to touch it. Holy shit, his body is epic. He pulls the shirt over his head and hands it to me, clearly pleased with the apparent look of awe on my face. I see one corner of his mouth pull up, but I can't take my eyes off his flawless body.

He leans forward and whispers in my ear, "You, too, look pitiful. You *really* need to get out of that wet shirt." I close my eyes and feel his warm breath on my ear and neck and faintly smell his cologne. My knees feel weak.

"I … I need to go change." I turn and run down the stairs, taking two at a time. I can hear him laughing above in the kitchen. This is way too much fun for him. He's driving me crazy and he knows it. I've been around guys my whole life; I should be able to control myself a little better. The problem is he's unlike any other guy I've ever known. I get wild butterflies in my stomach when I think about him, when I look at him, when I hear him speak, even when I smell him. I grab the first shirt I see in my closet and change. "Much better," I say to myself. I stand there and take a few deep breaths before stopping in the laundry room to put both our shirts in the dryer.

When I arrive back upstairs, I make sure that I appear completely under control. He's sitting at the kitchen table waiting patiently.

44

I make peanut butter and jelly sandwiches and we eat in silence. I feel his eyes on me from across the table. His gaze is heavy and increasingly intimate, but I flip through the newspaper casually. It probably doesn't appear casual though. I'm sure I look like a tense, inexperienced, naïve fool who has an enormous crush on the cute, cool guy sitting across the table from her. I don't dare look up. My eyes may literally jump out of their sockets if I look at him again, and I don't want to give him the satisfaction.

After putting our dirty dishes in the dishwasher, I retrieve our shirts from the dryer. He's bent over tying his shoes when I return. He stands up slowly and I don't resist staring this time.

"It's not quite dry, but it's a lot better than it was," I say apologetically. Hallelujah, I think. This time it sounded natural.

He takes his glasses off and sets them on the counter. I look into his eyes. They're shining, bright, and deep gray. They're breathtaking and they're the only thing prying me away from ogling his still shirtless torso. Again, it's as if everything is moving in slow motion, like a dream. He puts his shirt on, combs his almost-dry, envy-worthy hair back into place with his fingers and put his glasses back on. Perfect. He looks perfect. And it's not even work for him. He's some sort of phenomenon in the beauty department. It shouldn't be that easy to look that good.

"Thank you, Ronnie," he whispers.

I'm whispering too, and I'm not sure why. "You're welcome. Though my parents would kill me if they knew I'd just spent my lunch hour dining with a half-naked guy in their house."

He laughs and says, "They might surprise you." He pauses and winks. "They're going to love me, wait and see." He sounds confident, and it's hard to doubt him.

We return to school and the rest of the day is uneventful compared to lunch. I daydream about it all afternoon.

Life is sometimes … wet (and beautiful).

Chapter 3
Unannounced
And so very welcome

The moans and excruciating cries of pain are relentless and carried in on stretchers. There are so many of them and so few of us. I scan the room. It's full of battered and broken young men in fatigues. A wave of panic overtakes me. Which one do I help first? I look at the other two nurses rushing from one bed to the next doing everything they can to comfort, to make a difference.

"Veronica, we need you over here!" One of the nurses calls to me, extreme urgency in her voice.

I respond instantly, somehow suddenly focused. I hurry across the room to her side.

"What can I do?" I ask in a strained voice. She's walking toward the company's medic that has just helped carry one of the stretchers in.

The young medic looks at me with tired eyes full of concern. He speaks quietly. "We need more morphine. These boys are in bad shape."

I race to the other room, which is little more than a closet. There are vials and bottles and medical equipment. I scan the shelves, calling them, willing them to me, muttering, "Morphine, morphine, morphine ... " Then I find what I'm looking for—a dozen or so glass vials neatly lined up on a narrow shelf. I hold out my skirt with one hand and frantically clear the shelf with my other forearm, letting the bottles spill into it. I hurry back to the medic.

"This is all we have left." I say looking helplessly at the meager supply enveloped in my skirt.

The young medic is in his early twenties, but his eyes look tired and aged. "Some won't make it. Our platoon was hit hard. The town was supposed to be clear. They told us the Nazis moved north." Tears begin to swell in his green eyes. "There was one sniper and then two. They picked us off one by one." He bites his lip.

As much as this kills me to watch, I've seen it before many times and I know what I need to do. I read the name on his uniform and lock his gaze with mine. My words flow calmly and quietly. "Private Mason, these boys need you right now. You got them here. Please help me. Let's focus on those that can be saved, okay?"

He shakes his head, wipes his eyes and takes a deep breath. He looks at me apologetically. "Of course, ma'am. Let's go."

We move down the line of beds one by one, helping those we can and comforting those we can't. I've lost all track of time, but I realize that the room is much quieter now.

"Private Mason, these last three appear to have minor wounds. I can attend to them. You need to go outside and get some fresh air."

He looks at the floor, pauses, and then looks up at me slowly. "Yes, ma'am." He turns and walks out into the moonlit night.

I scan the room from one end to the other. Other nurses are already treating two of the final three injured men. The third sits in a chair at the other end of the room. I'm exhausted, but I walk quickly toward him. He's sitting patiently in the chair holding his right arm, which is wrapped in dirty makeshift bandages. I can see that they are blood-soaked, but the look on his face doesn't reveal a hint of pain. He is young and handsome. I kneel down in front of him and take his forearm gently in my hands. When I glance up his gray eyes pierce me from behind his glasses, but as he smiles his whole face softens.

"Hi, my name's Veronica."

"Hi, I'm Dimitri." His voice is quiet, but confident.

Blaring music jolts me awake. I reach across my nightstand, fumbling to find a button—any button—that will shut off the alarm. The music abruptly stops. I open my eyes and blink a few times. The dream was so real I half expect a Nazi soldier to walk through my bedroom door. I close my eyes and can still see Dimitri's face. I lay there for a few minutes concentrating on that face. That beautiful face.

Unfortunately, the day won't wait. It's Saturday and I have a long to-do list.

I drag myself out of bed, shower, dress, and trudge upstairs to get something to eat while my hair dries. My dad is sitting at the kitchen table eating breakfast and reading the newspaper.

"Hey, Ronnie, what's happening?"

I give him a kiss and a hug. "Morning, Dad. Not much."

Mom must have been up early this morning. The aroma of cinnamon rolls fills the kitchen. The pan is on table in front of my dad and all but two are gone. I slide the pan over and, not bothering with a fork, dive right in with my fingers. Some foods are more satisfying when eaten with your hands. The rolls are still warm, each bite is flaky dough infused with cinnamon and vanilla, topped with sticky, sugary, cream cheese frosting. There's a reason they call this type of deliciousness comfort food. It's bliss. Have I mentioned how much I love my mom?

Dad folds the newspaper in half and tosses it to the other side of the table. "So, how was the first week of school?"

"Good, really good. Looks like calculus isn't going to be as hard as I'd imagined, at least not yet. Besides, John's in my class so I know where I can get a good tutor if I need one."

My dad smiles. "That John's a pretty smart kid, but I bet you'll do just fine on your own. You'll probably be tutoring him by the end of the semester."

"John is a genius, Dad. I, on the other hand, apply myself to the best of my abilities. I don't mean to burst your bubble, but that's a fairly distinct and far-reaching difference. His brain is epic. Mine is functional."

"Functional and funny," he teases.

I laugh. "Aha, and there's the rub." I'm quiet while I take a few more bites of the heavenly cinnamon rolls. "So, how was your week? Mom said you ended up in Chicago?"

"It was a pretty good week. A few bad storms out east, but that's what makes it fun."

I shake my head and laugh. "Yeah, whatever. You do realize that you are the only person on the planet who actually enjoys driving in bad weather, don't you?"

My dad is unique, and I mean that in the best possible

way. He's opinionated and stubborn, but also equally kind and generous. He's very smart, though he barely graduated high school. I suspect a strong mix of boredom and a lack of interest were to blame for his poor grades. He takes a common sense approach to life and works harder than anyone else I've ever known. He's a perfectionist in every sense of the word. (The amount of time he spends doing and re-doing drives me insane. I'm critical of myself, but I'm a do-your-absolute-best-the-first-and-only-time type of girl.) He has an amazing sense of humor that gets quite juvenile at times and embarrasses my mom to death. But, most of all he's a great role model and, along with my mom, my biggest fan and supporter.

He laughs too. "So what's on the agenda for today?"

"I need to meet Piper and the homecoming planning committee at eight o'clock this morning at school, but it should only take an hour or two, and then I'm going to the library. I need a book to get started on a report for English."

"How is the Pied Piper?"

"Same. Wonderful. She's Piper, need I say more?" Because she really is pretty wonderful and my dad knows it. Of all my friends she's always been one of his favorites. She lives just down the street from us and we've been friends since her family moved here when we were both in seventh grade.

He smiles. "Did the Pied Piper bite off more than she can chew again? She needs help with homecoming?"

"Yeah, it's pitiful to watch her struggle though. And besides that she's so darn persistent, I think she's part honey badger. She never takes no for an answer. It's one of her best qualities." I lovingly roll my eyes.

This makes my dad laugh again. "Yeah, but we love her anyway."

I smile, too. "Yeah, we do."

I put the cinnamon roll pan in the dishwasher and hurry back downstairs to apply some mascara and do something with my hair. I decide to avoid the blow dryer and pull it back in a ponytail to save time.

I grab my bag and the list of books to check out from the

library. When I arrive back upstairs my dad is heading out to the garage, so we walk together.   "Bye Dad, love you."

"Love you, too, Ronnie." He winks. "Have fun and don't be too hard on Pied Piper. Tell her I said hi. I haven't seen her in a while."

"I will." I jump in Jezebel, turn my key in the ignition, and back down the long drive.

The homecoming planning meeting doesn't take as long as I'd expected. It's a follow-up to the meeting on Thursday afternoon that I missed, and it seems like everyone already knows what they need to do. Piper puts me in charge of selling tickets before school the week of the dance and taking tickets at the door the night of. I'm pretty pleased. It could have been much worse. I could've ended up with decorating duties. Decorating duties *suck*.

I head to the library, list in hand. I'm definitely a list maker. I make a list for everything. It comes to me naturally, too. I'm a second-generation list-maker, just like my mom.

The library isn't very busy so I decide to take my time and look around after I find the books I need. Time gets away from me and before I realize it, it's almost eleven o'clock.

During my drive home, I think about the books and the book report that looms ahead of me. Although I enjoy English and I'm a good writer, I always get anxious when I have a paper due. The satisfaction doesn't come until the paper is done. The entire process up to that point is nerve-wracking.

As I turn the corner and drive up my street I notice a car parked in front of our house. It isn't unusual to see cars in front of our house; we often have visitors, especially when my dad's home. But I've never seen this car before. It's nice—really nice. It looks out of place on our street. It's a shiny black Porsche with dark tinted windows. Maybe it's Daniel's car. He's a friend of my dad's, a car collector who's always got something new to show off.

I park in the driveway instead of pulling in the garage, because I still need to drive to the auto parts store for oil. I stack up the books and balance them in one hand while I put the strap of my bag over my shoulder with the other. My mom's in the kitchen making sandwiches for lunch when I walk in the back door.

"Hi Ronnie." She's flitting around the kitchen. My mom usually operates at 100 miles an hour. She doesn't know how to relax. She kisses me on the cheek as she breezes by.

"Hey, Mom. What's up, where's the fire?" She's making me dizzy.

Her laugh is nervous, giddy even. "I'm just making some sandwiches to take out to the garage. Do you want one?" The smile on her face could not be any wider.

I shake my head. "No, I'm not hungry right now, maybe later." I'm confused. I set my books on the counter and hang my bag on the hook by the door. "So, whose car is that outside?"

"That's funny, Ronnie." She looks at me and realizes I'm not laughing. She's confused. Good, now I'm not the only one. "You really don't know?"

"No, did Daniel get a new car? It's really nice."

She smiles again, "I think you better take these sandwiches out to the garage," and hands me two plates.

Her behavior is kind of freaking me out, but I take the plates and head out the back door. I need to ask my dad a question before I go to the parts store anyway and now I'm curious. My mom follows closely, like a hyper puppy, somehow carrying two full glasses of iced tea. I open the door to the garage and hear voices at the other end, but the TV is loud and I can't make them out. I can see that there are two people sitting in the chairs facing the TV, their backs to us.

My dad turns around first. "Hey, Ronnie, I was beginning to think you got lost." He reaches out to take a plate from me. "Thanks."

I look at the chair next to him and nearly drop the plate. Dimitri stands up and quickly grabs it before it slips out of my hand.

I can't speak. What? How? Too many questions are running through my head.

51

He looks at me like he can hear the incoherent babble in my mind. One corner of his mouth turns up into a boyish grin and he nods slightly. "Good morning, Veronica. Or is it afternoon?"

I'm still dazed. "Almost afternoon. Hi Dimitri. What are you doing here?" It comes out sounding rude and I want to take it back as soon as I say it.

"You said I should stop by this weekend to see the garage ... that your dad would be home ... remember? I apologize. I should've called, but you never gave me your number. I didn't realize you had plans this morning or I would've waited."

He's struggling and I have to interrupt him before this gets any worse. I force a smile. "It's okay. You just surprised me, that's all. I guess you've already met my parents, then?"

They all look at each other and smile. Suddenly I feel like an outsider.

Dimitri nods, the odd, knowing smile still on his face, as he looks from my parents to me. "Yes. We've met." The smile is the same one I saw on the first day of school when he asked me if I'd just come from French class. Only now they all seem to be in the on the joke and I have no idea what to think.

"Here's some tea, sweetie." My mom hands Dimitri a glass. "You let me know if you need some more. I just made a fresh batch."

"Thank you, Jo. And thanks for the sandwich. It really wasn't necessary. I've already made a pest of myself this morning."

A pest? That indicates some period of time has passed. How long has he been here? What the hell?

My mom gives my dad his glass of tea and pats Dimitri on the shoulder as she passes and goes back to the house.

I feel like I'm in a goddamn twilight zone. My mom is always hospitable and always friendly, but she's usually a bit more tentative with any new guys I bring home to meet them. Not to mention that this new guy brought *himself* home, unannounced—*without me*. And then there's my dad who, in the past, hasn't acknowledged any of my friends that

52

are guys unless it is blatantly obvious they aren't boyfriend material. A grand total of three have passed the test: John, Tate, and Teagan. My dad trusts me implicitly, but doesn't think anyone is good enough for his little girl. This is definitely weirding me out.

My dad pulls a chair up next to him. "Ronnie, why don't you sit down?"

I sit down mechanically. It's like I'm outside myself looking down on the scene. On one side I should be absolutely thrilled that Dimitri's come to see me. But on the other hand, my parents' reaction to him is so … *strange*. I know the effect Dimitri has on me. I'm completely spellbound in his presence, despite the fact that I've known him less than a week. I've noticed the way other girls react to him at school, too. His looks and confidence are intoxicating. But that shouldn't work on parents, especially mine. My dad is sitting here in his goddamn shrine, watching an old western, eating lunch with Dimitri like they are old buddies. For crying out loud—he's only known him for a few hours at most.

They eat their sandwiches in contented silence. My dad's eyes are glued on the TV and Dimitri's eyes are glued on me. He's sitting directly across from me and holds my gaze. His eyes run through a range of emotions, carrying on a one sided conversation: apologetic, then playful, then morphing into a look that's downright enchanting.

He's broken me again. If he could bottle this and sell it, whatever it is that so overpowers me, he would be a gazillionaire. I smile in defeat. He returns the smile.

"When are you going to change Jezebel's oil, Ronnie?" my dad asks. "You ready now? I've got some time before the basketball game starts if you need help."

"I need to pick up some oil first. Do you want to ride with me, Dimitri, or would you rather stay here? You two seem pretty cozy." I smile mockingly at him.

He concedes with a smile. "I'll go with you. I've taken too much of your dad's time already this morning. I'm sure he has work to do." He turns to my dad and extends his hand and chuckles, "It was so nice to … um … to meet you, Will.

Thanks for being so welcoming and sharing your garage with me. It's amazing, and the Spyder is incredible."

My dad shakes his hand and pats his shoulder with the other. "I'm glad you stopped by, Dimitri. Let me know when you're ready to get some paint on that Volkswagen, I'd love to help."

I wait until we're outside to start with the questions, but Dimitri beats me to it.

"Why don't you let me drive?" he offers politely.

Drive. Wait a minute—the Porsche out front. I'd completely forgotten about it. Could it be his?

"That is *not* your car," I say incredulously.

"That depends on which car you're talking about," he says quietly, a half-smile on his face.

We're nearing the end of the driveway, just past the house and the street is in full view. "That car." I point to the Porsche.

The smile turns up in both corners of his mouth now, "Oh yeah... *that* one's mine." I don't know how he does it, but there is a surprise around every corner with this guy.

"You're kidding me, right?"

The headlights flash as he clicks the remote on his keychain. "Afraid not, Miss Smith." He opens the passenger door for me.

I'm still in shock as I slip into the charcoal leather seat. It smells so good, like his cologne. I inhale quickly a second time before he gets in to sit beside me.

"Where to, Ronnie?" he asks as the engine roars to life.

"There's an auto parts store on the corner of Federal and 107th Street." I answer and then go quiet. We drive a few blocks before I realize how shallow and judgmental I've been acting about this car. I'm certainly impressed, but how does a guy my age have a car like this? I can't decide which direction my mind's going with it. I decide it's best for both us to drop it for now.

"So, what's this about a Volkswagen?" I ask, remembering my dad's comment in the garage.

"I'm restoring an old Volkswagen bug. I have everything finished except the paint. I was telling your dad about it and he offered to help."

"A bug? Really? That's actually pretty cool, you don't see them around very often."

My interest brings him relief and he opens up. "Yeah, I've always liked them. Maybe its nostalgia, I don't know. Anyway, I bought this one for next to nothing two years ago, and have been working on it ever since. It was supposed to be my first car, but it's taking a little longer than expected to put on the finishing touches—"

I interrupt, "Please tell me you're not one of those horrid perfectionists who dwells on even the smallest of details, details your average novice, or better yet even an expert, would likely overlook?"

He smiles, nonchalant and unoffended. "Guilty as charged."

I roll my eyes.

He smirks. "But I save it only for the important stuff."

"Ah, selective perfectionism." I shake my head emphatically. "Not horrid at all."

"I like to think of myself as perpetually patient. Good things come to those who wait, et cetera, et cetera."

"You may have a point; instant gratification is an ugly business."

His tone serious now. "In which much of our world, or at least this country, overindulges. Greed is open for business … and business is booming."

"Says the young man driving the Porsche," I say under my breath, but he hears me and shrugs. "Surely you see the irony in it?"

He sighs. "It's one of the reasons I'm so anxious to get the bug finished. Believe it or not, I favor inconspicuousity."

I raise my eyebrows. "You don't say?"

He shakes his head in mock dejection. "That's not a word, is it?"

"Nope. But maybe it should be. It sounded very convincing."

He smiles as though he's been comforted, as though maybe we've just touched upon something very real. "You, Mr. Glenn, are a paradox."

"Was that a compliment? My, but you're in generous form today."

Against my will, I blush crimson. "Shut up, or I may be forced to take it back."

He smiles. "Fair enough, I graciously accept that I am indeed a paradox, in the most uncomplimentary way of course." The smile fades. "Really, Ronnie, it boils down to preconceived notions. People tend to have them about people who drive cars like this. They're very quick to judge—good or bad. You understand?"

Unfortunately I do, having been guilty of it myself within the last five minutes, however fleeting it may have been. I like to think of myself as open-minded, but occasionally I can be very judgmental. It's a flaw of mine. I suddenly feel sorry for him and ashamed of myself. "That's why you always ride to school with your brother?" I ask quietly.

"Yes. I'd prefer people to get to know *me* before they decide if they like me or not. The car I drive, or the house I live in—money in general—shouldn't have any bearing on it, you know? I'm a very good judge of character and can tell almost instantly if someone is worth investing myself in, but a little insurance doesn't hurt." He's staring out the windshield at the traffic light waiting for it to turn green.

"So, why do you drive it?" I ask hesitantly.

"It belonged to my dad."

"Oh, did he get a new car or something? This is quite a hand-me-down."

We pull into the parts store lot and park before he answers. He looks at me and his eyes are suddenly tired. "My dad died last year."

My hand involuntarily flies to my mouth. "Oh my God, Dimitri." That is the last thing I expected him to say. I had no idea.

He takes my hand gently from my mouth and holds it in both of his. "It's okay, you didn't know. My mom drove it until we moved here this summer, but Sebastian and I thought she would be better off this winter in a four-wheel drive. We talked her into a massive SUV." A small smile flashes across his face as he thinks about it. "The thing is a tank, so at least we won't have to worry about her on the road, though I fear for everyone else in her path."

"That's really sweet of you and your brother to worry about her like that."

His smile grows. "You don't know Sunny. You'll understand what I mean when you get to know her. She takes a little looking after. Anyway, none of us had the heart to get rid of his car, so I ended up with it." He pauses and a devilish grin emerges. "It's fast as hell though and fun to drive. In fact, I just decided that you're driving us home."

My stomach flip-flops. "No, no, no ... I am *not* driving this car."

The devilish grin is still there. "We'll see." He's out of the car before I can counter.

After I find the oil and pay for it Dimitri takes the bag in one hand and tosses me the keys with the other. "I said no, Dimitri. Are you nuts?"

"Maybe. I really don't want to make a scene, Ronnie. And don't underestimate me, I'll do it." His mocking smile turns into a flirtatious smirk. "Besides, I bet you'd look damn sexy driving it. Humor me." He winks and runs the last few yards to the car and jumps in the passenger seat.

I stop at the rear of the car. "This is crazy. What if I wreck it?" I whisper to myself.

He opens the sunroof and yells, "Stop talking to yourself, Ronnie, people are going to think you're crazy. Get in the car, baby."

"I can't believe you're making me do this," I protest as I open the door and climb in. "Oh my God," I think to myself, "Did he just call me baby? He did. He just called me baby!"

He raises his eyebrows. "Oh come on. Don't tell me this doesn't excite you in the least?"

I can't help smiling ... a little. A crooked, terrified smile. But, buried deep beneath the paralyzing fear of driving this incredible car, I do feel excitement. Wild, deranged excitement. "Maybe a little," I confess. "But I don't want to hurt it."

He laughs. "You haven't seen me drive this thing,

believe me, you won't hurt it. I had her up to 150 miles an hour on the drive up from Texas."

"That's not what I meant; I don't want to wreck it," I say nervously.

He sighs deeply. "Have you ever wrecked a car, Veronica Smith?"

"No," I say quietly.

"Exactly. You won't today either," he says reassuringly.

I look at the steering wheel and can feel the nervousness ebbing as I start the engine. "Buckle up then," I command.

"Said like one compromised against her better judgment. Godspeed."

"I'm doing this under duress. Just so you know."

He's stone faced. "Of course you are."

I can't hide the excitement any longer, but I add emphatically, "Duress."

He nods and a faint smile bleeds through. "Duress. Now drive."

At Dimitri's urging, instead of driving straight home I drive toward the mountains. I weave up and down the winding highway for almost two hours. I can't wipe the silly smile off my face. The car is amazing. I feel so free. I don't think about anything but the speed, which far exceeds the posted limits, and the beautiful scenery—both outside *and* inside the car.

My smile is still spread from ear to ear as I pull his car up in front of my house. I kill the engine and sigh as I hand the keys to Dimitri, who's beaming in the passenger seat.

He's bright-eyed and staring.

I giggle. "What?"

"Duress seems to suite you. And I was right."

"Right about what?"

"You looked *very* sexy driving this car." The smile lights up his eyes.

I blush and look away, but he continues to stare. "Ronnie, will you do me a favor?"

I nod.

"Will you go out with me tonight? We can go to a

movie, or just hang out, whatever you want. Though I do insist on buying you dinner, you haven't eaten all day."

I nod again.

"Under duress this time?"

I shake my head.

"That's a relief. I'm not quite maniacal enough to bend a strong girl to my will to satisfy my *every* whim. Well, I'd love to stay and watch you work on your car. I could do with that sort of entertainment. You working on Jezebel would be very hot." He sighs. "Perhaps next time, it looks like I have a date to plan. I'll be back at 6:30 to pick you up. Will that give you enough time?" He looks as happy as I feel.

I'm still speechless, so I offer another nod. It's embarrassing how lame I can be sometimes.

We both get out of the car and he hands me the oil, which I completely forgot about. He takes my free hand and kisses it. "Thank you for an unbelievable afternoon. I'll be back soon."

I can't speak. My hand is tingling. I turn and walk slowly up the driveway. I know any moment I am going to wake up and the dream will be over. Someone pinch me already.

Reality sets back in when I walk in the door.

"Where have you been?" My mom's voice isn't mad, but there's an edge to it.

"Sorry, Mom. Dimitri drove me to the store and then kind of insisted on *me* driving home." I say sheepishly, waiting for the full wrath to come.

"It takes two hours to drive home? You could have called." She hesitates. "Listen, I really like Dimitri—"

"That was obvious," I interrupt, smiling at her.

"But ... that doesn't mean that all the rules get thrown out the window. All I'm asking for is a phone call to let us know that your plans changed." She's softening; I can see it in her eyes.

"I'm really sorry, Mom. I know I should have called. I lost all track of time. It won't happen again." It doesn't take much for my parents to coax a pathetic apology out of me. I hate apologies, but I hate disappointing them more, it makes me feel awful. Sometimes I wish they would just punish me like other parents.

"Good." Her eyes are beginning to twinkle now. "So, he actually let you drive his car? What was it like? Where did you go?" A childish grin spreads across her face.

"It was amazing. I ended up driving up into the mountains; you wouldn't believe how it handles."

My mom leans forward and kisses me on the cheek. "I'm glad you're safe, honey. So, are you going to work on your car now?" My mom refuses to call her Jezebel.

"Yeah, I better get out there and get it done right away." I can feel my cheeks warming. "I sort of have a date tonight that I need to get ready for." I look at the floor. I'm sure my face is bright red now.

There's a sly smile on my mom's face. She's staring at me and the silence is killing me. I'm embarrassed as it is and it feels like she's holding a spotlight on me.

I try to read her face. "You like him, right Mom?"

Her expression gives her away. The smile on her face doesn't falter as she nods. "Yes. I like Dimitri very much, Ronnie." The words are soft and entirely genuine.

I smile too. "So do I." I hug her and head out to the garage.

After I finish up I spend the next hour showering, scrubbing, moisturizing, and otherwise trying to beautify myself. I decide to leave me hair down and curl it. My thick, straight hair falls to the middle of my back, so working with the curling iron takes a while. I usually only do this for special occasions, and this definitely qualifies. Picking out an outfit is difficult because I have no idea where we're going. I choose my floral skirt because it matches my emerald green blouse. The modestly low-cut neckline is trimmed with delicate beading and the color makes my hazel eyes appear greener than their normal golden brown. It's my favorite piece of clothing and I always feel pretty when I wear it. Just as I put on my earrings I hear the doorbell ring. I freeze. My heart races. I slip on my sandals, grab my small purse, and take the stairs two at a time. I pause in the kitchen where I can hear my mom and Dimitri in the midst of comfortable conversation in the front room. I close my eyes and take a few deep breaths. My heart rate begins to settle. I walk slowly through the kitchen and turn the corner to the front room.

There he is.

Life is sometimes … a racing heart.

Chapter 4
Fairy tales are even better when they're real

He's spectacular. How does he seem to become more attractive every time I see him? This could get dangerous; he's on the verge of becoming *completely* irresistible. Forget actors or models. They have nothing on Dimitri.

His clothes, just like his casual school clothes, are not anything your average teenager would wear, but they're completely appropriate on him. His black tweed pants and pale blue vintage shirt look amazing against his tanned skin.

The smile sparkles in his eyes before it reaches his mouth and when it does it's slight but filled with awe, and I know it's only for me. "Hi Ronnie," he says with a wink. "You look beautiful." That's another odd thing I've noticed about Dimitri, he says whatever is on his mind, regardless of who hears it. Speaking from the heart never embarrasses him.

He's standing with one hand behind his back, which he extends to reveal a small bouquet of pink lilies.

I gasp as I reach for them. "Dimitri, I love them. Lilies are my favorite, especially pink ones."

He smiles that strange, knowing smile and nods once. "I know."

"Thank you."

"You're welcome," he says softly.

My mom reaches out to take the flowers. "Why don't I take those and put them in some water so you two can get going?"

"That's probably a good idea," I say as I surrender them.

My mom takes the lilies to the kitchen and races back in with her camera in hand. "I want to take a picture before you go."

"Mom, what are you doing? This isn't prom. We're just going out to dinner."

She herds us over to stand in front of the piano and points the camera at us. "Humor me, Ronnie. We don't take enough pictures." She looks from behind the camera at me. "This *is* an important event. *Trust me.*"

Chills run down my spine. My mom gets these uncanny, almost otherworldly senses. I wouldn't say she's psychic—nothing that corny—but she is *extremely* perceptive. She pays attention to subtleties that escape most people. She doesn't miss anything. It freaked me out when I was younger, but the older I get the more I've learned to respect and appreciate her perspective. Her life is ruled by a few simple rules: 1. There are *no* coincidences; *everything* happens for a reason. 2. What comes around goes around. You can call it karma or the Golden Rule (do unto others as you would have them do unto you), but it all basically boils down to the same concept. This one, she's assures me, is very important because it applies to this life, as well as the next. Whatever that may be.

Dimitri doesn't seem to mind at all and puts his arm around my waist as my mom clicks off a few pictures.

After she's satisfied, I walk over and kiss her. "Okay, time to go. Love you, Mom." We rush toward the door.

"Love you, too, Ronnie. Bye Dimitri. Have fun," she calls as we walk down the path to his car.

"Good bye, Jo. I'll take good care of her." Dimitri calls back over his shoulder.

"I know you will," she says as Dimitri opens the passenger door for me.

I blow her a kiss and climb in.

I allow Dimitri to drive for ten minutes before I break the silence. "Where are we going?"

He looks at me and raises an eyebrow. "To dinner."

"I know that. But where are we going?"

"To dinner." He's smiling. "Be patient. Take a breath, Ronnie. Sit back and enjoy the ride."

His words, like a mirror held up before me, make me realize how tense and nervous I am. While he, on the other hand, is completely at ease … as usual.

I look out the passenger window and watch the scenery fly by. We're on the highway, and he's driving very fast. The road is familiar though—I've driven it many times. I know where it leads.

"Are we going to Boulder?"

His answer is a grin.

"I've always loved Boulder. Look at that view. The Flatirons are unbelievable, especially at this time of day."

"I hope you're hungry, because we're here," he says, as we pull up in front of a small Spanish-style building on a residential street. The exterior is white stucco and the roof is covered in terra cotta tiles.

We walk hand in hand down the sidewalk. Just inside the front gate a narrow, stone path winds around an ornate fountain surrounded by a variety of flowers in full bloom. Twinkle lights wrap every tree and bush lining the path. It's enchanting.

Dimitri opens the door and I enter, still in awe. The inside is equally as charming. It's elegant, but not pretentious.

"Do I look okay?" I ask him quietly, suddenly feeling underdressed.

He squeezes my hand and whispers in my ear, "You're unbelievably perfect."

My cheeks warm and an electric current runs from my head to my toes as I look at him. He's wearing the most inviting smile.

Then, another voice seems to come out of nowhere, "Ah, Dimitri, so good to see you."

Dimitri holds my gaze a few seconds longer than necessary and then focuses his attention on the man standing before us. "Pedro, it's good to see you as well. Sorry, we're a little early."

"No trouble at all. Your table is ready. Follow me, señor, señorita." The man leads us to a small room in the back of the restaurant where there's a small table set for two. The room is bathed in the glow of hundreds of candles. "Is this what you had in mind?" the man asks Dimitri.

Dimitri nods and flashes an approving smile. "It's brilliant, well done. Gracias."

The man nods. "De nada, anytime my friend," he says as he pulls the chair out for me.

I take my seat, not quite comprehending where I am or what has just transpired. I'm quiet as I look around the room.

It's like a fairy tale. I look across the table to find him admiring me as I admire the surroundings.

"This place is amazing," I finally say, breathlessly.

He nods, "It's my favorite restaurant. I hope you like Mexican food."

"I love it. It's my favorite." I'm still trying to take in every detail: the candles, the fire in the fireplace behind Dimitri, the pink lilies that are not only on our table, but that fill vases all along the length of the mantle over the fireplace. I pull my eyes away from them and look at him. "You did this for me?" I ask quietly.

He winks and takes my hand. "I can only take credit for the idea. The credit for the execution goes to Pedro. He's something. This is even better than I envisioned. Though I can't imagine the candles meet the local fire code requirements," he laughs.

My eyes begin to tear up.

"What's wrong?" he asks softly.

My voice cracks. "Nothing. Absolutely nothing."

"Then why do you look like you're going to cry?"

"Most guys take girls to the movies, or to Applebee's for a first date," I say as a tear rolls down my cheek.

At this he raises an eyebrow and reaches across the table to wipe the tear away. "Well, in that case, pack up, Ronnie. We will leave this unsatisfactory, tear-inducing hell-hole for something much more upscale. There's an IHOP just down the street."

He smiles and I laugh.

"No, you don't understand. This sort of thing doesn't happen to girls like me. This is the sort of thing that happens in movies. How did I get so lucky?"

He squeezes my hand with both of his and his smile grows gentle, but there's something in his eyes—it almost looks like pain. He pauses, then says, "*I* am the lucky one. You have no idea how happy I am right now sitting here with you. It's the dream I've dreamt over and over again, and it's finally come true."

I hang on every word he's just said and commit them to memory. No one's ever spoken to me with such emotion and passion.

Dinner is fantastic. I order my favorite—chicken enchiladas—and they're the best I've ever eaten. Pedro offers us dessert and even though I'm stuffed I can't turn down flan. It's *homemade* and it's creamy and delicious. After Dimitri pays the bill and we fight over the mints, we talk. The conversation comes easy. It's not rushed. It's comfortable. Before I know it an hour and a half has passed.

"As much as I don't want to leave, Sunny will never forgive me if we don't get home soon," he says, his voice strained with a touch of reluctance.

"Do we have to?" I plead, my disappointment evident. "It's only nine-thirty. Don't tell me you have an early curfew? Wait, I know, you turn into a pumpkin at midnight, don't you? Dammit, I knew this was too good to be true," I say, an exaggerated frown on my face.

He smiles. "Wonderful guess, but sadly way off the mark. Sebastian and I don't have a curfew."

"Then what's the rush?" I'm whining now.

"My mom really wants to meet you." His smile is almost child-like.

I'm taken aback. "She wants to meet *me*?"

"Yes, it is tradition, when you are dating someone, to meet their parents."

I butt in, "I'm not a fan of tradition."

He glides along as if I haven't spoken. "I met yours this morning and you get to meet mine tonight." He's watching my face closely, trying to read my expression.

I shake my head. "You are so ... " I'm searching for the right word, but all I can come up with is "*weird.*"

"Weird was not exactly what I was going for. That sentence could've ended *so* many different ways: intelligent, sexy, charismatic, even charming, but weird ... really Ronnie, is that the best you can do?" His tone is playful.

"I didn't mean it that way, and believe me you are all of those other things and more, but seventeen year old guys don't act like you do. They don't plan unforgettable first dates like this one. They don't make a girl feel like the most

66

special person in the universe. They don't sweep her off her feet in less than a week. And they definitely don't want to introduce *me* to their mother."

He nods his head. "I've swept you off your feet, eh? That's good to know." He smiles and it quickly turns devilish. "Well, maybe all of those minor details will disappear when I actually turn seventeen. It looks like we only have a few more months to enjoy this, if that's the case."

"You're sixteen?" It rushes out a little louder than I might've liked.

He winks. "Yes, but only until November."

"But, you're a senior." I'm still shocked.

"Sunny thought Sebastian and I should start school early. We were a bit … advanced for our age. What's the big deal?"

What's the big deal? Other than the fact that he acts more mature and confident than any adult I've ever met, and now I find out he's even younger than I thought. I don't know how to respond. "I don't know. I guess I'm just sort of shocked. You seem so … old."

He's having fun with this. "*I'm* old? You're the cradle robber. Thirteen months is a *significant* age difference, Ronnie. I'm not the cougar here. I would never fault you for it though, there's something incredibly sexy about the idea—"

"How do you know how old I am?" I interject. "I never told you my birthday."

"I have my ways." He pushes his chair back and stands up. "We can finish this discussion in the car. We'd better get going."

I stand to face him and he takes my hands. The candlelight dances off his dark eyes as he looks longingly at me. This is it, I think, the moment I've been waiting for. We don't speak, but our eyes have this strange way of carrying on a conversation of their own. The things his eyes are saying are not discreet; they're purely seductive. My heart is hammering against my rib cage. He leans down and I close my eyes. My lips part in anticipation. He brushes the hair from the side of my neck and I feel his warm breath on my skin moving up toward my ear.

"May I kiss you?" he whispers.

Goose bumps instantly cover every inch of my tingling skin. My eyes still closed, I nod slightly once. His lips press gently against my earlobe and skim down my neck to my shoulder. I shiver with pleasure. He exhales softly. I don't hear it ... I *feel* it.

He releases my hands and softly lifts my face toward his. I smell peppermint lingering on his breath from the mint he's just eaten. His lips touch mine gently. They're soft and moist and delicious. My hands, which hang limply at my sides, move to his hips. He pulls me closer. I turn my mind off and let my body take over ... my hands glide slowly from his hips and unintentionally, but opportunely, find their way under his shirt. The skin on the small of his back is smooth and soft and *so* warm.

He emits a low moan. As if triggered, his hands move anxiously and become insatiably tangled in my hair. The soft kisses turn intense. My body is on fire. My hands ball up into fists at his back. His hands unclench from my hair and run down my back and circle up to my shoulders. And too soon his mouth parts from mine with a sigh. We stand motionless for a few seconds, only inches from each other, breathing deeply. His hands rest on my shoulders while mine are on his hips at his waistband under his shirt.

"This probably isn't appropriate; this *is* a family restaurant," he says through heavy breaths. He kisses my earlobe again and his lips trace my jawline lightly to my lips, which he kisses softly. "We should go, or Pedro will have to start charging admission."

I open my eyes to see two young bus boys standing just outside the doorway peeking in at us. They scurry away when they realize they've been caught. I drop my hands and my cheeks blush. I'm not usually so forward, but I'm caught up in the moment. Dimitri's hands still cup my shoulders. The corners of his mouth turn up sheepishly. He kisses my forehead and then leads me toward the door.

The car ride to his house begins quietly. The kiss has left

me dizzy. I look out into the darkness and replay it over and over again in my head.

As if on cue, Dimitri takes my hand. "What are you thinking about?"

I sigh and look at him. The faint lights from the instruments on the dash cast a glow on him. "I'm wondering when I am going to wake up, because I must be dreaming."

He squeezes my hand and smiles. "I assure you, you're awake."

"My dreams are really vivid though, you always seem very real in them." I'm slightly embarrassed at having divulged this highly personal information.

His hand tightens around mine. "You dream about me?" His voice is filled with shock and disbelief.

I look away, pause, and then say, "Yes, almost every night since we met."

"If you don't mind me asking, what are the dreams about?" His grip is surprising.

"They're strange … and short. In all of the dreams we're meeting each other for the first time, but each dream is set in a different place and time." My voice is distant as I try to recall them all.

"Can you tell me about one of them?"

"Well, last night I dreamt that I was a nurse and you were a wounded soldier that I was tending to."

"World War Two." It isn't audible, but I see his lips move.

"Yes, World War Two, good guess. It was so real: the images, the sounds, the smells … the pain … " My voice trails off at the memory of it. "It was awful … a nightmare really, until I saw your face and you spoke to me." I smile and look at him. His eyes look glassy, like there are tears in them. "What's wrong?" I whisper.

He takes a deep breath and blinks a few times. "Nothing." It's quiet for more than a minute and I assume he's dropped the subject. "I guess I was hoping for something a little less … dramatic and more … *pleasurable*." The corner of his mouth turns up into a devious grin.

69

I blush. "Sorry to disappoint you." I hesitate, then ask, "Do you dream about me?"

He looks out his window and then back to me. "Yes, for what seems years. And there's *no* drama. *Strictly* pleasure. Last night involved you and me, a cramped supply closet in the art building at school, and lots of paint creatively applied." He sighs faintly. "God, your body makes a beautiful canvas ... "

I clear my throat. My face burns and my skin tingles. "Um, yeah ... "

"What? You asked, I answered." He glances at me again and takes in my blush through the darkness. "I'm sorry if I embarrassed you."

"You certainly don't hold anything back, do you?" I have to shift the attention away.

"Why should I? I'll always let you know exactly how I feel."

"That's very admirable of you." There's a touch of sarcasm in my voice. "If you're only sixteen, how did you get so good at seducing women? You've obviously had a lot of practice."

"Seducing? Did you just say *seducing*? You haven't seen anything yet." His hand touches my thigh. "And there's been no *practice*, as you put it. I save this all up for you."

I laugh. "You expect me to believe that? You're too good at this. You've probably dated dozens of girls."

He smiles at me thoughtfully, but his eyes are completely serious. "I've never dated anyone else but you."

Life is sometimes ... like a dream.

Chapter 5
There should always be another kiss
And another after that

Dimitri's house, I soon find out, is located in a very exclusive neighborhood that's many miles from mine. We're not in the suburbs anymore. The neighborhood itself has always been somewhat of a mystery to me. It's a gated community surrounded by high walls, so access is limited and I've never known anyone who lived inside ... until now. We pull up to the security gate and we are greeted by a short, stocky, balding, middle-aged man who says politely, "Good evening, Mr. Glenn."

"Good evening, Charlie."

"How was dinner?" Charlie asks Dimitri with a sly smile. He's bent down peering at me through the driver's side window.

Dimitri is clearly amused by his direct curiosity. "Excellent. Charlie, this is my friend, Veronica Smith. The one I was telling you about."

Charlie raises a hand to wave. "Pleased to meet you, Miss Smith."

"Likewise, Charlie," I say.

Charlie taps Dimitri on the shoulder. "You sure were right, she's a beauty. How'd she fall for a guy like you?" he adds with a deep chuckle.

"Just lucky, Charlie ... I'm just lucky." He smiles. The banter is easy between these two. It seems Dimitri can get along with just about anyone.

Charlie hands a small handheld device to Dimitri. Dimitri pushes a few buttons and places his index finger firmly against the small screen and hands it back to Charlie. The security gates begin to open slowly.

"Have a great day off tomorrow, Charlie. You going fishing?"

"Of course! We don't have much good weather left— have to get out there while I can. You two enjoy the rest of your evening." He bends down again to look at me through Dimitri's open window. "Nice to meet you, miss."

"Nice to meet you, too, Charlie."

We roll slowly through the gate and into Dimitri's mysterious neighborhood. There don't appear to be many houses. The ones I do see all sit on very large lots, which is kind of a necessity because these homes are huge ... no, not huge ... *gargantuan.* And they're all different—some old, some new, but all of them are statuesque and meticulously well kept. Even in the dark I can see how immaculate they are. Each one looks as if it's been torn from the pages of *Home & Garden* magazine.

"All these years, I always wondered what kind of homes were behind those walls," I say quietly to myself. "And now I know." I look at Dimitri. "Do you realize how fantastic this neighborhood is?" I'm in shock.

"If you're asking if I realize how fortunate I am to have a roof over my head, the answer is yes. But, they're just people's homes, Ronnie. Just like your home. No better. Ordinary people live here." He points to a brick mansion on my right. "Well, except maybe them. They're pompous assholes."

I laugh humorlessly. "Well, these *ordinary* people have *extraordinary* homes." I continue gawking out the window. "Which one is your favorite?"

"My favorite is the house at the end of the next street." Dimitri turns the corner and drives down a dark street. As he rounds the bend, he points at the end of the cul-de-sac. "That's my favorite."

He stops in the middle of the road and before us stands the most incredible, grand-looking home I've ever seen. It's dark outside, but strategic lighting in the yard allows us to take in all of its detail and glory. The home is all stone and looks more like a castle than someone's house. It stands three stories tall and looks European—old, but perfectly preserved. The front yard is manicured to perfection.

"Wow, I can see why it's your favorite. It's beautiful. Are you sure it's a house though? It looks more like a hotel?"

We sit in silence for a minute, admiring like a couple of sightseers.

"Do you know the people that live there?" I ask, still in awe.

"Yes, they're a very nice family."

"Not pompous assholes?"

He smiles. "Not at all." The car starts rolling slowly down the street and stops just in front of the driveway. He looks at the house, his smile widens, and he points to the window next to the front doors. "And I think they're very anxious to meet you." There's a woman holding the curtain back waving at us through the window.

"That's your mom, isn't it? This is *your* house?" I'm dumbfounded.

He takes a deep breath and eases the car up the curb and down the driveway. "Yes, that's Sunny. And unless she sold the house today and didn't tell Sebastian and me, which knowing her is a possibility, this is still our house."

Then it dawns on me how far Dimitri lives from our school. "Don't get me wrong, I really love that we ended up in the same high school, but you are like, *way* out of district boundaries living here. Why don't you go to West Hills?"

"This life is all about choices, Ronnie, and this particular choice was imperative."

I wait for more, but nothing comes. "That's it?"

He smiles. "That's it."

The driveway is long and winds down behind the house and ends in front of a six-stall garage. One of the doors farthest from the house begins to open just as Dimitri raises his hand to push the garage door opener on his visor. He shakes his head. "Sunny must really be excited; she's not even going to let me open the garage door myself."

He pulls the Porsche into a very brightly lit and very clean garage. It reminds me of my dad's, but kicked up a few notches.

Dimitri takes my hand. "I really hope you like my family, because I know they're going to love you." His voice is gentle, hopeful, and reassuring.

I pat our interlocked hands. "If they are anything like you, I'm sure I'll love them, too."

He smiles that beautiful smile of his. "Wait there." He

exits his door and comes around to open mine. I take his offered hand anxiously.

"This must be the Volkswagen," I say, pointing to the car in the next stall.

He looks at me tentatively. "This is it. What do you think?" He seems to be holding his breath.

I walk over and peek inside. "It's great, very cool. I love the red interior. What color are you going to paint it?"

He shrugs. "Black. Is there any other color?"

I look back at his Porsche, and at the Mini Cooper, Mercedes, and SUV parked in the stalls on the other side of it, all of which are black, and raise my eyebrows. "Apparently not."

He squeezes my hand. "We can't put this off any longer or Sunny will have a stroke, and I'd hate for that to happen. I'm rather fond of her."

He leads me across the garage and into a breezeway that's connected to the house. The door opens suddenly and there stands a tall, slender woman with blond hair and big blue eyes. It strikes me how young and pretty she is. Of course she would be pretty, I think to myself. Look at her children! I tense up, which Dimitri senses immediately. He rubs my arm with his free hand and whispers in my ear, "She won't bite. She's completely harmless, I promise."

Sunny positively beams. Her smile is so friendly and warm that my nerves calm down immediately.

"Mom, this is Veronica. Veronica, this is Sunny."

Sunny closes the gap between us quickly and pulls me into a hug, as if I'm an old friend. Stunned, I stand there with my arms hanging at my sides. She doesn't seem to notice. She tightens her grip and then releases me. When she places her hands on my shoulders I realize how tall she is— Dimitri's height. I have to tilt my head up to see her face.

"It is so good to meet you, Veronica." Her voice is warm, tinged with a Texan accent, and flooded with excitement. "Welcome to our home. Won't you come inside?"

"I'd love to. Your home is beautiful, Sunny."

"Thank you." Sunny steps aside and gestures for us to

enter. She falls in step behind Dimitri squeezing his shoulders. She's trying to whisper, but her excitement makes it impossible, "She's so pretty, D. You two look precious together."

I step inside the back door and the loveliest feeling sweeps over me. Not only is the air filled with the aroma of freshly baked chocolate cookies, it's also filled with love. It feels like my parents' home. I've always thought that you can get a pretty good read on a person by visiting their family home. The house itself tells a story. Houses can be happy, sad, calm, angry, peaceful, or cold. This home is filled with love.

"Can I get you something to drink, Veronica?" Sunny offers.

"No, thank you. I'm okay right now; we've just come from dinner."

Sunny looks at me expectantly. "How was it? Did you love it?"

"Love it? It was perfect, like a fairy tale."

Sunny looks to Dimitri, her eyebrows pinched together. "Were the candles too much?"

Dimitri laughs. "I don't know how he got away with it without burning the place down. You should've seen it."

Sunny pulls her cell phone out of her back pocket, presses a button and holds the screen up for us to look. The phone displays a photo of the room we ate dinner in. "Oh, I saw it. You didn't think Pedro actually pulled it all off by himself, did you? Do you know how hard it is to round up two hundred candles and ten dozen pink lilies in two hours?"

Dimitri hugs Sunny. "Thanks Mom."

She kisses him on the cheek and ruffles his hair. "Clearly it was all worth it." Sunny turns toward me and takes my hand in hers. "My D. is a very particular young man. He knows what he wants and he's very driven, much like his father was. He's extremely selective about the company he keeps. I knew that you must be very special for him to have become so taken with you in such a short time. And after getting to meet you, I can see that you are. Please know that you are welcome in our home anytime you like,

75

and I look forward to seeing you often." She smiles warmly and her blue eyes glitter.

"Thank you so much, Sunny."

"Well, I'd better get to bed now. I need to play piano at church tomorrow morning. Sebastian's watching a movie in the theater. Good night you two," she says. And then, to Dimitri, "I love you, D."

"I love you, too, Mom."

"Make sure he shows you the gallery, Veronica," Sunny says over her shoulder as she disappears into the adjoining room.

"Mom," Dimitri groans, his voice tinged with embarrassment as he shakes his head.

She reappears around the corner for a split second, winks and disappears.

"She's great," I say.

"She is. Sebastian and I have been blessed this time." He's still looking in the direction Sunny has disappeared with a smile on his face.

"This time?" What an odd thing to say, I think.

He dismisses it airily. "Nevermind," he says, and turns to face me. "What would you like to do?"

"How about you show me around? Judging by the size of this place that may take the rest of the night and some of the morning. Apparently there's a gallery I'm supposed to see, too."

He takes my hand and leads me through the massive kitchen and dining room to a room near the front of the house. "This is the music room."

He turns on the lights to reveal a large room with very high ceilings. Everything in the room is bright white—the walls, the carpet, the drapes, the furniture; the only exception is the shiny, black grand piano sitting at the far end of the room. It's striking. He stands quietly just inside the room watching me as I look around. "You can come in, Ronnie."

"I don't want to get the carpet dirty," I say, looking down at my shoes.

He laughs. "We do *live* here. It's not just to look at. Take your shoes off if it makes you feel better."

I reach down and slip my sandals off and set them on the gleaming, dark hardwood floor just outside the music room. The carpet is plush and soft under my bare feet as I enter. "Do you play?" I ask pointing toward the piano.

"A little, but I'd rather listen to you play something." He takes my hand and leads me to the piano.

"Oh, I don't play."

He looks a little shocked. "You're joking, right?"

I shrug. "No."

He seems to be searching for words. "Oh, well … I saw the piano at your house and just assumed."

"My mom always wanted me to take lessons, but it never really interested me."

"Does she play?"

"Are you kidding? She's taken lessons three or four different times, but can never fully devote herself to it. If you couldn't tell by meeting her this morning, she's the type of person that has to be in constant motion. Sitting down is a struggle, so playing the piano is sort of out of the question. Maybe medication would help."

Dimitri laughs and flashes that knowing smile. "I think I understand. But seriously, you should learn to play. I know you would be great at it."

"Maybe someday you can teach me. I do love listening to piano music. Will you play something for me? Or will it wake up your mom?"

He walks back and shuts the double doors. "Sunny's bedroom is on the third floor. She won't hear a thing. With the doors shut the room is practically soundproof anyway. I come down and play when I can't sleep." He crosses his fingers. "Insomnia and I are like this, so Sunny took some precautions to ensure she and Sebastian get their beauty sleep while I roam during my sleepless nights. Any requests, what would you like to hear?"

With the doors shut, the room has become very intimate. Dimitri dims the lights, takes my hand and leads me to the piano bench. I sit down next to him and he begins to play. I'm mesmerized watching his hands move gracefully across the keys. He makes it look effortless and easy. He plays

77

several songs, a mixture of classical, current, and in-between, each running into the next. I've never considered pianists to be especially sexy, at least not until this very moment. But then again, almost everything Dimitri does is sexy. It must show on my face.

He looks at me out of the corner of his eye as he's playing. I'm shamelessly staring at him. He grins, clearly pleased with himself, and looks back down at the keys. "You're staring, Ronnie."

"How'd you learn to play like this? I thought you said you only played a 'little.'"

"Let's just say I've played for a very long time." He looks at me and the mischievous grin remains. He finishes the song and turns to look at me. "Let's go find Sebastian."

Dimitri opens the doors and I pick up my sandals and carry them with me. He leads me through a few more dark rooms to a staircase that descends down. "The theater is in the basement. Sunny kind of insisted on it. She doesn't seem to appreciate the fact that you can't enjoy a movie unless it's *really* loud, so she banished us to the basement."

At the bottom of the stairs there's a huge game room complete with pool tables, pinball machines, several oversized sofas, and two big screen TVs. At the far end of the room an old-fashioned cinema marquee hangs above a set of double doors. Next to the doors is a snack bar that would put a real movie theater to shame. It is stocked with candy, a soda cooler, and a monstrous popcorn machine.

"Do you want something to eat or drink?" Dimitri asks, as if everyone has one of these in their basement.

The popcorn smells so delicious that even though I'm still stuffed from dinner, I can't resist. "The popcorn does smell good."

He fills up a small bucket. "Butter?"

"Please."

He walks from behind the counter with a bucket of popcorn and a bottle of Dr. Pepper and stops to look at a small screen on the wall next to the theater doors. "Looks like they're watching a martial arts movie. Do you want to stay and watch?"

"Martial arts movies aren't my thing, but if it's something you want to watch we can."

"Sebastian and I have seen it at least ten times, I'm pretty sure I can sit this one out. Let's just let him know we're here. He wants to meet you, too. He's got quite a few friends over judging by all the cars on the street out front, so this should be quick."

Dimitri opens the door and I stand behind him. The noise is thunderous. I fully understand Sunny banishing the theater to the basement now. I peek around him to look inside. The screen covers the entire wall and there are several rows of recliners in the room. Though the room is dark I can tell about half of them are occupied with people intently watching the movie. They haven't noticed us yet. Dimitri cups his hands around his mouth and yells, "Sebastian!" Every head turns to face us. The volume lowers to a tolerable level and the lights rise slightly.

Someone stands up in the front row and walks down the aisle toward us. Sebastian greets me with the same familiar, warm smile he shared earlier in the week when I saw him through the gym window, and at the sight of it the same protective feeling rises up inside me.

"I was wondering if D. was ever going to introduce us. He won't shut up about you, you know?" His smile widens and he glances quickly to Dimitri and back to me.

I step from behind Dimitri, thankful for the dim lights— I can feel my face reddening. "It's nice to finally meet you, Sebastian." There's that nagging feeling again that I've met him before. He looks so familiar.

He laughs softly. "Finally ... "

We're interrupted by several shouts coming from within the room, "Veronica? What's up! What are you doing here? I know how you *love* martial arts movies. Come on in!"

I squint and look at the people standing or peering around the backs of their chairs. I recognize almost every face, though some I don't know by name. Most of them are juniors or seniors from school. Then I see my best friend Teagan standing up, and Tate right beside him. I smile broadly and wave. "Hey guys!"

Teagan, Tate, and I have been friends since grade school. They're like brothers to me. I give them advice, whether they want it or not (I can be bossy, I admit it) and they watch out for me, whether I want it or not (they're like brothers to me). It's a great arrangement that I wouldn't trade for anything. Teagan and Tate consider me to be one of the guys. Truth be told, I'm fairly certain they didn't realize I was indeed female until we'd already been best friends for several years. We talk about anything and everything. They don't censor themselves around me. In fact, they're brutally honest. Since our childhood days, they've grown into big, handsome young men—but we're just friends. They're certainly nice to look at though. And it is humorous to watch the girls at school fall all over themselves around them. These same girls either loathe me or love me depending on their method of approaching my boys.

Teagan walks toward us and holds out his hand to Dimitri. "Dimitri, right?"

Dimitri shakes his hand. "That's me."

I feel the need to intervene, because Teagan's manners suck. "Dimitri, this is Teagan."

Dimitri and Teagans' hands are still interlocked and Teagan's knuckles are almost white. "Nice to meet you, Teagan." Dimitri's voice sounds marginally polite, but there's a tense edge to it.

This isn't going well. Dimitri isn't the least bit intimidated and Teagan never backs down. I put my hand on Teagan's arm, which is rock hard, "That's enough, Teag," I say quietly through gritted teeth, trying not to make a scene.

Too late.

Tate is still standing. "Take it easy on him, Teag. Veronica can take care of herself."

Teagan drops Dimitri's hand harshly, but stares him down. "Listen chief, it's nothing personal, but if you hurt her I *will* kick your ass."

"Teagan!" I grab him by the wrist and pull him out into the game room. "What are you doing?" I'm trying to lower my voice, but the anger is bubbling up. "Are you insane?"

"I don't know about this guy, Veronica. He looks like

kind of a dick." The veins in his neck are standing out against his skin.

"Whatever, Teagan! I have a *dad,* thank you very much! I don't need protecting. Let's not judge the boyfriend, okay? I really like him. Don't screw this up for me. You'd like him too if you gave him a chance." My rage has somehow morphed into desperation.

The aggressive edge is fading from Teagan's face. "You'll tell us if he treats you bad, because I mean it. I'll fuck him up."

"Teagan, you know I don't put up with shit from anyone. Dimitri's not an exception. But trust me, this whole conversation is asinine; you don't have anything to worry about. He's amazing."

I've finally cracked him. He smirks. "Asinine, huh? That's a pretty big word. This must be serious."

I allow myself a smirk because I can't hold back some variation of a smile. "Jackass."

"You know you love it." He pulls me into a hug, which is like being crushed by a grizzly bear, and whispers in my ear, "Don't hate me for wanting to protect you. You're my best friend. I'd do anything for you."

My smile turns devilish as he releases me. "I'm glad you said that, because I really need you to do something right now."

He knows me. "Dude, what?"

"Apologize to Dimitri." It isn't a request; it's a demand.

He huffs. "Do I have a choice, Mom?" His voice is exaggerated, like a whining child.

My voice counters with authority and leaves no alternatives. "No." I smile, turn him around, and push him toward Dimitri who's still standing with Sebastian.

Teagan sounds defeated. "Sorry, man. Veronica's like a sister to me. I got a little carried away."

Dimitri is far more gracious than he probably should be, given the provocation, and I'm relieved and grateful for it. "I understand." He looks from Teagan to me. "She's easy to get carried away with. I have no intentions of hurting her." His eyes linger on mine for several seconds before turning back to Teagan and Sebastian. "We've interrupted your movie long enough; we'll let you get back to it."

Dimitri takes my hand and turns to go back upstairs.

I look back over my shoulder, first at Sebastian. "See you later, Sebastian. I'm sorry about that." Then I turn my eyes to Teagan. I scowl. Unaffected, Teagan just smiles with an innocent shrug of his shoulders.

When we reach the top of the stairs I let Dimitri lead me what I feel is a safe distance, through a room or two, before I stop him. The room is very dark. I turn him to face me. "I'm so sorry, Dimitri. I don't know what got into Teagan."

I can't see him, but I feel his fingertips brush my cheek. "I do. *You.* There's no need to apologize. It's not your fault you're so irresistible."

"What? No. No, no, no, it's not like that. I've known Teagan since we were six ... I ... " I don't feel like I'm explaining myself very well, but Dimitri patiently waits for me to finish. "He's my best friend. He doesn't think of me that way."

"Ronnie, I'm a guy. And I'm not blind or stupid. You don't think I see how other guys look at you and act around you?"

I wish I could see his face, even a glimpse; it's really dark in here. "Dimitri, I think you're exaggerating."

"Exaggerating? Even if I wasn't half as observant as I am, do you think it's gone unnoticed that we've been spending a lot of time together this week? Do you know how many guys at school have approached me the past few days to tell me what a lucky bastard I am? Sebastian's playing soccer this fall and has already warned me that half the team wants to get in your panties."

"Ha. Now I know you're lying. I know almost everyone on the soccer team, and—"

He interrupts me, "Apparently not as well as you think you do." His voice softens. "Listen, Ronnie, I'm not saying all of this to get a reaction out of you, or an explanation, or anything else. Your vulnerability—the way you just don't see how truly special you are—is one of the things I love most about you." He adds in a whisper, "And always have."

"You've only known me a week."

He doesn't miss a beat. "It seems like much longer for me."

I raise my hand and place it on his chest. I feel the slow, rhythmic beat of his heart under a layer of tight muscle through his shirt; my mind flashes back to the sight of him removing his wet shirt in my kitchen after the rainstorm a few days ago. I have to remind myself to focus. "Dimitri, I still think you're exaggerating, but I want you to know I don't want anyone else but you. And by the way, the picture you paint of me is nothing compared to the spell you've cast over ninety-nine percent of the female population at school. I may be oblivious to the way guys look at me, but I do notice the way girls look at you. They're all practically undressing you with their eyes."

He laughs softly and his response is playful and sarcastic. "Can you blame them?"

I blush, but answer anyway. "No … not that *I've* done anything like that."

He's still holding the popcorn and Dr. Pepper in one hand, but wraps his free hand around my waist and whispers, "Too bad. I'd even let *you* use your hands." I feel his warm breath on my face. He pulls me closer.

"Dimi—" His mouth on mine cuts off my words. I drop the sandals that I've been carrying and they hit the floor with a thud as I wrap both arms around his neck. Our mouths mold to each other in perfect harmony as if we've done this for years. I anticipate every movement of his lips and tongue. He pulls away only to focus his kisses on my neck, first one side and then the other. The sensations that run through my body are foreign and mind numbing. I've kissed other guys before, but it was nothing like this. My entire body reacts to his touch.

Suddenly Dimitri groans in protest and slowly pulls away. I slip back to reality and realize I hear someone clearing his throat behind Dimitri.

Dimitri speaks in a voice equal parts amused and annoyed. "Sebastian, you have remarkable timing. What do you want?"

83

I open my eyes to see Sebastian standing behind Dimitri. He's turned on the light in the stairway leading up from the basement and it casts a faint glow upon the dark room.

"Nothing. The movie's over and I was just running up to my room to grab my iPod so we can listen to some music. Sorry to interrupt." The wicked smile on his face contradicts his words and betrays the pleasure he's taking in irritating his brother. "Resume." Then he's gone.

I look up at Dimitri who is shaking his head and wearing that beautiful smile. My eyes are beginning to adjust to the faint light seeping in from the stairway, and I can see that we're standing next to the entrance to a long, narrow room. The room looks to be at least two stories tall, with upholstered benches in the center running parallel to the longer walls. I squint, looking from one massive wall to the next.

Dimitri takes my hand, clearly trying to coax me away. "Come on, Ronnie. Let's go up to my room. I'm on my best behavior now. We can watch a movie or listen to some music."

I ignore him, drop his hand and walk into the room. "What is this?" My voice is full of wonder and curiosity. The bright white walls almost glow, even in the dark, but dark shapes on them randomly break up the glow of the walls. I step closer to the nearest wall for a closer inspection and realize the dark shapes are paintings.

At that same moment, I hear Dimitri inhale and exhale deeply before he says softly, "This is the gallery." He turns on the lights, and I'm momentarily blinded.

But then, I look up and down each wall and turn slowly in a circle. The paintings are hung both high and low on all of the walls. There are dozens of them, most of them large, but some small. I walk to the far end of the room and back down the other side looking at each painting intently. Though all of the paintings are different, they all appear—at least to an untrained eye—to be painted by the same artist. When I complete the loop and recognize I'm looking at the first painting again I turn to look for Dimitri. He's sitting on one of the benches eating our popcorn.

84

He lazily extends the bucket toward me. "Do you want some before it's all gone?"

I walk over and sit down next to him and grab a few kernels, chewing as I talk. "I can see why Sunny wanted me to see her gallery. She should be very proud of it."

"You have no idea," Dimitri mumbles under his breath as he rolls his eyes and shoves another handful of popcorn into his mouth.

"Did the same artist paint all of them?"

He's still chewing very deliberately, but nods a confirmation.

"You'll have to excuse me; I don't know that much about art. I just know what I like or what I think is pretty."

"Do you like them?"

"Like them? They're fantastic! This is such an impressive collection. I guess she really likes the artist to have collected so many of his pieces."

His cheeks turn rosy and there's an impish grin on his face. He looks embarrassed. "You could say that. Which one is your favorite?"

"That's a hard question. I like them all, but I think my favorite is the small one of the Eiffel Tower. I'm kind of fascinated with Paris anyway, but that one, the way it's painted as if twilight has descended upon it … it's gorgeous. The dark background lends an eerie quality, but the Tower, bathed in moonlight, stands out in subtle contrast against it. The imagery is romantic, like a dark, beautiful fairy tale."

His smile widens and his gray eyes shine. "I was hoping you'd say that. I want you to have it. It's yours."

I involuntarily gasp, "What? No!" I catch my breath. "You can't give your mom's painting away."

He's still smiling, but the embarrassment has vanished and he speaks slowly, "These aren't *Sunny's* paintings, Ronnie."

"Then whose are they?"

He's silent. The smile fades and his eyebrows rise as if to answer my question and acknowledge guilt in the same humble instant.

"They're *yours*?" It comes out as a whisper and the

pieces all start to fall into place. I stand up and walk to the nearest painting to check out the artist's signature in the lower right hand corner. Though the script is small, it's legible. D. GLENN. My jaw drops and I turn around slowly to face him again. "You *painted* all of these?"

"Yes." He sits solemnly, looking at me. I'm suddenly staring at a much older man, someone with years of life experience, someone who has unmatched confidence and the accomplishments and talent to substantiate it. I see a flash of the man Dimitri's destined to be.

"Holy shit." Dazed, I walk back over and sit down next to him. I grab the last handful of popcorn from the bucket, chew it slowly, thoroughly, and swallow it. I pick up the Dr. Pepper and take several big gulps before I look at him again. "Is there anything you can't do? I don't know if we should hang out. I may not be qualified."

He laughs quietly, pauses, and thoughtfully says, "I can't cook anything but grilled cheese sandwiches, I don't know how to swim, and I can't spell to save my life. You're much smarter than I am. I could go on … "

I smile. "Seriously, Dimitri, this is *really* impressive."

He takes my hand and stands up. "It is what it is. I enjoy painting and it puts a little money in my pocket. It works out well for me."

I nod mechanically, still bewildered. "It works out well for you? That's a *colossal* understatement my talented friend."

He leads me to the Eiffel Tower painting and gently removes it from the wall and holds it pressed up against his torso, facing me. "I was going to save it for your birthday, but I guess now that you've already seen it, it wouldn't be much of a surprise."

"I can't take it, Dimitri."

His eyes blaze through me, but his voice is soft. "Ronnie, I painted it for *you*. See?" He points to the upper left corner of the painting.

The writing is small. I couldn't have read it while it was hanging up on the wall, but I can see now that it reads, *"To my darling Ronnie. Je t'aime. XOXO."*

My eyes fill up with tears that quickly spill over. I lightly trace my finger over the words and then look up at him. "Merci … "

He crouches to set the painting against the wall, then stands up and wipes my tears away with the gentle swipe of his thumb. "De rien," he says. He pauses and smiles. "You're welcome."

"You speak French?"

He winks and shrugs. "Oui … a little."

"A 'little,' huh? I've heard that one before." I glance at my watch just then, realizing that the concept of time has completely escaped me. I gasp in shock and disappointment. "It's two-thirty in the morning?"

Dimitri looks at his watch and nods, "I guess it is. Time flies … "

"I probably should go before Mom and Dad start to worry. I really don't want this night to end though; I didn't even get to see your room."

He runs his fingers absently through my hair and the corner of his mouth turns up in that mischievous grin that makes my heart skip a beat. "Let's save that for another time. I have a feeling I may not be able to keep my hands off you if I get you up there right now." He winks devilishly. "I don't want to tempt you into compromising your spotless reputation."

How does everyone seem to know I'm a virgin? My face reddens and I avert my eyes. My gaze lands on my feet, which I notice are still bare. "Oh. Where are my shoes?"

The smile still in place, I sense he's waiting for me to look at him so that he can taunt me some more. "I think they're on the floor in the other room. You may have dropped them when you became otherwise engaged."

My cheeks grow impossibly warmer. I whisper, "Oh yeah … I forgot."

Dimitri pulls his Porsche up into my driveway and puts it in park. Leaving it running, he quickly gets out to come around and open my door. I pry myself from the passenger seat; I don't want to say goodnight, even though by now it's early morning. He pulls me into the most comforting hug. His arms don't encircle me. They engulf me. I'm completely surrounded by his warmth, his smell, his kindness, and his love. I stand there in silence with my eyes closed and my head resting against his chest listening to the beat of his heart for several minutes. He squeezes me tightly, kisses the top of my head, and releases me. The cool morning air creeps in all around me and I shiver violently.

"You'd better get inside and get to bed."

While I unlock the back door of my house, he retrieves my early birthday present from his car. I turn and reach out to take the painting with both hands. I'm scared to touch it, afraid I might drop it. "Thank you so much … for everything. I'll never forget this night for as long as I live."

He rubs my back and his mouth turns up in a slight smile. "I'm counting on that, Ronnie." He leans in over the painting and presses his lips against mine and holds them there for several seconds before pulling away. "I'll call you after we get home from church later this morning. Sweet dreams."

He holds the door for me to get inside, walks to his car, and waves back at me before ducking inside and backing down the drive.

I walk gingerly down the stairs to my bedroom, being careful not to bump the painting against the walls. I set it on the floor of my room, propped up against the wall next to my bed. I slip my shoes off and lay down on my bed, staring at the painting.

I think about Dimitri. My mind begins to drift and my eyes grow heavy. Before I know it, I'm dreaming …

We are staring at each other across the dance floor of a large ballroom. Dimitri is dressed in a tailored suit. The room is crowded with woman in elegant, floor-length ball gowns. Couples glide around the dance floor to the music of a string quartet tucked away near the far end of the room. Dimitri makes his way slowly across the floor, gracefully dodging the dancers spinning and twirling around him, never taking his eyes off me. In a short time he's standing before me, bowing deeply. He gently raises my hand and kisses the back of it. "Good evening, Miss Smith."

I attempt to contain my smile, but it stretches from ear to ear. "Good evening, Dimitri."

In my dream, we are speaking in French, but I hear every word in English.

He gestures toward the dance floor. "Would you like to dance, Veronica? Or can I interest you in a walk this evening? The air is still warm and twilight draws near. The moon will be full tonight with plenty of light to walk by."

"A walk sounds lovely."

He turns and offers his elbow, which I promptly take and hold tightly. His touch, even through layers of clothing, is heavenly. I've not known him long and being near him is intoxicating.

We walk out into the warm evening air and dodge horse-drawn carriages as we cross the road.

"Where are we going?" I ask curiously.

"I want to show you something. I take this walk every night, but always alone. I thought it would be nice to share it ..."

I finish his thought, "With someone."

He smiles briefly and the ghost left behind coaxes a blush to my cheeks. He corrects, "With you."

The blush deepens and my arm that's touching his warms considerably. I walk as if on a cloud, barely seeing what's ahead, my world fuzzy with anticipation. His words bring me back and alert me to the fact that we've reached the river.

"I love a walk along the Seine at this time of day. At twilight, the water looks like a black mirror, ominous and beautiful. There's something very passionate and sensual about it. It's inspiring."

"Inspiring? How so?" I'm intrigued. Gentlemen do not talk this way in the company of ladies. It's intimate, and though I know it's inappropriate, I want to hear more.

"I am a painter. The river's dark allure inspires me. I do my best work after returning home from a walk beside her." His smile turns mischievous, "I perform brilliantly when I'm fully stimulated—my imagination aroused by

beauty. Especially late at night." He adds with a wink.

Heavens. Did it just get hot? Now my entire body is warm. I clear my throat. "I didn't know you painted? I mean, I guess I don't know anything about you really, since I've only just made your acquaintance a few weeks ago." I smile coyly. "Apart from the fact that you are partial to pistachio macaroons."

Dimitri began patronizing my parents' patisserie a month ago. He only ever buys pistachio macaroons. He stops in every Tuesday and Friday afternoon at four-fifteen. He didn't introduce himself until the second week, and by the third we engaged in friendly conversation. I learned he lives with his brother in the Latin Quarter, but visits this quartier twice a week for "personal reasons." This past week he asked me to meet him at the midsummer ball in the dance hall near Montparnasse. And I couldn't say no.

His knowing smile holds many secrets. "You know me better than you might think."

We walk with arms linked for quite a distance along the river. Soon, I began to look at it through a different set of eyes. It arouses something intense inside me, something that's new, yet familiar at the same time. It is beautiful at this time of day, I think.

Night has fallen completely and in the near distance I see the Eiffel Tower aglow in the light of the full moon. I love the Eiffel Tower. I stop and sigh, "I never grow tired of admiring it."

He follows my gaze to the Tower. "It's magnificent, isn't it?"

"It is. I remember watching it being constructed as a little girl. We've always lived in the 7th arrondissement, so I'd make my mother or father walk me here to the site every day. They took me to the fair when it was finally finished. It still takes my breath away, even after looking at it finished every day for more than ten years now."

"Have you ever been to the top? The view is spectacular."

"Only once. A couple of years ago, on my fourteenth birthday, my mother and father took me. I'll never forget it. I

could see Notre Dame, Arc de Triomphe, Jardin du Luxembourg, I think I could even see Sorbonne." I sigh again.

"I have a surprise for you."

"For me?

We begin walking toward the Tower, and excitement slowly builds inside me.

Just as we reach it, it a young man steps out of the shadows. The sight of him makes me jump.

"Good evening, Henri." Dimitri greets him in a friendly manner and is obviously not surprised to see him.

"Good evening, Dimitri. Are you ready? You won't have much time."

Dimitri looks to me and grins devilishly. "I'm grateful for whatever time affords me."

We ascend a set of stairs, Henri opens a lock and Dimitri and I are soon deposited in an elevator that opens up near the top of the Eiffel Tower. I gather my skirts in one hand and grip the handrail with the other as I climb the narrow staircase to the top. Dimitri follows closely. I'm out of breath as I alight on the observation platform. I look out and say, breathlessly, "Is that really Paris?"

It is, of course, but from up this high and beneath a full moon it's more magical than I could ever imagine. Gaslights twinkle as far as I can see.

Dimitri stands behind me and boldly slips his arms around my waist. My body tingles. He whispers in my ear, "There's no other view like this in the world."

I can't speak. I nod in agreement instead. I stand in his embrace admiring the view for several minutes until his faint voice stirs me back to reality.

"I can't believe I'm saying this, but we should leave. Henri could get in a lot of trouble for letting us up here."

The fact that we are indeed trespassing had not occurred to me until now. "Oh. Oh! Of course." I turn to face him, but turn and steal one more glance over my shoulder. I may never have this opportunity again and I want to remember this moment forever.

His whisper draws my attention back to him. "The most

91

beautiful thing I've ever seen."

I look up into his eyes. I can't look away. "It is. Paris is beautiful."

The moonlight dances off his gray eyes. "I was referring to you." His voice is soft and beckoning. There's longing in his eyes so strong I feel it as though it's inside me. He raises his hands slowly to place them on my cheeks. His hands are incredibly soft and they tremble as he strokes his thumbs across my skin.

"May I kiss you?" he whispers.

Goose bumps instantly cover every inch of my already tingling skin. I close my eyes and nod slightly once ....

Life is sometimes ... tingly and covered with goose bumps.

Chapter 6
Life's most important questions
Should always be written in ALL CAPS

Dimitri calls the next morning, but I don't get to see him. My English paper is my date for the day. The next two weeks ramble on much the same way. Work and homecoming obligations have completely taken over my schedule and thrown my life into a state of chaos, which—although short-lived—doesn't allow me much time to spend with Dimitri outside of passing periods, lunch, and study hall.

Homecoming has mutated and taken on a life of its own. Piper is so stressed out that I have to take on some additional commitments along with selling tickets to head off her certain and unavoidable nervous breakdown. She's always had an exceptional gift for biting off more than she can chew, so I see it coming and am not surprised at all when I'm literally begged (on knees) to take over soliciting donations from local businesses for the raffle and ordering the catering.

The extra favors normally wouldn't be such a big deal, except for the fact that I also have a job. I work for a small optometry clinic. Officially, I answer phones, schedule appointments, and take care of the filing. Unofficially, I run errands for the doctors—like picking up their dry cleaning or lunch or dinner; entertain small children in the waiting area; act as counselor to Rita, the flighty optician, whose life plays out like a soap opera; a shoulder to cry on for Dolores, the middle-aged doctor's assistant who recently lost her husband of thirty-two years to a heart attack; and run interference in an attempt to squelch any office gossip Helen starts before it gets out of hand. Helen's the other desk clerk, and we typically work side-by-side. Basically, I just do whatever is asked of me (and often what isn't) under the silly notion that it will keep everyone happy. The staff is small and, to put it lightly, quirky.

The past two weeks I've been covering for Helen while she's on vacation. I usually only work two afternoons a week and every other Saturday, but while Helen is out I'm working every day after school until close at eight-thirty, plus both Saturdays.

Dimitri is so patient and understanding and at my beck and call whenever a free moment presents itself. Unfortunately, they're just those ... moments. Every night I leave work to find a note tucked under Jezebel's windshield wiper. Dimitri comes up with something new every night. Whether it's a drawing, or a joke, or a quote, or a pointless trivial fact, it always makes me smile. I find myself almost running out the door every night with butterflies in my stomach anticipating that little piece of him waiting there to greet me. I save them all in my glove box.

I tell my coworkers good night as I walk out the door on Friday night. Helen will be back on Monday. *Thank. Goodness.* Freedom ... the thought puts a smile on my face. I'm struggling to get my jacket on as I jog through the parking lot and not paying attention as I approach Jezebel. My hand finally breaks through the sleeve as I look up expectantly at the windshield ready to strip the note from under the wiper. But there's nothing. My smile vanishes and my heart drops. I stand there staring at the wiper, willing a piece of paper to appear out of thin air. Finally I sigh in defeat and open up my bag to hunt for my keys so that I can unlock the door and sulk in privacy behind closed doors.

"Looking for something?" I jump at the close proximity of the voice, but it doesn't scare me. The voice is unmistakable. I smile and turn around to see him walking up from behind Jezebel. His right hand is extended out in front of him holding a folded piece of red paper. "I decided to hand deliver this one tonight rather than leaving it. I hope that's okay."

I nod and take the note. I open it up and read the words written in handwriting that has become very familiar to me. There, written in all caps as always—though this time a small heart doodle is there, too—are the words, *"WILL YOU GO TO HOMECOMING WITH ME?"*

I've been so focused on getting the work done for homecoming that I honestly hadn't given any thought to actually going to the dance. It's seemed more like a burdensome homework assignment rather than an actual event I might attend. I stand there looking at the words on the page in silence while butterflies take flight inside my stomach. *He* wants to take *me* to homecoming!

"Well? Do I have to beg, Ronnie? I'm not above that, you know." His smile is so sweet it leaves me silent a few seconds longer than I intend.

Finally I pry my eyes from the note, offer a sheepish smile and a shrug. "I'd love to. But I have to help decorate the gym before and then sell tickets during the dance. That's not very fair to you."

"You only have to sell tickets until ten o'clock and then you're all mine. I already talked to Piper," he adds with a wink. "I'll crash the party then take you to dinner after the dance, since we won't have time to go before." His words make it clear that he's done his research and has already planned the evening, even if I haven't considered the possibilities.

I feel guilty. "I'm so sorry, Dimitri. I'm going to ruin the whole night. I never should've let Piper sucker me into this one." I fold the paper and shove it in my jacket pocket.

"Alas, she admits it. She *is* a sucker." He laughs at my obvious irritation and takes my free hand in his, squeezing it and brushing my cheek lightly with his other hand. "You won't ruin anything. If I get to spend five minutes with you it will be worth it."

I gasp as a realization sinks in. I've been so busy that I completely overlooked the fact that I don't have anything to wear. Even if I was only selling tickets, and not going with this adorable, perfect guy, I still need a dress.

His eyebrows pinch together. "What's wrong?"

"I don't have anything to wear." Panic rises in my voice.

A smile of relief crosses his lips. "Already taken care of."

"What do you mean?"

95

"I talked to your mom last week and she's already sewn a dress for you. She's been secretly working on it while you were at work every night." His smile is smug now.

Relief washes over me, but suddenly I don't want to give him the satisfaction. My mom is an amazing seamstress and I know the dress will be beautiful. "How did you know I'd say yes?"

"You can't resist me."

"Is that so?" I'm teasing him. Of course I can't resist him.

He takes a step closer until our bodies are touching. His smile turns into the mischievous variety, the one that both excites and terrifies me at the same time. It excites me because it's so inviting and indiscreet and it terrifies me for precisely the same reasons. He lowers his head until our noses touch. He closes his eyes and his palms gently press against my cheeks while his fingertips graze my ears and weave into my hair. I close my eyes and wait for his kiss. I feel his steady breath on my face, while mine is wildly uneven.

We stand there for more than thirty seconds before he breaks the silence. "Perhaps I was wrong. It looks like you can resist me after all." I hear the smile in his voice.

I can't stand it any longer. I reach up and clamp his face between my hands and pull his mouth to mine. The kiss is urgent and not at all gentle. I've been waiting for this kiss since our first date, exactly thirteen days ago. Believe me, I've been keeping track. I dream every night about kissing him. Apparently the wait has been too long for him as well. His breathing increases to match my erratic pace. I cannot physically get close enough to him, though we are held tightly against each other.

"Perhaps we should go somewhere a little more private," he says, pausing only long enough to get the words out quickly before his kisses fall on my neck below my ear.

"Perhaps," is all I can manage before I pull his lips back to mine. My head is spinning. In the back of my mind I know I should be embarrassed to be behaving this way in a public parking lot, especially in front of my office. But I cannot come up with a single reason to stop.

Dimitri wraps his arms around me and squeezes me to the point that breathing becomes difficult before releasing me, reluctantly pulling his lips from mine.

I open my eyes to see his beautiful face only a few inches from mine. His cheeks are flushed and his smile is angelic.

"Don't stop," I whisper pathetically.

"Don't tempt me," he whispers as he kisses my forehead. "Can I take you to dinner tonight?"

It takes me a moment to realize that homework can wait until Sunday. I'm free for the first time in almost two weeks. "I'm starving, but you don't need to buy me dinner. We can just go back to my house and eat there."

"I insist. I haven't had any proper time with you in far too long. I know you need to get up early for work. I promise not to keep you out too late. I just want to talk, just you and I. I miss you." He rubs my upper arms as he speaks.

"I've missed you, too. Weird, huh? It's hard to believe we met less than a month ago. I never thought I could miss someone I'd just met this much."

He smiles his knowing smile and shakes his head. "Not so weird."

"Will you follow me home so I can change my clothes?"

He opens my car door for me. "Of course. I'll see you in a few minutes."

He follows me home and entertains my mom and dad while I go downstairs to change. I hear them talking and laughing. It's still strange to me how well they all got along. Aren't teenage boys supposed to be scared of their girlfriend's parents, to act awkward, at a loss for words? Not Dimitri.

He takes me to a quaint little Italian restaurant I didn't even know existed. We share a plate of ravioli and a piece of tiramisu. I'm beginning to think he magically conjures up these places and they mysteriously disappear after we leave.

97

We walk out to his car holding hands. He's swinging our hands back and forth. "Do you want me to take you home?" he asks politely.

I'm exhausted but I refuse to surrender. "No."

He opens the passenger door and I climb in. I'm never going to get used to riding around in a Porsche. He shuts the door, walks around, and climbs in beside me. "I was hoping you would say that. What do you want to do?"

"I don't care. Any ideas?"

The mischievous grin emerges. "Oh, I have *plenty* of ideas."

"Any PG-rated ideas?"

He laughs. "Yeah, lucky for you I have a one or two of those, too. How about some tea?"

We stop at a nearby coffee shop. I order a chai tea and sip it while we sit and talk. We're so engrossed in conversation that we don't realize that all the guests have left; the place is empty except for us, and it's closing time. One of the employees walks to the front door near us and rudely flips the sign to "Closed." We can take a hint.

Dimitri helps me with my jacket and holds the door for me to exit. Once we're back in the car, we drive in silence back to my house, which is only about a mile away—not far enough to steal more time with him.

I sigh as he pulls into my driveway. I look at him and can see his gray eyes in the glow from the dash. He looks happy. "Thank you."

He takes my hand in his. "You're welcome, Ronnie." After releasing my hand reluctantly he comes around and opens my door.

"I guess I'll see you tomorrow night, then." I say expectantly.

"Ten o'clock sharp." He cradles the back of my head in his hand and gently pulls my forehead to his lips. The kiss is sweet and brief and leaves me wishing it had been on my lips. "Sleep well, baby. Good night."

"Good night," I whisper.

I watch him back down the drive before I go inside. I almost ache. It feels as if he's taken a vital part of me with him. Tomorrow night will be too long to wait to see him again. I text him when I step in the back door. Only two words: "*Miss you*".

My parents are already asleep, probably have been for hours, and the house is dark. I fumble my way downstairs to my room. I flip on the light to find a black dress lying out across my bed. It's satiny, sleeveless, and short. I immediately love it. There's a note beside it that reads, "*Ronnie, I hope you like the dress. Love, Mom.*"

My phone beeps less than a minute later. The text reads, "*Miss you more.*"

The next day at work passes by unbelievably fast. Saturdays are always busy, which is definitely a good thing today.

I drive straight to the school after work and am pleasantly surprised to see that Piper has recruited several more people to help with the decorations. (I don't call her Pied Piper for nothing—the nickname has come to fruition.) Some of them, including Chloe Murphy, aren't exactly people I would've chosen to spend a Saturday afternoon with, but they're my ticket to getting out of here more quickly and that will give me a little extra time to get ready for my date with prince charming, even if I have to wait hours before he shows up.

Piper runs over and hugs me. "Veronica! Going awesome. Kicking ass. Out of here by six o'clock. Easy-peasy." She's talking *extra* fast this afternoon, so I focus *extra* hard to keep up. "No dinner reservations? Back at seven to sell tickets?"

Don't get me wrong, I love Piper, but good God, communicating with this girl is like speaking Pig Latin sometimes. It keeps me on my toes though—it's like mental gymnastics. You've got to be limber and on your game when you talk to the Pied Piper. "A whole hour to go home, shower, and get ready? Piper, why, how generous of you." She ignores the sarcasm.

I hear a snicker behind me. I turn as Chloe walks by with Gretchen Wills. They're a match made in heaven. Oh, did I say heaven? I meant hell.

"No dinner reservations, Veronica? Did I hear that right? I hope nothing's wrong with Dimitri. Is he bored already?"

Piper starts to open her mouth, but by some miracle I beat her to the punch. "Save it Piper, she's not worth it." Because she's not worth it. Nor is she worth our time. I turn to steer Piper away.

Then I hear Chloe say, "That's right. Take your crazy, psychotic friend and run away."

I know I shouldn't, but I have a general rule where my friends are concerned. No one, and I mean *no one*, makes fun of them when I'm around and gets away with it. I turn on my heel and with a sickeningly sweet voice I retort, "What's that Chloe? Couldn't find a date? Mmm, I'm sorry. No one left in the greater Denver area you haven't screwed? Or screwed over?"

"I actually have a date— "

I cut her off. "Fascinating, but it was more of a rhetorical question."

Hands on hips she faces up to me. "What?"

"It means I neither require nor desire a response."

She huffs. "It won't be long before Dimitri finds out he's dating a *little girl* and wants to hook up with someone *much* more experienced." Her mouth turns up into an evil smile.

I look to Piper, who I cannot believe has kept her mouth shut up to this point. I put on my best, over-exaggerated confused face and say, "Correct me if I'm wrong, Pied Piper, but I'm afraid this young trollop has confused 'experienced' with 'disease-ridden.'"

"You bitch! You're just jealous!" There's a vein throbbing in her neck. She's pissed.

And I'm bored.

Whereas apparently my tiny but fearless amigo Piper is not. Her longstanding silence comes to an explosive end. "Jealous?! Shut the hell up! Get the eff out of this gym!"

Chloe's voice is dripping with venom. "Piper, you're such a freak. We'll gladly leave just to get away from you two. Come on, Gretchen."

Piper steps forward, her hands extended like she may strangle Chloe. "So help me God … stupid twat! Incorrigible bitch!"

I grab Piper's arm and pull her back. "Bravo! Couldn't have said it better myself. But don't waste your time. Like I said, she's not worth it."

Chloe glares at me. "Have fun selling tickets tonight … *by yourself.*"

I curtsy dramatically. "The pleasure is all mine." I promptly drag Piper across the gym away from them.

Her little body is trembling. "Hate her," is all she can manage to squeak out.

"I know. The girl's pure evil," I say as we start unpacking the raffle prizes.

"Not evil. Effing Antichrist!"

"Is it just me? I'm confused … how do you think she hides her horns, Piper my dear?"

She tries not to smile. And then we break out into a fit of laughter.

Despite the unexpected excitement and loss of two workers, we still manage to finish up a few minutes before six o'clock, so I race home to shower and get ready. I curl my hair, put on my makeup, and slip into my dress all in record time before pausing to really look at myself in the mirror. The dress hugs every inch of my body and is very short, but I have to admit that though it makes me feel slightly uncomfortable, it also looks *really* good. I don't feel pretty; I feel sexy. It's like looking at a woman in the mirror for the first time—not a teenager. I pull my black heels out of a shoebox in the back of my closet. They're five-inch heels and won't completely give me the boost I need to look Dimitri in the eye, but it will be close. I put on a necklace and earrings and carefully walk upstairs. It's been a while since I've worn heels. My mom and dad are in the kitchen.

My dad's eyes widen as soon as he sees me. "Holy sh— "

My mom spins around at warp speed. She giggles and claps her hands excitedly. "I knew it was going to fit like a glove. It. Looks. *Awesome*. Turn around."

I turn around slowly, glancing cautiously at my dad out of the corner of my eye. His jaw has dropped … to the floor. The back of the dress dips dramatically from my shoulders to the small of my back, leaving a lot of skin exposed.

"Beautiful," she says, clearly pleased with herself.

"The dress is great, Mom. Thank you so much." I hug her quickly and kiss her on the cheek before turning to my dad.

He hugs me tightly. "You make sure Dimitri behaves himself tonight. I don't know if we should let you out of the house looking like this. Jo, did you have to make it so short? Does everyone need to see her *entire* back? Where's the rest of it?"

"It's perfect. And Dimitri is a gentleman." She smiles knowingly in my dad's general direction, but her eyes never leave the dress.

Dad doesn't look reassured. "Even so—"

I interrupt, because this could go on all night. "I have to go. I don't know when I'll be home. We're going to dinner after the dance. Love you both." I blow a kiss, grab my jacket and purse, and run out the back door to the garage.

Three hours never seemed so long. I try to enjoy myself and not focus on the fact that Dimitri will soon be here. No doubt he'll look unreal in a suit. I can't let my mind drift; it only makes time pass more slowly and exaggerates the torturous wait. Selling and taking tickets does provide me the rare opportunity to see everyone that comes through the door, so I keep my phone handy on the table next to me so I can take pictures of all of my friends as they pass through.

"Veronica, what's up? How'd you get stuck selling tickets?" It's Tate. He's here with my friend Monica. They've just started dating, though Tate's had a huge crush on her for years.

I laugh. "I pulled the short straw. It's not so bad." Thoughts of Dimitri surface and I glance at the clock on the wall. Nine o'clock—one more hour. I stand up and walk around the table to take their picture. "Where's Teagan?" I ask. "I don't even know who he's bringing. I've been a little out of touch the past week or so."

Tate laughs. "Teagan's parking the car. He brought this girl, Liz. She goes to West Hills. I don't think they're having much fun, though. I'm honestly not sure why he asked her. It was kind of a last minute thing."

I smile at Monica. "Monica, I love your dress."

"Thanks. Your dress is *amazing*. Did your mom make it?"

I nod.

I hold up my phone and gesture them together. "Okay you two, smile." I click off a few pictures.

When I pull the phone down I see Teagan. He's walking through the door behind a girl I've never seen before. I can only assume this is his date. I know the look on his face—he's thoroughly pissed. He's looking down at the ground, shaking his head and mumbling to himself. Mumbling is never a good sign.

"Chauffer tonight, huh, Teag? Did you borrow your grandma's minivan?" I try to lighten the mood.

He recognizes my voice and smiles, still looking at the floor. "So, now you're a comedian, Veronica? Actually—" He looks up at me and stops mid-sentence. I can't help but notice that his eyes quickly run from my face to my feet and back up—twice.

"Actually? Actually what?" I start to laugh. "You're rolling in Larry's Buick tonight, aren't you?" Teagan's dad, Larry, drives a thirty-year-old boat of a Buick. It's in pretty good shape, but definitely an old man's car. Teagan hates it.

Teagan's face is blank. He laughs, but it doesn't touch his eyes. He hasn't heard a word I've just said and is still staring at my legs.

I look to his date as an escape. "Hi, I'm Veronica," I say. "This goofball is my best friend. Do you mind if I take your picture with him?"

She smiles politely and says, "I'm Liz. And no offense, but I don't think a picture is a good idea. I'm not sure this is a night that either one of us wants to remember."

My eyes widen. "Oh. Okay." I set my phone down on the table and walk back to take my seat behind the ticket table. Awkward.

More people come through the door at that exact moment—thank goodness—and I send Tate and Teagan on their merry way.

It's busy between 9:15 and 9:45. It seems everyone's waited until the last minute to show up. I look at the clock at least every thirty seconds.

At 9:55 the butterflies in my stomach start to awaken, and by 9:58 I'm practically shaking with anticipation.

At 10:00 the excitement peaks ... but by 10:15 the fear sets in. I knew it was too good to be true.

I've just been stood up.

Maybe Chloe was right. Slowly sliding the chair back from the table I grab the zippered money pouch and walk over to Mr. White, one of the dance chaperones. He's also in charge of the ticket money and I'm glad to get it out of my hands. I'm struggling with the lesser of two evils: should I put on a brave face and head into the dance to spend the rest of the night with my friends? Or do I surrender to defeat and just go home?

The disappointment must be evident on my face by the time I reach Mr. White. "What's wrong, Veronica?" he asks.

I put on my bravest smile. "Nothing, Mr. White. It's just been a really long day. I'm kind of tired." I know immediately that it's a pathetic attempt and doesn't carry an ounce of conviction. So much for my valiant effort.

I turn before he can quiz me further and walk directly to the bathroom where I can steal a minute or two by myself to decide if I'm caving in and going home or staying here and toughing it out. If nothing else, I owe it to my mom to stay after she spent so much time on the dress.

The bathroom door opens just as I approach—and who should walk out but Chloe and Gretchen. They're laughing, no doubt at someone's expense. Probably mine.

Chloe stops and looks me up and down. "What a waste of a dress. I guess I was right. Dimitri must be bored with you already and found something better to do tonight than spend it with you. Maybe I'll give him a call."

My temper is usually fairly easy to control, especially with someone as inconsequential as Chloe, but she's picked the wrong time to mess with me. I've gone from sad to *pissed off* in less than two seconds. Piper was right; she is the fucking Antichrist. Tears sting my eyes, angry tears, and I blink trying to fight them back. I don't want to give her the satisfaction of seeing me cry. My hands tighten into fists, my fingernails digging into my palms. I'm just about to unleash my fury on her, to tell her in no uncertain terms exactly what she can do and exactly where she can go, when I hear a low whistle from somewhere behind me.

Chloe's jaw drops. I turn to follow her gaze and see Dimitri walking toward me with Sebastian trailing not far behind. I've pictured him in my head for the past three hours; he's drastically exceeded my expectations. The suit is classic; black and paired with a crisp white shirt and a dark gray tie that matches his eyes. He's so, so beautiful. His eyes are wide and he's wearing that mischievous grin.

Holding a pink lily in his left hand, he takes my right hand in his, kisses me on the cheek and whispers in my ear, "Ronnie, you look *gorgeous*."

I'd blush if I hadn't been boiling over with Chloe anger ten seconds ago. "Thanks. So do you."

He raises his eyebrows and exhales looking me over. "Your mother is a damn genius." He smiles and then blinks and shakes his head as if to focus his thoughts. "I'm sorry we're running late. Pretty-boy here couldn't decide what to wear." He gestures with a sideways nod to Sebastian who smiles and shrugs innocently.

Chloe and Gretchen remain frozen in place, speechless. Dimitri ignores them and turns to lead me to the gym doors. I give Chloe the finger behind Dimitri's back as we walk away. Sebastian chuckles quietly.

The gym is packed and the music is loud. We mingle through the crowd for a while, finding Teagan, Tate, and

105

their dates before moving to a quieter spot near a cluster of unattended tables.

Sebastian is working the unattached girls in the room with an impressive degree of success. They're putty in his hands. I have to admit it's entertaining to watch.

"Does he always act like this?" I point to Sebastian, who's only ten feet away flirting shamelessly with a pretty sophomore.

One side of Dimitri's mouth pulls up into a grin and he half laughs while shaking his head. "Yes. The kid is a machine. Sebastian has no shame. If there ever was a player … " His voice drifts a thousand miles away and his eyes look older and pained. "I don't understand the fun in it for him, though. He's never understood the benefits of committing himself to one person."

"He's what, fifteen? Cut him some slack."

"Sixteen actually; he just had a birthday. Remember? He drives," he adds with a wink. "We're only ten months apart." He shakes his head, then smiles gently. "Would you like to dance, Miss Smith?"

"I would love to." A slow song has just started.

The dance floor is packed but we manage to squeeze our way through the crowd of swaying bodies toward the center of the floor. I wrap my arms around his neck and his coil around my waist. The warmth of his hands on my bare back is divine. His fingertips trace the line of my spine up and down in a slow repetitive motion. With heels on, I'm only an inch shorter than he is, and can almost look him squarely in the eye. He's looking back at me. I don't know how to explain it, but his look is powerful and reverent. I *feel* his eyes on me; it's palpable, like a caress. And the rest of the world melts away.

"Have I told you how gorgeous you look tonight?"

I smile because this is the third time he's told me. "You may have mentioned it once or twice." I add, "Have I told *you* how gorgeous *you* look tonight?" I know I'm returning the compliment for the third time as well.

He nods and laughs. "You may have mentioned it once or twice."

106

His eyes turn intense again. He brushes the hair away from my neck and leans forward. My heart begins to race.

His voice is measured, serious and only a whisper at my ear. "Do you have any idea how *badly* I want to kiss you right now?"

My racing heart skips a beat. Not nearly as badly as I want to kiss you, I want to say, but I'm stricken speechless. I shake my head slightly instead.

He leans his head in and we stand cheek to cheek as we dance. His hair is soft under my fingers as I gently stroke the back of his head.

His face is buried in my hair, the warmth of his breath feathers across my neck increasing in frequency and depth. The tip of his nose teases softly up and down my neck and pauses to inhale deeply. "You smell so good. I love this perfume. I could devour you right here and now." The pressure of his hands on my back increases slightly. "I am trying *very* hard to behave myself. It's a Herculean effort at this point, Ronnie. Remind me again that I'm a gentleman."

My body is throbbing. The words come out monotone, with no conviction behind them as I whisper, "You're a gentleman."

Damn it.

He presses his lips to my neck and lets them linger a few seconds before pulling back to look at me. I'm convinced that his lips are magical, and my eyes plead with him to kiss me. If they could talk, they'd be shouting it; demanding it. We dance another minute, our eyes locked. The shouting intensifies. The next song, unfortunately, is much more up-tempo. The shouting ceases. I inwardly curse the DJ as Dimitri pulls me from the dance floor.

Dimitri looks at his watch. "It's almost midnight. I don't want to rush you if you want to stay, but I'm willing to bet that you haven't eaten anything since breakfast, which was technically almost yesterday."

He's right. I haven't eaten anything since seven o'clock this morning and I have to admit that my stomach is growling. "We can go whenever you're ready."

"You're sure?"

"I'm sure. Let's go."

He pulls his cell phone out of his pocket on the way to the car and quickly sends off a text.

Life is sometimes … gentlemanly. (Damn it).

Chapter 7
Sexy is up for interpretation

"Dimitri, it's so late. You really don't need to take me out to dinner," I say as he starts the car. "We can just go through a drive-through somewhere."

He shakes his head and laughs as he looks over his shoulder to back out of the parking space. "Seriously, Ronnie, have you looked in a mirror tonight? You're an absolute goddess! This is a special night; do you honestly think I'm going to take you through a drive-through dressed like that? Nice try."

We drive to his neighborhood and pull up to the secured entrance. The guard, Charlie, greets Dimitri politely and opens the gate to let us through.

I'm curious. We're going to his house—not a restaurant after all.

We enter his house through the back kitchen door. The room is dark, but it smells like heaven. Someone's been cooking.

His hands find my shoulders. "Can I take your coat?" He slips it off and takes my hand.

"What smells so good?"

"Dinner. What else would it be, silly?" he says playfully.

He stands behind me and caresses my bare back as he guides me through the dark to the dining room, which is dimly glowing with candlelight.

Prince charming has done it again. Yet another fairy tale has come to life. A long table glows like a dream in front of me. Pink rose petals provide the backdrop for dozens of flickering tea light candles.

"It's not drive-through, Ronnie, but do you like it?" he whispers eagerly. He's still standing behind me and squeezes me gently around the waist resting his chin on my shoulder.

I nod, mesmerized by the candles.

He urges me forward gently. "Let's eat before it gets cold."

The center of the table is already set for two. He pulls out the chair and I sit slowly. He lifts the silver cloche off my plate, and I instantly make the connection between the heavenly smell in the room and the food on the table— chicken enchiladas. And not just any chicken enchiladas. I smile and look up to see he's already sitting across from me. "Pedro?" I ask happily.

The corner of his mouth turns up in a grin. "Yes. Remember, I told you *I* can't cook."

"But this is fresh, and it's still hot. How did you manage that? Did you make Sunny stay up late and drive all the way to Boulder for this?"

"No, actually. Pedro often makes house calls." He smiles at my puzzled expression. "Pedro is an old family friend and he and Sunny are … well … kind of dating. Sunny won't quite admit it to herself yet though. I think she feels like it's too soon after my father's death. Sebastian and I have both told her we just want her to be happy, but we can see the guilt in her eyes. She truly loved my father, but Pedro is a good man and exactly what she needs right now."

His honesty surprises me. "You don't mind her dating? It's not weird for you?"

"Why should it be weird for me? Yes, I miss my father, but it doesn't mean that Sunny should grieve him for the rest of her life. She married very young. They only dated six months. She was almost nineteen and my father was forty-eight. Her family was in the oil business in Houston and very wealthy. My father, who was also in the oil business, had relocated to Houston temporarily from Wyoming to partner with Sunny's father on a deal. Sunny was working in my grandfather's office; she'd just graduated from high school. That's where they met. He swept her off her feet and when he left to go back to Wyoming they married and she went with him. I was born ten months later and Sebastian ten months after that. The rest is history."

"So you were born in Wyoming? I thought you said you moved here from Texas?"

"Sebastian and I grew up in Jackson, Wyoming. It's near Yellowstone National Park. We moved to Houston only after

110

my father died. We were there for about eight months before we convinced Sunny to move here." He smiles warmly remembering.

"Why did you want to move to Denver?"

He laughs quietly, as if at a personal joke, and pauses before proceeding. "We traveled a lot growing up, as I've mentioned before Sebastian and I have been very fortunate. Colorado was always one of our favorite places to visit. That, and I discovered there were certain people here that I needed to be near. Pedro had moved here about ten years ago from Houston and opened up his restaurant. He was the one who helped me and Sebastian convince Sunny to make the move."

The dinner conversation has taken an unexpected turn. Dimitri is always open with me, but I usually monopolize the conversation. He always has a lot of questions for me, but tonight it seems to be my turn. "Do you ever regret moving here?"

His eyes sparkle in the candlelight as he gazes across the table at me. "Never. It led me to you."

Wow. Just wow. I don't know what to say.

We finish our meal in silence.

Dimitri walks around the table to take my hand and leads me through the darkness to another candlelit room—the living room. It looks like a cozy lodge at an upscale ski resort complete with crackling fire, oversized leather sofas, and a furry rug.

Dimitri shrugs off his suit coat and loosens his tie as he sits down on one of the sofas. "Sunny really out did herself tonight. I asked for a little help with the table decorations for dinner, but I didn't expect all of this. I think she likes you," he says with a wink as he pulls me down to sit on his lap.

His arms tighten around me. "You're shivering."

"If you haven't noticed, I'm half naked here," I say almost resentfully. The novelty of the "sexy" dress has worn off. "Pretty" dresses are much more practical, and warmer, I've decided.

The mischievous grin emerges. "*That* fact has definitely not escaped my attention. It's been testing my self-control all night. The way you look tonight is a vision even I couldn't dream up in my wildest fantasies." His smile softens in reaction to my blushing. He strokes my cheek with his fingertips. "Your beauty ... *truly* ... astounds me. I've never seen anything else like it."

I feel indescribably special. My heart swells and a lump grows in my throat. "Thank you."

"Why don't we sit in front of the fire so that you can warm up?" He rubs my back and kisses the top of my head before saying, "I'm going to make us some hot chocolate. I'll be right back."

The dress is too short for me to sit comfortably on the floor, in so I decide to take my shoes off and stretch out on my stomach on the large rug. The warmth of the fire washes over me and I stop shivering. When I lie my head down, the rug is soft against my cheek. I close my eyes and absently stroke the rug with my fingers, listening to the fire crackle and pop. My mind begins to drift ...

Have I fallen asleep? I feel the softest kisses low on the small of my back. The kisses progress slowly and seductively up my spine, exploring every inch of uncovered skin. The journey takes several minutes—lips never losing contact with my skin. The breath is warm and the lips velvety smooth. They stop at my neck and I exhale softly. I want them to continue. I *need* them to continue. Why can't dreams just do what you want them to? But then, the light stroke of a tongue tracing the outline of my ear is far too arousing to be a dream. I'm indeed awake. Slowly, I open my eyes to find Dimitri hovering over me, his hands resting near each of my elbows.

I close my eyes in contentment. He whispers, "I leave for two minutes to make hot chocolate and you devise this plan to break down every last defense I have? You're devious, Miss Smith. Do you have any idea how sexy you look lying here in front of the fire?"

I smile wide without opening my eyes.

He settles in next to me and lightly traces the line of my spine with his fingertip.

112

I never want this moment to end. "That feels nice," I murmur quietly, mostly to myself.

I hear the mischievous smile in his voice. "Yes … it does." He leans over to place a kiss tenderly near the center of my back. It lingers. He sighs as he sits up. It's quiet for several moments.

I open my eyes to find him sitting beside me drinking deeply out of a huge mug with reindeer and a snowman on it. It makes me giggle. For the first time since I've known him, he actually looks sixteen or younger. So sweet and vulnerable, not at all the confident and mature Dimitri I know. I see the boy I met at the schoolhouse in my dream.

He pulls the mug away from his face to reveal whipped cream on his upper lip and nose. "What?" he says innocently.

He's so damn cute. I roll over on my back, holding my stomach with both arms as the laughter ripples through me.

He's still puzzled. "What?"

I catch my breath and open my eyes. He still looks so sweet and innocent, but the boyish look has vanished. In the blink of an eye he's the breathtaking, older Dimitri again. Coming to rest on my side, propped on my elbow, I watch the fire dance in his stormy, gray eyes. "You really are stunning."

He smiles.

"But you have a little something right here." I gesture to my own nose.

He reaches up and brushes his fingers across his nose. "Ahh," he says, smiling, as he licks his fingertips. "That would explain the fit of laughter."

"There's a little more … " I start to say, grabbing his wrist before he can reach for his face again.

I rise, resting on my knees directly in front of him, leaning in and unhurriedly—and most importantly, uncharacteristically brazenly—lick the whipped cream off his upper lip. I rock back to admire him. "There, now you look perfect."

He closes his eyes and moans, "You're killing me, Veronica Smith." He shifts his body slowly until he's

113

crouched on his hands and knees. He creeps toward me and my body answers until I'm lying on my back and he's hovering over me. Lacing our fingers, he guides my hands against the rug stretching them over my head. His palms are warm against my own. I see the fire, quite literally, reflected in his eyes as he closes in to kiss me.

He kisses me first on the mouth, then both eyelids, my forehead, my ear, and the hollow of my neck. The kisses are restrained, but there's an edge to them that promises much more to come. Finally I speak up, though I'm not sure how I find the words, "*You* … are killing me." I've never in my life been kissed like this.

I release his hands from my grip and reach up to remove his glasses, which I carelessly drop next to the sofa. I take his face firmly between my hands. The stubble on his cheeks feels rough on my palms. I pull his face fiercely to mine and put everything I have into this kiss. His response echoes mine, and suddenly our restraint turns to desire. His body lowers to rest on mine, perfectly aligned, and I bear the full weight of him.

I welcome it.

I delight in it.

The pressure awakens every nerve ending in my body. His hands are everywhere, but eventually find their way under me. And though it's not possible, he attempts to bring us closer together. He rolls to his back and pulls me on top of him. I'm vaguely aware of my dress hiking up—and then I hear a tear.

"That didn't sound good," I mutter, afraid to look. I don't want to ruin this moment, but I feel unexpectedly exposed. I glance over my shoulder to see that the seam has cleanly split from the hem at my upper thigh all the way up to my ribs. My panties are on full display. I know for most people this would be a huge turn-on, but I feel nothing but a wave of distress.

I am an inept sexual being.

"Close your eyes," I order, scrambling off him. I grab his suit coat off the sofa to cover myself.

"What? What happened?" He props himself up on his elbows.

My face is bright red. I can't decide if it's more a result of the torn dress or my reaction to it. "My dress tore."

He laughs at my embarrassment. "It can't be that bad, Ronnie. Let me see."

"Nice try. This dress left little to the imagination to begin with. Let's just say it leaves *nothing* to the imagination now."

He crawls over to sofa and kneels in front of me, putting his glasses on in the process. "My imagination is comprehensive, exhaustively so. I have quite a detailed picture in my mind of what you look like under that dress. Let's see how it stacks up against the real thing."

"Dimitri, it's not funny. My mom's going to kill me. And I can't stay here like this. What if your mom comes home?"

He stands up and turns his back to me. "Put my coat on and come with me." His hand is extended behind him in invitation.

I put the coat on. It does seem to cover my suddenly naked left side, and I take his hand. "Where are we going?"

He begins to walk toward the staircase. "To my room."

I stop dead in my tracks. "Dimitri, I can't go up to your room. Not like this."

Expecting his mischievous grin as he turns to face me, I'm comforted with an innocent smile instead. "You can borrow a shirt and some sweats. I know they'll be big on you, but at least they'll be warm."

The blush in my cheeks deepens and I avert my eyes to the floor. "Oh." I clear my throat, "That sounds good. Thanks." Incorrect assumptions are so embarrassing.

We walk up two flights of stairs in the dark. "We're almost there," he whispers.

He flips on the light and my jaw drops. "*This* is your room?"

I should be over the surprises by now, but the room is huge. It looks like a hotel suite, a really nice hotel suite. The kind someone like me has only seen on TV. There's a long red leather sofa with tons of pillows. A massive flat screen TV is mounted on the wall across from it and below the TV looks like a stereo and surround sound system. There are bookshelves on the far wall that are crammed full of CDs, movies, books, and magazines. Everything in the room is meticulously organized and clean. Through the double doors next to the bookcase I can see a simple bed, low to the ground and covered in a black silk bedspread.

He smiles sheepishly. "Yeah, this is it. Now let's find you something to wear."

I follow him through the double doors into the "bed" room. Dimitri doesn't turn on the light, but the dim illumination from the adjoining room aids me enough to get a look around. The room is large, but sparsely furnished. Apart from the bed there's only a chair and a huge, colorful painting of a bird, its wings spread, rising out of what look like flames. A phoenix, I think to myself; no doubt he's painted it. It's signature Dimitri, dark and sensual. Floor to ceiling red drapes cover the far wall of the room. While Dimitri disappears into a cavernous walk-in closet, I cross the room to look out the window. I pull back the curtain and stand in awe of the view outside the oversized picture window. It's a clear night. The view from his third story window goes on and on, unobstructed. The moon is full and exceptionally bright, I can see an outline of the mountains in the near distance. "Wow," I whisper to myself.

Dimitri's arms wind around my waist from behind and he rests his chin on my shoulder. "Pretty, isn't it?"

"Mmm, it really is." I place my hands over his arms at my waist and realize that they're naked. I turn to face him and he takes my breath away. He must have changed while he was in the closet. He stands before me in only a worn pair of jeans. I flash back to the day in my kitchen when he took off his wet shirt. Dimitri standing in the moonlight is even better. He is lean, but sculpted. Every muscle defined and visible across his stomach, chest, and down his arms. His jeans ride low and expose the tips of hip bones.

He retrieves a T-shirt and a pair of sweats from the bed and hands them to me. "These are the smallest clothes I

116

have. I know they'll be big on you. Sorry. You can change right here if you like … I don't mind."

I smile. "Yeah? You don't mind at all?"

"Not at all."

"Mmm, tempting. But the thing is I have a strict one striptease per year rule. And unfortunately for you, it seems I prematurely performed it just last week."

He smiles wryly and raises an eyebrow. "Last week you say?"

I'm enjoying flirting with him. "That's what I said."

"That's a shame."

"Tragic. Just me alone in my bedroom with not even a single, solitary, horny, perverted, desperate man ready to tuck dollar bills into my barely legal g-string; a complete waste."

He laughs. "Call me next year. I shall arrive utterly desperate and armed with loads of dollar bills."

My poker face has vanished and I'm half-laughing. "Awesome, because there's nothing I hate more than to put on a stellar performance and not be rewarded."

He's quiet for a moment and a sincere smile flashes as he shakes his head. "You're something else, Ronnie … I love being with you." It's unexpectedly genuine given our playful banter. He gestures over his shoulder. "You can use my bathroom."

I wink. "Thanks."

His bathroom is the size of my bedroom, maybe bigger. Again it looks like something from a movie, all marble and shiny fixtures. I can't believe real people actually live like this. I change into his clothes and pause to bury my face in the shirt. It smells like him—masculine and clean. It must be his cologne. Or maybe it's just him. The pants are big, but I cinch up the drawstring and cuff the bottoms. I throw my dress and his coat unceremoniously over my arm, turn off the light and walk back out into the bedroom. "Dimitri?" I whisper quietly. I don't know why I'm whispering; we're the only two people in this gigantic house.

"I'm out here," he calls from the adjoining room. He's stretched out on the sofa with his feet propped up on the coffee table. And I thank God (I actually say "hallelujah" under my breath) when I see he's wearing a T-shirt. I'll be able to focus, and perhaps carry on a semi-intelligent conversation now, instead of just ogling shamelessly at his body for the rest of the night.

"Here's your coat. Thanks."

"You can just hang it on the doorknob. I need to send it to the cleaners anyway. Let me see your dress. How bad is it?"

I hold up the dress and pull back the ripped seam to expose the damage.

He whistles. "Damn, Ronnie. There's not much left to it, is there? What are you going to tell your mom?"

"Maybe I'll tell her we were wrestling."

He responds with his mischievous grin, "We *were* wrestling ... and I think you may have even been winning."

My cheeks flush at the very recent memory.

He pats the sofa next to him. "Come and sit with me."

I sit down on the sofa sideways facing him, pulling my feet up and crossing my legs. Effectively restraining myself, it's not quite as tempting to continue the "wrestling" match if I'm not touching him. He turns sideways as well, pulling his knees up and casually wrapping them in his long arms. He rests his chin on his knees and the innocent, angelic smile that I love so much is there on his lips and beaming from his eyes.

A sense of calm has settled over me, and I notice he's turned on the stereo and there's music playing softly in the background. It's a live, acoustic recording of my favorite band. "I love this CD," I say smiling in recognition.

"I know. I remember hearing it playing in your car the day we went to your house for lunch. I decided to buy it. I was curious."

We sit in silence listening to the song play out. All the while he brushes the tip of his index finger along the leading edge of my toes, never taking his eyes off mine. As the song finishes he asks, "What is it about them, the band I mean, that's so appealing to you? Don't get me wrong, I like their music too, but why are they your favorite?"

118

My obsession with this band has not escaped his notice: the stickers on Jezebel's window and inside my locker, the patch on my bag, the T-shirts, the keychain … it's a legendary obsession. I listen to music nonstop, but this band is my absolute favorite. "Honestly?"

He nods. "Honestly."

"Honestly, it's because the lead singer may possibly be the sexiest man on the planet."

"Baby, I hate to break this to you, but I think you may have lost your mind. He's a great singer and a talented guitar player, but I've seen photos of him. He's nothing, if not average. I thought you were into handsome men?" he adds with a smile and a wink.

I roll my eyes. "Commercial beauty and sexiness are not mutually exclusive, Dimitri. I have to admit the first time I saw him I didn't look twice at him; he was just average, as you put it. But then I listened to his music and fell in love with him. His songs aren't just songs, he writes *beautiful* stories. I love to write stories myself, and admire anyone that can express themselves through words … or lyrics. He puts every ounce of himself into every song. His love songs aren't just sappy love songs either. You get the sense that he deeply loves women, or at least the one he wrote the song about—and not just horny, sex-driven love, but respectful, passionate, I-would-walk-through-fire-for-you love. Oh, and as you mentioned, he's a phenomenal singer and guitar player, too. I guess he probably is only average looking; I don't see that anymore. When you consider everything else—the whole package—*that's* what makes him incredibly sexy."

He tilts his head and rests his cheek on his knees. "Okay, I'm intrigued. What else is sexy?"

"Seriously?

"Seriously."

"That depends on the person I suppose, but there are a few things that are universal … " I pause.

"And they are?" He's still curious and patiently waiting. I have his full attention.

I proceed slowly and allow myself time to completely form each thought before speaking. "Number one is confidence—not arrogance, there's a distinct difference. Talent—especially when it's allowed to completely develop. Passion—the never-ending, unyielding pursuit of whatever drives and inspires you. Quick wit—a wicked sense of humor is always sexy. Genuine adoration—whether it is a man for a woman, a man for a man, or even a parent for his child—it's breathtaking when it's real. Acoustic guitar … beautiful eyes and lips—I'm a sucker for a great smile … oh, and Converse."

His eyes are full of wonder and contemplation until I complete my last thought and then he laughs. "Converse, as in the shoes?"

"Yes, Converse. Guys look really hot in them."

I don't think it sounds so crazy—guys do look really hot in Chuck Taylors—but he's still eyeing me suspiciously. After he's convinced I'm serious he nods and concedes with a smile. "I guess I'll have to buy a pair."

"Yes, yes you will. No respectable hot guy's wardrobe is complete without them." I'm curious now. "Your turn. What's sexy?"

"Mmm … your list is tough to follow. You're quite articulate. My list would make me sound like such a typical guy."

"Dimitri, you're the most *atypical* guy I've ever met. Let's hear it."

"The way you look tonight."

"I'm glad you enjoyed the dress, while it lasted."

"I wasn't referring to the dress," he says as he leans his head back, closes his eyes, and sighs before looking at me again. "Though that particular image will make its way into my dreams for years to come I'm sure." Then he squeezes his eyes shut and makes a face. "See, I sound like such a guy. I was talking about you sitting here, on *my* sofa, in *my* room, in *my* clothes. It's even better than the dress. You're just Ronnie, being Ronnie, and *that* is always sexy. You're so comfortable in your own skin. You are who you are, no

120

apologies. You were right; confidence is definitely at the top of the list. But I think you forgot a few."

I smile. "Enlighten me."

"Attitude—a *positive* attitude. Intelligence ... commitment ... genuine kindness ... brunettes ... black, lacy undergarments ... and a nice-fitting pair of jeans."

I laugh. "I was with you up until the jeans. Wait a minute ... stand up."

"What?"

"Stand up," I order.

He stands reluctantly.

"Lift your shirt and turn around ... *slowly*."

The corner of his mouth turns up into what I'm sure will end as the mischievous grin and he obeys. He lifts his T-shirt with one hand to reveal his perfect abs. His jeans hang loosely. A thin band of maroon boxer shorts peeks above the waistband of the jeans in the back as he turns slowly. He's enjoying this. He pauses as he completes the circle facing me again and drops his shirt. He raises an eyebrow. "And?"

It takes every ounce of self-control I possess to keep from leaping off the sofa and tearing his shirt off. Somehow I manage to keep my voice even. "I see your point. Maybe I'll add the jeans to my list." I can't hold back my own roguish smile any longer.

He takes off his glasses and gingerly places them on the coffee table next to him. Momentum brings him forward until he's leaning into me, his hands resting fully on my upper thighs. He stops when his face is an inch from mine and I inhale abruptly. I look forward to every second his lips are on mine, but this moment feels different. I'm alone with him in an empty house, in his *bedroom*. It's very late and this evening has already been very romantic: the slow dancing, the dinner, the episode on the rug, and the recent conversation. I know what he must be building up to—expecting even—and I need to speak up before I get caught up in the moment, myself.

I put my hand on his chest and hold him firmly before he closes the gap entirely. I look down at my lap and the words come tumbling out as an apologetic whisper, "Dimitri,

I can't do this … I mean, I know what you must be expecting right now and I am *so* sorry if I gave you the wrong idea … I mean, if I led you on in any way." I pinch my eyes shut. "I know I did. I'm so, so sorry."

He puts his hand under my chin and raises it slowly until it's even with his. Tilting his head he pulls his face back slightly from mine. He's studying me. There is no trace of a smile on his face. I wait. His eyes are so mature, but there's a softness that makes the knot in my stomach begin to unwind. His voice is low, that of a man twice his age, "Ronnie, please don't let me give you the wrong impression. I know I tease you a lot, but we aren't going to do anything that you don't want to do. I know you have boundaries." He pauses, obviously searching for the right words. He gently strokes my hair. "*You* are what I want … sex can wait."

I look down again fumbling with the frayed hem on the T-shirt I'm wearing, unable to meet his eyes. "What if it has to wait a long time? You're a sixteen-year-old guy. I know how sixteen-year-old guys think. My best friends are guys remember? We talk. It's almost all they think about. Don't tell me you're the exception to that rule. I'm sure there a dozen girls that I could call right now that would come over this minute and sleep with you without hesitation. It's not that I don't *want* to be with you that way … God, it's almost all I think about—kissing you, touching your bare skin. But I can't be *that* girl. Accidents happen. I *have* to be responsible. Everything has a certain order in my world."

His voice is soft and deliberate. "Ronnie … Ronnie, *please look at me.*"

I slowly raise my head. There are tears in my eyes. His eyes are pleading, "Ronnie, please believe me when I tell you this: even if you told me you would never sleep with me … if I had to trade that in return for spending the rest of my life with just you … I would choose you. You're right, I am a guy and you're the most attractive woman I've ever seen. I think about you physically, about you and me together physically, two hundred times a day. I dream about it. But that's enough for me for now. I can wait. Think about the conversation we just had, was sex on our short list?"

122

I shake my head.

He cradles my face between his hands with the lightest touch, as if I were breakable. "No, it wasn't."

A sense of relief washes over me. I whisper, "Thank you … for understanding. Most guys don't."

He smiles. "And those guys were incredibly stupid if they were willing to lose you over it. Lucky for me though," he says, winking, "Patience is one of my best qualities."

I sit there staring at him leaning on the sofa in front of me. It's as though I'm looking at him through a new set of eyes and he's more attractive than ever. It's funny how beauty radiates out of some people. It's at the core of their being and reveals itself bit by bit as you get to know them. Dimitri is flawless on the outside, but it appears the real treasure is inside. Where did he come from?

I wipe the tears from my cheeks and manage to find my voice. "I realize I'm pushing my luck here and this is going to sound incredibly bold, but can I ask you for a favor?"

"An-y-thing," he says, enunciating every syllable as if it is three separate words.

"Now that you know the rules … will you kiss me … now … please?" my whispers are practically pleas.

"You, my dear, may push your luck anytime." He smiles playfully, raising an eyebrow. "And I implore you to be bold more often."

We lay on the sofa facing each other. The kisses are sweet and go on and on into the wee hours of the morning. I've never been so comfortable or felt so safe with anyone before in my life.

To say that Dimitri is a dream come true is an understatement. I couldn't dream up someone this perfect.

Life is sometimes … sexy.

Chapter 8
It's me
Not you
Killing me

Perfect (pur'fikt) adj. *Complete in all respects; without defect or omission; sound; flawless.*

Sounds … well … perfect, right? Wrong.

Let me explain. My life has always been virtually perfect in all respects. Things generally go my way. Okay, they almost always go my way. I am admittedly spoiled and cannot remember a moment of true difficulty, let alone crisis, that I've personally experienced in all of my eighteen years. I've been there for friends who've been faced with some pretty unpleasant realities, though watching someone battle an inner demon is nothing like experiencing it yourself. There's a degree of separation, a buffer. As much as it kills you to know they're suffering, at the end of the day it's something you can distance yourself from if you choose. They can't. It's too intimate. I've never known that kind of intense turmoil and hope I never do. I'm not quite that naïve though. As the bumper sticker saying goes: shit happens.

I used to think of myself as a strong, confident, independent young woman who could meet any challenge head on. That was the Veronica in my mind. But lately, my belief in *that* Veronica is starting to waver, and it scares the hell out of me. Real life is rearing its head—a reality both beautiful and overwhelming—and I have no idea how to deal with the resulting stress. It's hard to know how much of that stress I've created in my over-active mind.

My life, on the outside, still appears perfect. This makes me feel even worse, which undoubtedly adds to the stress. My guilt drives me to strive for perfection to perpetuate the illusion. It's an exhausting cycle.

The past few months with Dimitri have been surreal. He's the type of guy every girl dreams about. He's gentle, kind, intelligent, and mature, all wrapped up inside a confident, attractive human being. One word sums up Dimitri—unbelievable. To anyone else, this sounds like an ideal partner, but to me, five months of "unbelievable" has gradually become *un*-believable. A distinct difference.

I don't know what to believe anymore. I haven't been able to find a flaw in Dimitri in the five months I've known him. It's not an act. He is simply, genuinely amazing.

Perfect.

For some reason this makes me incredibly anxious. He's so perfect that he doesn't seem real. I can't keep up. And I can't measure up.

This relationship isn't indicative of my past relationships (and I use the term "relationship" loosely within that context). I've dated several guys over the past few years. Attracting male attention has never been an issue for me. It's not that I go looking for it, at least not the way someone like Chloe Murphy does. I don't devise plans to lure boys in by being superficial or dressing like a slut. I just relate well to guys, they're easy to talk to. Attraction seems to be a side effect. At least that's my theory. I'm selective about who I date, though. I'm not generally one to date someone who pursues me. It somehow seems like settling or giving in if I'm not the one initiating the relationship. I realize that sounds completely self-absorbed and narcissistic, maybe it is, but I like to be in control. Obviously, I'm doing something wrong because none of the "past relationships" ever lasted. It's equally divided as to who pulled the plug:

If they didn't hold my interest or meet my expectations, I quickly broke it off (would it kill them to bring some interesting, intelligent conversation to the table? Or have an elementary grasp of manners? Kindness and wit seem to be in short supply as well). And if they did hold my interest, when they figured out I wasn't going to have sex with them, they broke it off. (My virginal status is legendary around school. It precedes me "like a police escort complete with flashing lights and sirens," so Teagan and Tate tell me. You'd think they would've known what kind of a dead end they were getting into. Why did they even bother? My name is apparently synonymous with "conquest." A challenge. A *game*.)

Even stranger, after the breakups, the guys and I almost always remain friends ... even after all of the weirdness. It seems I'm fantastic at being one of the guys, the buddy, the friend. I just suck at being the *girlfriend*.

And now, my dilemma. I'm now (*finally*) in a relationship with someone who I adore. He's well aware I'm not going to sleep with him any time soon, and he's actually sticking around. On several occasions he's been on the verge of using the *L-word*. I've stopped him. Maybe I don't believe he can really love me; maybe I fear the feeling is mutual ... or maybe (and more likely) I'm just a complete, fucking moron. I'm no good at this; I'm only supposed to be the friend, the buddy. Being the girlfriend makes me feel vulnerable.

And being vulnerable is scary.

Spending time with Dimitri is irresistible, but it's also alienated me from my friends. Keeping everyone happy has begun to feel impossible. The comments range from the genuine "I miss hanging out with you," to the snide "I guess you don't need friends anymore now that you've got a boyfriend." I know some of the girls are just jealous, but it makes their comments no less hurtful and cutting. And when my guy friends start commenting, I know there's something wrong. My world feels completely out of balance.

There's also the small matter of what to do after graduation, which looms on the ever-closer horizon. There are only four daunting months until I graduate. My grades have afforded me with the choice of many universities and I don't want to make a mistake and screw up everything I've worked so hard for by making the wrong decision. This is an expensive and life-changing decision. Many of the schools are out of state, and the thought of being away from my parents is terrifying. They're not only my support system, but they're also my friends. My mom just went through a breast cancer scare (which she didn't tell me about until after the fact) and even though it turned out to be benign (thank God), it made me painfully aware of the fact that my parents are fragile humans just like everyone else, not superheroes like I've always thought. What if something like that happens again, and the outcome isn't so good? I don't want to be away from her. So, where to go? How to pay for college? Student loans? Scholarships? What to major in? These are all questions that should've already been answered months ago, but I've procrastinated, and now I'm behind schedule. I can literally hear the clock ticking like a time bomb. The timeline is one pressure, and making the right choices is another.

Lastly, the optometry office where I work is closing in less than a month. One of the doctors has decided to retire, and the other is joining another practice on the other side of town. That means I'm out of a job. Looking for a new job doesn't scare me, but the thought of not seeing these people anymore makes me sad. I make it my job to take care of each one of them, and soon they won't need me anymore. I like to be needed.

I feel like a juggler who keeps adding more and more balls until there's no option but for some of them to drop. My boyfriend, my friends, my family, my future, my job … suddenly there are too many balls in my routine. The emotional and rational parts of me are at odds. The worst part? It's all *my* fault. I'm the one out of control.

I *hate* being out of control.

I spend the entire weekend locked in my bedroom and vow to come up with a plan to regain control. I don't answer my phone. I don't talk to anyone except my mom and that is kept to a bare minimum. In the end it appears that the only ball I can't juggle, no matter how desperately I want to, is … Dimitri.

Getting out of bed Monday morning is agonizing. It hurts, in a quantifiable and very real way. It feels like a five hundred pound weight is bearing down on my chest making it almost impossible to breathe. How am I going to face Dimitri? I've avoided his calls and visits all weekend. My mom told him I was sick, which is true. This decision has made me physically sick. I haven't eaten anything or slept in two days. The moment I decided to break up with him, my heart broke as well. How will he react? He never does anything like a typical teenager. Will he be angry? Hurt?

Maybe he'll be relieved that he's off the hook. My mind runs itself in circles. I can't think about any of the possibilities—they're all equally painful.

On my drive to school, I consider my terrible plan. It's January, which means a new semester is underway and Dimitri and I have two classes together: Literature and History (third and sixth period). I can avoid him for a few more hours if I don't go to my locker. I park in the lot on the back side of the school. I'm embarrassed by my cowardice, but I push it aside as I run across the lot and straight to my first class. My palms are sweating and waves of nausea roll through me. My first two classes pass by too quickly. It's all I can do to put one foot in front of the other to walk to Literature. I look longingly at the parking lot through the doors and consider making a run for it—but I can't. I need to face him.

As I open the classroom door, I keep my eyes glued to the dark tile floor. A tiny voice in my head reminds me that I am, without a doubt, the most horrible person in the world. I just don't know what else to do. I can't see any other alternatives. I take my seat and open a book and begin pretending to read. When I can no longer fight the urge, I risk a glance sideways through my hair at his seat. To my surprise, it's empty. I breathe a small sigh of relief. The room fills quickly and as the bell rings I steal another glance. Still empty. Mrs. Santo starts her lesson promptly, as always. Not two minutes later, she's interrupted by the creak of the door opening. She whips around to face Dimitri as he enters.

"Mr. Glenn, I'm so glad you decided to grace us with your presence today," she says sarcastically. Kind and understanding are not two words I would use to describe her. Tact isn't at the top of the list either.

"I apologize, Mrs. Santo," Dimitri says quietly. I don't know if it's just my imagination, or my guilty conscience, but he sounds tired … and worried … and sad.

I stare at a chip in one of the bricks on the front wall of the classroom the entire period. I don't listen. I don't feel. I don't even blink. I just stare.

The bell rings and a force outside my control propels me from my seat. My eyes burn, like a flame is being held to the backs of my eyelids, and the lump in my throat swells until I'm convinced I will suffocate. I pick up my books and begin walking toward the door. I flinch involuntarily from the hand that touches my shoulder.

"Ronnie, are you okay?" His voice is soft and concerned, but strangled by fear.

The tears begin flowing as I turn to face him. I can't meet his eyes ... his beautiful eyes.

He grips my upper arms firmly. Not with the intention of hurting me, but more with the intention of never letting go. It's agonizing. "Ronnie, what's wrong?" The fear is pronounced now. He knows this isn't good.

I struggle to catch my breath between sobs as I push quickly past him. I stop just outside the classroom. He trails closely behind.

"Ronnie, please tell me. What's going on? Jo said you were sick, but you're a mess. What's wrong?" He's pleading in a strained whisper.

I bury my face in my hands. I feel that crushing weight in my chest again. I don't know if I'll be able to speak. "I can't do this anymore," I sob from behind my hands.

He tries to pull my hands gently from my face, but I resist. "Can't do what?"

"Thh-iiss," I stutter through the sobs.

"I don't understand," he says softly, but his voice betrays him and I know he understands all too well. "Can we go somewhere and talk?"

"I have to get to class," I say turning away from him.

"Please, Ronnie." His voice cracks, and with it another fissure opens in my heart.

"I have to get to class," I repeat, though I don't take a step. "Later, maybe."

"After school?" His voice is equal parts despair, hurt, and anger.

I nod. "After school."

With that, he strides past me. I watch him go. He's frustrated, his hands balled up into fists. I stop in the bathroom before I make a late appearance in French. I know I'm quite a sight. Madame Lemieux's eyes grow wide when I enter but she doesn't say anything. She casts worried glances in my direction the entire hour.

Dimitri is a no-show in History, though that's the only thing I recall from the remainder of the school day. I drive home mechanically, strictly on autopilot. Thank God it's a short drive, because I could've run someone over and never even noticed. I'm only two houses away when I realize that Dimitri's Porsche is parked in front of my house. He isn't sitting in it. I pull slowly into the driveway watching the garage door rise before me in slow motion. I park and get out, leaving my bag in the passenger seat.

I walk quickly over the frosty ground to the back door with keys in hand and nothing else. I know he'll be waiting there for me and I don't like the idea of him standing in the cold. The irony of the situation hits me like a freight train. I'm willing to break his heart, but I don't want to keep him waiting in the cold before I do it? I shake my head at the absurdity of it. I look up tentatively as I approach the door. He's not there. Where is he? I turn around and quickly scan the driveway.

I unlock the door and run through the house to the front door. My heart begins to race. I open the door and look at his car again. He's not sitting in it. I start to panic. Two minutes ago I was dreading facing him and now I am frantic to find him. I shut the door and walk back to the kitchen to collect my scattered thoughts. As I pass by the sliding glass door to the backyard, a knock on the glass stops my racing heart.

There stands Dimitri.

I look at him through the glass, and in that moment of recognition my life with him flashes before my eyes: our first awkward day, the rainy day lunch in my kitchen, our first date, homecoming, and the dreams—all of it in an instant. And it's at that moment I know this isn't over, *unbelievable* or not. I can't be the girlfriend he deserves right now, but that doesn't mean I don't care.

He knocks again and mouths the words, "Ronnie, can I come in pl—?"

I pull the door open before he can finish. "What are you doing back here? You'll freeze to death."

"It's not that cold, Ronnie. I've been sitting on the swing waiting for you to come home. I've been here all afternoon. It's a good place to think. I've run through several scenarios of how this is going to all play out, and in the end I decided to just let you talk … *after* I say one thing."

The lump grows in my throat again and my voice cracks. "Go ahead."

He walks into the kitchen and sits down at the table. I follow his lead. He waits to begin until I'm seated across the table from him. He looks tired, and though his eyes are puffy they burn sincerely into mine and I can't look away.

"I love you. I'm not telling you this because I'm looking for you to say it in return. It's just something I need to say because I'll regret it for the rest of my life if I don't. You are the most amazing person I've ever known, and I absolutely adore you … despite days like today." He sighs, blinks twice and then adds, "That's it. That's all of it."

And there it was; the "I love you." I feel crushed. His gaze is still intensely focused on me. I pause for several seconds to put my thoughts in order before I speak. This conversation with anyone else would be rushed to spare myself the emotion, but I owe this to Dimitri. Talking to him has always been easy and I want to be completely honest with him. "Dimitri, I am so sorry. It's not you, it's me." And my honesty sounds cliché.

Dimitri looks down, shakes his head slightly and mutters, "Come on, Ronnie, you can do better than that."

"I know that is so overused, but it's true. I have so much going on in my life right now that I feel like it's literally driving me insane. Like I'm on the verge of a breakdown."

He's still looking down at the table. "What's going on?" he whispers.

The tears finally begin to flow and my voice is already strained. "My friends hate me. We graduate in four months and I have no idea where I'm going to go to school, what I'm going to major in, or how I'm going to pay for it. I'll be unemployed in a few weeks. And lastly, and most importantly, my mom found a lump in her breast."

His neck whips up and his eyes meet mine again. "Why didn't you tell me? Is she okay?"

I grab a napkin off the counter and sit back down as I wipe my nose. "She's okay. It was benign, thank God. She kept it all from me until she got the results back late last week."

His shoulders relax and his eyes soften. "That's good though, right? She's okay."

"I guess so, it's just scary. It wasn't cancer this time, but what if it happens again?"

"Ronnie, I don't want you to take this the wrong way. I know your parents mean the world to you. Will and Jo are amazing and I genuinely hope they live very long, happy, healthy lives. But unfortunately, that's life. That's why it's so important to seize the moment and make the most of each and every day. There aren't any guarantees and it's not always fair. Sometimes bad things happen to really great people."

He's talking softly and trying desperately not to upset me, but his attempt fails. "*That's* a nice thing to say. You're talking about *my* parents!" I'm raising my voice, which feels hollow in the empty kitchen.

His face is suddenly aged and even more tired if that's possible. He turns away from me, looks out the window and whispers, "I've lived it."

And there it is.

Regret.

If I could take it back, I would. I want to crawl under the table and hide my face. "Your dad," I say. Of course, his father. How inconsiderate can I be? "Dimitri, I'm so sorry. I wasn't thinking. I guess you would know better than I would. I *really* am sorry."

He continues to gaze out the window at nothing in particular, just a blank stare. "Don't be. Unfortunately that kind of loss is something I've had to deal with more times than I care to remember."

"Who else, besides your dad?" I whisper.

His eyes drop to the floor. "I don't want to think about that ... especially not today."

We sit in silence for more than two minutes. I'm watching the clock on the wall tick deafeningly in the stillness of the room.

Finally Dimitri breaks the silence. "Ronnie, I don't want to trivialize any of your problems, but your friends don't hate you. Beyond that, the rest are just the cards that life's dealt you right now. You just need to decide how you want to deal with them. It's not life or death ... it's just life. If you need help, why don't you just ask for it?" He's staring at me again and the sincerity has returned to his eyes.

I bite my lip and inhale and exhale deeply. "I'm not so good at asking for help."

He huffs and half smiles, but it doesn't touch his eyes. "I know."

"It's hard for me. I'm the one everyone else comes to when they need help." I look away. "I feel weak asking for it." I'm ashamed to hear myself say it aloud.

He closes his eyes and rubs his temples. Exasperated, he sighs. "You're such a goddamn martyr, Ronnie. Did it ever occur to you that people *want* to help you? I would do anything in my power to help you ... *anything*. Monica, Tate, John, Piper—they would all help you in a heartbeat. Teagan would probably cut off his freaking right arm if you asked him to."

The tears start up again. "I can't ask them for help, not after the way I've treated them lately."

"I don't know what you're talking about, but if there's an issue with your friends maybe it's time to address it."

I sob. "That's what I'm trying to do."

"I'm confused, Ronnie. Tell me what's going on."

I sit there and cry uncontrollably for several minutes before I'm contained enough to speak. "I can't be the girlfriend you deserve and the friend they deserve. I've spent all of my time with you this year and I've put them on the back burner."

His face drops and he whispers, "I don't expect you to sacrifice friendships for me, but has the time you've spent

133

with me really been such a bad trade-off? Because I don't regret a single minute I've spent with you."

The tears continue. "I just want to stop hurting everyone. I can't seem to balance all of the people in my life that I care about. I can't give each of them the focus they deserve. If I spend time with you like I have been, then my friends are hurt. And if I start spending time with them, then I hurt you."

His eyes are focused on mine again. "I'm willing to share."

The sobs start again. "Of course you are. Why do you have to be so *damn* understanding? I can't do it. I'm an all or nothing kind of girl. If I'm going to be your girlfriend I need to feel like I'm in it one hundred percent. I can't divide myself up."

He hasn't blinked. "So, what do you want me to do now? Please, tell me. Do you want me to leave and never talk to you again?" His voice cracks and a tear rolls down his cheek. "Because if that's what you want, I honestly don't think I can do it."

Seeing the tears on his face is worse than being punched in the chest. I want to hug him, to comfort him. But I know I can't. I'd get sucked right back in. "I don't need a boyfriend right now, Dimitri. I just need a friend. I know that's a lot to ask and I understand if you can't do it."

The tears trail silently down his beautiful face. "You're my best friend and you always will be." With that he rises, kisses me on top of my head, and walks out the front door.

I fold my arms on the table and my head drops onto them. I cry until I can no longer stay awake.

Life is sometimes … imperfect.

Chapter 9
Denial can be beautiful
But only when you're a fantastic liar

My stomach roars, protesting, painfully pleading for food. Hunger is a pain different from other physical pain. It's mental, the kind of pain that can drive you mad. It slowly gnaws away at you from the inside out, forcing out all other sensations. Attempts to divert your attention from it are short-lived and futile. I pull my knees tighter to my chest and stare at the shadowy blackness streaked across the backs of my eyelids. The dirt beneath me is cold but my skin is almost too numb to take notice.

I feel an arm around my shoulder tighten. "You okay, Ronnie? D. should be back any minute now. He thought he'd be able to get some bread from the vicar tonight."

The conversation draws me out of my hiding place within. "I'm okay, Sebastian. I just hope he hurries. We need to find some shelter before this bloody snow picks up."

Sebastian and I are huddled in an alley, which provides some protection from the wind. The snowflakes swirl around us like tiny dancers. Their beauty is temporarily mesmerizing. It's been nearly three days since our last meal, and even though the cold wind makes the hunger worse, watching the snow make its silent descent is peaceful and calming. It brings back memories of sitting with my mum and dad next to the fire in our little one-room house watching the snow fall on Christmas Eve. They're some of the most cherished memories I have of my parents.

I met Dimitri and Sebastian at the orphanage when I was five. When I was ten, we ran away. We've lived on the streets for the past five years. But we're a family, and that's what's most important. Even though I'm the oldest, Dimitri is a natural leader. He's ingenious for a fourteen-year-old and that's proven the difference between life and death on more than one occasion.

I hear footsteps on the cobblestone street at the opening of the alley. It's Dimitri. A huge smile spread across his soot-smudged face.

"I hope you two aren't too comfortable. I was thinking we could find someplace more proper to dine." With that he pulls loaf of bread as long as his arm from behind his back.

Sebastian stands up slowly and stretches as if his joints are frozen. "Brilliant! I told you he'd come through, Ronnie, didn't I?"

Dimitri smiles and says, "I always do, mate." His smile is infectious.

"Are you sure you want to share that with a couple of cheeky bums like us?" I joke.

This makes Dimitri laugh. "Cheeky bum or not, you're still my best friend and you always will be." He bends over and kisses the top of my head. "Now let's eat."

I sit bolt upright in bed and blink several times before my eyes adjust enough to read the clock on my nightstand. 10:37 … at night, judging by the darkness outside my window. The words echo in my head: "You're still my best friend and you always will be." How I pray those words are true.

I slowly get out of bed and stand there a moment, temporarily dazed. I think about the earlier conversation with Dimitri and his leaving and realize that I cried myself to sleep on the kitchen table. I vaguely remember my mom helping me downstairs to my bed. I glance back at my nightstand and see a plate with a sandwich and a glass of water. My stomach growls ferociously at the sight of it. It's been three days since I've eaten. I sit back down and attack the sandwich ravenously. It is, without a doubt, the best PB and J I've ever eaten.

I climb upstairs to the kitchen, and, finding it empty, decide to make another sandwich. And then another. After I'm finished, I sit in the dim kitchen, staring out the window. It's just starting to snow. For the moment, everything is quiet and calm, peaceful almost. It's funny how everything can change in the blink of an eye. How every new day can lead you down a new path. I begin to consider that life is ultimately just a series of choices—a game … with no instructions included.

The next morning at school is surreal. I feel so out of place. It's almost as if I'm the new girl at school, as if re-introductions to old friends are necessary. It's awkward, but I quickly learn most people are sincerely forgiving. Of course, news travels fast and by lunch it seems that the entire school knows Dimitri and I have broken up. How does that happen? I'm practically smothered by curiosity on a day that I really could have done without all of the attention. Piper, of course, wants the whole scoop—and Dimitri's phone number. I don't provide either. She understands and lets it go (only temporarily I'm sure). Monica is genuinely concerned and says to stop by her house after work so that we can talk. Tate tries to joke around with me. It's obvious he wants to avoid the breakup subject, which is just fine with me. John even stops by my locker to see if I want any help with my homework. Teagan is the only person I haven't seen. I don't have any classes with him this semester. I resolve to try to find him after school.

Seeing Dimitri at our lockers is the most surreal of all. He isn't "mine" anymore. He's only my friend. At least, I hope he is. The sight of him makes my throat feel scratchy and raw. I'm afraid to talk to him, suddenly intimidated by him. I've shared the most intimate conversations of my life with this person, and now I have no idea what to say to him—as if he's a complete stranger. It's as if our breakup has erased the last five months. He looks sad to me, but I wonder if my perception is merely a product of my own guilt.

The school day hasn't exactly been the disaster that I'd envisioned, but it's not one I'd care to repeat either. I walk to the parking lot head-down and deep in thought, not paying attention to anything except the pavement passing under my feet. I dig through my bag looking for my keys as I approach Jezebel.

"Did you lose your keys again?" The voice is unmistakable, mainly due to the overly sarcastic tone. But it is one of my favorite voices in the world. It's the voice of my childhood. It makes me smile. It's the one person I've been waiting all day to talk to. Teagan.

I run the last few yards and wrap my arms around his waist and everything comes spilling out. "I'm so sorry, Teag. I'm so sorry that I've taken our friendship for granted. That I haven't called. That we haven't been able to hang out ... " My words fail as I muffle my cries into his coat.

Teagan wraps his arms around me and interrupts my blubbering, "Veronica, stop being so damn stupid and shut up already. You don't have to apologize for anything." He grabs me by the shoulders and pulls back to look at me. "I only need to know one thing. Who broke up with who? What did he do? Do I get to kick his ass?"

"I broke up with him and you'd better not lay a hand on him. Dimitri didn't do anything wrong. If anyone deserves an ass kicking, I do. I just need a break. I need some time to get things straight. I need some time to spend with my friends because I've ignored you guys all year, and I'm sorry for that."

Teagan squints and smiles tentatively. "So, are you okay?"

I fake a half-smile. "I'll survive." And then I half-laugh, sniffing back my tears. "I've been through this whole breakup scenario enough times you'd think it would get easier each time, but this time it wasn't. It's not that I *wanted* to do it, but more that I *needed* to do it. Does that make sense?"

Teagan pulls me back into a tight hug. "Veronica, honestly, you never make much sense. But I'm here for you if you need anything."

I hug him back. "Thanks."

He rests his chin on the top of my head. "You sure I can't kick his ass?"

I reach back to punch him in the kidney and he lets me go. "Ouch," he says while rubbing his back. "That *almost* hurt. You're getting kind of strong."

I laugh. "I took weightlifting last semester, remember?" I start to rifle through my bag again. "I hate to cut this short, but I really need to get to work. Will you be home later tonight? I can call you then."

The smile fades and his face is suddenly very sincere, which is not like Teagan. He doesn't let his guard down very often. "You can call me anytime. Call me at three in the morning if you want to."

I can't help but smile. "Thanks Teag. You're a good guy, you know that?"

He smiles. "Yeah, yeah. Get to work."

Work has been weird lately due to the fact that we all know our days are numbered. Everyone is on edge and sad. It's depressing just stepping foot in the front door—and for someone who's already feeling down, that's saying a lot. Still, the thought of the office finally closing brings some relief. Maybe all of the prolonged waiting and sadness is just the universe's way of preparing me to cope, and to feel relief instead of dread. I guess I'll answer that question when I don't have a job anymore.

After work, I stop by Monica's house on my way home. She respects my privacy and doesn't ask about Dimitri. Instead, the conversation is focused on her and Tate. They've been together for several months now and she's totally enamored of him. She asks me a lot of questions about him, and the longer we talk the more I realize that I know Tate better than almost anyone else, except maybe Teagan. For instance, I know that he's allergic to bee stings (he puffs up like a giant marshmallow), and that he's terrified of Doberman pinschers (his neighbor's dog bit him when we were in fifth grade), and that he loved to roller skate when we were little (in his Superman cape). Sometimes you don't realize how much you really know about someone until you start answering random, trivial questions about them. She seems excited to see me and to talk so freely, and I'm relieved that we're not talking about me. It's been so long since we've done this. It actually makes me feel good. It's nice to focus on someone else's life for a while—someone who's actually happy.

The hour is like therapy for me. I should have paid her when I left.

139

I eat dinner with my mom, which is uncharacteristically quiet due to my "do not mention Dimitri" demand. This disappoints her. It makes me feel like I've robbed her and my dad of a friend by breaking up with Dimitri. They love him. I can tell it's killing her that I won't tell her what was going on, but I can't. Avoidance, at least today, is my coping mechanism.

I go directly to my room after dinner, finish my homework, and make a quick call to Teagan. He's watching a basketball game and even though he insists I'm not interrupting, I know I am, so I let him go.

The next few days progressively get better. I'm not feeling like myself yet, but I'm starting to feel somewhat human again. And that's a start.

On Thursday morning, my dad gets in from his latest trip. He's taking a long weekend off and the house feels a little warmer for it. My parents and I are all sitting at the table eating dinner that night when something happens. I'm like an alcoholic who's been clean, methodically embracing sobriety, when suddenly and unexpectedly a bottle of whiskey is thrust upon me, into unwanting yet *desperately wanting* hands. But instead of whiskey, it's the doorbell. When it rings, I offer to answer it so my parents can continue their conversation. I open the door. There standing in front of me is my addiction: Dimitri.

I feel like I've been punched in the chest and I can't help but reach up to clutch it. I've dealt with seeing him at school pretty well, mainly because I *expect* to see him there. Preparation is the key; that and the fact that he's just an amazing person and knows how much or how little to talk to me and relieve some of the awkwardness and spare me the guilt. All of the feelings come rushing back when he *unexpectedly* shows up at my house. I'm suddenly the recovering alcoholic with both hands wrapped tightly around a bottle. I'm consumed with need ... and guilt.

Upon seeing my reaction, he starts. "Are you okay, Ronnie?" He raises his hands, as if to place them on my shoulders—to steady me, maybe—but stops just short and drops them. His voice rings in my ears. "Ronnie?"

I drop my hands and blurt out, "I'm okay." My head is reeling. I take a few deep breaths. I can't look at him, but I ask quietly, "What are you doing here?"

He lifts my chin with the lightest touch of his finger so that I'm looking into his eyes; I'd almost forgotten how beautiful they are. "Can't I visit my friend anymore?" His smile is painfully kind, pleading.

"Of course you can," I say. The rest I continue silently in my head, thinking, "Except that it kills me to look at you and wonder if you hate me like you rightfully should."

"I also stopped by to see your dad. Is he home yet?"

My dad walks around the corner at that very moment. "I thought I heard your voice. Did you bring the car?"

"Yes, but if this isn't a good time I can come back tomorrow."

"Don't be silly, if you can give me a few minutes to finish eating we'll get it off the trailer and into the garage. Come on in and say hi to Jo." My dad urges Dimitri forward with a hand on his shoulder.

My mom is, as always, more than happy to see Dimitri. "Hi Dimitri. Have you eaten? Can I get you anything?"

Dimitri shakes his head. "No. Thank you, Jo. I've already eaten."

She gestures to the open fourth chair at the table. "Please have a seat."

"I don't want to impose. Really, I can just wait in the front room." He turns away from the kitchen and I exhale a sigh of relief. I wasn't aware of the fact that I'd been holding my breath.

My dad follows him, leaving his meal unfinished. "Nonsense, you're not imposing. Let's take a look at what you've got."

I watch through the kitchen window as they pull his Volkswagen into the garage.

I can tell my mom desperately wants to talk about Dimitri because she's quietly humming as she rinses of the dishes. Humming is a by-product of holding her tongue, always has been. It's filler. Her gaze returns to me frequently until she can't fight it any longer. "Your dad's really excited to help Dimitri paint his car this weekend. And I have to admit it will be nice to have him around again, even if it's only for a few days. I kind of miss seeing him."

If she's trying to make me feel guilty it's working. "I know you do, Mom. Sorry to ruin this for you and Dad."

She stops and turns to look at me. Her voice is timid. "What happened, Ronnie?"

"I broke up with him." I reluctantly divulge.

She sighs and looks to the ground. "I know."

I narrow my eyes. "How do you know?"

"Because I called him Monday night after I got you into bed." She peeks up tentatively waiting for me to unload on her, but I can't. This week has been too long and I don't have it in me. "You were a wreck and I thought he would know what was going on. He didn't give me any details, but said that he was worried about you. He said the two of you needed some time apart so that you could sort some things out. Do you want to talk about it?"

"No, I don't want to talk about it, Mom. Not now. I'm going to my room." When I get to my room, I feel lost. All I can do is lie on my bed. For some reason, my eyes are drawn to Dimitri's painting on the wall and I can't stop staring at it. I considered taking it down, but I can't bring myself to do it. I know it's stupid, but every time I look at it I think about the dream I had about me and Dimitri in Paris. It's as though I've actually been there. I can't bear to hide that memory away in my closet or under my bed.

There's a knock on my already open door. My back is to it, and I assume it's my mom. My voice cuts the silence. "I said I don't want to talk about it!"

"Sorry. I just wanted to return this." I roll over and see Dimitri standing in the doorway. He's holding up a CD case. "I forgot that I borrowed this. I found it in my glove box this afternoon."

Words are just out of my reach, so I stare at him instead. *Smooth*—God, I'm an idiot. I'm losing my freaking mind.

He takes a few steps into my room and puts the CD on my desk. "I'll just leave it here. Good night, Ronnie." He

142

turns and, walks out the door and climbs up the stairs. I cannot bring myself stop him.

The tears start as soon as I hear the door shut behind him. I want to chase him and stop him and hug him and never let him go. I want to tell him that I've made the biggest mistake of my life … but I can't. I need to deal with *me*.

Dimitri comes over that weekend and my dad helps him paint his car. I confine myself to my bedroom and try to stay out of sight as much as possible. I research colleges online and talk to Monica and John on the phone about their plans after graduation. I am feeling pretty good about things by Sunday afternoon. I have ruled out several schools and narrowed down the list significantly.

Needing a break, I head upstairs to get a glass of water and rest my eyes for a few minutes. I've been staring at a computer screen for hours. I pause and hear the TV in the living room. Over the noise, I can hear my parents talking and laughing. They sound so content and happy. They really enjoy each other's company. Curiosity gets the best of me and I decide to walk out to the garage and check out Dimitri's car. I slip on my coat and mittens. Despite the chill in the air the garage is nice and warm when I enter. My dad has the heat turned up. The air is slightly hazy and smells faintly of paint fumes. I walk to the far end where the car is parked. It's black and shiny. It looks amazing. All I can think about is how happy and proud Dimitri must be. His car, that he's worked hard on for so long, is finally done. It makes me smile. He deserves some happiness right now.

"What do you think?" A voice asks quietly.

I turn and there stands Dimitri. "I'm sorry; I didn't know you were here. I can leave."

"Please don't leave," he whispers.

I have to look away, back at the car. "The car looks awesome."

"I'm afraid it's too nice to drive now. The Porsche may not be retired after all."

"You must be really proud. You did a great job."

143

"Thanks. Your dad did most of the work. He's so talented. It's like watching an artist. I don't know quite how to repay him. He won't accept any money. Do you have any ideas?"

That sounds like my dad. "My dad loves to help people, even more so when he can teach them something in the process. Believe me, he probably enjoyed this more than you did. But I'll let you know if I come up with a good idea."

I feel him standing right next to me. He isn't touching me, but I can feel his presence. His hand comes within an inch of my arm, hesitates and then lowers before any contact is made; it's shaking. Tears fill my eyes and I know I need to get back in the house … quickly. I turn and head for the door.

I pause as I turn the doorknob and my voice cracks. "Cubs tickets," I screech. "My dad's always wanted to go to Wrigley Field."

Life is sometimes … consumed with guilt.

Chapter 10
Bruises that are ugly
And painful
And more than skin deep

During the next few weeks I try to keep myself as busy as I possibly can to keep my mind off Dimitri. I fill out college applications and even talk to my guidance counselor at school. He's actually a pretty cool guy and I find myself regretting that I haven't taken advantage of getting to know him before now. He answers a lot of questions and quiets some of my fears about the next four years, including scholarships, loans, and majors. I've talked to my friends a lot about their plans, too, and it is comforting to know that we all seem to be in the same boat. Everyone is a little scared and uncertain about the future.

At the beginning of February, the optometry office closes and my job ends. It's a sad day, but I'm relieved when the final day arrives. Being around depressed people is physically and mentally draining and I've had a hard enough time lately just being with myself. I am looking forward to something a little more positive. I can't help but feel like a mom watching her grown kids leave home and go out on their own. I worry about my former coworkers and what they'll do next.

A lot of my time has been spent with friends lately. I've gone to the movies with Piper and hung out at Monica's house a few afternoons. Teagan and Tate came to my house and watched a hockey game one night and even John stopped by to drop off a loaf of his famous banana bread and a new sci-fi book for me to read. I have friends again and it's great, but something is missing. I can talk to all of my friends and they are always there to listen, but they don't hear me the way Dimitri did. He "got" me better than anyone else ever has.

It's Thursday morning and all that's on my mind is the fact that my parents are going out of town for the weekend. I'm looking forward to having a quiet house all to myself.

145

My plans are simple: I'm going to sleep in and lie around in my pajamas all weekend and watch TV.

The school day is completely normal until after lunch. I realize that one of my textbooks is in my car, and I have to trudge through the snowy parking lot to get it before science class. As I'm running back to the building, I see Teagan opening the door just ahead of me.

"Teag, wait up!" I yell.

He holds the door, but doesn't respond or turn to acknowledge me.

I'm out of breath by the time I catch up. "Thanks," I say, panting.

He's still quiet and distant.

I put my hand on his massive shoulder and try to turn him. Impossible. "Hey, Teag? What's the matter?" I ask.

He turns slowly, but his eyes look past me.

I cup my hand over my mouth. "Oh my god!" I lower my voice realizing that the few people straggling in the hall are now staring at me.

He looks disfigured. The skin around his right eye is black and blue and bulging as if there's a golf ball lodged beneath it. The lid is swollen shut. He's still avoiding looking at me, with his good eye at least.

"What happened?"

He shrugs. "It's not as bad as it looks. Calm down."

"Not as bad as it looks? It looks awful! Teagan, who did this to you?" I'm shaking his arm, his shirtsleeve clenched in my fist. How can he be so calm?

"I got in a fight last night with a couple of guys from North Ridge. I'm fine, really." He's trying to put on his best macho Teagan face, but something is off and that worries me more than the black eye.

I know he's lying to me, but I don't know why. "Listen, we need to get to class, but this isn't over. We *are* talking about this after school, okay?"

He shrugs.

"I said after school, okay?" I can be bossy when I want to.

146

He half smiles. "*Okay,* okay Mom. Am I grounded, too?"

"Funny … Maybe ... Meet me in the parking lot after school. I'll take you home and we can talk."

He nods and the sight of him makes me feel sad and distressed all over again.

As promised, Teagan is waiting next to Jezebel after school. I see him from across the lot. He's so big he's hard to miss, even from a distance.

"Ronnie!" A voice calls from behind me. I chalk it up to my imagination and keep walking. The only person at school that calls me Ronnie is Dimitri and we aren't talking much lately.

Then I hear it again. "Ronnie!" I decide to glance behind me this time. No one else will realize I'm hearing voices, right?

Dimitri is jogging up to me, out of breath. He begins speaking breathlessly. "Damn, you walk fast. Where's the fire?"

I shrug, but can see Teagan waiting anxiously. He's leaning against my car with his arms crossed in front of his chest. I know him well and his body language is threatening. Unless I want a testosterone-induced confrontation, I need to keep this brief. "What's up? What do you need?" The words come out harsher than I intended because Teagan is making me nervous.

Dimitri seems taken aback by my tone. "Well, Sunny wants to talk to you and she was wondering if she could stop by your house sometime tonight? Will you be home?" The conversation has taken an impersonal turn.

I'm shocked. "Sunny wants to talk to *me*? Why?"

His answer is short. "That's between the two of you." The confused look on my face prompts him to elaborate. "It's not about us. Okay?"

I relax a little and nod. "Okay."

Dimitri's noticed that I keep glancing in the direction of my car and finally looks for himself. He sees Teagan standing next to Jezebel, and his expression morphs from irritated, to crushed, to pissed all within two seconds. "I see that I'm keeping you from something. I'll see you later." He turns abruptly and walks toward his car, which is parked next to Sebastian's on the other side of the lot.

Suddenly I feel irritated, crushed, and pissed, too. I stomp toward Teagan.

"What did *he* want?" Teagan asks. His voice is filled with disgust.

"Nothing. I don't want to talk about it," I say as I climb in my car. "Are we going to your house or mine?"

Teagan doesn't hesitate. He never hesitates when I ask this question. "Yours." I start the engine. Teagan and his dad live with his grandma in a rundown trailer home. I've only been there a few times in all the years I've known him. He's ashamed of it, and not many people aside from me and Tate even know where it is.

When we arrive at my house Teagan makes himself at home, like he always does. Teagan loves coming to my house. He turns on the charm, and though my mom can see right through it, she can't help but love him. Teagan adores my mom, too. He's spent a lot of time at my house over the years and I think he sees my mom as the mom he never had. When he was eight he even asked her if she would adopt him. He never knew his own mother; she left him and Larry when he was only a baby. Larry drinks a lot and has trouble holding a job. Teagan's grandma does what she can, which isn't much. Teagan's home life sucks, but he never talks about it.

"When does Mom get home?" he asks as he helps himself to a soda from our refrigerator.

I hand him some ice cubes wrapped in a dishtowel for his eye. "*Jo* gets home around four-thirty. Why, are you staying for dinner?"

He smiles and sits down at the table holding the ice pack to his eye. "I don't know. Is she making anything good?"

That comment earns him a smack on the back of the head as I walk by. "My mom's an awesome cook; everything she makes is good. You know that."

He removes the ice pack and sets it on the table in front of him. "Guess I'm staying then," he says, as he chugs down the soda in a few loud gulps.

I sit down across the table from him and stare at his black eye. He looks at me with his good eye for a while and then looks away. I know I'm making him uncomfortable staring at the bruises, but I'm trying to figure out what's really happened and how I'm going to convince him to tell me the truth about it.

"Does it hurt?" I ask quietly.

He shakes his head without looking at me. "No, it's fine. It doesn't hurt."

Slowly I get up from my chair and walk around the table until I'm standing in front of him. I bend over and look closely at his bruise. He tenses up, but doesn't move or say anything. It's deep purple in the center and more red around the edges. His eyelid is puffy but I can see his eye moving behind the swelling. Teagan closes his good eye and winces in pain when I gently brush my finger across the angry bruise.

My hand retracts at the first sign of pain. "I *knew* it. It hurts, doesn't it? Are you sure nothing's broken? What if your eye socket is broken? Or ... or your cheekbone?"

Teagan exhales loudly. "Now you're a doctor, too? For Christ's sake, nothing's *broken*, Veronica."

The staring commences when I sit back down at the table across from him. It's like I can't think straight unless I'm focused on his injury. Staring at it quiets every other thought in my head and enables me to give him my full attention. "Teag, you know you're my best friend, right? You know that I'd do anything for you, right?"

He nods.

I reach across the table and take his hand in both of mine. He lets me. "Then will you *please, please* tell me what really happened? Who did this to you? The truth this time."

He looks away, but his grip on my hands tightens. It's quiet for a long time. The expression on his face hardens, not in anger, but sadness.

The sadness hurts my heart. "Teag, do you remember that time, the summer after fourth grade, when we were riding our bikes on the dirt hills and I thought I was Evel Knievel and tried to pull off a double hill jump and ended up careening off and crashing into the chain link fence?"

His face softens a little and he nods.

"Remember how I split my leg open? I tried to tell you I was okay, but you knew I wasn't. I was bleeding all over and my left leg hurt so bad that I couldn't walk. You carried me six blocks to my house."

He nods again.

"When we got to my house you were barely out of breath, even though you'd just carried me all that way. Your shirt was soaked in blood and I remember wondering how in the world your grandma was going to get it clean. I felt so bad for ruining your shirt. It was your favorite."

He snorts out a laugh. "You were worried about my shirt and I was convinced that your leg was broken and they were going to have to amputate it."

I laugh too because I'd forgotten that part. "That's right. You kept telling my dad to take me to the hospital so the doctors could find a way to 'save' my leg."

We sit quietly for a few several moments just staring at each other.

He smiles again and says, "Remember how pissed Jo was when she came home and saw that huge gash butterfly-bandaged shut? I thought she was going to kill your dad for not taking you to the doctor to get stitches."

"I survived though, and got a pretty wicked scar out of the deal." I squeeze his hand.

"It *is* a pretty wicked scar." He agrees. "I'm kind of jealous of it actually."

"And you know what? To this day, every time I look at my scar I think of you. I think about how lucky I am to have a friend like you. Someone who cared about me that much, even at ten years old, to carry me six blocks and let me bleed all over him in the process."

He looks down at the table and blinks several times and then mumbles, "I'd do it again."

Now my eyes are tearing up and I am pleading quietly again, "And I'd do it for you, if I could. Please tell me what happened. Who hit you?"

His head has dropped to look at the table and I can't see his face anymore, but tears are hitting the table in rapid succession.

I jump up and circle the table to stand behind him wrapping my arms under his and around his huge chest. I press my cheek between his shoulder blades and hug him as tightly as I can. He places his hands over mine and holds them against his chest, which rises and falls with each sob. As the sobs lessen he pulls my hands away and turns to face me. He stands up pulling me into a hug. We stand there for a very long time. He cries and I hold him. I'm oddly calm until he stops and then I start to panic.

Finally, he takes a deep breath, looks me in the eye, and in a whisper tells me something I am not prepared to hear. "Larry."

I'm the one crying now. It's an angry sort of hysterical cry, completely unhinged. "What?!" I scream. "Your *father* did this? Who in the hell does he think he is?" Teagan grabs me by the shoulders. He's trying to calm me down now, but it's not working. "Does your grandma know about this? He can't do this to you!"

He turns his back to me. "She knows. It's been going on most of my life. He only does it when he gets really drunk and I mouth off to him. He's just never punched me in the face before. He knows better than to leave bruises … where people can see them."

I'm in complete and utter shock at this point. "This has happened before and I never knew?"

He nods.

It's a punch to my gut. "Teag, I'm so sorry. I can't let you go home. You're staying here."

"Veronica, are you out of your fucking mind? I can't stay here. Larry will know I told you."

"So? He should be rotting in jail for what he's done to you."

He grabs my arm and looks me in the eye. "We're not telling anyone about this. I'm not reporting this to the police … and neither are you. I mean it."

"Teag, this is serious."

A disgusted, humorless laugh escapes his lips. "No, this is my *life*, Veronica. It's always been this way and it always will be."

I interrupt him, still pleading, "But it doesn't have to be like this. Can't you see that?" Just then I hear my mom's car pulling into the driveway. "I'm telling my mom," I whisper.

I take his lack of response as approval.

As soon as my mom walks in the door and sees him, Teagan tells her everything. I'm floored that I never knew any of this before today. My mom listens intently, gives Teagan a hug, and then also refuses to let him go home. She calls his grandma and asks her to put Teagan's soccer gear, clothes, and toiletries in boxes while Larry is still at work and she races over and picks them up. She tells him he can stay with us as long as he needs too. He agrees … as long as we don't call the police. We find out Teagan has an aunt that lives about twenty miles away. He doesn't see her often because she refuses to speak to his grandma or dad. My mom tells Teagan she'll call her.

Teagan, Mom and I eat dinner after that, which, after all of the commotion, seems quiet and almost normal. My mom gives Teagan a pillow and blanket and apologizes over and over for our lack of a spare bedroom. There's a futon just outside my room in the basement, and he can sleep there. No one uses it except on the rare occasion that company visits. It's not very comfortable, but it could be worse. I'm helping Teagan make the bed when I hear the doorbell ring. I don't think much of it until I hear the voices coming from the front room above us and my mom yells down for me to come up.

It's Sunny. My stomach turns inside out. I haven't seen her since Dimitri and I broke up. "I forgot she was coming," I say under my breath.

"What? Who is it?" Teagan knows I'm nervous.

152

"It's Sunny, Dimitri's mom. I'll be right back." I start for the stairs.

Teagan booms, "Dimitri's mom? What in the hell is she doing here to see you?"

I turn and shoot him an angry glare. "Shh! Teagan, shut up! She can hear you. I don't know why she's here. Now be quiet so I can go talk to her."

I walk tentatively into the front room. Sunny and my mom are sitting and talking quietly. I overhear my mom asking about Dimitri. They both go quiet when I enter.

"Hi Sunny," I say softly. I feel a wave of guilt, and suddenly I fear she'll start yelling at me.

Instead, she walks over and gives me a hug, saying, "Hi sweetie. I've really missed seeing you. How are you doing?"

My guilt turns into relief. Sunny Glenn is one of the kindest people I've ever met. "I've missed you, too. I'm doing alright."

She's listening intently—the same way Dimitri does, I realize. She nods and takes me by the hand to sit down on the chair next to her. "I won't keep you long. I know it's getting late. The reason I wanted to talk to you tonight is to ask if I might get your help with something."

I feel my body tense up. At my reaction, she pats my knee gently.

"I'm opening an interior design firm next month. It's always been a dream of mine. I wondered if you might help me out after school and this summer. I need an assistant—someone to take calls, set appointments, file paperwork, that kind of thing. Would you be interested? Dimitri said you lost your job recently and I think you would be a perfect fit. That is if you don't mind working with me?"

I'm stunned. "You're joking, right?"

She smiles and shakes her head.

I jump up and hug her. "That would be amazing! I would love to work for you!"

"Great!" she says, laughing. "It's settled then. I plan to open in two weeks, so I'll call you next week and we'll discuss your salary and schedule." She gives me a big, genuine smile, and then turns to face my mom as she stands.

"It was so good to see you again, Jo. We'll have to meet for lunch next week and get caught up."

They say their goodbyes and my mom and I walk Sunny out to her car.

"Sunny?" I ask hesitantly.

"Yes, Veronica?" She's smiling at me.

"I'm sorry. About Dimitri, I mean. I never wanted to hurt him." I want to go on, but I don't know what else to say.

She pats my shoulder in her kind, motherly way. "I know, sweetie." She gives me one more smile, then turns and climbs back into her SUV and drives away. My mom and I go back inside, where she takes me in a huge hug and we squeal happily, celebrating my new job. Just then, Teagan walks in the room.

"What's going on?" Teagan says, laughing at the sight of us.

My mom speaks up first. "Dimitri's mom just offered Ronnie a job. Isn't that great?"

The smile vanishes from Teagan's face. "You didn't take it, did you?"

"Yes, I took it. Are you kidding?"

He looks annoyed. "Can't you see what he's doing?"

And now I'm annoyed. "What who's doing?"

"Dimitri. She's only doing this so that he can get you back. You can't see that?"

"Teagan, I'm sure Dimitri said something to his mom to prompt this, but I'm sure it was only to help me out. This isn't some kind of ploy to get me back."

Teagan throws his arms up. "Yeah right. Whatever, Veronica." He glares, then turns and stomps downstairs. When I find him later, he's sleeping on the futon.

Life is sometimes … bruised and broken.

154

Chapter 11
Disturbing touch
Unsolicited kiss

I wake Sunday morning not wanting to repeat the prior two days. Teagan and I have been alone together in my house and haven't said a word to each other. My parents are out of town until Monday evening and the house is so quiet. Quiet, but uncomfortably so, due to the grudge I'm holding against my basically homeless and beaten best friend. I feel horrible.

I lie still in my bed and listen for any signs of movement from the adjacent room. Finally I call out, "Teag, you awake?"

A pause, then his sleepy reply, "No."

"I'm sorry I'm such an ass."

I hear him laugh. Then he says, "It's okay, I'm used to it … *ass*. I'm sorry, too."

It's official. Everyone's forgiven. "What do you want to do today?"

Suddenly, my door creaks open, and he's standing in the doorway of my room rubbing his good eye. He's only wearing a pair of soccer shorts. My god, he's huge. I knew he was big under all those clothes, but it's been a couple of years since I've seen him without a shirt on. At 6'5", he looks like a bodybuilder.

"Teag, seriously, you really need to lay off the steroids. When did you get so big?"

He smirks. "That's what she said."

I throw my pillow at him, which he easily dodges. "You're such a pervert."

He laughs and flexes his biceps for me. "All natural, baby."

"Do you want to shower first, or should I?"

"Considering you take *forever* to get ready, you go first. But, do me a favor today and leave me some hot water."

I pull the covers back and jump out of bed. "Deal." I should've been a bit more selective in my choice of pajamas while I have a male friend sharing the house with me. I

155

watch his eyes pop and then run from my head to my toes and back up to my head again. Note to self— no more tiny tank tops and short shorts while Teagan's here.

He snaps back to reality, shakes his head, and turns to exit my room.

I shower as fast as I can. After I dress, I put on some lip balm and mascara. I'll let my hair air dry so Teagan can have the bathroom. I find Teagan sprawled out on my tiny twin bed. He has the pillows propped up and is lying with his hands behind his head, still only wearing the soccer shorts. His legs dangle off the end of the edge, making him look like a giant trying to sleep on a miniature bed.

"What's that say?" he asks curiously.

I'm bent over combing the tangles out of the underside of my hair and can't see what he's looking at. "What does what say?"

"The painting. Did your parents give it to you? It's got your name on it."

Here we go. I really don't want to discuss Dimitri with him again. "It says Je t'aime."

"No shit, Veronica. What does it *mean,* in English?"

My eyes are starting to fill up so I remain bent over. "Je t'aime is I love you in French."

He sits up and heads for the bathroom. "Cool," he says, in passing. "That's really nice of your parents, since they know you dig France and all."

I wait until I hear the door shut before I let the tears fall. God, I miss him.

That day, Teagan and I make grilled cheese sandwiches and watch a hockey game. Despite how the past couple of days have played out, today's been fun and we're joking around like old times. I order us a pizza for dinner, and he agrees to watch the movie I picked. We're sitting at opposite ends of the sofa, facing each other. His legs stretch almost from one end to the other, so I have to lay mine on top of his. I found the movie while we were flipping through channels. It's a love story that I've seen about a hundred times, but the

156

end always makes me cry. I'm trying not to sniffle, brushing away the tears inconspicuously.

"Veronica, do *not* tell me you're crying?"

Damn, he caught me. "So?" I say defensively.

"Dude, that's the cheesiest damn movie I've ever seen." He's relentless.

I sniff loudly. "It's not cheesy, it's romantic. You, my friend, wouldn't know romance if it hit you over the head."

"You doubt me?" he says, acting mildly shocked.

"In a word, yes." I'm only half joking. Teagan doesn't have a romantic bone in his body.

"Oh really? And which one of us has had sex? A lot."

I throw my head back and laugh. "What does *that* have to do with being romantic? I hate to inform you, but sex does not equal romance."

He looks confused. "Sure it does. How do you think I get girls to sleep with me? I'm romantic."

I'm still laughing. "Banging Sheila Kratowski in the back seat of Larry's Buick is not romantic. Easy maybe … but not romantic."

He shrugs and says, "Yeah, whatever." It's quiet for a few moments before Teagan asks thoughtfully, "Veronica, can I ask you something?" He looks too serious for Teagan … and that makes me nervous.

"Sure," I say apprehensively.

"Did you and Dimitri do it?"

I look down at my lap. "No."

"Why not? The douchebag was really into you. He still is. And you seemed really into him."

I can see that the joking is over and he's just being sincere. Nosy, but sincere. So I answer, "He's not a douchebag. And … I just can't. What if I got pregnant?"

"That's what rubbers are for; even I know that. I mean, didn't you want to?"

"Of course I wanted to." I feel myself starting to blush.

"You miss him, don't you?"

"Why are you asking me all this?" I ask, defensively.

"Because you seem bummed about it … still … it's been weeks."

157

The tears are coming again. "Yeah, well I can't be the girlfriend he deserves right now."

"I bet he'd take whatever you could give. Most guys would." He adds under his breath.

"It's not that simple, Teag."

"Why not?" He pulls his legs out from under mine. Without waiting for me to answer, he leans toward me and says, "You know what your problem is, Veronica?" I look up and into his eyes. "You think too fucking much," he says, and begins crawling over my legs. "Let your guard down a little. Get out of your head for once and let your body take over. Follow your instincts." His legs straddle mine and before I know what's happening, he's kissing me.

My first inclination is to resist, mainly because I'm in shock. His kisses are aggressive and exciting, and before I know it I'm kissing him back. I wrap my arms around his waist. He groans roughly and pulls my torso against his. I know I shouldn't encourage him, but I'm doing what I was told and I'm not thinking. He stops kissing me only long enough to take his shirt off. I can't help but touch his chest. The feel of warm skin suddenly brings an image to mind—Dimitri. I imagine it's Dimitri I'm touching, Dimitri I'm kissing. God, I miss the way his touch could make me … *feel*.

I'm lost in my fantasy … until Teagan reaches down and begins to lift my shirt. "This is Teagan, not Dimitri!" my brain screams over the other parts of me begging to continue. Fantasies are powerful, but this has officially gone too far. I push him back and crawl out from under him. I stand with my back to him, my face in my hands, and I start to cry again. I'm embarrassed and ashamed. And I'm sad … it's the grief associated with loss. The loss of Dimitri. The loss of myself.

Teagan is standing now, too, but keeps his distance. I can hear him pulling his shirt back on.

"I'm sorry, Teag," I say through the tears.

He strokes my hair from the top of my head and down my back. "I'm not," he says softly.

"I shouldn't have kissed you back. I don't want you to get the wrong idea."

Slowly he turns me around and pulls my hands away from my face. He smiles sheepishly. "Veronica, I know that it didn't mean the same thing to you that it did to me. For all I know, you were probably thinking about that douchebag the whole time. But you know what? I don't give a shit. I've wanted to kiss you since we were twelve years old; I just never had the balls to do it."

I sigh in relief and guilt. "I love you, Teag … just not *that* way. I'm sorry." I feel pathetic.

"It wasn't so bad though, was it? Admit it, I'm a good kisser." He still has that childish grin on his face.

"As much as I don't want to admit it, you're not bad," I say. I swear I just witnessed his ego grow … two sizes. I'm relieved that he's smiling, so I prod. "Are you mad at me?"

He laughs as if the question is absurd. "Hell no! I can finally cross kissing Veronica Smith off my list of things to do before I die."

That is such a "Teagan" thing to say that it makes me laugh out loud. "This is just between us, right? You won't tell Tate?"

"I was thinking about sending out a mass text or posting it on Facebook, maybe renting out a billboard … "

"Come on!"

"Kidding … I'm only kidding. I won't tell anyone."

"Thanks." I pause and think twice before I ask the next question, but I've never been in this situation before and I have an impartial jury here. I close my eyes and let it fly. "How was it for you? I mean, am *I* a good kisser?"

He smiles slyly. "On a scale of one to ten?"

I wince and nod. "Sure."

"A nine and a half," he says. His smile softens and his head tilts slightly to the right. "But if I'd been him, someone you were in love with, someone that you didn't hold back with … someone that wasn't like your *brother*," he pauses, grinning, "then on a scale of one to ten it would've been a twenty."

In a weird way, I'm flattered. "Thanks."

Life is sometimes … over-thought.

Chapter 12
What else can I say?
I eff'ed up

After my mom talked to Teagan's aunt, it was agreed that Teagan should stay at our house until graduation. She's more than willing to take him in right away, but she lives about twenty miles from school and he doesn't have a car, which would make getting to school difficult for Teagan. He's going to spend the summer with her and then he's off to college in the fall. He already has a soccer scholarship to a local college (as long as he passes all of his classes this semester; fingers crossed).

Teagan checks in periodically with his grandma just to let her know he's okay, but he doesn't speak to his dad. It's my hope that losing his son this way will encourage his dad to get sober, but I'm not holding my breath. To me, the important thing is that Teagan is safe. He seems happier now, but Teagan's always been really good at putting on the happy-go-lucky façade. He can't keep it up twenty-four hours a day though, and since we're now living in close proximity to each other, I can see the other side of him, too. I see the sadness on his face when he thinks no one is watching. His bruise has outwardly healed, but I worry about what's going on inside … emotionally. That will take more time.

The last few months of my senior year seem to pass so quickly. Prom is approaching and graduation is only six weeks away. Signs of spring are beginning to poke through the snowy ground, and the days are getting longer. I'm more optimistic than I've been in months and all signs indicate that my life is heading in a positive direction again. I'm gaining control. I'm still not so great at asking for help, but I am making baby steps. The things that make me feel good are keeping up my connections with my friends and family, and preparing for college.

I've applied to three local universities, and have been accepted to all of them. I have a 4.0 grade point average and I'm in the top five-percent of my graduating class, so things are looking up. My parents have set aside a college fund for me, but it's only enough for the first few semesters depending on where I go; I insist on paying for anything beyond that. I'm looking for any available scholarship money, but it's competitive. With budget in mind, the main concern is proximity to home. I would rather live at home and avoid housing costs if at all possible. It's stressful, but I'm working through it.

In March I started working for Sunny at her new office and have been there for about a month now. I love the job. Sunny is incredibly supportive. I learned quickly how smart and talented she really is. Her home is so beautiful; I've always thought so. But I never realized that she was actually an interior designer. For all of her intelligence and talent, she's also pretty quirky. She can be absentminded and make rushed decisions, sometimes without completely thinking through the consequences. Dimitri used to tell me that she took some looking after, and now I finally understand what he meant. I basically act as her assistant. I place orders with vendors, take calls from clients, make appointments, manage her calendar, and try to keep her organized to make sure she doesn't forget anything. I work every day after school, but I have weekends off.

Everything seems to be going well, with one exception: Dimitri. I thought that as time passed, things would get easier. But they haven't. He's always nice when I see him, but we're distant. He's friendly with people, but aside from hanging out with Sebastian, he seems to keep to himself. He's always been private. He has a few classes with Monica, so every once in a while I nonchalantly ask her about him. Of course, she sees right through me.

"Veronica, you're still not over him, are you?" Monica asks one afternoon as we're walking out of Literature.

I'm shamelessly watching him walk down the hall in front of us. All I can think about is how right he was about a nice fitting pair of jeans.

Monica waves her hand in front of my face. "Hey, Veronica?"

Startled, I blink and look at her. "What?"

162

"I *said*, you're still not over him, are you?" Her accusation turns consolatory, and there's pity all over her face. I hate that. Pity makes me feel even more pathetic.

"What are you talking about?" I make a weak attempt at playing stupid.

"You *know* what I'm talking about. Dimitri."

I don't answer and, correctly, she takes that as a yes.

"He thinks something's going on between you and Teagan, you know."

I can't hide my shock. "What?!"

"Yeah, Tate said he was over at their house last week with Sebastian, and Dimitri came home and hung out with them for a while. He said Dimitri was asking questions about you and Teagan. Tate told him that nothing was going on, but he said he didn't think Dimitri bought it." She takes a breath and looks at me. "Nothing is going on with you and Teagan, is it?"

"No! God, no! Teagan and I are just friends. I love him, but sharing a bathroom with the boy for over two months now is a *huge* turn-off."

Monica laughs. "I think I get the picture. I feel kind of sorry for Teagan though."

"What do you mean?" I know Monica doesn't know why Teagan is really staying with my family. Or does she? Teagan and I told everyone that his dad had to move out of state for a job and that Teagan needed someplace to stay so that he could finish school. Tate knows the truth, but beyond that, everyone else believes the story.

"Come on Veronica, Teagan's totally in love with you. He always has been." She's looking at me suspiciously.

My head shakes back and forth emphatically. "No, no, no, Teagan's totally in love with anyone whose pants he can get into. *We* are just friends." I will deny this to the end.

"Whatever. I know he's a man-whore, but he doesn't care about any of them. The boy *loves* you. You really don't see it?"

I shake my head. "No."

We part ways to head to our next classes and I can't stop thinking about everything that she's just said. I thought

Teagan had kind of gotten me out of his system after we kissed. It makes me sad if that isn't the case. But, what really has me thinking is what she said about Dimitri. He's *asking* about me, which means he's *thinking* about me, which means *maybe* he still cares? I know I shouldn't jump to such wild conclusions and I know I shouldn't get my hopes up, or even think about it at all for that matter, but I can't help myself.

I arrive at work a few minutes early after school. I'm still riding the Dimitri high, and I'm in a really good mood for a change. I don't see Sunny's car in front of the office, but sometimes she's out visiting clients when I arrive. She's given me a key to let myself in. I put the key in the slot, but the door is already open. I open it slowly and can hear someone moving around in the back. This makes me nervous. No one else should be here.

Stopping in the doorway, I yell loudly, "Hello?" I'm prepared to make a run for it if I have to.

I hear footsteps and then, "Ronnie?" Sebastian walks around the corner and into the front room.

I sigh in relief, and my body relaxes. "Oh, hey Sebastian. What are you doing here?"

He shakes his head like he really doesn't know either. "Oh, Mom texted me during last period and asked me to get here as quick as I could after school because she needed help with some orders that just arrived." He's rolling his eyes dramatically. "She sort of told me what to do and then ran off to some meeting. She said you could fill me in when you got here."

We walk to the back and start opening boxes. I actually do know what we need to do, and I'm grateful to have the help. This is going to take the rest of the day to finish, even with two of us, and it needs to be done by tomorrow morning.

It's a little uncomfortable at first, being here with Sebastian. Sebastian himself doesn't make me nervous. Friendship with him has come easily from the very beginning. Oddly, I've always felt some sort of unspoken bond between us. Maybe Dimitri was the common link. But I haven't talked to Sebastian much since the breakup, and I'm

164

not sure what he thinks of me for it. He and Dimitri are closer than any siblings I've ever met, and they're very loyal to each other.

We make small talk for a while and then the conversation takes a more serious turn. Sebastian doesn't beat around the bush. He's much more blunt than Dimitri or his mother.

"So, Ronnie, what's up with you and Teagan?"

This catches me off guard. "Teagan is staying with my family until school's—"

Sebastian interrupts, "Yeah, I know about the living arrangements. That's not what I'm talking about. What's going on? Are you two seeing each other?"

"God, *no*! This is the second time I've been asked that question today," I say, exasperatedly raising my voice. "What would give anyone the impression that *anything* is going on between us?"

He puts his hand on my forearm and half-laughs, "Easy, Ronnie. I forgot how easy it is to get you worked up," he pauses, "It's just that people are talking. I mean, he *is* living in your house and in pretty close quarters. It kind of makes me wonder."

I feel my heart rate increase. I'm getting pissed. "What exactly are *people* saying?"

He starts unpacking a box again. "Well, rumors are going around, and for the most part I ignore them because I think I know you better than that. Still, last week Tate was over at my house and D. came home and started asking Tate if he knew what was going on between you and Teagan. He hears the same rumors I do. Tate told him you two were just friends, but after D. left, Tate told me he wasn't really sure. He said that Teagan spilled his guts to him the weekend before when they got home from a party."

"Teagan spent the weekend with Tate two weeks ago. Teagan said they went to a party, but said he didn't remember much of it because he got so drunk." I'm trying to keep up and fill in the blanks.

"Well, I guess he was pretty wasted and going on and on about you. Tate kind of blew him off because he's heard it all before. I mean it's no secret that Teagan's into you. Anyway, Teagan claimed that he'd even kissed you recently, which I personally find hard to believe. So what's up?" He looks up from his box, waiting for my response.

I shake my head harshly. "Unbelievable," I say, talking mostly to myself.

He smiles thinking he's correct. "Right? That's what I told Tate. Teagan only wishes. I told Dimitri it didn't happen."

I'm still stunned. "Actually ... it did happen." I cover my face with my hands, feeling defeated.

Sebastian is shocked. "What the hell?" he says, slowly. "Are you shitting me?"

I rub my temples a few times, look Sebastian in the eyes, and inhale and exhale deeply before I answer. "No."

He shakes his head. "Please tell me this happened after you broke up with D.?"

I nod and answer quietly. "Yes."

"And please tell me that Teagan had *nothing* to do with your breaking up with D.?" He says through gritted teeth.

"He didn't." I feel so ashamed. Confessing all of this to Sebastian is almost as bad as confessing it to Dimitri himself.

He's still shaking his head and looks disgusted. "Ronnie, I know it's none of my business to pry into your personal life like this, but what in the hell is going on? What's the story with you and Teagan?"

I weigh my options and consider not answering him. He's really pissed at me and rightly so after what I've done to his brother. But, Sebastian is someone I trust. I also know this news has already made its way to Dimitri and I don't want him to get the wrong idea. This is my opportunity to air my side of the story, and telling Sebastian is second best only to telling Dimitri himself. Decided, I sit down and gesture for him to take a seat across from me. I look at the floor as I begin to explain. "Teagan is my best friend. We've been friends since we were little. I always thought of him as the brother I never had, and until very recently I assumed that he thought of me the same way. Due to an incredibly sad twist of fate, my family has temporarily taken him in."

166

Sebastian interrupts, "Right, because his dad moved out of state or something."

I bite my lip and ponder how to answer without compromising Teagan's secret. "It was something … a little more serious than that. I'm sorry, that's all I can say out of respect to Teagan. The official story is that Teagan's dad moved out of state though, so as far as you know that's what happened, okay?"

His face softens a little and he nods in agreement.

"Most people don't understand because they don't know the whole story. In ways, I'm closer to him than I've ever been, but not how you think." I shake my head; this is so hard to explain without saying too much. "Teagan needs me, but because he has feelings for me, I need to keep him at a distance. It's a fine line. How do you hold someone close just so that they can hold it together, while at the same time distance yourself so that you don't break their heart?"

Sebastian is poking at a hole in the knee of his jeans. He isn't looking at me, but he's listening to every word I say. It must run in the family—they're all good listeners. "So, let me get this straight," he says. "Teagan's been through some pretty bad shit and you're family rescued him and took him in. Now you feel bad because you know what he's been through and feel worse because you know he wants you. You want to help him, but you don't want to hurt him?"

"Basically, yes. I'm *not* attracted to Teagan. He's a nice guy, but I don't want *that* kind of relationship with him."

He's still playing with the hole in his jeans. "You left out the kiss. What happened there?"

I wait for him to look at me. "I don't know, sometimes things just happen. It would be pitiful of me to say I was vulnerable, but … " I trail off, searching for the right words. "Have you ever kissed someone you never intended to kiss?"

His eyes narrow. "You mean, something totally spontaneous?"

"I guess for lack of a better word, yeah, spontaneous."

He smiles. "Sure. I don't really plan things like that. If something happens, it happens."

167

"Well, it just happened." I'm thinking of the conversation leading up to the kiss and a sad smile crosses my lips.

"There's more. What?"

"I was just thinking about what we were talking about before he kissed me."

He raises his eyebrows. "What were you talking about?"

"Your brother." I suddenly feel very sad. The space in my heart that will always belong to Dimitri begins to ache.

"D.?"

My eyes are starting to well with tears. "Teagan was prying into my love life, and like a dummy I was letting him. This is really embarrassing, but he was basically chastising me for not having sex with your brother. He wanted to know why I never did, because he knew how much I liked him … and still do," I confess. "I shouldn't have even discussed it with him but it was completely selfish on my part. Sometimes just talking about Dimitri helps me remember that he was real. That what we shared really happened." I blink through the tears. "Anyway, he sort of told me I needed to stop thinking about everything so much and just let things happen. And that's when he kissed me."

"Did you kiss him back or punch him in the face?" Sebastian is trying to lighten things up. Tears have an uncanny way of making guys uncomfortable.

"I didn't at first, but—"

"But what?"

I clear my throat. "But then I imagined he was Dimitri instead." I put my head down, too embarrassed to look him in the eye. The tears keep coming. I swallow hard. "I know I'm an awful person, but he caught me off guard."

Sebastian's voice grows quiet. "So, what you're saying is … it didn't mean anything to you? The kiss?"

"No. It meant nothing. You can think whatever you want about me; at this point I probably deserve it. But, it's kind of hard to put your heart into it when you're thinking about someone else the entire time."

"No judgment here. If I had a dime for every girl I—" He pauses, and continues, "Ronnie, can I ask you something?"

I wipe my eyes and nod.

"Why did you break up with D. in the first place?" His anger has subsided. His voice is soft now.

"You mean aside from the fact that I'm a fucking moron?"

He smiles.

"I've asked myself that same question every day since it happened." He allows me a quiet moment to collect my thoughts. "Without getting into all the details, I just had so much going on in my life that I couldn't be the girlfriend he deserved. I was pretty lost. I mean, who am I kidding? I'm still lost. There were lots of things in my life that needed attention and that meant taking attention away from him. He deserves more than that. He *always* put me first. He was perfect. And I just ... wasn't."

Sebastian huffs loudly. "*Goddamn it!* I knew this all happened for nothing. Why do you two always do this?" he asks, clearly frustrated. "Ronnie, listen to me. Nobody's perfect. Though Dimitri certainly thinks of you that way, even though you can be a pain in the ass sometimes." His eyes flash to mine. "No offense." He exhales loudly again in frustration. "Oh hell, I don't know how to explain this in a way that will make sense to you. It would so much easier if you remembered ... " He searches the room as if trying to find the right words. "Do you believe in destiny?"

"Destiny?" What a strange turn this conversation has taken. What is he talking about when he says, if I *remembered*? Remembered what? "I believe that everything happens for a reason, if that's what you're asking."

He shakes his head. "No, that's not what I'm asking. I mean *destiny*." He's biting his lip and his eyebrows are pinched together. He's choosing his words deliberately. "Sometimes the universe has a way of making sure that things happen, that certain events are put into motion." The frustration is becoming even more evident. "What I am

169

trying to say is that if there ever was a couple that was supposed to be together, it's you and Dimitri."

I'm shocked, frozen in place, staring at him, hanging on every word.

Realizing the effect his words have evoked, he smiles and his voice softens. "Ronnie, it sounds like you're going through a tough time right now; that you're confused about a lot of things. *Please*, don't worry so much." He punches my shoulder lightly. "It's ruining everything."

I half laugh through the residual tears.

"Just remember who you are, deep down. The real Ronnie. Search for her again." He points at my chest. "She's inside there. And even though she's a pain in the ass, she's one of the coolest people I've ever known." He smiles. "Oh, and how about making up with D.? The guy's irritable as hell when you're not together. He's lost without you."

I look down at my hands which I'm unconsciously wringing in my lap. "But he probably hates me."

"D. could never hate you. He totally adores you. And if you were honest with yourself, you'd see that you feel the same way about him."

I'm starting to cry again. "I miss him," I whisper.

He stands up and wraps me in a hug. "I know."

We stand there in an embrace for a few minutes and he lets me cry on his shoulder.

Releasing me, he claps his hands. "Okay, back to work. I don't want you to get fired."

I wipe the tears from my cheeks again. "Thanks Sebastian."

He winks. "Anytime."

Life is sometimes … destined.

Chapter 13
A heart full of words
And an uncooperative mouth
Make an unfortunate pairing

Sebastian spends the next week after school at work helping me out per Sunny's request. Business is picking up, which is great, but Sebastian and I are having trouble keeping up working only a few hours a day. It's obvious Sebastian doesn't particularly like the work, but he's diligent and doesn't stop until the job is done. I know he has another job, though he's never said what it is. Although he's pretty strapped for time, I like having him around.

It's Friday evening and just about time for me and Sebastian to go home when Sunny arrives back from a consultation. She breezes into the office. "Hi, you two. Sorry I'm so late getting back; it took a little longer than expected."

I haven't seen Sunny in person since Monday. Something about her always makes me smile. "No problem, Sebastian and I finished the Murphy project and we're almost done with the Fitzpatrick project. We should be able to wrap it up on Monday."

She drops her bag on the sofa and walks across the room in a few easy steps. She can cover a lot of ground quickly with those long legs. She puts an arm around each of our shoulders and squeezes tightly. "Thanks for your hard work. You've been such a help to me." She pauses for a moment. "I do have another favor to ask."

Sebastian eyes her suspiciously. "What?"

"Can I ask ... no, beg for a few hours of your time tomorrow morning to finish up the Fitzpatrick project? They phoned me this morning and asked to have everything ready for a secondary consultation tomorrow afternoon." She's smiling, but looks almost scared as she anticipates our reaction.

Before I can speak Sebastian unleashes a flurry of anxious words. "Mom! Tomorrow is prom! You know I have a lot going on already."

She cringes, but I know she expected this from him. "I know, I know, and I'm sorry, honey. Can you give me two hours between nine and eleven? I'm going to be here too, so it shouldn't take us too long."

Sunny is so sweet that I wonder if anyone has ever denied her anything. She's one of those people that you just want to help as much as possible.

As usual, Sebastian's bark is worse than his bite. He gives in. "Fine, but what about Ronnie? Did it ever occur to you that she might be busy tomorrow?"

Sunny looks over at me anxiously, but I interrupt before she starts pleading. "It's really okay, Sunny. I'll be here. I'm not going to prom. So I can stay as long as you need me."

Sunny hugs me and thanks me over and over.

It's almost embarrassing.

After another squeeze she continues, "And I want you to know that I've recruited some help for you, Veronica." She glances at Sebastian and winks. "I thank you, Sebastian, for helping Veronica out this past week, but you are officially relieved of your duties—after tomorrow of course. I talked to Bob this afternoon and he's agreed to come in and help us out starting Monday. He'll work mornings and Veronica will work afternoons until school's out and then the two of you will be here together."

Sebastian looks up at the ceiling and mouths the words, "Thank God."

I'm curious. "Who's Bob?"

Sunny beams and says, "Bob is a lovely older gentleman who attends our church. He lost his wife a few months ago, and he told me that he's looking for something to get him out of the house and keep his mind occupied. I think you're really going to like him."

Sebastian chuckles. "Bob's actually a really cool guy. Dimitri and I have been trying to talk him into coming down and helping out the two of you for the past couple of weeks." He looks at his mom. "He finally gave in, huh?"

Sunny nods. "He finally gave in," she says. "I can be very persuasive."

"Is that what you call it?" Sebastian needles her.

172

Sunny doesn't give him the satisfaction of a reply, only an exaggerated smile and widening of her big blue eyes. "I think it will be good for him, too."

As we clean up and gather our things to leave, Sebastian's mood seems to have lightened with the news of Bob. Sunny stops us when she hears us open the front door. "Would you two like some pizza? I can pick it up on my way home. I'm sure D. hasn't eaten yet either. It would be nice to have you over again, Veronica."

The sound of his name, even his nickname, makes my stomach flip-flop. I look to Sebastian for guidance with my answer. He sees the plea for direction in my eyes and nods slightly.

"Sure," I say, nervously.

"Wonderful. You two go on ahead; I'll be right behind you." Sunny says as she waltzes to the back room.

I call my mom to tell her I won't be home for dinner. As I expected, she's thrilled with the news.

Once in my car, I follow Sebastian down the familiar route to their neighborhood. God, it's been a long time. Too long. It feels strange to drive through the guard gate in my own car. And once I'm inside, waves of panic pulse through my veins. The panic increases exponentially with every revolution of the tires. I'm talking to myself like a crazy person as I coast down their street. By the time I bring Jezebel to a halt in front of their house, my body is trembling. I feel elated, terrified, and so nervous I could puke. I'm full-on manic. I cut the engine, close my eyes, and take several deep breaths. I open them again and look out the passenger window at Sunny's house, contemplating the position I've just put myself in. The fact is, it isn't too late to turn around and go home. But then Sebastian gets out of his car and walks down the driveway, motioning for me to come around to the back of the house.

"Don't be such a coward, Ronnie," I tell myself, coaching my body to open the door and deposit myself on the asphalt. Sebastian has disappeared. I take a last deep inhale to calm my nerves, and then walk quickly down the driveway. I can't give myself time to chicken out, but I remind myself that running to the house would make me look pathetically excited—which, of course, I am. (Well, either pathetically excited or masochistically deranged. Yeah, okay I'm glutton for punishment). The back door leading into the kitchen is open. Cautiously, I enter, utterly terrified of what I might find on the other side.

"Hello?" I call out timidly as I step inside. There is no one in the room.

As I look around the kitchen the memories come flooding back. The Glenn home had been a secondary sanctuary for me during the several months that Dimitri and I dated. Remembering the time I spent here makes me realize how much I miss it. Not the house, necessarily, but the feeling it gives me when I'm here: warm, safe, and loved. The nervousness subsides somewhat as I lose myself in the familiarity of the place and the memories it provides.

Resigned to stay (what did I say about being a glutton?), I take off my coat and drape it over a chair at the table. I set my bag on the chair, and then walk over and sit down on one of the stools at the counter. I don't know how else to explain it, but I feel comfortable. I've spent countless hours in this kitchen and always sat on this particular stool. One of Dimitri's car magazines is lying on the counter and I start flipping through it, a diversion while I wait for Sunny to arrive with the pizza.

"Ronnie?" It's an exclamation of shock, surprise, and disbelief. I know the voice, of course, and my heart is racing again (yup, I'm *definitely* masochistically deranged).

I turn on the stool to see Dimitri standing in the doorway leading in from the dining room. His snug-fitting shirt is covered in paint. Splatters of black stain his pants, too. My mouth is as dry as the Sahara and I don't know if I'll be able to speak. I smile quickly, although I'm somewhere between nervous and straight-up-terrified. When he doesn't respond, I lose the half-smile and just stare. I give both of us a moment … a reprieve.

A moment turns into several moments … and several more moments.

174

Dimitri hasn't moved—not a fraction of an inch. Is he breathing?

Silence is now the elephant in the room.

It's too much for me to bear. "Sunny invited me over for pizza," I blurt. "I ... I hope that's okay. She should be here any minute. You know, with the pizza ... " I trail off, trying to conceal the fear in my voice. The words are rushed, and I feel my tendency toward nervous rambling kicking in. I need to shut up.

Dimitri blinks a few times, as if my voice has finally broken through to him. "Wow. Pizza. Okay ... " His voice is monotone and filled with shock.

I rise and start to reach for my coat. "Maybe this was a bad idea."

He looks at the floor, closes his eyes as if he can't bear to watch me walk out the door, and pleads softly, "No, stay. Please. I'm just ... surprised."

The desperation in his voice seems to cut right to my heart. I don't want to go, and I don't think he wants me to, either. So I set my coat back down on the chair and return to the stool. It's only after I'm seated that he blinks. He's watching my every move intently. "Thank you," he whispers.

Suddenly, Sunny walks through the door carrying two large pizza boxes and a two-liter bottle of soda. She sets them on the counter next to me and the apologies begin. "I'm so sorry to keep you waiting, sweetie. I forgot how busy *Mile High Pie* can be on a Friday night. I had to wait a few extra minutes."

Hesitantly, Dimitri steps into the kitchen from the doorway. "Oh, hi honey!" Sunny's eyes always light up when she sees him. She walks over and kisses him on the cheek.

"Hey Mom," Dimitri says. The shock is receding from his voice but still abundantly clear in his eyes.

Sunny's suddenly cautious. "I invited Veronica over for dinner tonight."

Dimitri takes a seat on the stool at the other end of the counter from mine. "I see that."

175

I know she isn't oblivious to Dimitri's mood—the shock would be obvious to a complete stranger—but she tries to act casual. "I see you've been painting. Is the Fitzpatrick piece done?"

He reaches for a piece of pizza from the box in between us and takes a bite. "I just finished it. I'm not happy with the way it turned out though. It needs something, but I'm not sure what yet. I'm going to take a look at it again later tonight."

Sunny pats him on the back as she walks behind him. "I'm sure it's perfect. You're always so hard on yourself." She takes a seat between us and I can feel both Dimitri and myself relax a little at the buffer.

It's quiet until Sebastian returns to eat. He's changed out of his school clothes and into a pair of sweats and a T-shirt. He looks at me, and then Dimitri. I pretend not to notice the apologetic, minute shrug he aims at Dimitri. He fills the awkward silence as he stacks six pieces of pizza on a plate. "So, D., did you hear that Bob finally surrendered? Mom wore him down." He looks to Sunny with a teasing smirk. "I mean, she *skillfully persuaded* him." He wraps the words "skillfully persuaded" in air quotes with his fingers.

Dimitri's voice softens and begins to sound more like himself. "No kidding? That's great. When does he start?"

Sunny smiles in satisfaction. "On Monday. Veronica will get some well-deserved help and Sebastian can get back his normal routine."

The rest of the dinner conversation centers on Bob. I stop eating after one piece of pizza; I can't trust my uneasy stomach to any more than that. Throwing up would put a bit of a damper on the evening, and right now I need all the help I can get.

Sebastian disappears to the basement and Sunny wraps the leftovers in plastic wrap to store in the refrigerator while announcing that she's leaving to meet Pedro for a movie. "Thanks for joining us tonight, Veronica. We really enjoyed having you." She smiles warmly. "That stool has gone empty far too long. Stay as long as you like." She winks at me as she pulls the door shut behind her. I'm beginning to think this is a set-up and the terror returns.

The silence is deafening, and I take that as my cue to make an exit, even though, deep down, leaving is the last thing I want to do. Leaving will relieve the near-nausea that my body is struggling against at the moment, but that unpleasant feeling is almost welcome—a fair trade for the way sitting near him makes my heart feel. It doesn't ache the way it has the past few months. It feels alive again. And for the moment I'm selfish. I need this.

Suddenly, Teagan's advice rings in my ears: "Get out of your head for once and let your body take over. Follow your instincts." The sudden urge to walk over and kiss Dimitri is overwhelming. There's nothing in this world better than kissing Dimitri Glenn. *Nothing.* Time hasn't erased the smallest detail of his kisses from my memory. Truthfully I dream about them often, very often: his taste, his smell, his touch … the all-consuming desire. I wonder if my thoughts are written all over my face. The heat is rising in my cheeks and my heart is flying.

I steal a glance down the counter at him. He's staring at me. "You know she's right," he says, his voice steady and calm.

He holds my gaze, and I can't look away. "Right about what?"

"That stool *has* gone empty far too long." His eyes are serene and the corner of his mouth hints at a smile.

"It's been a long time, hasn't it?"

He just nods.

This is your moment, Ronnie, I think to myself. You may not get this chance again. Okay heart, you ready? Mind's going to shut up now, heart's got the floor. "Dimitri, I'm sorry … about everything." I want to hug him, to feel his arms around me again, to feel his warmth. I want to follow my instincts.

"I know. I am too," he whispers. I know his face well, there's a struggle flashing behind his eyes.

I'm almost certain he's wrestling with the same feelings I am. There are so many things I want to say. I want to tell

177

him how much I miss him. I want to tell him that my life is better when he's in it. But I don't want to push my luck and ruin this moment. My heart steps down off the soapbox and forfeits control to my mind again. We sit in silence for more than a minute before I opt for the safety of a subject change. I am such a coward.

"My dad got the Cubs tickets in the mail last week. He was so excited, you should've seen him. It really was a nice thing for you to do. Thank you."

He smiles, either at the change of topic or maybe just the topic itself. "It was the least I could do. He called a few days ago to thank me. He said they're leaving early the morning after graduation and making a weeklong vacation out of the trip. It should be a good time. I'm glad you came up with the idea. Your parents work hard and deserve a vacation."

I smile and nod. "Yeah, they do. Thanks again."

After a few more minutes of small talk the nervousness subsides on both sides and we settle into comfortable conversation. We cover a wide range of topics without ever touching upon anything too personal. The past few months melt away. The awkwardness, at least for the moment, has vanished. And laughter returns. It's encouraging, consoling, kind; like an old friend returned from a long time away. I forgot how much we used to laugh together.

I *love* his laugh.

There isn't a moment of silence and we don't move from our stools seated ten feet from each other—not until I excuse myself to use the bathroom. I glance absently at the clock on the wall when I return to the kitchen. "Is that clock right? Is it really 1:37 in the morning?"

Dimitri looks at his watch and confirms. "It is indeed."

I'm pleasantly surprised. The past several hours have passed effortlessly. "I had no idea it was so late. I guess I should probably get going."

Dimitri's face is peaceful and angelic as he rises to help me put my coat on. "Thanks for coming over tonight, Ronnie. You don't know what it meant to me. I feel like this is the first time I've been able to breathe in months." He lifts his hand, but hesitantly stops just short of brushing my

178

cheek. He smiles and lowers it. "Can I walk you to your car?"

My heart is soaring and my palms are sweaty. "I'd like that."

We walk slowly down the long driveway, our bodies so close that our arms brush against each other. I think back to the first day of school and smile; personal space is *so* overrated.

He opens the driver side door and stands behind it at a safe distance so as not to make the situation awkward. I throw my bag through onto the passenger seat and stand with one hand on the door and the other on the steering wheel. When I look up at him he's staring down at me. His eyes glitter in the streetlight.

It's at that moment that my life comes into focus, like flipping a switch. The entire world tilts back onto its axis. Call it an epiphany; the rare type of realization that changes your life absolutely. I *need* this man in my life. I need him like I need air and water. He *is* part of me—my past *and* my future. Since the day we met I've given my heart to him ... piece by piece. And it's at this exact moment that I realize he has all of it. My heart is no longer mine; it belongs to him and always will.

I can't help but smile.

He returns the smile—his beautiful smile. "What?" he asks softly.

"Thank you for being you, Dimitri."

Not much escapes him and I know from the look in his eyes that he understands. He nods humbly. "You're welcome."

I duck down into the driver's seat and look back up at him. "Maybe I'll see you tomorrow." I don't know if it's a question or a declaration, but it's hopeful.

He winks. "You can count on it."

Slowly he shuts the door and moves to the sidewalk. I wave and pull away, watching him in my rearview mirror as he begins to fade into the distance. He stands there glowing under the streetlight like an angelic statue. When I turn the corner, he's gone.

Life is sometimes … an epiphany.

Chapter 14
Falling in love
... again

The night is long; sleep eludes me for hours. When the dream finally comes it's about him, as they always are now. The dream is a succession of still images, like a slideshow. Each image captures Dimitri and me at different ages and in different situations. Many of the images are borrowed from actual events or past dreams I've had, but some, like us at a wedding that appears to be ours, are obviously just my mind taking liberties. Unconsciousness usually affords my imagination the privilege of conjuring up fanciful stories, but this dream is the scrapbook of a storied life—fulfilled, content, and lovely.

To say I'm disappointed when the alarm clock halts my visions is an understatement. "Back to reality," it buzzes. "Life and work won't wait." Don't I know it.

Sunny is already at the office when I arrive at 8:45. I'm thankful to see donuts and hot tea waiting for me. I feel like the walking dead after only getting two hours of sleep. The caffeine and sugar will at least offer a jumpstart.

Sebastian, Sunny, and I start working promptly at nine o'clock. The morning flies by with not much progress made. Complications that Sunny had no way of anticipating arise. It slows us down. Sebastian stays an extra two hours and leaves at one in the afternoon, at which time we break for lunch. Sunny calls for Chinese to be delivered.

With a box of steaming Hunan beef in my lap, I sink into the sofa in the back room and enjoy my lunch. Sunny sits on the sofa next to me. We're both exhausted and for a while we don't speak—just work with our chopsticks, focused on food.

"Veronica, I'm so sorry this is taking so long," Sunny says, chewing around bites of sweet-and-sour chicken. I had no idea we would run into so many problems. If you need to leave, I understand. You look like you didn't get much sleep last night." She winks and says, "Late night?"

I laugh. She doesn't miss anything. Or maybe she's just hopeful. "Late night," I confirm with a nod. "Thanks for inviting me over. It was very ... fortuitous."

She smiles softly. "I don't want to interfere, but D. has been miserable without you and you haven't seemed yourself, either. I thought it would be nice for the two of you to spend some time together."

"It was nice, thank you. And I can stay as long as you need me today. I told you, I'm not going to prom. I don't have any plans tonight."

She reaches across the sofa and rests her hand on my shoulder tenderly. "Veronica, you're an angel. Thank you for all the help you've given me. I don't know what I would've done without you these past few months."

I smile. "You're pretty easy to want to help. Maybe if you weren't so nice and wonderful all the time—" I say sarcastically. "No, even then I'd still probably want to help you."

She giggles. "Okay. You finish up your food. I need to run to the hardware store to pick up the paint. Will you be alright here by yourself?"

"Of course, go ahead. I'll be fine."

After Sunny leaves, I turn up the music and my body grudgingly picks up where it left off. I'm singing along (loudly) to one of my favorite songs when I feel my phone vibrate in my pocket. I pull it out and the text reads: "Can you keep it down in there? :) And please come and open the front door." It's from Dimitri. My pulse accelerates and the smile on my face is instantaneous. I turn down the music and run to the front door.

He's standing at the door holding a large frame wrapped in brown paper. It's taller than he is, and almost as wide. It must be a painting. I hear his laughter as I open the door. He gently slips the painting inside first.

"What's so funny? You don't like my singing?" My tone is mockingly defensive, but I can feel the blush rising in my cheeks.

He laughs again and shakes his head as he gingerly steadies the painting against the wall. "I love your singing … but don't quit your day job. I just forgot how loud you belt it out when you think no one's listening."

My face is beet-red. I know I'm a terrible singer, which is one of the reasons I never sing in front of anyone. But when I'm alone, it's a different story. Without an audience I sing at the top of my lungs. "You've never heard me sing before, so stop trying to embarrass me."

He turns and winks at me. The odd, knowing smile returns to his lips. "That's what you think." He proceeds to the back room. "What smells so good? I haven't eaten all day. I'm starving." He's peeking in the containers still open on the table. "Do you mind if I have some? Are you finished?" Unable to wait for an answer, he begins scooping the last few spoonfuls of Hunan beef into his mouth with my chopsticks.

"All done, help yourself. I need to get back to work."

He sits on the sofa and I return to the stacks of contracts I'd been organizing before. I like having Dimitri nearby. His presence calms me. It's something I realize I've known all along, but I'm only now appreciating.

Just as Dimitri finishes his lunch, Sunny returns. She walks in the room with two buckets of paint in each hand and her keychain in her mouth. Dimitri jumps up and takes the paint from her and sets the buckets on the table.

"Thanks D.," she says as she takes the keys from her mouth. As she turns to close the door, she claps her hands in delight and gasps, her eyes wide with excitement. "The painting's done!" She pushes past him and into the front room for the unveiling. "Let me see it! Let me see it!" Sunny is one of those rare people who never lost her childish innocence or wonderment. It's one of her most endearing qualities.

Dimitri drags his feet to prolong her agony. Her unbridled pride in everything her sons do embarrasses him, but I know that deep down, he loves it, too.

"Close your eyes," he orders Sunny. He unwraps the painting carefully, but the painstaking process drives his mother crazy.

She practically stomps her foot in anticipation. "Oh D., hurry! I can't wait!"

I'm standing behind her, trying not to laugh at her impatience.

Dimitri does laugh, and says, "Okay, before you wet your pants, open your eyes."

Sunny puts down her hands and gasps, "Oh, D. it's beautiful. It's just perfect."

Dimitri rolls his eyes. "You say that every time, Mom."

She kisses him on the cheek. "That's because they always *are* beautiful and perfect, my talented boy."

As she steps back, I finally catch a glimpse of the entire painting, and cannot help but gasp, myself. Dimitri reflexively reaches for my arm. "What's wrong, Ronnie?"

I shake my head slowly. "Nothing ... it *is* beautiful." And it is. It's an abstract painting. The black background is so soft it appears to glow. Black shouldn't glow, but it does. It's contrasted against sexy shades of purple and blue boldly applied in a deliberately haphazard fashion that lends to the overall highly sensuous vibe, the dominant versus the submissive. I'm at a loss for words. "It's just ... really ... beautiful," I say quietly.

Dimitri accepts the compliment humbly with a sincere nod of thanks.

The moment feels intimate, even with Sunny in the room. His paintings are so revealing, and the style so distinct and entirely his own. He pours his soul into each of them and it radiates back out at its audience—raw and unforgiving, yet somehow ... pure.

The three of us stay in the office and work until the work is done, which is just after seven-thirty that evening. Sunny leaves after thanking me for the five-hundredth time. And then Dimitri and I are alone in her studio. The sun is beginning to set outside and though I'm a little hungry, I don't want to leave. I don't want to leave *him*. Not even for a second. Time with him, especially alone, is precious. I'll never take it for granted again.

As I put away the last of the paint buckets and brushes and am clearing off the worktable, Dimitri breaks the silence. He's examining his painting on the other side of the room. "Do you really like the painting?"

I stop what I'm doing and rest my back against the table turning to face him. "Are you kidding?"

He shakes his head. "No, I'm just asking for some honest criticism."

"I don't like it … I *love* it. Why do you even have to ask? You are so, so talented. Don't you see that?"

He smiles half-heartedly. "Not every painting is a masterpiece, Ronnie. I think you're a little biased."

"Maybe I am, but you obviously have no idea how special they are."

He raises an eyebrow. "How so?"

It takes me a moment, but I close my eyes, push any internal censors aside, and speak from my heart. "I don't know how to describe the way I feel when I look at your paintings," I begin, trying to find the right words to continue. My eyes still closed as I bite my lip in thought. "They're … provocative … verging on carnal. Not the subject necessarily, it's just your tremendously passionate style. Something about the colors you choose. The way they work together … while fighting against each other. Harmony in the throes of agony. It's always sexy … so much so that in a way you should feel somewhat violated when people are done viewing your paintings. Looking at your paintings is an almost interactive and highly personal experience that leaves one slightly out of breath, yet aching … just short … of fully satisfied." I open one eye and risk a peek at him.

He's standing directly in front of me. His eyes are burning, no hint of a smile. "That's quite descriptive for a virgin." He twines his fingers with mine, one hand and then the other. "Painting is very emotional and very … physical for me … the perfect outlet for pent-up desires." He flexes his arms sharply and pulls my body abruptly against his.

185

I gasp; it takes my already shallow breath away. My face is against his chest. I inhale, taking in the faint scent of cologne on his shirt. As I look up he's already looking down at me and our lips brush. My voice is low, rough. "Pent-up desires?" I've picked up his habit of making questions sound more like statements.

He's pinned me against the long table in the center of the room. The heat of his body radiates through my clothes. His lips lightly graze mine as he answers, "In a sense, painting is quite ... satisfying." He reaches behind me and clears the table with a quick stroke of his forearm. Bolts of fabric roll off and across the floor. "You ... " he starts to say as his strong, fast hands pick me up by the waist and place me on the table directly in front of him. His hands come to rest on my straddled thighs as his forehead touches mine, "... are mind-blowing." We reach for each other's faces at that exact moment and collide.

My head spins. He takes a commanding lead, but I enthusiastically keep up. The months apart have fueled an explosive reunion. We act without restraint. Clothing is removed ravenously piece by piece. Lips are hungry. Fingertips explore, one moment light as a feather and the next commanding and willful, finding places on my body that trigger spasms of pleasure—places that I'd never expect: the skin beneath my ear, the inside of my wrist, and crease of my thigh. Touch has never been so affecting.

In the end, virtue remains scarcely intact, but the moment is no less life changing and magical.

I dress quickly and sit down on the sofa. My heart is still flying, but my breathing has returned to normal. He's buttoning his shirt slowly, watching me. A hint of his mischievous smile plays at the corners of his mouth. His face is flush and his hair is rumpled, but he looks beautiful in an entirely new way.

He kneels down silently on the floor in front of me, a look of undeniable adoration in his eyes. His voice sounds different too, more mature, older. "Ronnie, I love you."

"I love you, too." No truer words have ever been spoken.

186

Life is sometimes … mind-blowing.

Chapter 15
Hearts can physically shatter
Ask me
I'll tell you

Dimitri and I are virtually inseparable after that night. He visits me at Sunny's office almost every afternoon, and we do homework together almost every evening. Well, I do homework while he sits with me. He says that homework is a waste of time and assures me that with his amazing memory he's the ultimate test-taker. A passing grade is perfectly acceptable to him. He's looking past high school to the real world that awaits us on the other side. For him, that means his art.

Dimitri has made the decision to forego college and pursue his blossoming career as an artist. Who can blame him? Galleries are beginning to request showings, his paintings are selling for thousands of dollars each, and clients are lining up at his door. I find all of this out from Sunny naturally; Dimitri though exceedingly confident is equally as humble. He doesn't brag and even when I ask he downplays the degree of his success.

I, on the other hand—born with no innate and freakishly obvious talent—have decided college is my best avenue to success. At my parent's urging, I'm all set to attend the University of Colorado at Boulder in the fall. I'm nervous, but I allow myself to feel some excitement as well. I've earned a partial scholarship and have saved up some extra money to help supplement the college fund my parent's set up. As long as I can live at home and continue to work while I attend school, then financially everything should work out without the necessity of taking out any major student loans— at least for the first couple of years.

A week before graduation, Teagan moves out of our house to live with his aunt. She's letting him use her extra car to commute back and forth to get to school and to his job. We're sad to part ways, but we're both relieved. Sharing a bathroom with him was utterly disgusting and I'm glad to have it back to myself. And his huge appetite meant that there was never anything left in the refrigerator worth eating. He wasn't all bad though. I imagine it's like losing a sibling. I'd grown so used to his snoring at night that it's hard to fall asleep in silence now. I bought a fan and the white noise seems to help. Teagan is even beginning to treat Dimitri differently. The tense, ready-for-a-fight aura is gone and he's much more relaxed around him. There's a reason behind his behavior, though, and her name is Andi. She's sweet and innocent and nice ... and not at all Teagan's type. Which means she's *perfect* for him. They've been dating for a couple of weeks. He met her at a soccer clinic. He confided in me that he isn't going to rush things with her, even though it's killing him to be a gentleman. He *really* likes her. I think it's changing him for the better. He's still Teagan, but he seems more focused and gentler. I couldn't be happier for him and I have to admit it's a relief to have the focus taken off of me. We have a healthy friendship again.

Graduation isn't as climatic as I'd always envisioned it would be. The ceremony is *long*—unnecessarily long—and the speeches sound methodical in both content and delivery. I imagine they've been regurgitated, with very little variation, by thousands of people, at thousands of schools throughout modern history. The only real gratification the afternoon holds is the look on my parents' faces after I receive my diploma. I have no other family members, so my parents are my only relatives in attendance. My mom is crying, which is to be expected, and they both look as if they could, quite literally, burst with pride. I'll remember the look on their faces—those looks of pure joy—for the rest of my life.

After the ceremony, my mom takes dozens of photos of me with friends and classmates in our black graduation gowns. We're all there: Teagan and Tate, Monica, John, Piper, and of course, Dimitri.

Due to our lack of extended family, rather than hosting a graduation party for me, my mom conspired with Sunny to plan a joint party honoring me and Dimitri. The party is held at Sunny's house. She claims she's going to keep it simple, but I know better, simple is not in her vocabulary—it's over-

189

the-top. It looks more like a wedding than a graduation. A huge white tent is set up in the driveway with very formal looking decorations on the tables. Pedro's restaurant caters the late afternoon lunch, turning me into an enthusiastic glutton.

At the party, there are over one hundred attendees: fellow graduates, Dimitri's family from Wyoming and Texas, and a wild horde of Sebastian's friends. My parents stay for a few hours, eating and mingling, before heading out on their vacation to the long awaited Cubs game in Chicago. They're driving, rather than flying, and my dad wants to get a few hundred miles behind them tonight so that they'll have more time to spend when they arrive in Chicago.

My parents depart just before twilight falls. And the adults begin moving into the house. That's when the real fun begins. We clear all the tables to the outside perimeter of the tent and turn it into an impromptu dance floor. Sebastian acts as deejay and is quick to lure everyone out onto the dance floor. Predictably, someone has snuck in a bottle of booze. It's a plastic bottle of Smirnoff, passed around freely in between swinging hips and clapping hands. When it comes to me, I take a discreet gulp, coughing as it burns down my throat. Dimitri holds up a hand to decline, and passes it along. Despite the liquor, no one gets belligerent and no one gets sick. Liquid courage does incite a few harmless dares, a few declarations of unrequited love, and a few stolen kisses. But for the most part there's just a lot of silliness, a lot of laughing, and a lot of memories made.

As Dimitri drives me home I run the past several hours through my mind and can't help but smile. Dimitri catches me and asks thoughtfully, "What are you thinking about?"

I turn my tired head that is nestled heavily against the headrest of what Dimitri affectionately refers to as "Ronnie's seat" in his Porsche to face him. My mind is fuzzy, but not from the vodka (that buzz wore off an hour ago); just from a long, fun, happy day. He's smiling through heavy, exhausted eyes.

"I was just thinking that this is one of those days that I will probably remember for the rest of my life. Not because I graduated, but because I got to spend it with all of the most important people in my life. It's a rare moment in time when the planets align and your favorite people are all gathered in one place simultaneously experiencing pure happiness. I've been blessed, and I want to make sure I don't forget the details. My life has taken incredible twists and turns these past few months, but now ... now I would say it's just about perfect."

The smile widens and he laughs quietly.

"What? It was a really great night, right?"

He concedes with a nod. "It was. I'm not disagreeing. Leave it to you to get philosophical on me at four-thirty in the morning. I can barely focus on the road and you're pondering life's finer moments. That's one of the things I love about you. You never stop thinking do you?"

"Nope, only when I sleep. Wait ... no, not even then." With that I let out a wide yawn.

He pulls into my driveway and leaves the car running while he gets out and comes around to open my door. He takes my hand and helps me out, and we walk slowly to the back door of my parent's house. He strokes my hair as I rummage through my bag for my keys. With some effort I finally locate them.

His arms wind around my waist from behind as I open the door, effectively trapping me. I feel his warm breath on the back of my neck and it raises goose bumps all over my body.

"It seems a shame to waste this opportunity. Your parents are gone and the house is empty," he whispers in my ear and a ragged sigh escapes him. "But Sunny is expecting me back." He pulls the hair back from the side of my neck and kisses it ... again ... and again.

My knees grow weak as I turn slowly to face him, not wanting to interrupt the sensation of his lips on my skin. "I don't want you to leave either." His kisses continue under my chin. "But we have all week." My breath is shallow. "It's

191

only Sunday morning. Go home and get some rest and come back this afternoon. I'll be waiting."

His lips finally find mine and though we're both exhausted, we kiss with passionate energy. We grudgingly part after a few minutes. His eyes are intently focused on mine, though his eyelids are drooping.

"You need to go home and get some rest, Mr. Sleepy Face."

"I can sleep when I'm dead."

"You might get the chance. If you don't get home soon Sunny may kill you."

He smiles. "You might be right. She should've let you sleep in the guest room at our house tonight, but my mom's pretty old fashioned."

"Old fashioned or smart? She knows you too well. She knows you wouldn't be able to stay away from me. I'm too tempting, remember?" I kiss him teasingly.

I suddenly find myself coiled in his embrace again. "Okay, when you put it that way, Sunny's a genius." He kisses me on the forehead.

I hug him tightly. "I love you … now go."

He kisses the top of my head and releases me. "I love you more. Sleep well, baby."

He waves as he backs down the driveway.

Sleep comes seconds after my head hits the pillow, and with it, a series of the strange dreams I've grown accustomed too. A predictable graduation dream ensues with Dimitri and me in the starring roles. The setting is right—a high school auditorium—but the clothing is all wrong. We look like a bunch of hippies. It's almost embarrassing to watch even though I'm distinctly aware it's only a dream. Dimitri is still unbelievably good-looking, but his long hair and clothes are ridiculous. My parents are there in the audience, looking exactly as they did yesterday, overflowing with pride. My eyes return again and again to their faces. I just can't get enough, wanting to remember every detail; their smiles, their looks of pride, the way my dad claps and my mother wipes her eyes. The memories seem to almost be frozen in time.

192

I'm positive I'm dreaming with a satisfied smile spread across my face. I'm sleep-smiling.

I wake with my mom and dad's happy faces still swimming through my head. The clock on my nightstand tells me it's almost noon. I decide I'd better shower and get dressed; hopefully Dimitri will be over soon to spend the day with me. That thought makes the smile on my face grow even wider.

Just as I finish up in the shower and turn off the water, I hear my cell phone ringing. I wrap myself in a towel and hurry to my room, sure it will be Dimitri. It isn't. It's a number I don't recognize, a number that I normally would ignore but the instantaneous knot in my stomach prompts me to answer it. Maybe it's my parents calling from a hotel.

"Hello," I say quietly.

It is a man's voice. "Veronica Smith?" he asks, sounding official.

The knot in my stomach grows. "Yes."

His voice grows gentler, but in a rehearsed and official sort of way. "Are you the child of William and Josephine Smith?"

My mind is racing. His voice isn't right. This doesn't feel right. "Yes," I say in a quivering voice. A wave of nausea rolls through me.

"Miss Smith, this is Officer Ryan Johnston with the Nebraska State Patrol. I'm afraid I have some bad news. Your parents were in an automobile accident this morning near Lincoln, Nebraska—"

I burst in before he can finish, "An accident? What kind of accident? Are they okay? Can I talk to them?" Suddenly I'm frantic.

"I'm afraid their vehicle was struck by a semi, head on, at 75 miles per hour on Interstate 80." He pauses, and I know the rest before he says it.

For a moment the world stops. Time stops. My heart stops. I inhale deeply and speak in a voice that doesn't sound like mine anymore. "They didn't survive, did they?"

The man's voice turns weary, human, and sad. "I'm very sorry. They were killed instantly."

193

I allow the words to wash over me. I feel numb, as if I'm outside my body, disconnected, watching this all play out.

"Miss Smith, are you there?"

My voice is monotone. Dead. Like my family. "Yes."

"Miss Smith, I will arrange to have local law enforcement officer visit you as soon as possible. Are you home?"

The shock is setting in, seeping in through every pore. "That won't be necessary." I want to be alone.

"Miss Smith, this is protocol." His voice is calm.

"That won't be necessary," I repeat.

"Miss, your parents have been taken to the Lincoln Mortuary in Lincoln, Nebraska. The director there—a mister Russell Clark—will be in contact with you later this afternoon to make arrangements." The formal, official voice flips back to the human voice. "I am so sorry, Miss Smith. Do you have a family member that we can call? I see here you're only eighteen. In times like these, we are able to phone family members if need be."

"No ... no, sir I don't ... it's just me ... call me ... just have them ... call me." The room is starting to spin. A vortex that I'm certain will suck me in whole.

"Miss Smith, are you sure I can't have someone local stop by to check on you?" His voice is still calm but laced with concern.

"No one ... thank you." I hang up and drop the phone on the floor, where it shatters into pieces.

I stand there, half-wrapped in a towel. *Shattered.*

My mind is numb, yet my senses are momentarily heightened and I'm acutely aware of the smallest, most inconsequential details. I feel the wet carpet beneath my feet where I've been dripping since I got out of the shower. I hear the hum of the air conditioning unit just outside my window. I smell the floral scent of my freshly-washed hair. I see the tear in the wallpaper above the switch plate on my wall.

I don't know how long I stand there, not moving an inch, still half-wrapped in the towel, still staring at the tear in the wallpaper. Everything else has faded away, except that tear.

I don't hear.

I don't smell.

I don't feel.

And then … I drop.

I drop to the floor and begin to cry. It isn't a hysterical cry, just a quiet, almost detached cry. I hug my knees to my chest and lie there, helpless. I close my eyes and see nothing. I decide I like that better. The tears subside.

I am not sad.

I am not scared.

I just *am*.

And that is enough, preferable even.

Time goes by.

I am vaguely aware of sounds outside and a voice. I do not allow myself to receive them, or try to decipher them.

I just *am*.

I am vaguely aware of someone's hands on my face shouting at me. I do not allow myself to focus on them.

I just *am*.

I am vaguely aware of my body shaking violently and the sensation of something heavy and soft draped around me. But I do not allow myself to feel.

I just *am*.

And then I hear cries of pain, someone shouting my name as though being tortured. I snap back to reality, opening my eyes to see Dimitri's agonized face hanging over me.

"Veronica," he sobs. "Ronnie what's wrong? What happened?"

I can't move. I realize how *warm* it is. I'm under a blanket. "How did you get in here?" is all I manage to squeak out.

He pulls me into his arms and sobs. "You didn't answer your phone. You didn't answer the house phone. I thought you were sleeping, but I've been calling for three hours," he gulps, swallows, and continues, "I was worried, so I came over. You didn't answer the door when I rang the bell. I went around to the back and peeked in your window, and saw you lying on the floor." He sobs again, coughing and sniffing. "I

195

broke out the window in the back door. What happened? Are you hurt?"

I don't answer. My brain has completely shut down and I have to focus to even remember why I'm lying on the floor in the first place. A hollow, disengaged voice begins retracing my steps. "I was in the shower, and then there was a phone call. And then I got the carpet all wet, and did you realize that there's a tear in the wallpaper by the door?" I point weakly at the wall.

He takes my shoulders firmly in both hands and sits me up to face him. He looks at me with wet eyes. "I don't care about the damn wallpaper, Ronnie. Are you okay? What happened?"

And then the curtain drops. The barrier that's allowed me to feel nothing for the past few hours disappears. It all comes flooding through, uninvited, and completely overwhelming. The man's voice in my head repeats over and over, "I'm very sorry. They were killed instantly. I'm very sorry. They were killed instantly. I'm very sorry, they were killed instantly." The tears are immediate and fierce. I begin pounding the floor with my fists and repeating along with the incessant chant in my head, "I'm very sorry. They were killed instantly. I'm very sorry. They were killed instantly." It's almost unintelligible, but grows in volume with each iteration. "I'm very sorry. They were killed instantly. I'm very sorry. They were killed instantly." The chant nears a blood-curdling scream.

Dimitri has taken me by the wrists forcefully and effectively restraining me, afraid I'm going to hurt myself. He's shouting my name over my endless rant. "Ronnie!" His primal scream brings me out of my trance. I collapse forward into his lap and sob uncontrollably.

He strokes my hair gently. His voice is suddenly calm. "It's your parents, isn't it?"

Words don't come, so I nod instead.

"They were killed? Is that what you're trying to tell me?" The calmness radiates through his hand as he continues to stroke my hair.

196

I peek up at him through puffy, tear-filled eyes and nod again.

"Ronnie, I am so, so sorry." He takes a deep breath. "How did you find out? What happened?" His voice cracks again and I see his eyes welling with tears.

I swallow hard against the lump in my throat, unsure if I'll be able to speak. "A highway patrol officer called. He said there had been an accident. They were hit head-on by a semi. They were—"

Dimitri finishes my sentence. "—killed instantly."

I nod, and my bottom lip begins to quiver uncontrollably again.

Dimitri bends down and kisses me gently on the cheek. "What else did the officer say? Where are they now?"

I sit up slowly, cocooning myself in the blanket. "He said it happened near Lincoln, Nebraska. They're at the mortuary there … oh, damn it!"

"What?" he says urgently.

I point at the shattered remains of my cell phone on the floor. "I broke my phone. They're supposed to call me this afternoon."

"Baby, it's six o'clock at night. The afternoon is gone."

"What? Six?" I glance at the clock on my nightstand— 6:07. "How'd it get so late? What should I do?" I start gasping for breath; the hysterics are starting in again.

Dimitri takes my face in his hands, shushing me gently. "You put some clothes on while I go upstairs and check the phone for messages. Someone probably called the home phone when they couldn't get through on your cell." He kisses my forehead. "Will you be okay? I'll only be gone a minute."

I nod slowly. After Dimitri leaves, I pull a T-shirt and jeans out of the dresser drawer and dress as quickly as my sluggish mind will allow my body to move.

Once upstairs, I drop into one of the chairs at the kitchen table and watch Dimitri making us tea while he talks quietly on his cell phone. The conversation is a gentle hum in the background. Numbness has permeated every inch of my being. I unthinkingly drink the tea he presents and feel the

197

mild sensation of being warmed from the inside. It is neither pleasant nor unpleasant.

I begin to wonder if my life, as I've known it, is over. What happens when your world's torn apart? What happens when everything changes in the blink of an eye?

Dimitri finishes his call and sits down next to me. He takes my hand and wipes away the tears I didn't realize are trickling down my cheeks.

"I hope you don't mind, but I called Sunny and she's on her way over now. There was a message on the answering machine from the Lincoln Mortuary and one from the Nebraska State Patrol. I called the mortuary to let them know you received the message and that you would call them in the morning. Is there anyone else you need me to call, anyone you would like to talk to?" His voice is calm and gentle. Rational.

"No. Thank you for being here. I don't know what to do."

He strokes my hair. "I know. You have me and Sunny and Sebastian. We'll help you through this. You aren't alone. We love you."

I hug as tightly as I can, fearful he'll slip away. He's all I have left. Letting go scares me to death.

There's a knock on the back door and through blurry eyes I watch Sunny appear. She leans down next to us and begins to rub my back, but I still can't let go of Dimitri. She doesn't speak for several minutes.

Finally I find the strength to let go and turn to face her. Her eyes are puffy and moist with tears. "Veronica, honey, I'm so sorry."

Sunny and Dimitri insist that I come with them to spend the night at their house. Dimitri boards up the window he broke out earlier and Sunny packs a bag with some clothes, pajamas, and my toothbrush. We all leave in Sunny's car.

The majority of the night is spent sitting around Sunny's kitchen table. Sebastian joins us and they don't let me out of their sight. The evening is a blur.

The next morning Sunny guides me through a maze of complex questions with delicate, efficient precision.

Unfortunately, she's been in my shoes not so long ago after losing her husband, and she knows what I'm in for. She makes notes of everything we talk about because she knows I'm in no condition to remember my own name, let alone the decisions that are being made. Anything she overlooks Dimitri and Sebastian add to the list.

I'm so grateful that my parents shared their wishes with me after my grandmother's death two years ago. It wasn't a morbid conversation at the time; my dad said that death is a fact of life, and one of the only things that we are all guaranteed. My parents made it clear that they wanted to be cremated and have their ashes spread in a place of the surviving family's choosing, someplace we would enjoy visiting—not a depressing cemetery. And there is to be no funeral—they made that very clear.

I quickly learn, in the sleepless days that follow, that death is not an easy process for anyone, save one: the deceased. My own grief is somewhat postponed, due to the sheer amount of time and focus I have to expend on planning and doing what needs to be done. There are meetings with a lawyer to administer the will and grant me power of attorney over all of my parents' assets. There are meetings with insurance companies and banks. Sunny or Dimitri accompanies me to each meeting. I'm surprisingly composed given the overwhelming severity of the situation. It's mechanical. Dealing with finances is preferable at the moment to dealing with my emotions. I'm grateful that my parents had the forethought to ensure that I'll be taken care of financially for a while.

Their bodies were cremated in Lincoln and then shipped to me. I make Dimitri handle the boxes at first, which are rectangular and heavy, like shoeboxes filled with sand. Their wedding rings are in a small envelope wrapped in bubble wrap. I don't think I'll ever look forward to receiving another package in the mail after having to sign for my parents' ashes.

I return home on Thursday—four days after I received the phone call. Sunny begged me to stay with them, but I insisted on some time alone. I haven't slept since Sunday, and my mind and body are beyond exhaustion. Putting off returning to my parents' home, to *my* home, is only delaying the inevitable grieving process. I can only hope that the house will provide me a haven to rest.

Dimitri drives me home and hesitantly drops me off at the back door only after my repeated insistence to be left alone for the night. His familiar hug is warm and comforting, a security blanket. With my ear pressed against his chest, the beat of his heart becomes almost hypnotic. My own breathing and heart rate slow and the world begins to dull and fade. Then everything is quiet.

Life is sometimes ... dead.

Chapter 16
Occasionally I think better at night

I wake from a dreamless, seventeen-hour sleep to the reality that is my new life. Just me, alone ... in *my* empty house. I stretch and my body, still wrapped in sheets, protests painfully. Apparently, so much time in a prone position is not good for the back.

As I head for the bathroom I notice a vase of pink lilies on my desk. Beside it are a brand new cell phone and a note from Dimitri. It reads, "I hope you had a long, peaceful rest and that these flowers make you smile. Call me when you are up and about. I Love You!'

The lilies do make me smile.

I take a long, hot shower and relish in every second of it. Even though the previous days at Sunny's had felt like staying at a luxury resort, returning to my own home is comforting, even my tiny bathroom with its old, thin, faded towels.

Walking upstairs and through each room is like reacquainting with a childhood friend I haven't seen in a long time—familiar, yet different. It's like I'm seeing things through older eyes. Tragedy has an aging effect. Maturing decades in the mere span of a couple of days is not something I welcome, but given the situation, I don't have a choice. I can face this head on or I can submit and fail miserably. I've never been much for failure.

After walking through every room, I stop in the middle of the front room and stare at the piano. It's an opponent, a confrontation in the making. Determined, I walk to the piano bench and lift the top. My mom's music books are piled loosely inside. She attempted to learn how to play several times, and there are numerous lesson books inside. I select one of them, mainly because the white margin on the cover has my mom's handwriting on it.

With trembling hands I open it, place it in the music holder, and sit down. I played tenor sax in my elementary school band, but it's been years since I've even looked at a page of music, and even longer since I attempted to play the

201

piano. Luckily, the book is written for a beginner and illustrates the keys, so I'm able to follow along. I spend the better part of an hour fumbling my way clumsily through the exercises. I lose myself in my concentration, and when I finish the book, I pull out the next one. I like this book much better because my mom has notes written on almost every page, most of which don't even pertain to her lessons: "Pick up Ronnie at 4:00;" "Make dentist appointment;" lists of groceries; doodles. My mom could never focus on one thing at a time. I imagine her stopping her instructor in the middle of a lesson to jot down whatever popped into her head. It's *so* her. It makes me smile through teary eyes.

I flip through book after book. My fingers grow more confident, and reading the music is coming back to me like riding a bike. Hours go by and it's only when my stomach begins growling louder than the music that I decide I'd better stop for the evening.

My appetite, like sleep, has eluded me for days. I can't remember the last time I ate anything. I call Dimitri to see if he wants to join me for dinner.

He answers on the first ring. "Hi baby." His voice is sweet and cautious.

"Hi Dimitri. Thanks for the new phone and the flowers." It feels like days since I've seen him. His voice is comforting.

I can hear the relief in his voice. "You're welcome. We can exchange it for another model if you don't like it."

"No, no, it's great, really. Much fancier than my old phone though. It may take me a while—and apparently a degree in computer programming—to figure it out. But I'm sure I'll get there eventually."

My joking relaxes him and he laughs. "It's just like Sebastian's. He can tutor you on it. He probably won't charge much."

"Not much." I smile. "Have you eaten dinner yet?"

"Actually I haven't eaten all day. I was kind of waiting for you to wake up so that I could take you out for breakfast or lunch, but dinner's perfect."

"I was hoping we could just eat here if that's okay. Looks like I'd better get used to cooking for myself, so I may as well start right now."

His voice is tentative again. "Are you sure you're ready for that?"

I peer in the refrigerator as I consider this. Bleak—it is almost bare, and what is there looks beyond expiration. "Don't have a choice, do I? Looks like Jo was planning on being gone for a while … huh, that's irony for you … because there's not much here in the fridge."

"No problem, I'll stop at the store on my way over. Anything specific you need?"

I half laugh. "Everything. Do they sell that at the store?"

He laughs at my sad attempt at humor. "I'm leaving now. I'll be there as soon as I can."

I clean out what remains in refrigerator while I'm waiting. He arrives with the Porsche completely full of groceries, which isn't saying much. It maxes out at a five bag limit. Dimitri even has bags under his feet on the floor. Clearly Porsches were not manufactured for mundane, domestic chores.

He helps me put all of the food away and we decide on spaghetti for dinner. He starts boiling water for pasta while I cut up a head of romaine lettuce, a tomato, and two carrots to make a salad. Dimitri dumps a jar of spaghetti sauce into a pot and heats it on the stove. Food has never smelled so good—even just store-bought pasta sauce. As it turns out, when you don't eat for days on end your appreciation for food only grows. When it's all ready, we sit down and devour our food in silence. When we're both satisfied, we clear the dishes. Dimitri makes us tea as I load them into the dishwasher. Then we talk.

It's dark outside and a good time for reflection. "I never imagined a week like the one I've just lived. Was it like this when you lost your dad?"

He's thoughtful. "Much like this I suppose. It was chaotic. I don't remember a lot of specifics, even from the funeral, but I do remember emotions. My mom was devastated. I was sad. Sebastian was distant. Death is a confusing creature."

I stare at the table and nod. "That it is." I hesitate a few moments before asking my next question. "Where do you think they are now?"

He tilts his head to one side. "What do you mean?"

"Well, you've always gone to church every Sunday with Sunny, right?"

He nods.

"I've never set foot inside a church, aside from the occasional wedding or funeral. Since you're the only religious person in the room, I thought you might know. They talk about death and heaven in the Bible, right?"

Another nod. "They do talk about death and heaven in the Bible."

"Then where do you think my parents are now? Are they in heaven?"

His smile is slight and thoughtful. "Ronnie, just because someone attends church every Sunday doesn't mean they know what happens after we die. There are theories, certainly—every religion has its own."

"What is your church's theory?" This is important to me, so I keep prodding.

He exhales and I'm not sure if I'm testing his perfect patience. "Ronnie, do you know why I go to church every Sunday?"

I'm prepared for a sermon of sorts. "No."

His smile softens. "I go because Sunny enjoys it and I like to see her happy. But I also go out of pure curiosity. It fascinates me."

"What do you mean, *curiosity*? I always just thought you were really religious and that we'd never discussed it because you knew I wasn't."

He chuckles and says, "Let's just say that I tend to have a very clear set of beliefs and what I like to call 'knowns.' Occasionally these do coincide with the ideology preached at the church I attend. But usually they do not. I sit back and watch the congregation closely every week and it always astounds me how different they all are. I don't mean

204

physically. I mean spiritually, religiously. They're all reading the same Bible, hearing the same sermons, yet each person in the room interprets it differently. No two people practice exactly the same, even though they huddle together under their chosen religion's umbrella. Some are there for purely social reasons, some because they're coerced by their spouses, some because they truly believe. But even the true believers believe variations of the story. People by nature are all wired differently; it's what makes us individuals. Variety is beautiful. But with that kind of variety, how can any two people possibly have exactly the same beliefs about something as intangible as religion?"

I shrug. I'm following him, but admittedly shocked by the philosophical turn my questioning has taken.

He knows he's just given me a lot to think about and he pokes my chest gently with his finger. "Where does *your* heart tell you they are?" He pauses. "Because that's all that matters."

I hesitate and take a deep breath. "I don't know. I mean, I'm *supposed* to say heaven, right?"

He shrugs. "That is a widely popular view, at least in western civilization." He says this in a mock-official tone, as a history teacher might. "People in eastern civilizations may beg to differ. But really, east and west don't matter. Religious and spiritual views are highly personal. What did your parents believe?"

I shake my head and shrug. "They never really talked about death, aside from making it clear that they wanted to be cremated and didn't want a funeral. As far as religion, they didn't practice anything specifically. My mom was spiritual, but she focused more on how we live our lives, how we treat each other, and how our thoughts and actions affect future thoughts and actions. She believed there was definitely a larger force at work in the universe and she talked about life as if it were unending. She acknowledged the fact that death is inevitable, but the idea never seemed to frighten her. My dad was the same way. He just said 'death is a part of life.'"

He smiles. "That sounds like Will and Jo."

205

I let out an exasperated huff. "Exactly! Profound maybe, but extremely vague, which leaves me with no answers."

His smile softens and he narrows his eyes. "What is it that Veronica Smith believes? You've had many years to ponder life. You can't tell me you have no ideas. I know you too well—you analyze *everything*. The fact that you've never attended church makes you no less competent than any theologian to formulate your own theories. Religion and spirituality arise from within. And you, my dear, have an opinion ... *about everything*."

I hesitate and take a deep breath. "It's going to sound silly to you."

He winks. "Probably not, so let's hear it."

I bite my lip, unsure if I should share my thoughts. "Well ... I would like to believe that my parents are still with me." I eye him cautiously.

"They're always with you," he says in a comforting voice. "In your heart and especially in your memories." He strokes my cheek and an almost pained look emerges in his eyes. "Memories are more meaningful and powerful than you can imagine."

My eyes begin to burn with tears. "I don't want them to be only a memory. I want them back." I wipe the tears from my cheeks with my shirtsleeve and look down at the table. "I know it's not possible, but deep down I feel like they haven't left us. That they're nearby. Not in heaven, but here on Earth." I wait for a response but he doesn't offer one. "You think I'm crazy, don't you?" He doesn't answer until I raise my head to meet his gaze.

His expression is gentle. "No."

I'm relieved. "So, where do you think they are?"

"I think they are wherever *your* heart tells *you* they are; *that* should be all that matters."

That statement is the single-most reassuring and comforting thing I've heard in days. Countless people have offered their condolences over the phone and through personal interactions. Even mere acquaintances have tried to reassure me with their own religious beliefs as if they are a universal truth we all share.

Guess what? We don't all share one truth.

Religious sentiment, even, or especially, in the case of something as monumental as death isn't always necessary, wanted, or warranted. I wish everyone realized this.

Dimitri's words unknowingly sum up and shape a lifetime of my spiritual beliefs. It's something I will always remember and look to for guidance. My beliefs are not in a book or a speech, but in my heart ... and that should be all that matters.

Life is sometimes ... whatever your heart tells you.

Chapter 17
Old guys are cool
And so is Billie Holiday

I finish out the week at home, but when Monday morning rolls around I force myself to go to work. Sunny, of course, insists that I take another week off, but the thought of another day alone with my grief and self-pity is nauseating. I need a distraction and though the house is paid off, I still need money for utilities and food. Work is a necessity now. I don't want to touch my parents' savings unless absolutely necessary.

I'm 18, and I'm officially grown-up.

I pack my lunch and grab my bag. As I turn the doorknob to head out the back door to the garage, anxiety grips me. I stand in the driveway, staring through the open garage door at Jezebel parked next to my dad's truck and his old Porsche. It dawns on me that I haven't been out to the garage since before graduation. Dimitri or Sunny drove me everywhere I needed to go for the past week. The cars are yet another reminder of the loss, but what aches most is the gaping hole where my mom's Subaru is usually parked. It, of course, was the car they died in. It was completely destroyed, along with them.

Without realizing it, I've dropped to my knees on the driveway. Suddenly the nerve endings begin to scream in protest against the rocks now embedded in my right kneecap. I ease myself up and lift my skirt to get a look at my knee. It's bleeding, but overall it looks worse than it feels. I brush away the rocks and pick up my bag. I'll clean it up at work. I've got an early start, and Sunny won't be there yet to fuss over me.

I put the imaginary blinders on and walk straight to Jezebel, getting in without a sideways glance at the other two cars in the garage. I blink through tears, but the cars are like a neon sign flashing in the darkness of my peripheral vision. The sign flashes: "Your parents are dead. You are alone."

My tires squeal as I hit the gas and back down the driveway. I hit the button to close the garage door on my way down the drive, and I don't look back making a promise to myself at that moment never to park in the garage again. The idea of opening that door and seeing the void is too painful.

As I suspected, I don't see Sunny's car parked out front. I sling my bag over my shoulder and gather my skirt up to avoid getting blood on it from the scrape on my bruised knee. I unlock the front door and march directly to the back room of the office. I drop my bag on the floor in front of the sink and wet a paper towel with water. A thin line of blood has trickled down my shin. Normally, the sight of blood makes me a bit light-headed, but I prop my foot up on a nearby chair and inspect the cut for rocks before I start wiping it off. No rocks. No nausea. Bonus. I dab at the cut cautiously.

"Hello young lady. You must be Miss Veronica."

I jump back and the chair my foot's resting on tips over with a crash. I turn to look behind me, in the direction of the unfamiliar voice, quickly running over escape options in my mind.

A short, white-haired man with a gentle smile stands in the doorway with his hands up in surrender. "I'm sorry to have frightened you, miss. That was thoughtless of me. Allow me to introduce myself properly." He lowers his right hand and extends it tentatively toward me. "My name is Bob Carruthers. It appears we have the happy coincidence of finding ourselves co-workers." He has a friendly, southern accent.

I unclench my fists—which I'd unconsciously raised to chest level, and exhale deeply. I'd been ready for the fight if escape wasn't an option. I approach Bob and shake his hand. "I'm Veronica. It's nice to meet you, Bob. I apologize; I'm not usually so jumpy; I just didn't think anyone else would be here yet." I walk back and set the chair back up on four legs.

"I realize it's probably inappropriate for a gentleman of my age to be looking at your legs, Miss Veronica, but are you all right?" His face is creased with concern.

I swallow hard against the lump in my throat. "Yes, I had a ... an accident of sorts this morning. I'll be fine."

His features soften. "Does Miss Sunny have a first aid kit around here somewhere?"

I pause, fighting against tears threatening to erupt. I cannot and will not cry in front of this man I've only just met. I'm sure he knows about my situation and I don't want or need his pity. I clear my throat. "I think Sunny keeps one in the bathroom."

Bob disappears to fetch the first aid kit before I can look up. When he returns, he looks anxious to help. He hands me a cleansing wipe, some ointment, and two bandages.

I glance quickly at his dark eyes, slightly magnified behind thick spectacles, and then look away. "Thank you."

"You're welcome, miss."

I clean up my knee and Bob briefly brings me up to date on the project he's working on. It's something new since I've been away. Bob and I work side by side without speaking for almost two hours. The radio plays softly in the background. It's tuned to some jazz station that Bob appears to be fond of.

Our silence is uncomfortable at first. I feel rude for not striking up conversation, but the tightness in my throat is relentless. Bob, on the other hand, seems completely at ease with the silence. He works at a consistent and steady pace with a perpetually peaceful look on his face that always hints at a smile. He's calming.

I began to relax as lunchtime approaches. Bob hums along to a song on the radio. His voice is unexpectedly pleasant. I look at him and smile.

He looks up, blushing. "I'm sorry, Miss Veronica, does my humming bother you?"

I shake my head. "Not at all."

"Do you like Billie Holiday?" he asks.

"Is that who's singing?"

He nods.

I smile. "It's not bad. Different from what I usually listen to, but it's ... familiar in a way. I think I like it."

He smiles triumphantly. "Tomorrow you'll have to share some of your music with me. Sometimes I get stuck in a rut and forget that music has been made since 1950. I tend to stick with my favorites."

The thought of this sweet older gentleman listening to "my" music makes me chuckle. "We have a deal, Bob. We'll alternate days. You can school me on pre-1950 and I'll bring you up to date." I pause to look at his enthusiastic expression and smile. My heart softens a little. "Sometimes I forget music was made before the last five years. I could stand to expand *my* horizons."

He nods. "Wonderful."

The morning brings about an unpredicted, serendipitous friendship between an eighteen-year-old girl and a 75-year-old soul. By lunch we're engaged in light conversation. Bob eats a peanut butter and butter sandwich on white bread, which he had wrapped in wax paper, and an apple sliced in quarters. When silence returns in the afternoon it's accepting and legitimate; the kind of silence that can only be appreciated fully by the best of friends. We've also established an unspoken rule: he doesn't ask about my parents and I don't ask about his wife.

Sunny arrives just as we're cleaning up to go home for the day and she's surprised to see me there. "Veronica, I didn't expect to see you here today, honey. I would've stopped by earlier if I'd known." She's clearly distressed in her usual motherly way.

"You do pay me to actually work, remember?" I change the subject before she has the chance to question my state of mind further and smile in Bob's direction. "After we got introductions out of the way, Bob and I had a very productive day."

"Oh heavens, I feel awful for not being here to introduce the two of you." She's fretting.

Bob is quick to defuse Sunny's guilt with a gentle smile. "Miss Veronica and I were quite capable of introductions," he says gently. "Though I'm afraid I may have frightened her near to death when I arrived. She's feisty though, and was prepared to put up a fight. I can see why Dimitri fancies her. He's smart, that boy of yours, always thought so. I must say I approve wholeheartedly of this match." He winks at me

211

before pulling on a felt fedora. He tips his hat to each of us. "Good evening, ladies. I'm off to catch my bus."

We answer in unison, "Good evening, Bob."

The door shuts behind Bob and I feel Sunny's worried eyes on me. Hurriedly I offer, "Bob's really nice. I like him a lot."

Sunny smiles. "He is." I can see that she is struggling with how to broach the subject.

I let her off the hook, trying to answer her unasked questions and concerns. "Sunny, I'm okay. I don't need anything. I'm fine." The words are unsettling, and hard to get out. The lump returns to my throat and I can't continue. Hurriedly I hug her, grab my bag, and walk out the door.

I'm in tears by the time I reach Jezebel. Driving out of the parking lot I find myself unable to go home. Suddenly I want to be anywhere but home. I turn my phone off and drive until sunset. Eventually, not by conscious effort, I find my way home and park on the street, keeping my promise to stay out of the garage, and enter the house through the front door. I cannot remember ever unlocking the front door. We *always* use the back door.

This moment is symbolic.

I have to do things differently if I'm going to get through this grieving process.

Process. What an impersonal term for such excruciatingly intimate and gut-wrenching feelings. Whoever coined the term clearly hadn't been through the "process" firsthand.

The only familiarity I cannot do without is Dimitri. I turn on my phone and see that he's tried to call several times. I dial and he answers on the first ring, his voice verging on desperation, almost breathless. "Ronnie?"

The churning in my stomach subsides with the sound of his voice. "Hi baby."

He exhales, relieved. "Ronnie."

"Have you eaten dinner yet?" He's come over and eaten dinner with me the past few days, beginning a trend that I discover I want to continue.

212

"Nope. I'm starving. Can I come over? I have a new recipe to try out."

I smile; the pain of the past few hours releases its clutch on my heart. "A new recipe? Okay."

He knocks on the back door exactly seven minutes later, even though the drive from his house should take at least fifteen.

I open the door to a bewildered expression on his handsome face. "Why is Jezebel parked out front?"

I fumble for words. "Um, yeah, I just decided I wanted to park out front tonight. The garage door is … the garage door is broken."

He turns to go back outside. "I'll take a look at it before we eat."

I grab his shoulder. "No, you're starving and so am I. It's late, let's eat. You can look at it another time."

He turns and steps back in the house eyeing me suspiciously. "Okay." He knows I'm lying, but he doesn't push it.

Dimitri pulls out a recipe card from his pocket, and we set to work. It's a recipe of Sunny's—chicken cacciatore— and though he is admittedly challenged in the kitchen, he's trying so hard to impress me. He told me once that he couldn't cook anything but grilled cheese and I've discovered this past week that wasn't far from the truth. We're polar opposites in the kitchen: I measure ingredients by sight and taste. Dimitri measures ingredients with painstaking accuracy, using any and all available utensils or devices. I don't follow recipes. Dimitri never deviates from them. Cutting, chopping, even using a can opener seems foreign to him. It's almost comical to watch him struggle with something, especially something I'm good at. It definitely doesn't happen often.

Surprisingly, the meal's not too bad. "Good job, Dimitri, this is almost edible."

He glares playfully at me.

"Kidding."

"If you must know, I watched the Food Network all afternoon," he says.

I raise my eyebrows.

"I'm determined to figure this cooking thing out, alright?"

I smile at the effort. "It's actually pretty good. Thanks for cooking. I had kind of a hard day, and I wasn't really looking forward to making dinner. If it were up to me we probably would've ended up eating cereal and toast."

He frowns. "I suspected you probably didn't have a good day when I couldn't get you on your phone earlier. Do you want to talk about it?" He reaches across the small kitchen table to take my hand.

"No, I don't think I do. But thanks for asking." I have trouble looking him in the eye. I almost always feel better when I talk to him. But tonight, I just feel sad and don't want to even try.

The saddest smile crosses his lips for only a second, and he waits patiently for me to speak again.

I don't.

"You did get to meet Bob though, right?"

Bob, sweet Bob. "Yes, Bob's great. Very cool. We listened to jazz. Have you ever heard of Billie Holiday? She's good. You'd like her."

He smiles that knowing smile. "Yes, I've heard of Billie Holiday. She's amazing. What song did you hear? Good Morning Heartache? Lover Man? God Bless the Child? That one's my favorite."

I'm astounded. I realize everyone doesn't live in my insular world, but Dimitri always surprises me. Excellent memory aside, he's a walking, breathing encyclopedia.

He's smirking at me and knows I'm impressed. "Well, Ronnie, which song was it? I could name a few more to jog your memory."

"I don't remember the name of the song. Bob hummed along, and it was lovely," I say. Suddenly, I'm agitated.

He's still smirking. "You have to be careful of Bob, always the southern gentleman. He's incredibly charming. I'll have to watch myself or I may end up losing you to an older man."

214

Funny, but where did this vast knowledge mid-century jazz come from? I finally shake my head and the agitation begins to wane. "How do you know Billie Holiday anyway?"

His smile widens. "I like to think of myself as ... cultured."

I can't resist his confident smile and the twinkle in his gray eyes. I exhale completely as he reels me in with his charm, though I haven't lost my sarcastic edge. "You're *something* alright."

"Hah." It's guttural and unforced. "You know you secretly love it ... I impress you."

Was that a question? "Incessantly," I say.

His voice drops and the corners of his mouth allude to his notorious, mischievous grin. "Incessantly ... I like that."

The flame is rising through me and it awakens my body from the numbness that's consumed me for over a week. Slowly, life, or more accurately lust, is inching its way back into my veins. My ears begin to hum. Life, lust, whatever it is—I'll take it. I stand up and walk around the table to stand in front of him, leaving myself completely unguarded and vulnerable, waiting for a further invitation, ready and willing for whatever may come. His eyebrows pinch slightly as he tries to read my face. The flash of a smile ghosts across his lips so quickly I wonder if I've only imagined it. Finally, without taking his eyes off mine, he pushes back his chair and extends the invitation, pulling me down to sit on his lap.

I hitch up my skirt slightly and straddle his legs with mine. I take off his glasses and set them on the table behind me without breaking his gaze. My hands move to his cheeks, softly over his ears, and to the nape of his neck where his hair is so, so soft.

His hands, which have been hanging limply at his sides, brush lightly over my calves, slowly pausing with a gentle squeeze at the backs of my knees, before shifting and grazing the top of my thighs. The pressure increases slightly as his hands move up, up and over my skirt, except his thumbs, which clasp unapologetically under the hem. My skirt inches its way up ... creeping deliberately.

He leans forward and kisses the hollow of my neck. It's an electric shock. The slightest touch puts my body into overdrive, hyperaware. His hair feels like silk under my hands. I feel the gentle pull of my skin under his kisses as his lips move their way up my neck.

I bow my head until my lips just touch his ear and whisper, "Incessantly ... yes, you incessantly impress me," before pulling his mouth hungrily to mine.

I don't want him to leave. I want him. And I give in to the want.

Life is sometimes ... incessant.

Chapter 18
Hiding and waiting
For the worst
Or the end

In the end, it turns out lust only numbs the pain for a short time. Dimitri went home that night around eleven, like every other night, at my gentle insistence.

The routine continues, an endless loop. Every day is the same unless he's out of town at a gallery showing or an art sale. Variety has ceased to exist in my world, and it seems I've forced it out of his as well. He *always* comes over when I get home from work; we *always* eat dinner; we *always* watch TV until around eleven, at which time he *always* offers to stay, but I *always* decline. I have to get through this on my own.

Days turn into weeks, summer passes. Weeks turn into months, then winter passes. I find myself withdrawing into my own inner world of despair. In the beginning it wasn't so difficult to put on the "happy" face for work, the occasional visit with friends, and for Dimitri. Months later the desire to care has evaporated. The "happy" face is gone. I choose not to enroll in school, much to Dimitri and Sunny's dismay. Merely waking and going to work has become a monumental struggle, and school feels completely out of the question.

Isolation and utter numbness have replaced the sadness. Sadness is pain; it's something you physically feel in your heart. Depression is something different altogether—*it's destructive*. It creeps up on you and strangles you and before you even realize it you're paralyzed and nothing matters anymore. It transforms entirely.

I can still manage to lose myself in my work, though I've become a new, different me. We're always busy and Bob is very intuitive. He knows I don't want to talk and he never forces it. We have yet to finish a lunch in silence, though. He always has a bit of news to share, or a story about one of his grandchildren, or a volunteer project he's working on. He's brief and has learned that the stories are better if he doesn't expect a response from me in return. It's just Bob's kind way of keeping the channels of communication open between us, which is extremely generous given that it's been one way for months.

My friends called and visited during the first few weeks after my parents' deaths, but my attempts to stay connected waned as summer passed and then their respective colleges stole them away in fall. And then they forgot about me, or at least that what I told myself. The distance I put between us was certainly more to blame, but the idea that they simply forgot about me eased my guilt at first. That guilt slowly faded to indifference, and then I began to forget about them. As the months passed, even Teagan stopped sending text messages because I never responded. That one hurt. But I no longer have the strength to bridge the gap. Gap? The Grand Canyon pales in comparison to this one. It's monumental at this point. Impossible to bridge.

Dimitri was and remains the constant in my life; a saint sent to endure me. There's no other way to put it. He simply … lovingly … *endures* me. I want him. I need him. He's all I have in this world, the only thing that rouses any emotion inside me. But feeling this dead inside, it's become hard to convey, to show, to share any type of emotion with him. When he's around I *have* to touch him, but I can't bring myself to be intimate. Passion is dead. I love him, more than anything, certainly more than myself, but I can't bring myself to physically show him. That desire is gone. All desire is gone. The desire to live is gone.

Every night after Dimitri tucks me into bed on the sofa (because even after almost a year I can't bring myself to sleep in my own bed), he kisses me on the forehead, tells me he loves me and leaves, and I pray to God and I thank him for Dimitri Glenn, for sending this angel to me. I used to pray for my own happiness. When that didn't work I started praying for the sadness to leave. And when that didn't work I pleaded for the constant, aching, all-consuming hopelessness to lessen so that I could breathe—*just breathe*. It didn't. I'm still choking. So through tears, sometimes silent, sometimes sobbing, but always present, I pray every night for everything good in this world to be bestowed upon Dimitri,

218

especially happiness ... even if that happiness cannot include me.

On the one-year anniversary of the accident, I make up my mind to do something radical. Dimitri is out of town for a week at an art gallery exhibition, and I manage to pull it off while he's away. I sell or give away everything in the house and garage except a few items of clothing, a blanket, a towel, a pan, a few dishes and a small box of mementos: photos and my parents' wedding rings. The furniture is gone. The TV is gone. Jezebel and the other cars are gone. I tell myself I don't need these objects anymore. I would feel almost relieved, *if I could feel.*

It's not until Dimitri returns and breaks down into tears when he sees the house empty that it hits me. It's been decided. I've surrendered. I'm done. Through his crying and my haze it's hard to understand everything he's saying until he's kneeling before me, clutching at my pant legs and I hear the words: "I won't let this happen."

He's still pleading. "Ronnie, I've helplessly watched you destroying yourself every day and it's breaking my heart. I've tried everything to make you happy again, but I keep failing. All the classic signs were there. You don't eat like you should, you don't talk, you walk around in a fog, you just ... exist. And now this," he gestures to the empty house. "This final preparation scares the hell out of me. What can I do? You *need* help."

I kneel down and blink in disbelief. "Dimitri, *you* haven't failed me; *I've* failed me." The tears, which I almost never notice anymore, start flowing. "None of this is your fault. Please don't blame yourself; that would kill me. I'm already dying. I have been for a year now. I just didn't realize it was completely unavoidable until now."

He pulls me tightly against him and we sit on the floor crying and holding each other in the empty, echoing house. After nearly an hour, Dimitri pulls back from me. He wipes my cheeks with the sleeve of his shirt. "I have to get you out of here. We're leaving tonight. We're going somewhere for a few days, just the two us, until we can get this figured out and come up with a plan."

I begin to protest, but I don't have it in me to do much of anything, let alone put up a fight.

He stands up and goes downstairs for a few minutes, arriving back in the living room with my bag, the remains of my clothes, and my toothbrush under his arm. He helps me up. "Where are your house keys?" he asks.

I feel around on the outside of my pants pockets. "They're in my pocket. Why?"

"Good. Come on, we're leaving." With a final, desperate look around at the blank walls and empty hallway, he ushers me out the front door to his car (he stopped using the back door months ago, when I did). After he opens the door, deposits me in the passenger seat, and gently buckles me in like a parent would for a small child, he runs around the car and jumps in the driver's seat. He's already dialing his phone before the car is in gear.

"Mom, Ronnie and I need to leave town." I can faintly hear her questioning, but he doesn't let her finish. "I just can't let this go on any longer. I'm taking her away for a few days. Maybe a change of scenery will … I know … just until I can get her some real help." His voice is controlled but tense. "I don't know where we're going yet, but I'll call you when I know more."

I drift off to sleep and when he wakes me we're in the airport parking lot. He skips the clothes and stuffs my toothbrush in my bag and says he'll buy me some clothes when we get where we're going.

"Where are we going, anyway?" I ask sleepily.

The fear and pain is still in his eyes though I can tell he's trying very hard to keep calm. "I don't know yet." He smiles weakly. "I thought we'd leave it up to fate. Are you up for an adventure?"

My voice is dead. "Whatever."

He takes my hand and leads me to the United Airlines ticket counter. It's late and there's no line. "When does the next domestic flight leave?" he politely asks the woman at the counter.

The woman is confused. "Where are you flying this evening, sir?" she asks.

"It doesn't matter. When does the next flight leave?" His composure is fading.

The woman narrows her eyes a bit, and asks again, "Sir, I need to know what your destination is?"

Dimitri's voice is low and harsh, and his composure is gone, but he manages to display the authority of someone twice his age. "I don't care where the next damn flight is headed, I would like to purchase two seats on it, preferably first class." He slides his American Express and United Airlines frequent flier card across the counter at her.

She starts pecking away at her keyboard and looks sufficiently annoyed but it doesn't seem to slow her down. "Las Vegas, flight leaves in fifteen minutes. The plane is already boarding."

"Perfect."

In two minutes, the transaction is finished and we have our tickets in hand. We literally run through the concourse for the gate, Dimitri clutching my hand and practically dragging me. We arrive just in time to squeeze through before they close the doors. I hear the sound of seatbelts clicking just as the plane begins to taxi away from the gate.

I'm sitting next to the window in the comfortable and generous first class seat and mutter quietly to myself as I watch the lights of Denver grow smaller and smaller as we rise high into the sky, "This is my first time on an airplane."

His voice is pained and probably not meant for me to hear. "And I'll make sure it's not your last."

I stare out the window for ten or fifteen minutes until the clouds grow thick and blot out the twinkling lights far below. My ears pop, and the sound of the jets roaring seems to get louder. I glance at my watch, as is always my habit around this time.

Dimitri has been silently watching me. "What's wrong?" he asks gently.

I tap my watch. "It's eleven o'clock; time for you to go home."

His arm circles around me protectively and a kiss falls on my temple. The whisper is so soft, I have to strain to hear the words, "I'm never going home again," he says. "I promise. Now, get some rest, baby."

I snuggle in against his shoulder and fall quickly into a deep, dreamless sleep. The dreams, once so vivid, have been absent for months and sleep feels heavy, dark, almost drug-induced; a barren wasteland of nothingness. It is not restorative, but merely a preferable alternative to consciousness.

"Wake up baby, we're here." Dimitri whispers in my ear. I'm lying across his lap drooling on the thigh of his pants.

I wipe my cheek and mouth with the cuff of my shirt and look up at him out of the corner of my eye. "Sorry about your pants," I say, groggily.

He's still hovering over me and the corners of his mouth turn up in a gentle smile. "No problem." He kisses my temple again before helping me sit upright.

I yawn widely and rub my eyes trying to chase away sleepiness as I look out the window as we taxi toward the gate. The sky is dark, but the airport lights are bright. "What time is it?" I ask through another wide yawn.

"It's eleven-thirty, Vegas time."

"Oh," I say. Time has also become somewhat irrelevant in my world unless I'm at work.

The chirpy flight attendant welcomes us to Las Vegas and instructs us we're allowed to unfasten our seatbelts and disembark the plane. Dimitri gathers my bag from the overhead compartment. Since we're in first class we're able to quickly exit the plane before the rest of the passengers. With one arm tightly around my shoulders, Dimitri removes his phone from his pocket and begins reading and responding to text messages as he guides me through the airport. He's been here a couple of times over the past year to meet with clients commissioning paintings, so he knows his way around.

The air outside the terminal is hot and dry. It's almost midnight, but it feels like a summer afternoon. The lights are bright and taxis line both sides of the street. Dimitri walks to the front of the line of endless taxis, opens the door and motions for me to get in. When the driver asks, "Where to?" he responds with what I only assume is the name of a hotel.

Though I don't value my life much these days, I certainly fear for it during the next several minutes. The cab ride is terrifying. The driver excessively breaks the speed limit, runs red lights, and cuts other vehicles off by mere inches. The tires squeal against the hot pavement in protest, trying to gain purchase. I close my eyes after the first few minutes and when we screech to a halt Dimitri whispers in my ear, "You survived your first cab ride. Would you mind getting out here and taking a short walk with me, Ronnie?"

"A walk sounds nice." Especially if it means getting out of this cab.

He pays the driver with a folded up wad of cash, and we step out of the taxi.

For the first time I really open my eyes to the Las Vegas strip. The place is surreal, crawling with people and neon. Everything is huge, loud, and bright. The lights are colorful and ever-present in all directions, competing, tempting, and overwhelming. It's sensory overload, but it's beautiful in a strange way.

Twirling in a slow circle, I look around, stunned. "Wow."

Dimitri's arms wind around my waist from behind. "Crazy, isn't it?"

I nod my head in agreement. "Crazy."

He takes my hand and turns me toward him. "There's something I want to show you," he says.

He leads me down a sidewalk to the background noise of screeching tires and honking horns. The tourists we pass are dressed in everything from evening gowns and heels to shorts and flip-flops. Someone tries to hand me a flyer. They're insistent, so I take it. Dimitri chuckles. It's for a strip club. Embarrassed, I deposit it in the nearest trashcan. And then we turn a corner and there stands the most beautiful sight alight, rising in front of me like a dream. "It's the Eiffel Tower." The words escape inexplicably as I exhale, because for a moment I'm unable to take another breath.

His smile lights his eyes and he squeezes my hand. "Oui va la voir, ça vaut le coup." He releases my hand and stops walking.

I continue on alone, drawn in by a thousand lights. Stopping at the base of one of the four massive legs, I peer straight up. Tears begin rolling down my cheeks and for the first time in months I realize these aren't tears of pain, the ache has temporarily subsided.

I am standing beneath the Eiffel Tower.

I do understand that what I'm looking at is halfway around the world from the real thing, but it feels so real. I tune everything else out—the people, the flashing cameras, the music coming from the direction of the casino. I don't know how long I walk around and under it but I take in every angle.

"C'est magnifique," I say under my breath.

After a time, I tear my gaze from the structure and turn back to look for Dimitri. I search the faces in the surrounding crowd, and find him standing ten yards away, staring intently at me with tears streaming silently down his cheeks and the most angelic smile on his lips. His eyes trace a line from the top of the Tower down and back at me with a subtle shrug of his shoulders.

I blink through the tears as I run to him, knocking him back a few steps as my body collides with his. I bury my face in his chest.

He hugs me tightly and kisses the top of my head. "Sorry it's not the real thing. I swear you'll see Paris someday. I thought while we were here this might be a good substitute." His eyes are shiny with tears.

"It's lovely, more beautiful than I ever imagined. Thank you."

"Are you ready for bed or do you want to walk some more?"

I yawn at the suggestion. "Ready for bed if that's okay. Are we staying here at the Eiffel Tower?"

He smiles and laces his fingers through mine. "We're staying across the street … where you'll have a better view of it."

We cross the street and walk past a series of gigantic fountains before entering a seemingly endless casino. It's a labyrinth. After following a series of signs that I swear walk us in circles, we locate the guest services desk to check in. I stop near a huge vase of orchids and let Dimitri deal with checking in alone. It takes several minutes and after talking to three different attendants it's evident by the set of his shoulders that he's tense. He looks irritated when he returns with key cards in his hand.

"What's wrong?"

He shakes his head. "There was a mix up with the room. We'll be in this room tonight and tomorrow," he says, holding up the key card between two fingers. "But on the third night they're going to move us into the room Sunny requested."

"Sunny?" I'm puzzled.

He sighs softly and the irritation vanishes. "Sunny made the hotel reservation while we were on the flight. That's who I was texting while we were walking through the airport."

I yawn, my eyelids are fighting gravity. He smiles and his arm falls around my shoulders. "Come on Sleepy Face. Let's get you to bed."

The room is opulent. I peek in the bathroom first, which is larger than my bedroom at home. The floors, walls, counters and shower are covered in shiny marble. The tub is as large as a hot tub. I never take baths, but the idea of taking a bath in this tub is tempting. I open the glass door to the shower and step inside, in awe of all the controls. They look like they could launch a space shuttle, not assist me with cleanliness and personal hygiene. I take a quick inventory of the showerheads and stop counting at five, though I wonder if there are more hidden that I just can't see. I push one of the buttons and water rains down on me from the ceiling. I shriek as cold water showers down from directly overhead. Dimitri rushes in as I poke the button angrily.

Panic turns to relief and then amusement as sees me standing there, fully-clothed and dripping wet. "Most people undress before stepping in the shower, Ronnie."

225

I scowl, and as I look at the sweet smile on his face sadness tightens around my heart, thinking of an earlier, happy time when this situation would've elicited a completely different response from him. The smile would've been mischievous and seductive. I haven't seen that smile in almost a year. The comment that accompanied it would've been equally forward and saturated with innuendos, veiled or bold. He's always on guard around me now. Sincerely kind and relentlessly patient, the friend I desperately need, but playfulness, romance, and desire have been neatly put away in a box buried somewhere deep inside both of us.

He takes two towels from shiny chrome racks beside the shower, and drapes one around my shoulders. With the other, he begins drying my hair. Since when did he become the parent? I feel utterly useless. "There are usually robes in the closet," he says. "I'll be right back." He's gone only a matter of seconds and returns with a fluffy, white robe, which he drapes across the sink. "You can sleep in this tonight. We'll get you some pajamas tomorrow." He leaves, gently closing the door. I step out of my damp flip flops and peel off my wet clothes, laying them over the edge of the giant bath tub. I wrap myself in the fuzzy robe, and finger comb my damp hair. I brush my teeth with my toothbrush and some toothpaste from the basket of assorted, fancy toiletries on the counter.

Tentatively I reenter the bedroom. It's twice the size of any hotel room I've ever stayed in. We're clearly out of motel territory. There's an armoire, two sofas, and a king size bed. Dimitri's clothes are in a pile next to the bed and he's lying under the covers, propped up against several pillows with his bare chest and arms exposed. He must've been exhausted because he's already asleep. He looks so young when he sleeps, so peaceful. His calm approach to life envelops him as he sleeps. I remove his glasses and set them on the nightstand, kiss his forehead, and whisper, "I love you."

I grab an extra pillow and blanket out of the closet, throw them on the sofa facing the windows, open the curtains, and turn off the light. I wrap myself in the blanket and lean back on the pillow staring out at the hotel next door. It isn't the Eiffel Tower, which must be in the opposite direction, but the lights are hypnotic. I watch them for several hours.

For the first thirty minutes I think about where I am and who brought me here. How lucky I am to have been blessed with him, even if only for a short time. Then I think about all of the family vacations I took with my parents. We never went anywhere like this. We always visited distant relatives or my grandma in Nebraska and though we had fun, the trips seemed, at least for my parents, to be more about obligation than enjoyment. Those memories lead to the inevitable tears and the crushing hopelessness runs like ice through my veins again.

The hopelessness is relentless and I resign control. It takes over my mind, opening up possibilities I've never let myself consider in detail before. Fleeting thoughts, put quickly out of my mind so as not to linger on them previously, I allow myself to dissect and examine. The physical relief that suicide would offer is so tempting, intriguing almost. The solution seems too simple, too easy; a tangible end to unmerciful despair. Suicide had such a negative connotation in happier times. I used to pity people in such a state that they would take their own lives; I used to think that they were weak.

Guess what? Weakness doesn't knock. It doesn't ask to be invited in. It bears down until you surrender.

Briefly I mourn the life I will not live out: the wedding vows I will never speak, the child I will never hold in my arms, the people I will never help in my work. I weep over them and then tuck them away in the back of my mind. The decision has been made, I'm tired and I'm ready to wave the white flag … to surrender.

I close the curtains as the first glimpse of dawn peeks over the horizon and curl up in my blanket on the sofa. Exhaustion is overwhelming and sleep comes moments later.

I wake to a room submerged in darkness. How long did I sleep? I still feel tired, but that's no longer a good gauge for

227

how long I've slept. I can sleep for 30 minutes or 14 hours and still feel tired. Quantity, and obviously quality, are irrelevant where sleep is concerned. I feel around blindly on the side table for a lamp.

"Good morning, baby," croons a voice through the darkness. I hear him rise and walk to the window and pull the curtain back slightly letting a sliver of light cut through the center of the room. I'm sheltered in darkness on one side of the divide and Dimitri on the other.

"What time is it?" My voice is scratchy and my eyelids and throat are swollen from crying half the night.

"Eleven-thirty. How did you sleep? I see your fondness for sofas extends to Vegas." There's no contempt in his voice, but he doesn't mask the sadness.

I'm ashamed. "Yeah, I guess it does."

He crosses the light beam and sits next to me on the sofa taking my hand. "Are you hungry? You didn't eat last night."

Hunger is another thing I've learned to suppress or ignore at will. "Not really."

"Sorry it was so cold in here last night. I didn't realize the air conditioning was cranked up until I woke up this morning. I turned it off after I got out of the shower. The shower, by the way, is awesome, once you figure out how it works."

Gesturing toward the bathroom I reply dryly, "I think I'll just take a bubble bath in the swimming pool."

The tub is huge and takes almost 20 minutes to fill completely. The bubbles are six inches deep, clinging to the surface of the water. They smell like lilies and vanilla. I climb in and wonder if this is what little kids feel like in a normal tub. I don't remember taking bubble baths as a child, though I know I did because I've seen actual photographic proof. I close my eyes and submerge myself completely underwater. The soap stings my eyes but I ignore the irritation and concentrate on the isolation the water provides. It's a barrier; a barrier between me and reality. The idea of never surfacing crosses my mind briefly; drowning wouldn't be such a bad way to go, would it? I break through the bubbles gasping for breath; gasping not for lack of air, but at the gruesome thought. It scares me. I close my eyes and try to block everything out, which is difficult because the gnawing ache in my chest and head is ever-present. I close my eyes and concentrate solely on the warmth of the water.

Time passes. I'm not sure how much, but I'm just beginning to notice the water cooling down when I hear a knock at the door. "Ronnie? I had room service bring up a chai latte. Can I bring it in to you while it's still warm? They even put whipped cream on top, just the way you like it."

I look down, taking inventory of the remaining bubbles. They've diminished considerably, but the water looks murky, hardly translucent. I'm covered. "Okay."

The door opens slowly and Dimitri walks in. His approach is timid. He looks only at my eyes, no attempts to peek at the naked body in the tub. He no longer wants me, I'm sure. At least not that way. The realization hurts me. I'm surprised how much it hurts me, though the rational side of me knows it shouldn't. I caused this disconnect. I caused us to drift apart. "Do you want me to set it on the counter or would you like to drink it in the tub?"

"The water's getting cold. You can set it on the counter; I think I'm ready to get out." I rise to reach over the side of the tub for the towel on the floor.

He bends down and hands it to me before any of my body is exposed and quickly turns his back on me and exits, shutting the door behind him. Rejection. I feel nothing but rejection. Tears trickle down my right cheek. If I'm feeling this way, how must he feel? I've barely kissed him for months and even then they've lacked even a hint of intimacy.

I ... am ... awful.

We spend the afternoon eating lunch at a French café and shopping for pajamas and a new outfit at an exclusive store in the hotel lobby. Dimitri insists on paying for them, though after I saw the price tags I only let him buy one sundress instead of two. The dress costs more than I make in two weeks. I also squash the idea of new shoes. The flip-flops I left home in will be fine.

We walk outside briefly after dark to get another look at the Eiffel Tower, at my request. The city that never sleeps offers dozens of options, but all I really want to do is return to the room. I'm tired.

I change from the dress into silk pajamas, a camisole and pants. I've never worn silk pajamas, or silk anything for that matter. Dimitri picked them out (and wisely kept the price a secret). The sensation of the cool silk sliding against my skin is soothing. I can't help touching the fabric. Even while I brush my teeth with my right hand I stroke my thigh with my left.

Dimitri's already in bed when I return. The scene is reminiscent of the previous night—his clothes crumpled up in a pile on the floor next to the bed. He lies propped up against several pillows under the covers with his bare chest and arms exposed; but tonight, he's awake. The boyish, sleeping Dimitri has been replaced by an alert, virile man. Anxiety swells within me. What am I supposed to do? The familiar comfort of the sofa has become habitual, but the sight of Dimitri lying in the huge bed alone is so tempting. If my days are truly numbered, can I allow myself this one night?

Back in the days when my nights were filled with dynamic, picturesque visions, I dreamt repeatedly of lying next to him in bed and sleeping, just sleeping, until dawn. I loved the feeling: secure, warm, content. I know I will die a virgin, that part of me is already dead, but the part of me that remains desires his touch. My needs and wants are entirely innocent now, minimal.

"Ronnie?" I'm lost in thought and his whisper breaks through the dilemma rattling inside me. I look up and meet his eyes. They're dark, but sparkle in the dim light. "You're beautiful." His words are so sincere it almost hurts. My looks have suffered right along with me over the past year: my depression shows in the hollowness of my cheeks, shadows under my eyes, my skin is pale, and my hair is dull and lifeless. I haven't cut it in over a year and it's usually pulled back in a ponytail. Makeup is another thing I've given up on.

I'm a raw, sickly version of my former pretty self. His words are too generous.

My responding smile is slight and meant to appease, but he sees through it. I shrug.

Patting the empty side of the bed he beckons sweetly, "Come here, baby ... *please.*"

I pull back the fluffy down comforter and climb in beside him, letting his arm curl under me and around my shoulder. We're both propped up against the pillows, but I'm facing him while his eyes are fixed on the ceiling. A peaceful silence fills the room. He's relaxed, his chest rises and falls rhythmically; I watch it. The sudden urge to touch him overwhelms me. With trembling fingers I reach for his chest. Dimitri's surprise is evident in his immediate flinch at my touch, followed by a faint moan as he bows into it, welcoming the contact. The muscles are hard and tense, tight, as I my fingers draw lines along his chest to his shoulders, down each arm to his fingertips, and back up to his neck.

His voice is rough and low when he speaks. "Do you know what I miss most?" His gaze still fixed on a single point on the ceiling.

"This?" I meekly guess.

His chest rises as he huffs in strangled amusement. "No, though your touch is, to say the very least ... arousing. I miss it more than you can imagine." So I do still affect him physically, I think. He does still want me. He sighs almost painfully, as if he can read my thoughts, and continues in a low voice, "Your laugh. I miss hearing you laugh."

"I laugh," I say weakly.

He cocks his head and looks at me, correcting me tenderly, "No. You don't. The last time I remember hearing you laugh was graduation night. That was a year ago." He returns his gaze to the ceiling and smiles. "One of the funniest things I've ever witnessed is you trying to get through telling a funny story. Half the story is lost in laughter."

I pinch my eyebrows together. "I don't do that." Inflection near the end indicates my response is more a question than denial.

He smiles again and steals a glance at me. "Yes, you do. Jo is exactly the same way. You two, especially together, cannot tell a funny story without breaking out into hysterical laughter, then dissolving into happy tears—and this is before you're even halfway through! The story is always more for your entertainment than your audience's, which ironically makes it even funnier for us."

I think about it a moment. "Really?"

He laughs at the curiosity in my voice. "Ronnie, I know you better than you know yourself. Trust me, yes."

I prop myself up on one elbow and challenge him, "Oh really? How well do you know me? Let's hear it." I'm caught up in the innocent argument.

There's no hesitation. "You lick your lips unmercifully when you're deep in concentration."

I pause momentarily to contemplate; my lips are always chapped when I get done writing a paper or reading a good book. I concede, "Okay, I'll give you a point for that. I guess I do."

"You have a black speck on the iris of your right eye, where the green fades to gold, and you have a birthmark shaped like a paw print on your back over your left kidney."

"I'll give you a half point for being so observant."

"Your favorite scent is sandalwood."

I stop to think. "When did I tell you that?"

"You didn't." After a short pause he adds, "You sigh half a second before you drift off to sleep."

My response is quiet and questioning. "No I don't."

He nods and smiles faintly, as if remembering something pleasant. "Yes, you do ... every night."

Do I? I don't know. And how does he know? He always leaves before I fall asleep.

"You've always dreamed of visiting Paris—"

I interrupt this time. "That's easy. I award you no points."

232

"You didn't let me finish," he objects. "You've always dreamed of visiting Paris with the man of your dreams." He glances at me for approval. "Too bold if I presume that the man is me?"

Wrapped up in our game, I shake my head. "No, not too bold."

"You've always dreamed of visiting Paris with me, near the end of summer. Of walking hand in hand near the Seine at twilight when the air is still warm, and kissing me at the top of the Eiffel Tower under a full moon."

I'm lost in his narrative. Goose bumps rise on my arms. It is *exactly* as I've pictured it a thousand times, though I've never shared any of this with him. I whisper, "Another point."

"You're a magnificent piano player and have a soft spot for Beethoven."

"I don't play, remember?"

He winks. "Not yet. You can give me that point in a couple of years when this little prediction becomes reality." He continues, "You secretly yearn to be a mother someday." He clears his throat and exhales softly, his voice cracks, "You've always wanted a son."

My throat tightens at this. He's right. I have, but this is something I've never told anyone. Ever.

He looks at me through misty eyes. "Ronnie, you have *so* much to live for."

I glance down at the sheets, at nothing in particular, and realize I'm licking my lips.

"What are you thinking about?" His voice catches near the end.

"I guess you do know me better than anyone else."

"I'm not one to say I told you so, but—" the ghost of a smile is faint.

"—I told you so," I say, the corners of my mouth twitching. I'm drawn back to his eyes searching optimistically for answers I desperately need. "Well, since you seem to know everything," I continue hesitantly, "How does my story end?"

His eyes are bright again. "That's easy," he says as he kisses my forehead. "You and I live happily ever after."

Life is sometimes ... finding something to live for.

Chapter 19
Misery loves company
Tragically

I sleep in his arms that night and though it's a dreamless sleep, I feel safe in a way I never have before.

I wake to find that the all too familiar, painful void remains in my chest. Foolish of me to think that a conversation could change my perspective, clean the slate. Kind words don't erase depression, not when it's hijacked your mind and taken your body hostage. I'm surviving, day by day, hour by hour, minute by minute, at its unforgiving mercy.

Upon awakening Dimitri ushers me to the hotel spa where he informs me I'll be spending (and I quote) "a well-deserved day of pampering". Well-deserved is an extreme exaggeration, when what he should have said was, "Ronnie, you look like hell and need a haircut and a really thorough scrubbing." My entire day is meticulously scheduled and he has ensured that I'll be looked after every second. I have the odd feeling I'm being babysat.

I've never been to a spa before and don't know what to expect. After a few hours I begin to liken myself to a lab rat in the midst of an experiment. I'm stripped, scrubbed, massaged, wrapped, and polished. They polish peoples' bodies you ask? Why yes, yes they do. I realize many people think this experience is relaxing and pleasurable, but it makes me self-conscious, embarrassed, and raw. Those feelings carry over nicely to the massage. I cannot get over the fact that a complete stranger is rubbing down my naked body. I feel exposed and vulnerable. That coupled with the fact that the masseuse has a brutally heavy hand does not make for a relaxing hour. I'm pretty sure she views me as a tough steak that needs tenderizing. Mission accomplished— I'm tender. And sore.

Admittedly the manicure and pedicure, on my end at least, aren't offensive. Though I pity the woman scrubbing my feet; this really isn't something we should ask other people to do for us, even if they are being paid. It's degrading and humiliating. She picks out the colors without asking and I'm pleased to see my toenails covered in pale pink polish and my fingernails covered only in a clear coat. The conversation is limited, but unlike the masseuse I actually find myself liking this woman, maybe because she hasn't violated me yet.

The last of my "handlers" finishes up with my hair and make-up. His name is Ian and he's by far my favorite pseudo-babysitter. He's young, friendly, and kind. My only instructions to him are: "Make me look human again please; the rest is up to you."

He responds with a fiendish smile, as if ready for the challenge. And he goes to work mixing up a concoction that he methodically applies to small sections of my hair before wrapping them in pieces of foil. After letting the stinky stuff work its magic, or so he says, he shampoos me. I decide in that moment that a scalp massage is *so* much better than a body massage. I could sit at this shampoo bowl all day. Too soon we return to his chair and I watch eight inches of hair drop to the floor. We chat easily the entire time. He's complimentary and encouraging in a way that an old friend might be. He's believable. He makes me feel good … and I allow it. For two hours, I don't think about the past or the future—only the present. And for the first time in months, the stranglehold loosens. I can breathe. Ian turns my back to the mirror, not allowing me to watch as he styles my hair and applies my make-up. He insists on surprising me.

Ian bends down, his hands on my shoulders, looking me squarely in the eye, a slight pout on his lips. "Veronica, I must admit … you don't look human." The frown slowly draws up into a dazzling smile and his eyes sparkle. "You look *fabulous!*"

He turns the chair around slowly, and I barely recognize the woman in the mirror. She's beautiful—and much older than eighteen. The hair that falls just past her shoulders is shiny and full of body, golden highlights woven through the chestnut brown. The eyes are golden green, lined in black— much larger than my own. Her skin is flawlessly glowing, and her cheeks are rosy. And she's smiling ... smiling while a single tear rolls down her cheek.

I turn to Ian and hug him. "Thank you," I whisper in his ear. "For everything ... more than you can imagine ... thank you."

His eyes are shining in triumph and he winks. "You're welcome. We're not quite finished though. Your knight in shining armor will be here soon to rescue you, but he's requested that you change into this first." He retrieves a large white box from the table next to us. "You can use the dressing room in the back, love."

The box contains a very revealing, silky, burgundy dress. My hands tremble as I undress and slip the dress over my head. I haven't worn anything this pretty, this sexy, since homecoming, and that feels like a lifetime ago. Or maybe just a different life altogether. The dress fits as if it's been custom made just for me. It's short and backless, exactly like the homecoming dress my mom made for me. The neckline plunges, embellished with intricate beadwork. It's a work of art. I slip my feet into the suede, toeless, five-inch heels. They're the same color as the dress. My pink toenails peek through and compliment the shoe color so well I can't help but suspect that Dimitri has orchestrated every last detail to perfection. The last thing remaining in the large white box, amongst all the tissue, is a smaller black velvet jewelry box. With shaking hands, I open it—and gasp. It contains a jaw-dropping pair of earrings. They're delicate: dozens of dangling, translucent pearls set in yellow gold. It takes some time to feed the posts through my ears since my hands are shaking so much. As I slide the second back in place I look at the woman in the three-way mirror in front of me, and she's even more a stranger than the woman in the salon chair staring back at me minutes earlier. This woman is stunning. Her face reflects a look of surprise and awe.

I return to much "oohing" and "aahing" from the salon staff. As I smile at the group of smiling faces, I find that there, standing behind them all, is Dimitri. The crowd parts and we meet in the middle. The rest of the world drops away, except the two of us. His smile is joy, desire, and triumph ... and it's all for me.

Wearing the heels, I meet him eye to eye, smile, and then brush my lips gently across his. I close my eyes, pull back slightly, and revel in the moment. "Thank you, Mr. Glenn."

His lips nudge the hair away from my ear and he whispers so softly I wonder if he's speaking aloud or directly into my subconscious. "You take my breath away. Not the clothes, or the hair, or the make-up. Just you." The ghost of a kiss touches below my ear and his face drops to nestle against my collarbone. His warm breath seeps in and elicits a delightful shiver that resonates just beneath the surface of my exposed skin.

Our fingers interlace and his face comes level with mine. "Shall we go to dinner, Miss Smith?"

I nod, unable to speak. I wave to everyone and blow a kiss to Ian. His hands are clasped in front of his chest and his eyes are glassy. He blows a kiss back, smiles and nods, as if to say, "You're welcome."

After dinner I request a walk outside to admire the Eiffel Tower. The sun has set and the Tower twinkles with light. It makes me smile. My heart feels less heavy. Dimitri stands with me, his arms wrapped around me, the entire time.

"Do you think it really looks like this? The real one, I mean."

"For the most part, yes," he says thoughtfully. "I'd expect a slightly different ambiance in Paris these days, and probably a lot less neon."

I smile at his joke. "I think I'm done for tonight. We can go inside now."

He kisses my forehead. "Okay. It doesn't have to end here. I have something to show you. Something I think you might like."

We walk through the casino, but instead of walking toward the bank of elevators we've used for the past two days, Dimitri leads me toward a different set of elevators on the other side of the hotel.

We ride the elevator in silence. I can't take my eyes off Dimitri. He's dressed in a black suit, with a dark blue shirt and tie. His gray eyes shine bright and deep. He smiles at me, gentle and content. I feel satisfied, calm, and actually … happy.

It's not until we exit the elevator on a floor near the top and walk down the hall that the light bulb goes off. "We changed rooms, didn't we? Since this is our last night?"

We arrive at the end of the hall, and he slips his key card into the slot to the side of the door. He looks at me and nods, smiling. The room opens up in front of me. It's huge, just like the last, but I don't see any of it because the curtains are drawn on the far wall and only a faint light pours in. But through the curtains I can see the Eiffel Tower directly across the street. I walk to the wall of windows and ignore my fear of heights pressing my hands to the glass as if I can reach out across the space and touch it.

I turn back to Dimitri and smile. He's standing across the room watching me, letting me enjoy the moment. "We can push the sofa over in front of the window and sleep on it." He winks. "That way you won't miss a moment of it."

I pinch my eyebrows together and walk toward him. He closes the gap. "I think sofas just might be overrated," I say, looking at the floor before turning my eyes back up to him. "The view from the bed would be spectacular."

His arms wrap around me and caress my exposed back. "Spectacular," he murmurs. His finger traces the line of my spine from the nape of my neck down to the small of my back, where it's halted by the zipper of my dress. His hand disappears over the fabric and grasps the zipper. It slides down slowly and my breath catches. His sensuous touch sets my skin aflame. He leans in to kiss on the top of my shoulder, and then hollow of my neck, and then under my chin as I lift my head.

Just as our lips are about to meet, his phone rings. It's demanding, competing for attention. The ring dies away only to start up again, and again.

"It's Sebastian's ring tone," Dimitri says.

239

"Maybe you should answer it," I say, forcing the words. I don't want this to stop.

"No," he groans softly capturing my ear lobe between his teeth.

The phone rings again.

I can't believe I'm saying this, but Sebastian obviously isn't going to give up. "Please answer it."

He sighs and the tug of his lips releases my ear lobe. With one hand still under my dress fondling the top edge of my panties, he answers in a harsh voice. "What?"

As he listens, his face softens. Suddenly his eyebrows begin to lift, and his lips part slightly. He says nothing.

His hand slips free of my dress and he looks at me. As desire drains away, something else pours in. This is a one sided conversation. He's only listening, though a range of emotions are chasing each other across his face. Shock and dismay have replaced the hungry look in his eyes. I hear Sebastian's voice die out on the other end. Dimitri exhales roughly and says, "Eleven o'clock tomorrow? Our flight arrives in Denver at ten-thirty. We'll be there. Text me the address, will you?"

Sebastian talks some more. Dimitri ends the conversation as Sebastian quiets again, "Okay. Thanks man. Later."

He slips his phone back in his pocket and studies me. He tilts his head and looks from one eye to the other and back again. Clearly he's deciding how to say what needs to be said. This seems serious. It's starting to scare me. He rubs his lips together and takes a deep breath before taking my shoulders firmly in his hands. I'm holding my breath, waiting. "I don't know how else to say this, so I'm just going to say it. Teagan died."

I exhale loudly, something between a cough and a sob. And then room begins to spin and static fills my ears. Dimitri's lips are moving but I can't hear him. My muscles betray me and I feel myself beginning to fall, but Dimitri's arms hold me upright, clutching me tightly to his chest.

I cry.

I sob.

Eventually I sniffle.

I don't know how we made it there, but when my eyes finally clear, we're sitting on the sofa. I'm on Dimitri's lap, cradled like a small child. I find my voice. "What happened?"

Dimitri strokes my cheek and looks outside at the Tower. "He committed suicide. Sebastian said he hung himself. It happened two nights ago." He sounds one hundred years old.

I think about where I was two nights ago. On a sofa, contemplating the very same fate for myself. My own end … It makes me shudder. "Does anyone know why?" I ask. *I should know why*, I think to myself. I shouldn't have to ask someone else why my best childhood friend felt the need to end it all.

I.

Should.

Know.

But I haven't spoken to him in months.

"Sebastian said his girlfriend—the one at the graduation party last year, Andi—he said that she died last month. She had a rare heart disorder that nobody knew about. It had gone undetected all her life. One day she had a massive heart attack, and it took her instantly. I guess Teagan was with her when it happened." Dimitri's voice has grown thick and he stumbles over the last few words. "Sebastian said that she died in his arms."

My eyes start to sting again, and I feel the tears scraping harshly against the backs of my half-closed eyelids. "I can't believe it. I should've been there for him. I shouldn't have let him slip away. I'm a horrible friend."

He brushes a stray hair off my cheek. "Don't be so hard on yourself, baby. You've had your own demons to fight this past year."

I rub my eyes angrily with the backs of my hands. "I was selfish. Goddamn it! I was only worried about myself!" My voice softens. "And now he's gone. And he's never coming back. And I didn't get to say goodbye … to tell him I loved him."

241

Dimitri's stroking my hair and it's soothing in a way nothing else at this moment could be. I close my eyes. He kisses my shoulder and whispers, "He knew. He always knew. You were his best friend. That's what best friends do, they love each other."

I think about growing up with him. The trouble we got in together, the fun we had, the fights we had, and the secrets we shared. "I hope you're right. I hope he knew."

"So tell him now." He raises his voice. "Teagan Marshall!" he shouts toward the window. "I know you're listening! Veronica has something she wants to tell you!" He gestures to me with a sad smile. "There. I think I have his attention; the floor is yours."

I huff out a humorless laugh, but when I look at Dimitri his eyes are serious and sincere. He whispers, "It's okay. Say what you feel."

I look up at the ceiling. I don't know why. I guess I'm talking to heaven. "I love you, Teag."

Life is sometimes … just a series of goodbyes.

Chapter 20
It feels like it feels
Nothing more
Nothing less

I snuggle up with Dimitri in the bed and we both fall asleep shortly after our heads hit the pillows. Bad news has an uncanny way of bringing exhaustion with it.

The next morning is a crack of dawn rush to buy funeral appropriate clothes, dress, check out, and catch a cab to the airport. Thank God our flight is right on-time. At this point I'd probably commandeer a plane and pilot it myself to get to Teagan's funeral. We arrive in Denver five minutes early and run through the terminal to the parking garage. Although have exactly 25 minutes to drive the route that normally takes closer to 45 minutes, Dimitri's driving the Porsche. I'm not too worried.

We pull into the church parking lot at eleven o'clock on the dot.

We take a seat in the last pew just as the priest is walking up to the pulpit. The church is about half full, but as I look around, I can see that everyone who mattered to Teagan is here.

The service is fairly non-descript and quite generic, lots of praying and singing dull hymns that Teagan would've hated. I suppose it's the type delivered when the priest has no personal relationship with the deceased. It's one-size fits all, insert name here, blah, blah, blah. It makes me sad. The last straw comes when the priest calls him Teagan James Marshall. His name is Teagan *Michael* Marshall for Christ's sake. (No offense, I know I'm in a holy place). Moments after this faux pas the priest asks if anyone has anything they would like to say before the final prayer.

I clear my throat, unsure how I'm going to get through this, and I squeeze the life out of Dimitri's hand. He squeezes back and I know this gesture is meant to give me strength and urge me on.

I clear my throat again as I stand. "His name is Teagan Michael, not Teagan James. He was the brother I never had.

243

Well, I guess technically we were blood brothers. At least that's what he called it. One summer day when we were ten years old, he cut our palms with a pocket knife we found at the park, and we sealed it with a handshake." I hear a lone, low laugh and look up to see Tate smiling at me from a few pews away. Tate was at the park that day with us, but he was smart enough not to agree to cutting himself with a dirty, discarded knife. His cheeks are wet with tears. "Teagan never thought of me as a girl back then, so of course we had to be blood *brothers*." My voice starts to get croaky, but I forge on. "Teagan wasn't perfect. He was crude, and rude, and … and boisterous. But, he was Teagan, which also meant that he was funny, protective, honest … even when I didn't want to hear it." I look at Tate again, who's wearing a knowing smile. He's remembering too. Remembering *our* Teagan. "Teagan was fiercely loyal and caring in a way only Teagan could be." I take another deep breath before I finish the most un-eloquent eulogy in history. "I wish I wasn't here right now. I wish this didn't happen. But please know that I love you, Teag. I always will. You'll always be in my heart. And tell my mom and dad I said hi."

Dimitri squeezes my hand as I sit down. The look in his eyes says *well done*.

One by one people stand to say their own words. I hear my sentiment repeated over and over again. "I love you, Teagan." "I love you, Teagan." "I love you, Teagan." Over and over.

The service wraps up when the church falls silent, which takes a while because Teagan is loved.

A lot.

The crowd moves to their cars, and each vehicle proceeds slowly, single file, to the nearby cemetery. Once there, the priest says a prayer, reads a passage from the Bible, and asks Teagan's family members to each place a rose on top of Teagan *Michael* (he remembered) Marshall's casket before it's lowered in the ground. His father weeps uncontrollably the entire time. I should probably offer my condolences, it would be the right thing to do, but I can't get over the violence and pain he brought to Teagan's life. Now

244

he's the one suffering. I hope he realizes what a beautiful child he brought to this world. As I watch him, I can only think of one word—redemption. I hope for his sake he finds it somewhere, anywhere, and that it's enough to lead him to get help he needs.

Teagan's aunt hands me a rose and nudges me forward toward the casket. Dimitri's hand rests against my lower back reassuringly. Seeing the casket in the church was sad. Seeing it here makes it real. *So real.* He's gone. I place my rose with the others, gently, like I might disturb Teagan if I move too fast. The gesture feels final, but comforting. Offering this tangible token is like being allowed to leave a piece of my heart with him. I like that. "Bye Teag."

There's a small gathering back at the church, but no one's in the mood to socialize. Pain hangs heavy in the air and the crowd disperses quickly.

I'm exhausted as Dimitri drives to my house. My head rests heavy against the seat back and I close my eyes. Dimitri drives silently for what must be ten or fifteen minutes before he clears his throat and rouses me from a groggy fog.

"I'm sorry if you were sleeping, but I just wanted to tell you how proud I was of you today, Ronnie. What you said about Teagan was beautiful. And if he didn't know how much you cared about him before, well ... no one can deny it now."

"Thanks. He was a really good guy."

"He was. If I needed proof of that I could see it in how seriously he took his friendship with you. And for someone who looked for any excuse to kick my ass, I have to admit I even liked him."

A tired chuckle escapes me. "He really did look for any opportunity, didn't he? I'm sorry."

"It's okay. He meant well, for you at least." He smiles through tired eyes.

We pull up in front of my house shortly, and Dimitri walks me to the front door. I hesitate as I insert the key in the lock. I pull the key back out. "I think that maybe I need to use the back door today."

He's surprised, but understands and nods in agreement.

245

I open the door to the empty kitchen. For a moment I'd almost forgotten everything is gone. It seems like I've been away for a lifetime, not just a couple of days. A lot can happen in a couple days.

Dimitri holds up my bag. "I'm just going to put this in your room. Do you want to come?"

"Sure."

I stop at the top of the stairs when I realize he isn't following. "You coming?" I ask.

He walks toward me without a word and takes my hand, leading me away from the basement and down the hall to my parents' room. The door is shut. "Close your eyes," he says. "And please don't be mad at me, Ronnie."

I close my eyes and hear the door creak open. He nudges me forward over the threshold. He moves to stand behind me, and rests his hands ever so lightly on my shoulders, whispering in my ear. "Before you open your eyes, please know that I love you more than life itself. I'm nothing without you. Please allow me this." He takes a deep breath. "Now, open your eyes."

I take in my parents' room. What was an empty room before is no longer empty. It's filled with Dimitri's bedroom furniture: the bed, the chair, and the painting of the phoenix. The walls have been painted and red drapes have been hung over the window. The room still smells slightly of fresh paint.

I'm at a loss. "It's your room."

He corrects me. "It's *our* room."

"*Our* room," I say, mulling it over. "Our *room*."

Acceptance begins to overtake my shock, and I nod. "Okay."

He kisses the back of my head. "Thank you." He tosses my bag on the bed. "If I'm correct, I think Sebastian, Sunny, and Bob moved a few more things in yesterday. Let's take a look in the living room."

The front room is still empty without the chairs and piano, but Dimitri's sofa, tables, TV, stereo, and bookshelves have been set up in the living room. The walls have been painted, too, and there are new drapes hanging over the windows.

"Wow, Sunny really went all out. It's definitely not my parents' house anymore, is it?" I don't know what else to say. It looks great. It's better than great. I never pictured myself living in a house this nice, this hip. But it's still weird, even sad in a way.

Dimitri's eyes are pleading with me. "Ronnie, you *were* running a little low on furniture. I mean, I can appreciate minimalism, but ... " He trails off. He's trying to lighten the mood with some humor, but my uncertainty is killing him.

I shrug. "It was unintentional minimalism anyway, does that even count?" He smiles slightly at my sad counter attempt at humor. "I'm sorry. I'm being an ungrateful bitch. After all that's happened the past few days, I completely forgot I was coming back to an empty house. To be completely candid, I didn't really intend to come back ... here, or anywhere. It's all a little shocking. I'm sorry." My emotions tighten like a fist within me, choking off my words.

He takes my hands as we stand in the middle of the empty front room. It's just Dimitri, me, my pain, and my honesty in the barren space. "Ronnie, baby, I think you need to see a doctor. Someone you can talk to, someone that can help you, someone with medicine ... " His words trail off again, but his gaze is steady, unwilling to release its grip on mine. And his eyes tell all. Behind his words lay total anguish. This is harder for him than I ever imagined, and the past few days have been the hardest yet.

I reach up and stroke his cheek with my hand. He's so beautiful, even when he's tired and broken. "I've been thinking a lot today. I mean, my mom always said it, but I am pretty sure I've been presented undeniable proof." I pause as I watch his Adam's apple move up and down, swallowing the lump in his throat. "There *really* aren't *any* coincidences. *Everything* happens for a reason. I don't know why I'm supposed to suffer through this depression. I don't know that yet. But I do know that three nights ago, I lay awake all night crying, staring out at the Vegas strip thinking about every possible way to kill myself. Which would be the least painful, the quickest, the least … messy? And later, I found out that Teagan killed himself that very same night. That's uncanny timing, don't you think?"

Dimitri nods in agreement through misty eyes.

"The funeral today was awful. It gutted me. We shouldn't have been there … any of us. He shouldn't have done it. Don't get me wrong I, of all people, can't exactly fault him for it. Suicide is so *fucking* tempting. It's, it's … " I'm searching for the word, and notice Dimitri's wincing at my explicitness. "It's relief from the excruciating pain that bears down every single day. We all have our burdens to bear, and God knows Teagan had more than most. But if he could've sat there in that church and at the cemetery today and watched the emotional torment his death caused the people he loved—" I shake my head. "—I don't think he would've done it."

The tears are in Dimitri's eyes now. "It would be the same at your funeral, you know?"

I'm eerily calm. "No, I don't know that. But I assume it would be. And I know what you're going to ask next." I bite my lip. "After seeing their faces, and picturing you in that much pain," I shake my head at the ground before looking into Dimitri's eyes, "I don't think I can do it. Today was a horrible reality check." My thoughts are getting ahead of me and a humorless chuckle escapes me. "It's funny. I always thought I was the one taking care of Teagan, I mean he called me Mom, for God's sake. In an ironically auspicious twist I think the scale was tipped more in my direction than I ever realized. In a strange way I feel like Teagan was, and is, my guardian angel. He always looked out for me in life and now his death has prevented mine." I heave a heavy sigh.

Dimitri's eyes are searching mine. "I guess I'm indebted to Teagan for the rest of my life."

I take his hand in mine, and place them both over my heart. "I'm not going to lie to you. The pain is still here. And it's still heavy. I've been carrying it so long that it feels like an extra limb. It's part of me. And it still scares the hell out of me. I pray to God it's not permanent, but I do feel different today. I can't say it's hope, but it's something close.

248

It's not total despair, and that feels almost human and *lovely*. I can't allow Teagan's death to have happened in vain. I owe it to him to fight. I owe it to *you* to fight." At this, I squeeze his hand, and bring it up to my lips to kiss his fingers. "You've stood by me the past year when everyone else abandoned me. I know it wasn't for my sparkling personality or my shitty conversation skills. What I want to know is, why?"

He pulls my hand toward his lips and kisses my own fingers. He sniffles as he says, "You know why, Ronnie. Because I love you. I'm undeniably devoted to you. You have no idea how special you are to me. I don't think that most people could even comprehend a love this intense."

"I think maybe I can ... and do. I love you, too. Thank you, from the bottom of my heart, for everything—especially for being Dimitri Glenn. I wouldn't be here without you." Our eyes are both heavy with tears and exhaustion. I nod my head toward the hallway. "Come on Mr. Sleepy Face, you need some rest. I hope this bed of yours—" I stop to correct myself. "I mean, *ours*, is comfortable."

The corner of his mouth twitches and lifts precariously into his familiar old mischievous smile as he eyes me. "Oh, I'd say it's plenty comfortable enough for just about anything."

Life is sometimes ... auspicious.

Chapter 21
Pain endured
Light ahead

Despite the innuendos and the fact that, for the first time, we are sleeping together in our own bed, we both fall asleep instantly. And tonight, my dreams return.

The snow is heavy on the ground and in the air. The wind is biting and evil—the kind of wind that gets into your bones and freezes you from the inside out. I have to lift my layered skirts, which are sodden and heavy, to walk up the hill through the freshly-fallen, knee-deep snow. Normally Dimitri wouldn't get the horse and buggy out of the barn in this type of weather for anything short of an emergency, but this is an important day. When I reminded him of it this morning, I knew he wouldn't deny me the three-mile drive.

It's been snowing like this all morning. I blink against the sting of the snowflakes as they strike my face like a million tiny needles. "We're close. It's there—just beyond that tree."

Even though the storm is violent, the snow on the ground is so fresh and undisturbed that it feels almost criminal to trudge through it. I pull the wool blanket tighter around my shoulders and feel Dimitri's hand strong against my back, steadying me. The walk from the road up the hill is challenging in the snow, but I'm determined. Dimitri holds on to me with one arm, and carries a small shovel in the other. We trudge on.

We arrive at the top of the hill, where a mighty oak shelters us from the worst of the storm. From its trunk, I walk three paces north and rest my hands on my knees bending over to shield my face from the driving snow and to catch my breath.

"Good thing we didn't wait another hour or it would have been covered and we wouldn't have been able to find it. I think they were waiting for you," Dimitri says, stepping around me and reaching down. The top of a gray stone marker is just visible, and he begins to brush away the snow. Then, he takes his shovel and deftly removes the rest of the

snow, revealing the bare earth in front of the marker. I step into the clearing wiggling my toes in my thin, ankle-high boots to bring some feeling back to my feet. Then I kneel down on the wet dirt, looking directly at the marker as Dimitri continues to clear the snow behind me. I brush my glove across the surface until I can see what's written there:

William Smith
Born May 25, 1824
Died January 12, 1867

Josephine Smith
Born May 23, 1824
Died January 12, 1867

I visit them once a week on foot if weather permits, but each time I look at their names it brings on a momentary wave of terror. These days, it's over as quickly as it comes, but the finality of their names in stone is always disturbing. "It's been exactly a year, but not a day goes by that I don't miss them terribly," I say, almost as if I'm speaking to the stone itself.

Dimitri's standing behind me in the clearing now and I feel, through the layers of sweaters and blankets, his hands on my back and shoulders attempting to sooth me. "I know. I miss them, too."

I reach deep in my pockets and empty two handfuls of small rocks on the frozen ground. I work quickly but diligently. When I'm done the word LOVE is spelled out in rocks at the base of grave marker.

I look back at Dimitri and shrug. "No flowers."

He bends over and kisses the top of my hat. "I think it's brilliant. They would love it. No pun intended."

"You know I still believe they're with me."

He nods. "They're always with you," he says in a comforting voice. "In your heart and especially in your memories."

I stand and turn to face him, squinting against the bombarding snow. "Their death has been very difficult for me to deal with this past year, but you've stood by me. And you're here today, in the middle of a blizzard. Why?"

He squeezes my hands and sniffles, "You know why, Ronnie. Because I love you. I'm undeniably devoted to you. You have no idea how special you are to me. I don't think that most people could even comprehend a love this intense."

"I think maybe I can ... and do. I love you, too."

My eyes open to total darkness. I blink several times. I blink twice more just to be sure I'm awake and release the death grip I have on the sheet covering me. I hear soft breathing to my left and it takes me a moment to realize it's Dimitri. We've slept all afternoon and all night in our clothes. So much for the nap. He's sprawled out on his back, taking up a good two thirds of the bed. His hand is resting on my shoulder. Good thing the bed's a king size, or I may have been forced to the floor. I slip out as quietly as possible to avoid waking him.

I return from the bathroom to find him awake, propped up against two pillows. It's almost dawn.

"Did I wake you? I'm sorry." I talk quietly as if there are others in the house I might disturb if I don't keep my voice down. I guess I'm used to silence in the morning after spending a year alone in this house.

He smiles. "It's okay. I have trouble sleeping when you're not with me."

I crawl across the bed and lay my head on his chest. "I thought you told me once you were an insomniac. You've slept like the dead these past few days."

He flashes his knowing smile and winks. "Like I said, I have trouble sleeping when you're not with me. I wish I would've found you years ago; it would've been much easier on my constitution. The real question is, how did Ronnie sleep in her new, oh-so-comfy bed?" He's rubbing the sheets on either side of him for added effect.

"I dreamt," I say, smiling. I know he'll be pleased. He's always been interested in my dreams, and I haven't had any since my parents died.

He sits bolt upright and catches my head in his lap. "You did? What was it about?"

I sit up and wrap my arms around his waist. "Visiting my parents' graves. It was like a hundred years ago and there was a blizzard."

He nods. He always looks like he's trying to conjure up imagery when I tell him about my dreams, like he wants to share every detail with me.

I muster up courage from deep within. "I think it's time."

He brushes a few stray hairs behind my ear. "Time for what?"

"I think it's time to spread their ashes," I say, my voice wavering.

He stokes my hair. "Where?"

"Well, after my grandma died, they told me when they passed away they wanted their ashes spread somewhere the family would enjoy visiting them. So, I was thinking about their favorite places and mine. I think they would really like it in Glacier National Park. We drove through the park on vacation when I was nine or ten, and I remember thinking it was the prettiest place I'd ever seen. We all loved it." I sit up and look into his eyes. "What do you think?"

"Are you sure you're ready for this?" His eyes are penetrating and he's analyzing everything my words and face are and aren't telling him.

"I think I need to do it. To get some closure. In the dream, it was scary at first to visit them, especially with their names glaring out and memorialized in stone, but it was also kind of comforting to have somewhere to go to honor them. I think I need that, and I think they deserve that. They should be honored somewhere beautiful, someplace they loved."

"Let's do it. When do we leave?"

He's always so eager and quick to please me. I think he'd do anything for me. I truly don't deserve him. I'm thankful that I didn't just tell him I'd like to rob a bank.

253

"Maybe in a couple of weeks?" I say. "I really need to get back to work before your mom fires me. By the way, do I work today? I don't even know what day it is."

He winks. "It's Sunday. You're safe."

Getting back to some semblance of normalcy during the following two weeks is strange. I don't even know what normal looks like anymore. But I'm willing to try to create it anyway. My heart is still heavy and the pain continues, though there are moments when peace visits me. It comes at unexpected times: when I'm reading a book Sunny gave me (I haven't read in months), when I'm riding the bus to work (I don't have Jezebel anymore, remember?), or when I'm washing the dishes with Dimitri after dinner (our new plates have cherry blossoms on them; Dimitri picked them out). Peace is an unbelievably satisfying companion. I haven't mastered the art of cultivating it yet, but I've learned to nurture it when it makes a serendipitous appearance. It helps to balance out the moments of despair. But those moments are diminishing, and come only at night after Dimitri's fallen asleep and the house is so, so quiet. Quiet enough to think … and remember … and grieve.

At the office, Bob welcomes me back with warm smiles. Eventually, I start participating in his lunch conversation again. He's been kindly talking *to* me for the past several months, but I've been horribly remiss on my end. Bob has invited me to volunteer at a local homeless shelter this month. Bob goes once a month and though he didn't say so, I know he thinks it would be good for me. And I think that maybe I need to trust Bob and accept whatever help he wants to offer. The thing with Bob is that he has this unquestionable humility and kindness about him. Helping people is not only what he does; it's who he *is*. With a lot of people there's an ulterior motive, there's something in it for them. Not with Bob. I think he helps because that's what he thinks he should do and it makes his heart feel good. He's completely selfless. I haven't met many people like him. He's precious. And I've   finally noticed.

254

It's Friday, the day before Dimitri and I leave on our trip to Montana. It's sunny, hot, and dry—a perfect June day in Colorado. I'm sitting with Bob at the table in the back room of Sunny's studio and we're eating lunch— a peanut butter and butter sandwich on white bread and an apple sliced in quarters for Bob (as always), and a leftover stuffed bell pepper for me. But today, Bob seems quiet and deep in thought.

"Bob, is everything okay?"

He looks up from his piece of apple. "I'm sorry, Miss Veronica. I'm not much in the way of company today, am I? I've just been thinking about your trip this weekend."

I'm startled at his mention of the weekend. I haven't told Bob about my trip. The topic of my parents and his late wife has always been off limits—a mutually, unspoken rule. I suspect he's been talking to Sunny or Dimitri.

He acknowledges my discomfort with his usual gentleness and pats my arm. "Miss Veronica, if I asked you to go somewhere with me after work today, would you? It will only take a half hour, I promise." His wrinkly skin creases around his eyes as he smiles and I can't say no.

"Sure, where are we going?" I ask curiously.

"I have someone I want you to meet."

After work we lock up and I join him at the bus stop.

I don't ask questions when we board the bus that takes Bob home every evening.

I don't ask questions when we stop at a small floral shop and he buys a single white rose.

I don't ask questions when we board yet another bus and ride ten blocks before hopping off.

I don't ask questions when we walk three blocks to the edge of the cemetery.

And I don't ask questions when we stop in front of a simple headstone engraved with the name Alice Marie Carruthers.

Bob kneels down and lovingly places the rose atop a pile of assorted colored roses, some freshly wilted and others dried completely. He turns to me after gently stroking his shaky fingers across her name. "Alice, this is my very good friend, Miss Veronica. Miss Veronica, this is my Alice."

I smile through the pooling tears in my eyes. "I'm very pleased to meet you Alice."

He smiles approvingly and removes a handkerchief from his back pocket and blots his watery eyes. He returns his loving gaze to her name and strokes it again. "I brought you a white rose today. They looked magnificent, for first time all week." He looks back at me and whispers, "White is Alice's favorite." He returns his gaze to the stone. "Alice, Miss Veronica is a wonderful young lady. She's dating Dimitri, Miss Sunny's oldest boy. I brought her here today to meet you because she has a difficult weekend ahead of her. I thought she might gain some strength by making your acquaintance." At this, he turns to me. "My Alice is proof that although death may have taken her from me physically, it did not take her spirit. Or mine. The love I feel for her will forever fill my heart. And I have a feeling the same is true for you, Miss Veronica." He turns back to the grave. "I feel your love around me, my sweet Alice, like a soft, warm, comforting breeze that smells of roses." He kisses his fingertips and places them on her name. "I'll see you tomorrow. Sweet dreams. I love you, darling."

He extends his hand to me and I take it. His hand is cool to the touch despite the warm temperature. It's veined and liver spotted, and his skin feels almost waxy. But his touch brings me peace, and I smile. Peace, like the book, or the bus, or the dishes … peace, like a white rose on a grave. We walk hand in hand to the bus stop. Bob doesn't speak, he just gazes upward toward the sun through squinted eyes, and he smiles too. We arrive at the bus stop and before he boards his bus, I kiss him on the cheek. His smile widens and he tips his hat, and then he disappears.

I didn't thank him. I probably should have said it, but I think he knew.

He always knows.

I think about Bob and Alice on the bus ride home. He doesn't grieve her death; he celebrates her … every day. Love can endure all things, I think.

256

Even death.
Life is sometimes … enduring.

Chapter 22
Shedding fear, fault, and failure
Because love's a lighter load to bear

The plane ride is relatively short, but stands in sharp contrast to those I took to Vegas and back only a few weeks ago. This time we aren't racing to save my life; we're taking steps to heal my spirit—a very distinct difference.

The park is only a few hours drive from the airport. Dimitri, as always, is my strength. He's calm and stable, though a few layers below the surface I can see nervous energy buzzing. He's so even-tempered that after spending the past few weeks almost nonstop with him, I'm able to detect the smallest shifts in his demeanor. He's more controlled than anyone I've ever been around. He rarely worries. I think it's because he doesn't have time for it. It's not that he doesn't care—he cares with every inch of his being. He just doesn't let worry consume him the way I do. He deals with it, whatever *it* is. He's an amazing human being, so centered and mature. A role model, really.

My thoughts are interrupted when I look up and see it—the perfect place. "That's the spot," I say, pointing to a waterfall in the near distance. It looks like a painting.

Dimitri smiles at my decision. "The spot indeed."

Even though it appears to be a stone's throw away, it takes twenty minutes to reach it. Dimitri parks our rental car on the shoulder of the road and I grab my jacket, my bag, and the urn from the back seat and we set off down the footpath. Though most of our drive was made under cloud cover, they're beginning to recede. By the time we reach the base of the falls, the sun is shining brightly overhead and I've shed my jacket. We've gained some elevation during our walk, and when I look back toward the valley I see that it is covered with purple and white wildflowers, thousands and thousands of them. The setting is perfect. It's time.

I ask Dimitri to hold the urn while I reach into my bag to pull out a resealable plastic bag. I crouch down and empty its contents, rocks, on the ground. My hands are trembling, but I manage some quick rearranging. Dimitri rubs my back as I stand and brush off my hands. Small rocks spell out the word *LOVE* at my feet.

I shrug. "No flowers."

He smiles that knowing smile. "I think it's brilliant. They would *love* it. No pun intended."

My eyebrows crinkle together and I smile curiously. "That's what you said in my dream … and I *don't* remember telling you that part."

He winks. "You didn't," he says, and kisses me on top of my head.

I've accepted that weird things just happen with Dimitri. He always seems to know more than he should. That's just the way it is, so I don't really question it anymore.

"Can I have the urn?"

"Of course," he says, handing it to me. "I'll see you again my friends," he says, lifting it to his lips and kissing it softly before handing it to me.

His gesture brings a lump to my throat. I swallow hard. With shaking hands, I hug the urn against my chest. I kiss my fingertips and rub the container tenderly. "I miss you both, every day. And I love you both, every day." I smile through silent tears. "And I'm going to be okay." I sniffle, unscrew and remove the lid, and walk to the water's edge. The breeze picks up just as I tip the urn. I watch their ashes catch on the wind, disappearing into the air and water. "I really hope you like it here," I whisper.

I blow a kiss and turn to see Dimitri standing a few yards behind me with arms wide open. I walk slowly to him. He draws me up inside his arms, and I'm enveloped in his warmth and his love. I stand for a long time letting it seep in through every pore. And when I feel it in every cell of my body, I step back and look into his gorgeous gray eyes and I thank him and I tell him I love him. And we walk back to the car in silence.

And we drive back to the airport in silence.

And we wait for the next flight to Denver in silence.

And we board the plane in silence.

And it's okay.

I'm sitting in the window seat looking at the scenery far below, thinking about everything that's happened with my parents, not just today, and not just this past year, but a lifetime. And that's when I feel it. There's a quantifiable shift. The pain, dull but ever-present, is love, a love that's heavy but real. A love that feels almost one sided, but that's enough. It fills me up. Love.

My lips lift into a smile just as the tears begin to fall. Dimitri puts his arm around me and holds me tightly as I cry, my head resting on his shoulder. The tears force their way out and with them, I say goodbye to the sadness, the anger, the grief, the guilt, and the fear … but not to the love. I keep the love for myself.

Dimitri digs a tissue out of his pocket and hands it to me. (He's in the habit of carrying tissues with him at all times these days.) I blot my eyes and cheeks, and blow my nose.

Dimitri gazes at me with a face so serene I would swear he's forgotten that we're sitting on a very crowded plane. He's looking at me like we're the only two people in the world, completely oblivious to the crying infant in front of us or the snoring man behind us. It's just us. He brushes his fingertips from my temple to my jawline, across my lips and down my throat, his eyes studying me as if he's trying to memorize every detail of my face. I'd forgotten how amazing his touch feels. It must show, because he smiles slightly and it lights up his eyes.

We stare into each other's eyes for a long time until all at once he leans forward almost urgently, like he can't hold back, and whispers in my ear, "Will you marry me?" He kisses me softly just below my ear before he pulls back to look into my eyes again. His eyes are bright and sincere.

The words don't register at first. It's as if he's just said something in a foreign language I don't speak well and I have to translate the question word by word into English.

Will.

You.

Marry.

My heart skips a beat—

Me?

I've just been proposed to. I can hardly believe it.

Dimitri's expression is expectant, and I realize he's waiting for an answer or at the very least, an acknowledgement. And I'm sitting here with my mouth gaping open, looking at him like an uncomprehending fool. *Say something,* I tell myself. But I can't. Dimitri Glenn wants to marry *me.* After everything that's happened today, it's all I can do to nod. *Yes.*

Relief washes over him. He leans forward to kiss me, gently at first, but then takes my face in his hands and his kiss becomes euphoric and frenzied. When he stops and pulls away, his lips are full, dark pink, and smiling.

"I promise to love you every day ... every yesterday, every today, and every tomorrow ... forever." He kisses me again.

I'm dizzy when I finally come up for air. I'm not a veteran air traveler, but I'm fairly certain this is not proper airplane etiquette.

The flight attendant announces we'll be arriving in Denver shortly and instructs us to fasten our seat belts. Dimitri sits back against his seat and holds my hand. His smile cracks me up. He looks like he's hiding the world's greatest secret behind it, like it's just on the verge of bursting out.

What's even funnier is that I know I'm wearing the exact same smile.

The setting sun outside the terminal looks different—brighter and glowing. The walk to Dimitri's car feels different—lighter and floating. And Dimitri is different. He's more. He's mine. He's holding my hand, swinging it back and forth between us, and I feel like the luckiest girl in the world.

I wait until the drive home to start asking questions. When the first one slips out, I feel silly for bringing it up so soon. We've only been engaged for 30 minutes, after all. I'm not one of those girls who's always dreamed of having a huge wedding. They're ridiculous if you ask me. You're just as married if you spend $100,000 on a day-long production

261

or if you drop $50 on a courthouse appointment. But, I am a planner at heart. I can't help it. His eager answers let me know it's okay, so I proceed.

By the time we get home and Dimitri parks the Porsche in the garage (because I've decided it's okay to start using it again), the most important decisions have been made. Though Dimitri enthusiastically suggested we go to Vegas next weekend, I exercised my right to veto that idea. After that, the brainstorming began. We agreed on August 25th (the two-year anniversary of our very first date) at the Glenn house. (The location is still a point of contention. He votes for outdoors, and I really want the ceremony held in the gallery, even though he thinks that is too pretentious. Keeping his talent under wraps is of paramount importance to him. But I'll have Sunny on my side, so I know I'll win.)

It's getting late so we decide to wait until tomorrow after Sunny gets home from church to tell her the good news. After I put a load of laundry in the washer, I find Dimitri stretched out on the sofa with his laptop in his lap, listening to music. His stereo is so nice it's unbelievable. It sounds like the band is playing in our living room.

"Whatcha lookin' at?" I ask as I plop down next to him.

"Well, it seems I'm faced with an insurmountable challenge." He's glued to the screen.

"Tell me about it. Maybe I can help. I have a lot of expertise in the challenge department."

He's still looking at the screen though the corner of his mouth hints at a grin. "So, there's this girl," he begins. "It always starts with a girl, doesn't it?"

I nod as seriously as I can manage. "It always starts with a girl."

"Here, here … " he concurs. "Well, there's this girl, and she's not just any girl … she's the most amazing, fantastic, phenomenal girl I've ever met—"

"*Phenomenal?*" I interrupt. "Wow, this sounds serious."

He nods. He's playing along, but his eyes are still on the laptop screen. "That's just it. It is serious." At this his mouth twitches closer to a grin. "This phenomenal girl just agreed to *marry* me and I don't even have a proper engagement ring to secure her hand. I'm the consummate prognosticator, but alas the timing, though perfect, was spontaneous, and has left me looking like some kind of inept romantic fool."

This makes me smile and I can't hide it. "Quite a conundrum."

He looks up now and grins. "Quite." He turns the laptop around and he's on the Tiffany & Co. website. The screen is filled with sparkling diamond engagement rings.

I shake my head. "Dimitri, it's not important."

His face is serious now; the playful banter is over. "Yes, it is important. You're the most important person in the world and I asked you to marry me, and I don't even have the ring yet."

"I'm serious though. The ring isn't important to me. You are."

"I just want it to be perfect."

"It will be. We'll be together."

He smiles.

I tilt my head and narrow my eyes. "Have you been planning on asking me to marry you for a while, or is this just something that happened today? You said it was spontaneous."

He sets the laptop on the coffee table and looks at me for several moments before he answers. I feel his eyes looking into the depths of my soul. This is real. "The first day we met I knew I was going to ask you to marry me. Today was just … right."

Life is sometimes … just right.

Chapter 23
I love you more
And even more than that

We're in Sunny's kitchen waiting for her to arrive home from church. Sebastian's home and has already been clued in. When Dimitri tells him the news he responds with, "Took you long enough to ask her." Then he winks at me and says, "Destiny. I told you so." Sebastian, the eternal romantic.

Sebastian is waiting with us. He wants to see Sunny's reaction. There's a bet riding on it—fifty bucks. Sebastian says she'll cry and babble on incoherently and Dimitri says she'll do her happy dance and hug him until he breaks in two.

Dimitri edges out Sebastian for the win. At the announcement, she does indeed do her happy dance (it's really, really cute), she squeezes him just short of breaking him in two (and me too), and she does babble, but it's brief … and coherent. There are no tears though, so a tie is avoided. She's ecstatic.

Sebastian slips Dimitri a fifty.

After she settles down, she sits on a stool at the kitchen counter next to me. "I can't believe my D. is getting married," she says, still giddy. "There's so much to plan—."

Dimitri interrupts her, "Mom, we want to keep this simple. I know this is a big event, but we aren't going to make a spectacle out of it. Are we clear?" He's smiling. He adores his mother, but he also knows her well. This could turn into the royal wedding pretty quickly.

She nods. "Of course. You want to keep it simple. Simple can be beautiful, too. It will be perfect. What can I help with? Do you have a date yet?"

Dimitri nods. "August 25th."

She gasps. "That's only two months away!" She runs to the calendar on the refrigerator and flips the pages. "And it's on a *Monday*?" She looks back at us, puzzled.

I intercede, "It's the anniversary of our first date."

She smiles and claps her hands. "How romantic. I remember that day well." She sighs, fondly recalling, "All those lilies and candles. I still have the picture in my phone."

Dimitri breaks her out of her reverie. "We'd like to have the wedding here at the house if that's okay with you."

At this she does start to tear up. She walks over and hugs him again. "Of course. I would be honored to have you two married in our home."

Dimitri returns the hug. "Actually I was thinking *outside* our home … in the backyard."

She releases him and wipes her eyes, "Of course, the backyard would be lovely. We can set up chairs and tables by the waterfall, and—"

I interrupt, "And *I* was thinking inside the gallery."

Sunny looks at me and her smile widens. "The gallery would be absolutely perfect. It's long and narrow—just like a church. And it's so white." She looks at Dimitri and he's pretend-scowling at me. "But Dimitri doesn't want it in the gallery?"

He shakes his head.

"*Because?*" she presses.

"The backyard would be better," he answers quickly.

"You mean your artwork isn't on display in the backyard, which makes it better."

His checks blush. "Maybe." As I look on, I think to myself that it's cute the way only Sunny can truly embarrass him.

She rubs his shoulder and I can tell already it's an act of apology. "The backyard would be fabulous, don't get me wrong, but I'm with Veronica on this one. The gallery would be perfect. It's the one room in this house that's truly yours. It's you, on the most intimate level. Your wedding should take place there." It's final.

Dimitri can never say no to Sunny. He gives in. "Okay."

Sunny has many, *many* ideas. We have to rein her in several times. She clearly isn't familiar with "simple." Ice sculptures and horse drawn carriages are *not* simple.

She calls Pedro and shares our news and puts me on the line. He's such a nice man and he's more than happy to grant my request— chicken enchiladas, *lots of them*—for our reception. He also recommends an outstanding bakery that has killer cupcakes. The food is going to be amazing.

Sunny wants to take care of the flowers; we hesitantly acquiesce. "Simple," I keep repeating. "Simple is your new mantra. Simple, simple, simple."

She smiles. That smile frightens me. I know simple will be stretched unrecognizably to the outer limits of its literal definition.

Dimitri is going to design the artwork for the invitations. They'll be the greatest invitations ever, so nothing to worry about there.

Sebastian knows a photographer.

I'm ticking items off on my fingers: "We have a date, a location, food, flowers, invitations, and a photographer; that about covers it, right?"

Sunny has her own list in front of her. "I think you forgot a few things, honey."

This is supposed to be simple, right? "Like what? No cupid ice sculptures, remember?"

She laughs. "Okay, but what about a guest list?"

Dimitri and I look and each and answer in unison: "Small."

"We want family and close friends only," Dimitri says. "30 to 35 guests, tops."

"Okay," Sunny says, jotting down the figures on her list. "And what about a best man and maid of honor?"

Dimitri nods to Sebastian. "Obviously."

Sunny asks, "Have you *asked* him?"

Dimitri sighs, it's exaggerated. "Sebastian, would you do me the honor?"

Sebastian rolls his eyes. "Yeah, whatever." Then he smiles genuinely at Dimitri. "You know I wouldn't miss it." They bump knuckles across the table.

Sunny nods approvingly and looks to me. "What about you, Veronica?"

"I have something in mind."

She nods. "Okay. What about the honeymoon?"

266

Dimitri's quick to answer. "That one's all mine." He winks at me. His mother clucks her tongue but looks pleased.

"Alright then. What are you both going to wear?"

We look at other and shrug. I speak up first. "I'm kind of a jeans girl."

Dimitri smiles. "Jeans are simple. And sexy. I like it."

Sunny looks horrified. "Jeans? *At your wedding?* I guess we'll talk about the dress another day."

After a few hours of wedding details, Dimitri and I decide to head home. He takes a detour downtown, stopping at a jewelry store. From the manicured bushes out front to the ornate signage and tall windows, I suspect that it's a fancy jewelry store. *Scary* fancy.

It looks so intimidating I don't even want to go in. This is the type of place rich men buy their wives and mistresses rings and necklaces that cost more than my house. This isn't my type of place; this is a whole different world.

He's opening my door but I don't want to leave the safety of his car. He bends over and peers inside at me. "Come on, baby." He holds out his hand.

I take it reluctantly and slowly peel myself from the seat. His grin is so eager that it makes me anxious. "Dimitri, we really don't need to look for rings here," I say in a whisper, as if the people inside the store can hear me. "This place looks *way* too expensive."

Dimitri looks at the front door and back at me. He's not intimidated at all. He never is … *by anything.* "I did some research last night. This is supposed to be the best place in Denver to buy an engagement ring."

I'm still whispering, "I don't need the best. I'm just fine with good. Mediocre, even." I smile anxiously.

He kisses my forehead. "Don't be silly. Besides, this is for me too. I've never been able to buy you a ring from a store like this. Let me be selfish just this once. Besides *I* gave in on the gallery … " He trails off, wheedling me with his gray eyes. He's got a countenance that walks a line between a roguish teenager and a mature adult. He's so sure of himself right now that I can't deny him.

267

I huff softly. "Okay, but *please* Dimitri, nothing extravagant. Simple, remember?"

He kisses me on the lips. "Simple."

We walk in, and I'm terrified we'll either be ignored or laughed at. We're just kids. We're dressed in jeans and T-shirts and—aside from the Porsche parked outside—we hardly look like the type of people who have enough money to even window shop here. Dimitri gives my hand a reassuring squeeze and all my fears vanish as I watch him take control.

He walks up and introduces us to a man in a nicely tailored suit. It's so easy for him. He's been conducting his own business since he was fifteen. He knows how to talk to people. It's not some kind of put on act either. He's confident, straightforward, witty and charming; and people eat it up. I feel like I'm seeing a different side of him that I've never seen. I have seen it of course, but watching him interact in a professional setting with a stranger is different. He's Dimitri with me, and he's confident, and straightforward, and witty, and charming, but watching him now is impressive, to say the least, and all kinds of sexy. I forget for a moment that we're ring shopping.

The salesman, Francois (I have a sneaking suspicion he's just Frank at home, but Francois sounds better for peddling rings with diamonds the size of my fist) shows us several cases with settings minus the diamonds. Apparently you pick the setting first and then you pick the diamond separately. That way you can pick the exact size and quality you want. The options are unlimited.

Francois takes in my blank expression and mistakenly confuses overwhelmed with dissatisfied. "Miss Smith, if none of these settings pleases you we have designers in house that would be happy to set up a consultation. They can design a custom ring that's tailored specifically to your taste and style. We wouldn't want your big day to be any less than absolutely perfect."

I smile obligatorily in response and I know it looks fake because it feels weird and strained.

This is *way* too fancy.

It's all too much. I pull Dimitri aside. "Dimitri, these are all *really* beautiful. And I think it's *really* nice, and just a touch crazy, that you want to drop insane amounts of money on an engagement ring for me. But," I pause. "I don't think any of these rings are *me*. Can we forego the whole big, obnoxious engagement ring thing and just buy matching wedding bands instead? I would be paranoid every minute of the day that someone was going to mug me with a fifteen thousand dollar ring on my finger. You shouldn't wear fifteen thousand dollars. You should put it in the bank ... or drive it."

He smiles, but I can tell that he's hurt. "I want to show you how much I love you."

I squeeze his hand. "You show me every day."

His face relaxes. "Wedding bands, huh?"

I nod.

"You're sure?"

I kiss his cheek. "Positive."

He smiles, and it's real this time. "Okay." He turns to Francois. "Change of plans, Frank."

We pick matching platinum bands (no diamonds) and make plans to pick them up a few days before the wedding. They have to be sized. Though Dimitri pays for them with his debit card on the spot, he won't let me see the total, which is probably good because I'd have an instantaneous aneurism.

He smiles the entire drive home and it makes me happy. "We're really doing it, aren't we?" I ask happily.

"Yup, we're doing this, Mrs. Glenn."

I correct him, "Mrs. Smith-Glenn."

He looks at me and raises an eyebrow. "Hyphenated, eh? Progressive. I like it."

I'm worried. "Really, or you just saying that?"

He nods. "Really."

"You don't think it's too, I don't know, pretentious?"

"Nope. I like it. It's your past and your future combined."

I smile. He gets it. "Exactly. I can't give up who I am. I'll always be Veronica Smith."

"Yes, you will. Forever. I think your parents would be touched by the gesture, Mrs. Veronica Smith-Glenn."

I grimace. "Wow, it sounds long when you say it like that."

His hand is resting on my thigh, a gesture that's recently become comfortable for us again. He squeezes my leg gently. "It's perfect. It's who you are."

The next several weeks are busy. Sunny is consumed with every detail of the wedding, which has been a huge help. I've found time most weeks to volunteer with Bob. It takes my mind off the stress of the wedding. We've gone to the homeless shelter, to his church, and an assisted living center nearby. I even donated blood for the first time in over a year. It makes me feel good in a way I haven't felt in a long time. Helping others is something that used to come naturally to me, but somehow I moved away from it ... or it moved away from me. Either way, I'm glad it's back. Plus I get to spend extra time with Bob, which is a bonus. Bob's like my new best friend. We have a lot in common, which is a bit crazy considering the 50-year age difference. Bob has a quiet wisdom that I admire.

So when I ask him an important question about the wedding a week before the big day he listens contemplatively ... and then he answers ... and it's the answer I need to hear. "Yes."

Life is sometimes ... your past and your future.

Chapter 24
Marriage is a beautiful arrangement
To which weddings are mandatory

The big day is here and Dimitri, Sunny, Sebastian, Bob, and I are taking the day to prepare. The wedding isn't until six-thirty tonight, but there's a lot to do. The weather couldn't be better, and there's not a cloud in the sky. The temperature this evening forecasts seventy-five degrees and no rain, so Sebastian's setting up the tables and chairs for the reception in the backyard near the waterfall, and Dimitri's stringing twinkle lights in all the trees. Bob is setting up chairs in the gallery, and Sunny is arranging flowers. And I'm trying to stay out of the way and not freak out.

We break for a late lunch, but I can't eat. I'm too nervous, so I excuse myself to the backyard to enjoy the weather and take a breather. The good thing is that everything is ready, and all we can do now is wait for the guests to start arriving around six. Three hours to burn, the majority of which I should probably spend showering and getting myself ready (that's what brides do on their wedding day, right?). I graciously and gratefully refused the fancy spa appointment Sunny tried to set up for me. (I have a one spa visit per lifetime rule. Quite honestly, they still frighten me). Besides, I want some time to myself to reflect on just how lucky I am to have arrived at this day.

Dimitri finds me sitting on a boulder in the backyard by the waterfall. It's quiet out here. He sits down next to me and hands me a bottle of water. "Hey you."

I take the water and smile. "Hey."

He puts his arm around me and kisses the top of my shoulder. "You ready for this?"

I lean my head on his shoulder. "Ready to be married to you, yes. It's just the wedding itself … " I trail off. "I think maybe I should've taken you up on your offer to go to Vegas weeks ago."

I feel his chest rise as he laughs quietly. He pulls my hair back from my face and tucks it behind my ear. "I can't

271

promise it won't be painful ... and extravagant. Sunny *is* involved, after all. But it will all be over in a few hours."

"We still have time to elope. They'll all have enchiladas and cupcakes to eat. Pedro's enchiladas are so freaking amazing, they won't even miss us." He's so easy to joke around with that I feel better already.

"Weddings are all about the food, right? That's the biggest reason why everyone is coming, anyway. Didn't you know? The whole wedding ceremony is just a sidebar. A precursor, if you will. They definitely wouldn't miss us."

I burst out laughing. This is what I needed: time alone with Dimitri. I raise my head to look at him. "I love you."

As he leans in to kiss me he whispers, "And that's a good thing, because you're stuck with me forever now."

The kiss is unexpectedly passionate. It's the best kind of distraction. Several minutes later I stop to catch my breath. He moans and pulls me back. I kiss him once and rest my forehead against his.

"Let's go upstairs," he pleads.

I put my hands on his cheeks and hold him, my forehead still resting against his; it takes everything I have to not take him by the hand, run upstairs to his old bedroom and rip his clothes off. "We can't."

He runs his hand up under the back of my T-shirt, under my bra strap and back down. It's hot. "We can."

"But we shouldn't." I run my hand down his cheek to his throat, to his chest, to his stomach, to the waist of his jeans. I curl my fingertips over the inside edge, my thumb hooking through a belt loop.

His voice catches. "Oh, we *definitely* should." He kisses my neck, over and over.

Every inch of my body is buzzing. I thought these sensations were gone forever, but they've made a miraculous comeback these past two months.

And then we hear someone clear his throat. "Jesus Christ, save it for the honeymoon already." We both jump at the sound of his voice. It's Sebastian. He loves to ruin a moment. He smiles. "D., Mom needs you. She needs help

272

moving the piano or something. I'm going to run Bob home. He forgot his tie."

Dimitri's cheeks are red. I don't know if it's from the kissing, or the heat, or both. I let go of Dimitri and stand up. I guess we do have a wedding to get to. I can't resist kissing him one more time as he stands. "I'm going to go shower while you help Sunny." I wink. "I've got this thing, this really important thing, that I need to get ready for."

He bites his lower lip, smiles and nods. No witty comeback, he just smiles. It's one of those special moments that hits you like a freight train. For that moment in time, everything is perfect. Not perfect in the true sense of the word, but it's exactly the way it should be. That's what this moment is. It's genuine and lovely. I wish I could wrap it up and tuck it away in a box so I could open it up later, over and over again. When I blink, it's gone. So, I say, "See you in a few hours, Mr. Glenn."

And he says, "I'll be the handsome one in the black suit, standing next to the priest."

I shower and do my hair and make-up and paint my toe nails in the bathroom in Dimitri's old bedroom. Sunny stops in a few times to check on me and to see if I need any help. I secretly think she's just dying to see what I'm wearing because I haven't told anyone. I want to surprise Dimitri. Not that I'm really into tradition, but that is the tradition, isn't it? He's not supposed to know. Just as I slip into my shoes I hear the doorbell ring. It's 5:57 and the first guests are arriving. All there is left for me to do now is wait.

At 6:20 there's a knock on the bedroom door. "Miss Veronica, may I come in?" I open the door to Bob's familiar smile.

"Miss Veronica, you look like a picture."

I blush. "Thanks, Bob."

"Place is filling up down there. Are you ready?"

I nod.

"Before we head down, I brought something for you. There's an old saying that goes along with weddings. I don't remember all of it, and I may not be remembering it

273

correctly, but I'm fairly certain there's a line about something borrowed and something blue."

I nod again. "I think I've heard that one."

He reaches into his suit coat pocket. "Well, I would be honored if you would wear this tonight. I don't know if it matches your dress—I'm not real good with that sort of thing—," he looks down, chuckling a bit to himself. "But it is blue." Lying in the palm of his hand is a delicate gold and sapphire bracelet.

The tears are welling up in my eyes and I take a deep breath in hopes of pushing them back. "Bob, it's beautiful. I would be proud to wear it."

I extend my arm and he fastens it around my wrist and then raises my hand and kisses the back of it. "It belonged to Alice. I know that seeing you wear it on this day would make her very happy, Miss Veronica."

All I can do is smile.

He looks at his pocket watch. "It's time." He smiles, eyes glistening, and thrusts his elbow out proudly. I slip my arm through. The polyester fabric of his suit coat is scratchy against my bare arm. Bob and Alice never had any daughters, so when I asked him if he would walk me down the aisle, it was something especially important for him. It's a big deal for me, too. I can't do this alone.

When we get down all the flights of stairs, I see Sunny sitting at the piano at the back of the gallery. She's fidgeting on the bench. She sees us as we approach and smiles sweetly before looking down at her sheet music. The wedding march begins and the priest asks everyone to stand. It's time.

The room is dimly lit overhead, but there are literally hundreds of candles strategically placed throughout the room. The gallery is absolutely glowing, and it's breathtaking.

Bob's pace is slow and steady, which is perfect because I'm about ready to blackout. High heels may have been a bad idea. I decide to focus on the faces around me. The crowd is small, about thirty people. The majority of them are Dimitri's family and friends, but I spot my guests quickly. Tate and Monica are first. Tate is giving me the thumbs up

274

and Monica is smiling. Her eyes are glistening. John and his mom are next. His mom blows me a kiss and John waves. And then there's Piper who's never hard to miss. She's bouncing in place, practically vibrating with nervous, happy energy. I'm smiling now. I'm glad they're here. This feels right.

We're near the end of aisle before I look up. The first thing I see is a wall of pink cascading from the ceiling to the floor. I have no idea how Sunny pulled it off, but it's extraordinary. She's a genius with flowers. And then I see the handsome guy, standing next to the priest, in front of the lilies. And all my worries melt away. He's beautiful. His suit is black, paired with a crisp white shirt. He's wearing his burgundy tie—the one he wore to dinner when we were in Las Vegas—just as I requested. His eyes are shining, and he's wearing a faint smile. It's the kind of smile that originates in the depths of your soul. So deep that by the time it reaches the surface it's faint, but so emotional it's almost painful. I know because I'm wearing it too, and I feel it.

Bob and I stop when we reach them. Directly before us is the priest, and to his left is Dimitri, and to his left is Sebastian. Sebastian smiles at Bob and me. The music stops and I hear Sunny's heels clicking up the aisle behind us as the crowd is seated.

"Who here gives Dimitri and Veronica to marriage?" The priest asks.

Sunny is standing beside me now. She reaches out and gives Dimitri's hand a squeeze. "I do." Then she whispers too low for anyone except Dimitri and me to hear. "I love you. Both of you."

The priest looks to Bob, whose arm is still interlocked with mine. Bob clears his throat. "I do, on behalf of William and Josephine."

I smile. I didn't realize he was going to say that. My hand involuntarily clutches the locket I'm wearing around my neck. The locket belonged to my mom, a gift from my dad on their wedding day. I've kept it stored away until today. It contains their wedding photo. I wanted them here with me. It seemed the best way.

The priest nods to Sunny and Bob to take their seats. Bob pats my arm before releasing it.

As they're taking their seats the priest leans forward and whispers to me, "Where is your maid of honor, dear?"

I pat the locket hanging over my heart. "They're right here."

He concedes with a nod and begins the ceremony. It all passes in a blur. I can't focus on anything except those gorgeous gray eyes locked with mine. They're shining with tears and happiness. I'm not taking in individual moments, just those eyes.

I repeat the priest's words when I'm asked to, as does Dimitri. And I place the ring on Dimitri's finger when I'm asked to, as does Dimitri. But when I hear the words, "You may now kiss the bride," I'm fully alert. All of my senses come back in a rush. I smell lilies and sandalwood. I see Sebastian grinning ear to ear. I hear whistling and cheering from our friends and family. And I feel the warmth of Dimitri's hands on either side of my face as I breathe in his kiss. His lips are soft and taste like vanilla. It's heavenly.

The priest looks to our guests and gestures toward us. "I now present to you, Mr. and Mrs. Glenn."

Dimitri takes my hand. "Shall we, Mrs. Smith-Glenn?"

I smile and nod. I can't believe I'm married to this precious person. How did this happen? What makes me so special to deserve someone like him?

As we walk down the aisle to the cheers of our family and friends, he leans in and whispers. "I love the dress, though you may have warned me. I was prepared for floor-length white, something concealing and chaste … and virginal. Instead, you look *hot*. Do you think anyone noticed that I had to pick my jaw up off the floor when you walked down the aisle?"

I wink. "It's your own fault. You picked it out." I decided to wear the burgundy dress Dimitri gave me in Las Vegas. I realize it's not standard issue white and it is very revealing, but I'm not a big fan of tradition. I wanted to feel pretty on my wedding day and this is the prettiest dress I've ever seen. So, I thought, why not?

We stop outside and he pulls me aside before the crowd follows. "I love that you asked Bob to walk you down the aisle. Well done. He was *so* proud. Wait until you see the pictures."

"He's special. And since my dad couldn't be here … " I trail off sadly.

He gestures to my locket. "May I?"

I nod.

He opens it gently and smiles knowingly at the image inside. "I knew it." He snaps it shut and kisses my forehead. "They made it after all."

We are interrupted by hugs and kisses and photos and more hugs and more kisses and more photos. Then we all proceed outside to enjoy the evening reception. Dinner lives up to its reputation and exceeds my expectations. Everyone finishes up their cupcakes as darkness descends. The twinkle lights act as backdrop for us to circulate the yard and personally thank everyone individually for coming. I am so blessed to have reconnected with Tate, Monica, John, and Piper this summer. Teagan's death was the unfortunate catalyst, but I am so, so grateful to have them all in my life again. I won't lose them twice. Tate, Monica, and John are all leaving to go back to various out-of-state colleges next week, and Piper's moving to Puerto Rico next month, so the wedding's timing couldn't have been better.

At ten-thirty, Dimitri reminds me of the time. "We'd better get going or we'll miss our flight."

The majority of them have gone home. It is a Monday night after all, and most of them have to be to work in the morning. A few of Dimitri's relatives from Texas are staying with Sunny for a few days and have moved into the kitchen to talk. We say our goodbyes and give our last hugs.

Sunny hugs us both at once and kisses each of us on the cheek. "I want you to know how much I love you both. Congratulations. Be careful on your trip and have fun. Take lots of pictures."

Sebastian hugs Dimitri next and says something I can't hear and then he hugs me, "Welcome to the family, Ronnie.

It's strange to say that, because I've always thought of you as family, just like my sister. I love you."

I feel the same way. "I love you, too."

We wave to the rest and run out the back door to the garage. Dimitri packed our suitcases yesterday (he's being very secretive about our trip) and put them in the Porsche so they'd be ready to go tonight. Just as I'm about to click my seatbelt in place I look down at my wrist and see the bracelet winking at me in the light. "Hold on a minute, I'll be right back."

I run back inside, to Sunny's surprise, "Where's Bob?"

"I believe he's sitting in the living room."

He is. He's sitting on the big leather sofa watching an old sitcom, and from the look of the unnatural angle of his neck I would bet he's asleep. I tip toe around in front of him and find that he is. I kneel before him and jostle his shoulder gently. It takes a moment for him adjust to wakefulness.

"I'm so sorry to wake you Bob, but I wanted to return the bracelet." I take his hand and turn it palm side up curling his fingers around it. "It was so thoughtful of you. It meant a lot to me to wear it during my wedding day"

He smiles and his tired eyes twinkle. "You're welcome, Miss Veronica. Alice will be pleased to hear you wore it. I'll tell her tomorrow when I visit her."

"You'll tell her thank you for me?"

He nods. "I will."

I pat his knee and stand. Before I exit the room I stop. I turn around and say, "I love you Bob."

He turns his head stiffly. "I love you too, Miss Veronica."

Life is sometimes … ceremonious.

Chapter 25
L'attente est terminée

The flight departs at 12:45am. I still have no clue where we're headed, though I suspect it's international since Dimitri insisted I get a passport. Dimitri covers my eyes as we approach the gate so I can't read the sign and then places me strategically in a seat in the waiting area without a clear view of it. I can't hear any of the announcements that are most likely being made over the concourse speakers, because I'm listening to his iPod with earbuds. He's thoroughly keeping me in the dark. I don't mind. He put a lot of thought and time into planning the honeymoon so I don't want to ruin the surprise.

As soon as we take our seats in first class I remove the earbuds and ask the flight attendant for a blanket. I'm still wearing the dress and have Dimitri's suit coat on over it, but my legs are chilly. "We should've changed clothes," I tell him.

He shakes his head.

"Why not? We would've been more comfortable."

"I don't think you understand how incredible you look in that dress. It does crazy things to me. I'm thinking about calling the store in Vegas to see if I can buy six more in your size, so that way you can wear one every day of the week." He looks like he means it.

"It's more a special occasion dress. I don't see myself pushing the shopping cart around the supermarket in it."

He coils his arms around me. "You know, I'm never going to think about grocery shopping the same way again. I might even take up cooking to encourage extra trips," he says, smiling roguishly.

"Thanks for always making me feel beautiful and loved."

"You are. Always," he says, kissing my forehead.

The flight attendant returns with a blanket. "Is there anything else I can get you?"

"A pillow, if it wouldn't be too much trouble," Dimitri requests.

279

"No trouble at all." She looks to me. "And you, miss?"

"I'm fine, thank you."

She nods. "Well, let me know if you change your mind, the flight to Paris is a long one."

I'm stunned. "Can you repeat that please? I'm not sure I heard you correctly."

She looks puzzled, but repeats, "I said, let me know if you change your mind."

"No, the last part, can you repeat the last part please?"

"The flight to Paris is long?"

"Shut the front door! Are we really going to Paris?"

She's looking at me like I have two heads.

Dimitri is sitting in the aisle seat closest to her. He cups his hand to his mouth toward her as if to hide what he's about to say, but he doesn't lower his voice. "We were married tonight and we're going to Paris for our honeymoon, somewhere my wife has always wanted to visit. The destination has been a secret ... until now. You'll have to excuse her; she may be experiencing symptoms of temporary shock."

The flight attendant smiles. "I'm sorry to have spoiled the surprise." She looks apologetically to me. "Can you forgive me?"

"Are you kidding? Of course! I'm on my way to Paris! I'd kiss you if you were closer."

She laughs. "Well, congratulations to both of you."

"Thanks so much," Dimitri says, and glances at her nametag. "Gabrielle, you can call me Dimitri." He gestures toward me. "And this is my wife, Veronica."

I wave.

She smiles. "Very well Dimitri and Veronica. I'll be right back with that pillow."

I'm trying to keep my voice down as I turn back to Dimitri and say, "Oh my God, we're really going to Paris?" Despite all the excitement of my wedding day, this news has given me butterflies all over again.

He smiles and nods. "Where else would we possibly go? It's our honeymoon. I thought you figured it out weeks ago."

"No. I know it's going to sound stupid, but I thought we were going to a beach, somewhere tropical. Isn't that what people do on their honeymoons?"

"A beach? We don't even swim." He pauses. "Although that would have meant you in a bikini for a week." He hits the heel of his hand against his forehead. "God, I'm such an idiot, why didn't I think of that? You're planning all the honeymoons from here on out." He looks at me and winks and then reaches down to squeeze my knee. "Paris is the most romantic city in the world. What better place for a honeymoon?" He whispers in my ear, "And honeymoons aren't just about beaches. They're supposed to be all about romance, and love, and sex … and romance, and sex … Did I mention sex?"

I giggle. "I thought the point of traveling was to see the sights and have experiences you wouldn't normally have at home."

He kisses my neck. "Oh, I intend to return home quite experienced."

Judging from the playfulness in his voice I don't think he's referring to the Eiffel Tower or brushing up on his French.

We sleep for most of the flight. It's direct: Denver to Paris. I've been spoiled by first-class seats and all the hot tea I want, which makes the nine hour trip breeze by. We eat a meal about an hour before landing—croissants wrapped in plastic with small cups of yogurt and small, waxy apples. Over the intercom our captain tells us that there's patchy fog and that the landing will be bumpy. "The time in Paris is seven o'clock in the evening," the voice crackles.

Our plane lands and we're off and into baggage claim in no time. Airport signs are in French obviously, but it's still surreal, something I never dreamed I'd ever see. I'm in the midst of sensory overload and we haven't even left the airport yet. As we step outside I'm picturing all of the landmarks I'm going to see while we're here. I stand on my tiptoes and peer around like I'm going to be able to see the Eiffel Tower from here. The fog is thickening and the sun, though barely visible, is getting low, not exactly perfect sightseeing conditions even if we weren't standing on a sidewalk outside the airport. I remind myself we have five days.

My French is rusty, but as I chat with the cab driver it starts coming back. The ride ends at a hotel that appears to be hundreds of years old yet pristine. Three doormen descend as the cab pulls to the curb. They have our suitcases loaded on a cart before Dimitri has even paid for the ride.

"Merci," I say, waving to the cabbie as I crawl out of the backseat. I'm already enjoying this trip more than I thought possible. I feel like I'm back in school on some sort of far-fetched field trip and Madame Lemieux, my former French teacher, is going to pull up in a bus behind us with the rest of my class any minute now.

The doormen greet us in French and whisk us inside to the check-in desk. The lobby is fancy, *really* fancy and déjà vu creeps over me. Dread squirms deep in the pit of my stomach. It's the same feeling I had outside the jewelry store when we went ring shopping. This place is too nice for me. And then I watch Dimitri; he isn't fazed in the least. And his French—his *French!*—is amazing. He told me once that he spoke a little French. But he lied. He's *fluent*. And he's confident, straightforward, witty, and charming … *in French*. This is unbelievably impressive, and beyond sexy. I'm stunned. And I'm no longer feeling inadequate. I'm feeling turned-on.

Five minutes later we're on our way to our room.

"Why didn't you tell me you spoke French?" I ask as we enter the tiny elevator. He's swinging our hands back and forth between us.

He smiles like he's just given up a secret. "I did tell you."

I narrow my eyes. "You said you spoke a little French. That was *not* a little … that was *goddamn sexy* is what that was."

His eyebrows raise and he grins wickedly. "Well then, any chance I might get lucky tonight, *Madame?*"

I nod slowly. "Oh, *oui*," I say, forcefully pinning him against the elevator doors with my kisses. He answers without restraint. We stumble out when the doors open.

Dimitri fumbles with the heavy iron key as he tries to open the door. It takes several attempts and I hear grumbling under his breath before the door finally cooperates and opens.

Our bags are already stacked neatly just inside the door, so there's no chance of an interruption from hotel staff. Nice.

He stops me before I step inside, and sweeps me up in his arms in one gallant motion. I gasp as my feet leave the ground. "What are you doing?" I ask, giggling.

"I'm carrying you over the threshold." He winks. "It's tradition."

I feel the heat of his body through the fabric of his shirt and my dress. His arms are strong around me. I run my hand up through the hair at the back of his head. "I think I'm warming up to tradition."

"That's good, because there's one last wedding night tradition that I'm dying to try out."

He kicks the door shut behind us with his foot and carries me to the king size bed. It's covered in a gold silky comforter and lots and lots of pillows. The bed is tall and he doesn't have to lean over to lay me down upon it.

His body never leaves contact with mine as we hit the bed. He's on top of me; though it's not the weight of him that's taking my breath away. It's him. Everything about him. My body, from the tips of my toes to the top of my head, is on fire. The heat is rising slow and steady, filling me up.

His hands slide over the slippery surface of my dress from my waist, up over my ribs, and across my chest; they pause before touching bare skin where the neckline plunges. His touch is hot, as if the blood pulsing through him has risen in temperature several degrees. His hands stop to rest at my temples as his fingers lace into my hair. He smiles before he lowers his face to kiss me. I close my eyes and inhale as I anticipate his lips on mine.

There's a hitch in my breathing as I feel the tip of his tongue at the hollow of my throat instead. It traces a line slowly downward where it stops between my breasts, restrained by the fabric of my dress. Kisses make the return trip and fall on every square inch of exposed skin until they reach my collarbone. I feel the strap of my dress pull aside and the kisses continue across my shoulder leaving my skin burning with sensation in their wake. The last kiss lingers and I feel the faintest bite on my upper arm and the devilish impression of a smile sinks into my skin. I keep my eyes closed and focus completely on his touch.

The tip of his nose brushes softly following the line below my collarbone, up my throat, under my chin; back down my throat to my other shoulder where he pulls the remaining strap aside with his teeth.

I have not moved up until this point, in a state of paralyzed arousal. I exhale loudly and pull up his shirttail to release it from beneath his waistband. He's already unbuttoned the top few buttons so I strip his shirt off over his head and throw it on the floor next to the bed. My hands explore his torso like a sculptor working clay. The muscles across his chest and stomach are rigid. I can feel the excitement pulsing through him. He's coiled up tighter than a spring.

Before I know it, every piece of clothing has been removed and we're pressed against each other, breathing heavily, completely committed to this animalistic act of lust and love.

The kissing is so exacting and intense I have the feeling it's not really kissing anymore. Like we've crossed over into a whole new world—a place no one's ever been before. Then suddenly the kissing slows and softens … and pauses. Dimitri is breathing deeply, gritting his teeth. A few seconds later the look of concentration passes and he whispers, "Are you ready?"

My heart is slamming against the inside of my chest and the sensation of burning has engulfed me. I nod and whisper, "Say something in French."

He moans, "Je ne peux plus attendre. Je te veux tout de suite," as his mouth descends on mine and I feel flooded with an urgent heat and desire like I've never felt.

Life is sometimes … burning.

Chapter 26
Forget not
Regret not
Live

The night is the best night of my entire life. Some things are worth waiting for. In fact, I would have waited a lifetime for last night. Ten lifetimes even.

We fall asleep just as the sun's beginning to rise and rest blissfully until noon. When I open my eyes, Dimitri's awake and propped up on one elbow, gazing at me and sweeping my hair away from my eyes.

"Bonjour, Madame Smith-Glenn."

I smile. "Bonjour, Monsieur Glenn."

He smiles. "You're right, speaking French is sexy."

I laugh and rub my eyes. Mid-yawn I ask, "What are we going to do today?"

He wraps me up in his arms. "Someone wise once told me—" he says, kissing my temple, "—that the point of travelling—" he kisses me again on the neck, "—is to have experiences—" and again on my shoulder.

"I think that I'd like," I say, as he nuzzles his nose into the crook of my neck, "some more of that." I kiss the tip of his nose. "But I think she also said something about sightseeing."

He sighs and rolls over on his back, releasing his hold on me and looking at the ceiling in mock defeat, "There is also that I suppose." He looks at me and winks. "Where do you want to go first?"

The next five days are a whirlwind of unforgettable sights during the day and unforgettable experiences during the night.

We recount it all on the plane ride home: the Eiffel Tower (kissing at the top under a full moon), the Seine (walking hand in hand at twilight when the air was still warm), Notre Dame, the Louvre, the Arc de Triomphe, the Champs-Elysées, the Jardin du Luxembourg, the Sorbonne,

286

the Panthéon, the patisserie in the 7th (I think Dimitri is addicted to pistachio macaroons), and the hotel. God, I'll *never* forget that hotel.

I loved every moment of Paris, but I'm so glad to be home. Our home. *Mr. and Mrs. Glenn's* home. I'm so happy to share it with him. Sometimes it feels like he literally gives me the world. Even though I know money isn't important to him, the scales are extremely out of balance. I don't want to be a burden, but I know I'll never make the kind of money he does. So it gives me some satisfaction that I'm able to provide us with a home, albeit sparsely-furnished.

Sunny remodeled the kitchen while we were in Paris, our surprise wedding gift. And over the weeks following the honeymoon, we manage to purchase all of the items we'd been lacking. Our house looks amazing. I guess that's what happens when your mother-in-law is an interior designer though. I swear she's half fairy and uses pixie dust or something; she's magical. Over the next few weeks, Dimitri converts half of the garage into his art studio and office and can now work from home full time—except for when he's traveling. The gallery remains at Sunny's for obvious reasons, but the walls of our home slowly become covered with paintings. Some are permanent (gifts to me), and others are on rotation; I'm sad to see them go when they're sold, because I get attached.

My birthday comes in October, and I'm reduced to tears when I come home from work to find Dimitri sitting in the front room playing "Happy Birthday" on a brand new upright piano—*my* piano. He's serenading me with a cheesy rendition of the song, singing loudly and finishing with "you look like a monkey and you smell like one too."

"Why are you crying, baby?" he asks, laughing, when he finishes. "I was only joking." I walk over to the piano bench, where he pulls me down to sit on his lap. "You don't really smell like a monkey," he says softly, wiping my cheeks with his thumb.

I laugh through the tears. "You didn't have to do this." It's been months since I've shed a tear and I seem to have opened the floodgates. "Thank you. I'm sorry I'm crying.

287

It's just overwhelming to see a piano sitting here again. I didn't realize how much I missed it."

He strokes my hair. "I know. But you're twenty years old today. I hear that's the perfect age to start taking piano lessons. Twenty's the new ten," he says, smiling sheepishly. "Or something like that. And I know this incredibly handsome, and talented, and patient piano teacher who works for next to nothing. Did I mention he's really handsome? I know that may be a little distracting, but you're a married woman and would never be tempted by such—"

I interrupt him with a kiss. "Thank you. It was really thoughtful. And I would love for you to teach me."

He acts playfully shocked. "What? Me? How'd you know?"

There are two small pieces of paper folded over and safety pinned to his shirt. I flip the one on the left with my finger. It says: "Incredibly handsome, talented, patient piano teacher for hire."

He rolls his eyes mockingly. "Oh, I completely forgot I was wearing that."

Then I flip the other one. "Can I work off a tab or do you demand payment at the time services are rendered?" It says, "Will work for sex." I laugh. Sex is still new and exciting for us, *really* exciting for him—to the point of near preoccupation. But what can I say, he is a boy, and he waited a long time for me.

He's still in character. "I'm glad you noticed. I try to be upfront. It's a bit embarrassing when my clients aren't privy to my terms ahead of time and then there's this whole, 'Oh my God, what are you doing?' reaction when I take my clothes off at the end of the lesson. Believe me," he says, shaking his head and exhaling dramatically. "It's much more enjoyable for everyone this way."

"It's come to prostituting yourself in return for piano lessons? For shame, Dimitri. Clearly we need to find you a hobby." I pause, and then kiss his temple. "Really … I mean it, thank you."

He hugs me tightly and kisses me on the cheek. "You're welcome, Ronnie. Happy birthday. I love you."

"I love you, too."

The lessons begin the next afternoon, and we manage to fit them in at least twice a week, though Dimitri insists I practice every other day. I don't mind; in fact, I enjoy it. It's an escape. And to my surprise I'm good at it. It comes easy, just like Dimitri always said it would. Dimitri's an excellent teacher. He's talented and patient, just as advertised (he's also handsome, and contrary to terms, he rarely demands payment on the spot. He's taken to keeping a running tab on the back of my sheet music, though).

I also decide it's time to start taking colleges classes. Dimitri is thrilled. He was understanding, but disappointed, when I let my scholarship to the University of Colorado slip away after my parents' death, and I think the more time that passed, the more he thought I had resigned completely. I've decided to apply for my first two years at a community college near our home. Tuition is a fraction of the cost of a state university, and all of the credits will transfer. My goal is to finish up my degree at the University of Colorado eventually. I'm registered to start classes in January, and I've worked my class schedule around my work schedule. Sunny's very flexible and encouraging, and it will allow me to continue working full-time for her while taking a full load of classes. I'll be busy. But I like busy.

Come January, I realize that I'm not just busy. I'm *crazy* busy. But I guess I got what I wished for. Working and going to school is a huge commitment, but Dimitri and I adjust quickly and get into a routine. I take classes through the spring and into the summer, too, in hopes of making up for lost time. Dimitri travels a lot, showing his art at exhibits in several East Coast galleries. He's even asked to display paintings at two contemporary art museums. He's so humble and never makes a big deal of it, but it *is* a big deal. And if he's not going to be outwardly proud, then I'll be proud enough for both of us.

Dimitri also starts taking guitar lessons. He said he's played for a long time, but he wants to improve. I've never heard him play, even though I've begged him to many times.

289

He says he'll play for me when he feels up to par. Knowing him, that will be at the point that he could easily join a rock band and tour the world. And I thought I was critical of myself. Dimitri is the real perfectionist.

We ramble on blissfully through our first year of marriage. God, I love him. He's my best friend, my other half. He makes me happy like no one else can. We never argue. And aside from the fact that his clothes can never quite make it *in* the clothes hamper (it seems they always fall short … like two inches short … on the floor *next* to the hamper), there's nothing irritating about him. I know no one's perfect, but Dimitri's perfect for me. We balance one another. And we've been through a lot. It feels so good to be at peace, taking care of each other day-to-day.

Our first wedding anniversary is low key, mainly due to the fact that I'm going to school non-stop and he's buried in his work. When Valentine's Day approaches months later, he insists we take a long weekend and get away from our obligations.

"Where do you want to go?" I ask, excited by the prospect of a reprieve, if only for a few days.

He wraps me up in his arms and says, "I would love to go back to that hotel in Paris. We saw all the sights last time, so this time we'd only need to concern ourselves with the—what did you call it—experiences?"

I confirm with a nod, "Experiences. I'd love too, but that's a long trip for a weekend. I think we'd better settle on somewhere closer."

"Damn time constraints," he mutters under his breath. He stares off, thinking of alternatives.

I wink. "Experiences can be had just about anywhere," I say, suggestively.

He smiles wickedly. "True. What about Jackson, Wyoming? We could stay at Mom's house." Sunny kept the house they lived in with Dimitri's dad, and she uses it as a vacation home now. We've been there a few times, mostly over the holidays. It's great, but it's full-on winter in Wyoming.

"I'd really like to go someplace warmer, where we can be outside. I'm *so* over winter."

He nods. "*Outside* experiences. I like the way you think."

I roll my eyes. Though the idea kind of excites me, at the moment I don't let on.

He's deep in thought again. "Warmer, like beach-warm, or southern-states warm?"

"Umm … southern states warm would work."

His eyes search mine. "Ever been to the Grand Canyon?"

I smile. "You would be safe to assume that if I haven't been there with you, I haven't been there."

"The Grand Canyon it is then. It's so impressive; I think you'll love it."

"Any math exams or research papers due at the Grand Canyon?"

He smiles. "I haven't been since I was a kid, but no, not that I recall."

"Perfect."

The Grand Canyon is impressive, to say the least. The colors are so vivid. The formations so vast they seem to go on forever in the distance. It looks like a painting. We spend the first day hiking and are famished by dinnertime. After consuming stupid amounts of food we return to the hotel where we immediately fall into a state of sleep so near comatose it's almost scary. We are exhausted. I'm definitely out of shape.

The second day is Valentine's Day. The first half of the day is spent on a long drive around the canyon taking lots of pictures. Dimitri informs me this is the "sightseeing" portion of the day.

The "experiences" portion of the day is spent at a five star hotel in Phoenix that evening. That particular evening may go down in history as one of my favorites. There's Champagne, pink lilies, candles—lots of candles. And Dimitri—lots of Dimitri.

The trip ends all too quickly, and a couple of weeks later I'm lost in school and work. One morning before a test, I wake up with something tugging at my memory. It's heavy. Like there's something I've forgotten. I scan my brain for clues but just feel an overwhelming sense of urgency. For the life of me, I cannot figure it out. Even after my test, the feeling follows me through the day. I try to shrug it off, but it clings to me. It makes me feel uncomfortable, like I'm walking around without pants, or like I've lost something without knowing what the thing is.

I'm unlocking my car (I finally broke down and bought one this past summer. Her name is Hazel, because she's not at all "sexy" but more "reliable" and "solid") after finishing up from work when I feel a sudden knot in my stomach. And then I feel incredibly dizzy, like I've just stepped off a roller coaster. I open the car door and take a seat behind the wheel, digging through my bag for my phone. I open up my calendar, it's my lifeline, and look at today's date, tracing back one day, two days, three days … panic begins to gnaw at me. I continue to count: four days, five days, six days, seven days …

"Shit!" I say to myself. I close my eyes and take a deep breath. My period is a week late. I'm *never* late. But, I can't be pregnant; I've been on The Pill since just before our wedding. And I take them faithfully …

Except when I forgot them at home when we went to Phoenix.

"Shit!"

This cannot be happening, I think. We haven't talked much about having kids. I know he thinks getting pregnant is a long shot. When we first discussed birth control over a year ago he mentioned he had some fertility concerns due to a childhood illness, but he never went into detail about it. Which was fine with me, I always assumed, though I never vocalized it, that we'd adopt if it wasn't possible for me to actually get pregnant. He knows I want a child, but I want one when it's time, after I've graduated from college and started a career. When I'm a real grown-up and prepared for the responsibility.

I sit for several minutes trying to decide what to do. After some intense internal dialogue, I decide it's best not to worry Dimitri until I know for sure. I stop at the drug store on my way home and buy a home pregnancy test. I feel self-conscious buying it. I know nobody's paying attention and nobody cares, but I feel like everyone is staring, judging me, like I've done something wrong. I want to scream at the top of my lungs. "I may be knocked up, but I'm 21 years old and I've been married for over a year, for Christ's sake!"

Dimitri is home when I arrive, so I put the box in my bag and try to act normal.

He's washing paint off his hands at the kitchen sink when I walk in the back door, but makes a point to stretch his neck out for a kiss as I walk past him. "Hi baby, how was your day?"

"Great," I say, in an unnaturally high-pitched tone. He looks concerned. I clear my throat. "I mean, it was good. You know." Desperately, I point to the hall. "I really need to use the bathroom. I've been holding it all the way home."

He nods, but eyes me suspiciously. "By all means, go ahead." He knows something's up.

Once out of the kitchen, I run to the bathroom and lock the door behind me. I read the instructions; because this is important ... actually I don't think important covers it. Momentous, serious, life-changing ... there isn't a word readily available in my vocabulary, possibly the English language, to describe the significance. I've never been so nervous in my life to just pee. I take a deep breath and remind myself of my mother's mantra: "Everything happens for a reason."

And I pee.

And I wait.

It's the longest five minutes of my life.

Life is sometimes ... a waiting game.

Chapter 27
Biology is simple
Babies are not

Sitting on the edge of the tub is uncomfortable, but it affords me the most space, within the confines of the tiny bathroom, I can put between myself and the pregnancy test perched precariously on its box inside the sink basin. I swear the walls are moving, closing in on me, as the last minute of the five ticks by. Time's up. I give the second hand another trip around the dial before I stand.

My legs feel like rubber. I'm feeling that strange dizzy feeling again, and the knot in my stomach seems to have expanded. I take two short steps to the sink, but my eyes refuse my brain's command to look in the sink. My eyelids pinch together tightly, and I wonder momentarily if I'll ever be brave enough to open them. I place my shaky hands firmly on the countertop, where the trembling isn't as noticeable. That gives me strength. I breathe two deep inhales and exhales, tip my head down directly over the sink, and ...

On the count of three I'll open my eyes, I tell myself.

"One."

"Two."

"Three ... "

"Four."

"Five."

"Six ... "

Another deep breath ...

Open. I see the symbol. It's glaring, bright, and bold. It's unmistakable, undeniable ...

I'm pregnant.

We're pregnant.

Ten separate emotions bombard me simultaneously, each distinct and palpable, appealing their case: fear, hope, apprehension, relief, guilt, excitement, shock, joy, denial, and humility. They roar against one another in a tempest and a lone survivor evolves and emerges ... acceptance.

I can deal with this. I *have* to deal with this. There's a tiny human being growing and multiplying deep inside me at this very moment. And I swear, now that I know, now that it's been confirmed, I feel different. I feel pregnant. I know I can't feel the baby, but I *feel the baby*. It's there, and it's *ours*.

What will Dimitri's reaction be? There's only one way to find out.

"Dimitri, can you come here please?" my voice quivers.

His voice comes immediately from the other side of the door. "I'm here." I should've known he'd be waiting outside; I've been in here for a long time. He's probably worried, especially with my strange behavior earlier.

I open the door slowly.

"Is everything okay?" he asks, his voice heavy with worry.

I shrug. "That depends." I attempt a smile.

Not the right answer, he's beyond concerned now. "Depends on what?"

I glance down at the test and box still lying in the sink. "Depends on whether or not—" I pause, looking back into his eyes. "—you're ready to be a father."

He takes two big steps back from me, his body hitting the wall behind him with a soft thud. He slides down slowly until it slumps in a heap on the floor. His face rests in his palms.

I suck it a sharp breath and reach toward him. I don't know what I expected him to say, but we're probably both in shock. This is unexpected to say the least; it's life changing.

He rubs his eyes, and at this sign of movement I kneel next to him and rub his back. "Dimitri, I—"

Before I can continue he wraps his arms around me so tightly that I can hardly breathe. His face rests against the base of my neck and all I register besides the strength of his embrace is the wetness of his cheeks. He's crying. I feel it rippling through him like waves.

His grip on me lets up to a comfortable embrace, and I stroke his hair. "I'm sorry Dimitri. I should have been more careful."

He pulls back instantly at my words and looks into my eyes as if he's searching, so anxious he can't contain himself. "Sorry ... you're *sorry?*"

I nod as confusion takes over.

He grips my shoulders and, although it seems impossible, the look in his eyes intensifies. "This is quite possibly the single most significant bit of news I have *ever* received, and for me that's saying a lot. Ronnie, I never in a million years thought I would be a father. I had a severe case of the mumps as I child, and sterility is the consequence I live with. At least that's what the doctors have always told me. And you've always wanted a child—the one thing I couldn't give you ... " His voice trails off. The tears are shining brightly in his eyes. "By some miracle I can't understand, we've been blessed with a child. The last thing you should be is sorry. Today we are the two luckiest people on the planet." He places his hand tenderly on my stomach. "I love you, Ronnie. And I promise to be the best father I can be."

I'm crying now, too. I feel happy, and relieved. I hadn't realized how much I wanted him to say those words. "You will be, baby. You'll be amazing."

The pregnancy immediately takes over our lives and becomes the most important thing in our world. Sunny's world, too—from the moment she hears the news, which is about one hour after we find out, she wins the prize for proudest, most enthusiastic grandparent-to-be. Sebastian, after being roused out of shock, is thrilled for us. I suppose he knew about his brother's condition and thought biological fatherhood would be impossible, too.

Doctor's appointments become yet another piece to fit into the complex puzzle that is my busy schedule. Sunny insists I cut back my hours at her studio, which makes everything much more manageable. If only it relieved morning sickness and a constant state of fatigue, I'd be golden.

By the third month, my nausea subsides and my waistline begins growing noticeably. I can no longer hide it—and even my favorite, loose sweat pants don't fit anymore. Dimitri is absolutely, obsessively in love with my belly. Every night when we go to bed he lays with his head resting on my ever-growing midsection. He listens to the gurgles and talks to the baby. It's sweet, especially since I can't feel the baby moving yet myself.

At the halfway point of the pregnancy, twenty weeks, we have an appointment for an ultrasound to determine the sex of the baby. It is now only a week away, and I can't wait. There are lists and preparations to be made. I know some people want to be surprised at the birth, but I feel a deeply rooted need to have everything decided, planned, and purchased at least one month prior to my due date (which is November 16th). I'm neurotic and I know it, but I'm proud of it at this point in my life. There are already enough unknowns that come along with bringing a baby into this world. Those still scare the hell out of me, so you better believe anything and everything that's under my control *will* be under control by the time this baby makes an appearance.

The subject of names has come up a few times, but it never went anywhere. I thought Dimitri's boy names weren't unique enough, or if they were unique they were just too weird. And he said my girl name sounded like a prostitute. After that we didn't discuss it again. We refer to the baby only as "Baby." The subject is put to rest for a month or so until the night before the ultrasound.

I'm lying in bed propped up against several pillows and Dimitri, as is his ritual, is lying with his face toward me, his head resting just over my belly button. His hand is massaging the area of my belly just in front of his nose (he jokes it gives him good luck). He's looking at me. "Are you going to be disappointed if Baby isn't a boy?"

"Yup, and I'm blaming it all on you. Father determines sex, right?" I raise my eyebrows and he knows I'm kidding. "Growing up I always pictured myself having one child, a boy. But, you know what? After carrying Baby around for a few months and enjoying every moment, good or bad, of this miracle that is taking place inside me, I really don't care. A boy or a girl would be equally... exceptionally ... wonderful."

He smiles. "Good. That's how I feel, too."

We enjoy the silence for several minutes until I notice that Dimitri is staring intently at the painting hanging behind me over the bed. He stops rubbing my belly and asks, "Have you given anymore thought to names?"

I shake my head. "No, I don't think I'm ready to burden myself with the guilt of perpetuating career choice in the direction of solicitation or stripper. So no, no I haven't."

He laughs; clearly he remembers the prostitute comment. "We agree it has to be unique though, right?"

"Yes."

"But not *weird* unique, like outrageous spellings that no one would ever figure out?"

"Yes."

"And it would be nice if it meant something to us, if it was special?"

"Of course that would be nice," I say.

He returns his gaze to the painting, "I think I have the perfect name, boy or girl. It's unique and special and has significance to us."

I follow his eyes, turning my head so that I can see the painting on the wall behind us. We say it in unison, "Phoenix."

"Phoenix," I repeat quietly. He smiles hearing me say it aloud. "I love it," I say. And I do.

"I do too," he says, kissing my belly.

"Plus, there's a good story to go along with it," I say, winking.

He narrows his eyes. "You mean, aside from the awesome painting and tales of fantastical birds that rise from their ashes to live again?"

I tilt my head and look at him suspiciously. "Actually I was thinking of the story that involves a fantastical city that rises from the desert. You know, the one where your baby was conceived?"

He winks. "Aha, there is that, too." He presses himself up and sits beside me, taking my hand in his. "Here's to fantastic experiences, fantastical cities, *and* fantastical birds."

I smile. "Phoenix it is then, boy or girl."

We arrive at the doctor's office the next day anxious to find out if our Phoenix is a he or a she. Apparently Phoenix is ready too, because I feel Baby moving for the first time. I've pulled my shirt up, and a technician has applied generous amounts of slimy gel to my belly. The technician places a cold instrument to my skin. It's attached to a twisty cord that runs up to a machine with a display screen. After a few blips and blurry lines, an alien-like figure appears on the screen. The sight is more emotional than I was prepared for, and tears emerge from my wide eyes. The figure is our baby, complete with little fingers and toes. I watch in awe as Phoenix moves on the screen. The technician looks for critical information first, taking measurements and tracking development of organs and bones. We are relieved to hear everything looks perfect.

The technician looks at us, smiling, and verifies, "You would like to know the sex if I am able to determine it, is that correct?"

We both nod, holding our breath.

She repositions the instrument and Phoenix moves to reveal his anatomy. There's no mistake. I see it before she confirms, "Well, it's pretty obvious ... " she begins to say, smiling.

Dimitri is tilting his head back and forth squinting at the screen. "Obvious? I can't even tell what we're looking at here."

In his defense, the image is very grainy and blurred, and Phoenix is upside down. The technician points to the screen at a specific area, and says, "You're having a little boy."

His eyes widen in realization. "Oh ... *Oh! We certainly are!*" He squeezes my hand and we both cry little sobs of joy, staring at our tiny little one on the screen.

My tears have dried by the time we get to the car. Dimitri opens the car door for me and helps me in. Getting in and out of the Porsche is not as easy as it once was. He climbs in next to me, but doesn't start the car. He just stares at me and his eyes are radiant.

I return the smile. "So, we're having a baby boy."

He leans over and kisses me on the lips, then leans down to kiss my belly once again. "Phoenix William Glenn, we love you." He sits up and places hands on either side of my face, "Veronica Josephine Smith-Glenn, I love you," and he kisses me again.

"Phoenix William?" I ask tentatively. Suddenly I'm flooded with emotion. I feel as though I may burst.

He nods and confirms confidently, "Phoenix William."

Twenty weeks later, Phoenix William arrives as foretold on his due date, November 16th, five days after Dimitri's birthday. I struggle through twenty hours of labor without the aid of drugs (I'd been determined to have the child without them), but it is without a doubt the most empowering hours of self-discovery I have ever experienced. The pain is other-worldly, and time is in a state of suspense, but getting through it with Dimitri at my side is one of the proudest moments of my entire life. And we are rewarded with the ultimate prize—a beautiful, healthy baby boy with an angelic face, a head full of dark hair, the most perfect pink lips I've ever seen, and a serious set of lungs. He's precious, a gift ... and he's ours.

Life is sometimes ... a gift.

PART II

Chapter 28
Life depends on a lot of things
Of which love is the most important

Looking back on the last 18 years ...

Phoenix is a gift, and has been the most incredible addition to our family over the past eighteen years. It's moved faster than I thought possible, and suddenly, here I am thinking back on it all.

Ever the perfectionist, I wanted to make sure that every detail of my child's life was as perfect as possible from the very beginning. I was prepared—or so I thought—to be that perfect mother. As much as I thought I had prepared myself, I was reminded at breakneck speed that motherhood, like so many other things, cannot really be planned for, and was completely out of my control. Sure, I read books, took classes, and talked to Sunny, the whole time thinking, "I've got this under control. I can do this. People become mothers every day. It can't be that hard, right?"

Wrong. I was delusional.

Hospitals should start posting signs that read "Godspeed" (or maybe just "Good Luck – you're going to need it!") at the exits of the labor and delivery ward.

Despite the challenges of caring for and raising a child, there's nothing else that compares to the pure joy they bring to you as a parent. The love I feel for Phoenix? There aren't words to accurately describe it. "Love" simply doesn't seem like a big enough word.

Phoenix loved music from the very beginning. His swing sat next to the piano and he loved listening to Dimitri or I play for him. (He turned out to be a big fan of Beethoven, too. Good thing I learned to play a few of his songs.) Late at night as Phoenix got older, I frequently heard the sounds of acoustic guitar coming from his room—the sounds of Dimitri playing him to sleep. It worked just about every time. For me too, God I love acoustic guitar.

301

Children are magical, wondrous little creatures. But they're not exactly predictable. Phoenix excelled at being unique.

He was always tall for his age (whatever age that was).

He started walking the week he turned ten months old.

He painted his first masterpiece at age two (a fingerpaint piece on canvas will hang in our front room forever).

He started playing piano at age three-and-a-half.

He started reading at age four.

He started kindergarten a year early.

He won his third grade spelling bee.

He started playing guitar in middle school.

He's an avid volunteer.

He played striker on his high school soccer team.

He graduated with honors.

He's currently attending New York's Pratt Institute on scholarship studying graphic design.

Every day he makes us more proud than the day before to be his parents, but we didn't need achievements to make us proud. He is Phoenix, and that in and of itself, is enough.

Dimitri cut back on his work the minute Phoenix was born. He didn't travel until Phoenix was almost a year old. He was (and still is), as promised, the best father he can be. Which means he's the best father *ever*. I took a break from school to be home with Phoenix, too. Dimitri and I made a good team. While I worked part time for Sunny, he stayed home and Phoenix and I spent a lot of time in the studio with him late at night while he worked. Sunny also insisted on getting in lots of "Nana time." She took off every Tuesday and Thursday morning and spent the time at our house to be with Phoenix.

Sunny has been an amazing mother-in-law, but to her credit, she's an even better friend. She continues to be the loving, caring, intelligent matriarch of the family, although she'll forever need some looking after. That job fell full-time on Pedro, when they married fifteen years ago. He adores her and they complement each other well. Pedro, with his unassuming, gentle manner, brings joy to everyone he encounters. And he still makes the most amazing chicken enchiladas.

I received my Associates of Arts degree from the community college the summer semester before he was born, and I returned to college at University of Colorado in Boulder the fall that Phoenix turned one. Attending a big university was intimidating, to say the least, especially as a twenty-three year old, married, working mother. I felt old and out of touch, even though my classmates were only a few years younger. Still, I managed. It took five years, but with Dimitri and Sunnys' support, I received my Bachelor's degree with a double major in secondary education and English and a minor in psychology. I think Phoenix and Dimitri cheered louder than anyone else at my graduation (complete with fist pumps and cow bell). It was one of the proudest moments of my life (right behind Phoenix's birth and marrying Dimitri).

I got a job teaching English Composition and Literature that fall at the same high school Dimitri and I graduated from, just down the street from our house (yes, we still live in my parent's house. It's home, and we love it. We could never leave).

Dimitri continued to paint, and the demand for his work never diminished. If anything, his contracts and commissions increased when he returned to work full-time as Phoenix got older. His passion and intensity inspired me as I began my own fledgling career as an educator. He simply loved his work. He taught me that if you make your work your passion, your work is never a job. I carried that very motto over into my teaching career, and it made a world of difference. He continued to play guitar and, as I suspected, grew to be a phenomenal talent.

Sebastian is, well, Sebastian. He has always been independent, charismatic, and confident. He's never wavered. He got his degree in finance and is currently filthy rich working as a stockbroker. I never realized his gift was working with money until he went away to college. That's when Sunny told me that he'd been doing her personal accounting and managing Dimitri's investments since he was in high school. Crazy. He lives in New York City and has a new girlfriend almost every month. He comes home to Colorado for a visit once a month and talks to Dimitri, Sunny, Phoenix and me on the phone almost daily. I love him like a brother.

Our friends are doing well, too. Tate and Monica married after they both graduated from college. They live in Seattle and have two daughters. They're a happy, picture-perfect family, complete with the dog, SUV, and the white picket fence. It's nauseatingly cute (and I mean that in the most complimentary, loving way). John has become a surgeon at a prestigious hospital in Boston. He's still as shy as ever, and to my knowledge he's still single. Maybe he prefers it that way, but I'll never know. He sends us a loaf of banana bread every year at Christmas. (And it's still awesome). Piper has gone through many iterations and evolutions. She is currently a performing artist in Los Angeles. I'm not kidding when I say that she swallows knives and breathes fire—the stuff of traveling circus legends. And she's established quite the following, with fans that loyally follow her from show to show—still the Pied Piper. I love her for all of her quirky, effing goodness.

And Bob, sweet Bob. He was a friend, a mentor, a father figure, and a grandfather figure. Most of all, Bob was a lovely, honorable man. He died when Phoenix was ten after suffering a stroke. The good thing is that he's with Alice now. Dimitri, Phoenix, and I visit their graves every month. We always take a white rose and an apple—cut into quarters, of course.

And now, Phoenix, my baby boy, has grown almost into adulthood. He is bright, curious, and confident (taking after Dimitri). He's kind, and has a wicked, wonderful, sarcastic sense of humor. He's absolutely beautiful—his face takes after mine, but he got his height, his build, and most importantly his gray eyes from his father. He's absolutely, stunningly Phoenix. He has many talents and hobbies that have always come naturally, like art (though he prefers drawing to painting), French (he was fluent by age 11), playing the piano, and his love for reading and writing. I would read to him every night at bedtime until he was old enough to read himself. Then, he began reading to me. This continued through elementary school. Even in middle school and high school, he would frequently sit on my bed beside me late at night and we'd read to one another. Those are some of my fondest memories.

It strikes me that my life would be so different had I never met Dimitri. There is no limit to the love, gratitude, and admiration I feel for him. He is still caring, patient, and calm like no one else can be. His confidence is magnetic and his presence is practically larger than life. His hair is graying at his temples now, but he's still as sexy as ever. Even after all these years, the sight of him still makes my heart race (and he still looks really good in a nice-fitting pair of jeans and Converse).

My life has been so blessed. And to think it could have ended all those years ago before it every really began ... and I would have missed all of this. I would have missed lifelong friends and family who love one another with their whole hearts. I would have missed the hundreds of students who passed through my classroom and touched my life. I would have missed the happiness and sadness, the challenges and triumphs. I would have missed my life—all of it—and most importantly, I would have missed my time with Dimitri and Phoenix.

I've learned that to love means giving everything, body and soul, and expecting nothing in return. The beautiful thing is that if you're loved in return, it will all come back to you ten-fold.

I owe Dimitri everything. From the beginning, he has loved me tirelessly. And I have returned the love. I still do, because it's what I'm destined to do. I will for the rest of my life.

Life is sometimes ... looking back.

Chapter 29
Never misconceive that which is real

Living in the present ...
Learning the truth

I'm 40 years old, and the rest of my life can now be measured in days. At least, that's the doctor's best guess.

Days.

Three months ago, cancer violently crept into my body—into our lives—and I am now faced with my inevitable end, measured in mere days.

Days.

My mind now functions apart from the rest of my body. It's as if my spirit's already on its way out. The doctors and nurses say I'm in a comatose state, which I suppose is a pretty accurate description. The pain that wrecked my body unmercifully is gone now. The haze of the painkilling drugs has cleared. The unfortunate aspect of my newly limited timeline seems to be the fact that at the precise moment focus and clarity returned to my mind, my ability to communicate and move just ... disappeared. Now that my mind is free, my body is restricted to a hospice bed. Seems like poor timing if you ask me.

I am now faced with living out the remaining hours (let's face it anything measured in days, can also be measured in hours) in bed, unable to speak. And you know how hard it is for me to keep my mouth shut. I suppose there's a lesson here, somewhere.

Although I feel flooded with helplessness, I have no regrets. I have already told everyone I care about how much I love them and how much I'll miss them.

I'll miss them *so* much.

The senses that remain have been heightened by this newfound focus and clarity. I maintain my ability to hear and to feel another's touch. It's as though I've gained greater awareness despite my lost abilities.

Phoenix is home on winter break from his first semester of college. He's spending the majority of his time at the hospice with me. He's been here at my bedside all day and has refused breakfast and lunch. He still talks to me as if I'm participating in the conversation (it reminds me of Bob, chatting at me over lunch, all those years ago). The fact that I don't answer his questions or offer my end of the exchange doesn't faze him, and makes me feel warm inside. Today he told me in detail about all of his favorite memories growing up: our vacations to Disney World, Paris, and London; Christmas holidays in Jackson; visiting Grandma Jo and Grandpa Will in Glacier National Park every summer; fishing and skiing with Uncle Sebastian; going to the park with Bob when he was little; eating homemade flan with Nana and Pedro on Sundays; watching Dimitri paint in his studio; and reading in bed with me.

After telling me all about this, my baby boy—now a fully-grown man, even taller than Dimitri—climbs on to the bed and reads to me from my favorite book, *The Catcher in the Rye*. I can feel the impression of Phoenix's body on the mattress next to me, and the warmth of his bare arm against mine. The sensations are heavenly. If I were able to outwardly cry, the beauty and sincerity of the moment would have brought tears to my eyes. Instead I feel them, locked in my heart.

I hear Dimitri's voice soon enough. He's coaxing Phoenix to take a break and get some dinner in the cafeteria. Phoenix kisses me softly on my cheek and the words "I love you, Mom" ring sweetly in my ears.

Dimitri refuses Phoenix's invitation to join him for dinner. Dimitri, like Phoenix, hasn't been eating. He hasn't eaten in two days. He rarely leaves my side. I hear the desperation in his voice when he speaks to the doctors and nurses. When speaking to Phoenix, his voice is slightly stronger and more hopeful—almost believable, if I didn't know him so well. The voice he saves for me when we are alone is both despairing and valiant. It's pure love.

It's the voice I hear now.

"Ronnie, baby. They tell me it's not long now and I know they're right. I have a sixth sense where you're concerned," he says, his voice cracking. He coughs to clear his throat. "I know you can hear me. I have a lot to tell you before you leave me."

His chair scrapes across the linoleum floor as he stands up, and the mattress yields to his body on the bed next to me. The right side of my body tingles where he lies beside me. His fingers slide between mine and he gives my hand a gentle squeeze, though I cannot return the gesture.

His lips are so near my ear it tickles as he begins to speak. "This may, or may not, come as a surprise to you, but this isn't our first rodeo. I guess I should start from the beginning.

"I'm an old soul, Ronnie—extremely old, over 600 years old, at least. This isn't my first go at life. I know it's hard to believe, but I've been living, dying, and coming back again over and over as long as I remember. My first few lifetimes were rough. I lived in what's now Russia, virtually alone, afraid to open myself up to anyone; afraid I was insane because I was all too aware of my abnormality—of the process of reincarnation. I was born to a different set of parents each time, but always on November 11th, and always given the same name, Dimitri. I remembered my past lives, everyone I'd known, everywhere I'd been, everything I'd learned ... and I was convinced I was mad.

"That was until I met a nice couple in London in December of 1467 and knew instantly there was something unique about them. They were different. I was right. They were just like me. They'd already been through the cycle for over two hundred years, so they understood it. They helped me make sense of it all, as much as possible, and helped me accept it. They are my oldest friends, and I've managed to find them in every lifetime since. Just like me, they're born to different sets of parents each time, but there are always a few details that time has never changed. They are always born within a few days of each other, if not on the very same day. They find each other very young, fall in love, and their love for each other grows—it seems like it grows more with every incarnation. And just as they live together, they die together—always at exactly the same time. His parents always bear the same last name—Smith. They name him

William. Her parents always name her Josephine. And every lifetime, for the past 300 years, they give birth to a daughter on October 14th and name her Veronica Josephine Smith.

"I'll never forget the first time I met you. It was love at first sight. I was fourteen and I had tracked down your parents in the outskirts of Paris. The early 1700s in France were brutal. Will and Jo had a small cottage in the country where they raised pigs. It was a fall day, but unseasonably cold and rainy. I can't say they were surprised to see me show up on their doorstep, but the moment we meet in every new life is a little jolting. We were just catching up in front of the fire when you walked through the door. It was late evening and you had just come in from feeding the pigs." There's a smile in his voice now. "You were soaking wet and muddy from head to toe. When Jo introduced you as their fifteen-year-old daughter, I almost fell off my chair. You were beautiful, even with mud caked in your hair and dirt smeared on your cheeks. But I didn't see any of that. You looked exactly like you do today and in every lifetime in between—tall and slender with shiny, chestnut-brown hair, hazel eyes, and those gorgeous, full lips." A small sigh escapes him and he kisses my temple. My skin warms at the touch. "From that moment on, for all of these hundreds of years, I have loved you.

"And in case you're wondering," he says, as though he can see my quizzical look, "we've been through a lot. We've lived many, many lives in many different places: twice in Paris—which, incidentally were your happiest, most contented lives—four times in the United States, and all of the rest in England—mainly around London. I don't know why, or who chooses, or what affects the locations. Sometimes we're rich, but more often than not we're poor. But we always find each other. Of course, I'm already madly in love with you when we meet. The cruel twist in all this is that Will, Jo, and I remember all of our past lives. But you never do. To you, the memories are nothing more than blips of déjà vu. They come to you as flashes of intuition in your dreams. You, of course, don't realize the significance of those glimpses. How could you? But Ronnie, all of those

309

dreams you had, all those flashes of intuition that you chalked up to your vivid imagination—those were *real* memories. Those events actually happened in the past, exactly as you dreamt them.

"Your past also visits you in the form of your preferences and predispositions. You've always loved reading and playing the piano, especially after you discovered Beethoven. As a young girl, you're athletic and prefer sports to playing with dolls. Pink lilies have always been your favorite flower and sandalwood your favorite scent. Artwork, especially my paintings, will forever intrigue you. You've always learned to speak French during your lifetime, even if you didn't live in France or particularly have the need to do so. It's just that your preoccupation with Paris is part of you. You've always been a talented writer and a whiz at math. All of these things you thought just came easily to you were in fact the very things you've *always* been good at and enjoyed. They were easy for you because deep down, you already knew them.

"Oh, and you've always fallen in love with me," he chuckles wistfully. "Usually, it happens quickly—like with Will and Jo. Sometimes, though, you really make me work for it." I can hear the smile in his voice.

"And with my extreme luck, not only are you always the same gorgeous, intelligent girl, but you're also caring, giving, and kind. You take care of everyone else before worrying about yourself. You're confident and opinionated, which means you've never been one to bite your tongue or hold back. You choose your friends carefully and keep them close for life due to your sense of commitment and loyalty. And your wit and sarcasm make being around you so much fun. You have a birthmark that always appears on the left side of your back. It's always shaped like a paw print. There's a black speck in your right iris. The habit of licking your lips when you are in deep concentration has followed you for hundreds of years, and I cannot remember a night ever that you haven't sighed just before you've fallen asleep." He clears his throat and silence settles over me. I feel his warm breath on my ear. "And … " his voice trails off, croaky and broken. He clears his throat again and takes several deep breaths. Suddenly I don't know if I want him to proceed. His words are filling me up and breaking my heart at the same time. Finally he clears his throat again, and then continues in a whisper, "And I love it … *all of it.*"

I feel him squeeze me closer to him. I feel him take a deep breath, I feel him swallow, and I feel his chest rise as he continues. "You're probably wondering," he says, after a pause, "about now how Sebastian fits into this picture. I know from the start you've felt a strong connection to him. Sebastian came to us in your second lifetime. It was the mid-1700s and I found you, Will, and Jo living in England. They had more money than most, since Will was a successful blacksmith. Will and Jo took in an abandoned, orphaned newborn baby two years after you were born, and they named him Sebastian. They raised him as their son and you never knew him to be anything other than your little brother. You two were very close. By the time we met you were thirteen, I was twelve, and Sebastian was eleven. Sebastian and I bonded instantly. He felt like the brother I'd never had. It's funny— in each lifetime since then, Sebastian has been born as my own brother. He is always born on September 4th the year following my birth. He is always named Sebastian, and looks and acts like only Sebastian can. And like Will, Jo, and me, he remembers every detail of his past lives. He has always considered you his sister; he loves you very much, Ronnie. I'm sure you know that.

"I've saved the best for last," he says warmly. "*Our Phoenix.* I wish I knew what to say, or how to explain it. Phoenix is still a bit of a mystery to me. The most *beautiful, life-changing, wonderful* mystery I have come across in 600 years. I honestly don't know where he came from." I can almost hear the blush in his voice. "I mean, I *know* where he came from … but I was never supposed to be able to father a child. In all my childhoods, I contract a severe case of the mumps, even despite modern day vaccines, and in each lifetime I am sterile as a result. So, although you and I have had many experiences, as you once called them—*hundreds* of years of experiences—we've never had children. Not until

311

now. I don't know what was miraculously different this time, but I only hope that we are blessed with him in every lifetime to come. The thought of leaving him behind is too much to bear.

"I know how smart you are, Ronnie. By now the wheels are turning and you're putting together all the pieces inside that lovely head of yours. Everything is starting to make sense. The way I always knew everything about you and your past even before you told me. The fact that Sebastian looked familiar to you the first time you saw him. All of your likes and dislikes and all of your dreams. I also know that you must be working through the mathematical details. I'll lay it out for you. Will and Jo died 22 years ago, which means—taking into account their reincarnation from birth—they must be 21 years old now. No doubt they found each other young, as they always do, and have married. You are always born on October 14th, and given that today is January 7th, your end is drawing near." He inhales deeply and wipes his nose with a tissue. I feel the wetness from his tears seeping into the pillow we're sharing. "You always pass in January, but never on the same day. You'll be born this coming October 14th to Will and Jo, again." His voice catches again. "It's times like these I almost hate them for being so anxious to put their family back together. But after having Phoenix in our lives, I can no longer begrudge them. They'll be *so* happy to see you again." A quiet sob escapes him. He's stroking my hair now with his free hand. The other is still gently clutching mine. "Inevitably, I'll be born to my new parents the following November 11th, and Sebastian will come along the following September 4th. The flip side to our re-birth is, of course, that this life must come to an end. We know it's coming which, in the past, has somehow made it easier to prepare for. I know that probably sounds strange, but without you, life is *lifeless*. During our time apart I think of nothing else, except being with you again. Poor Sebastian is lost when we're both gone. I feel sorry for him. He always has to finish out the last year alone. I think that's why he never lets anyone else into his life for long; it's too painful for him to lose them. And he knows loss better than any of us.

"The one variable this time around is, of course, our son. The thought of Phoenix losing both of us over the next year, the thought of leaving him alone, is almost unspeakable. I promise to make the most of my last year with him. And then, Sebastian will watch over him after I'm gone. We've already talked about it at length. And he will make sure that Sunny and Pedro are there for Phoenix when his time comes to an end." Dimitri sobs silently as the weight of the situation bears down on him. His body shudders next to mine. I wish I could comfort him, hold him, and tell him everything will be okay, because after hearing everything that he's shared with me I know that it will be okay. Everything makes sense now.

It's then that I hear footsteps enter the room. It's Phoenix. I would recognize his relaxed gait anywhere. Dimitri hears him, too, and raises himself off the bed, blowing his nose in the process.

Phoenix talks quietly, as if I can't hear him for the moment. "Dad, are you okay? Did something happen?"

Dimitri draws him into a hug and his voice is muffled. "Nothing happened. I was just chatting with your mom. We don't have much time left with her and there was a lot left I needed her to know before she moves on."

It's quiet for several minutes, and so still in the room I wonder if I'm alone. Then I hear shuffling and feel weight descend on either side of the bed. My two favorite people grasp my hands, Dimitri is on my right side and Phoenix on my left. I feel their love pulsing through their hands into my own, and I wonder if they feel mine flowing out in return. My focus is beginning to wane and I feel myself nodding off, as if I'm just too tired to stay awake. It doesn't scare me. It would be almost comforting if I didn't know what I was leaving behind.

But I *will* see them again. My Dimitri, my soul mate— he will find me. My hope is that I take everything I've just learned into this next life: all of the memories, and the knowledge, and the feelings ... and that I *remember* it. And I know deep in my heart that I will see Phoenix again. He is

313

destined to be our son, again and again, over and over. He is part of us now. He's part of our recurring story.

As darkness creeps into my subconscious I hear the heart monitor next to the bed stutter and slow.

I hear Phoenix begin to cry. He's squeezing my hand in both of his now and his head is resting on my chest. His warm tears soak through my thin hospice gown.

Dimitri is brushing his thumb lovingly across the back of my other hand and he's stroking my hair gently. I hear him sniffle and gulp as he tries to hold back the tears.

The heart monitor is beeping an alarm now and has almost come to a standstill. My time has come.

All at once, I feel their lips on my cheeks at the same time, and their whispers in my ears.

"I love you Mom."

"Je t'aime Ronnie. Forever."

Days.

Then hours.

Now seconds.

Seconds left to tell them goodbye.

I squeeze their hands. I know it's weak and barely perceptible but unbelievably, my fingers grip theirs. They both squeeze back. My eyelids flutter open and they swim into focus. Their beautiful faces are only inches from mine. I look at Phoenix first. His eyes are wide. "I am so proud of you, my beautiful boy," I say in a voice as clear as day. "I love you more than you'll ever know. I'll see you again." His tears have given way to sobs.

Then, with great effort, I look to Dimitri. Tears are streaming down his cheeks now, but he's smiling. "Thank you for sharing your life with me … and for loving me … always. I'll be counting the days until we meet again. I love you forever and ever … and the lifetime after that."

My eyelids are too heavy now, and as they collapse they take everything with them, plunging into a deep, peaceful nothingness.

Life is sometimes … just life … and death.

Epilogue
Invariably my story ends as it begins

I love coming to the art museum; I always have. We used to rush through it all, moving from gallery to gallery, all the images blurring together, because my mom, Jo, can never seem to slow down. Even a day at the museum is condensed down into an hour-long affair, skimming past most exhibits while lingering (I use the term loosely) on the ones she loves. It's not that she doesn't appreciate the beauty of it all, it's just that standing still in one place for more than two seconds is challenging for her. My father, Will, used to come along, but I suspect it was only to spend time with the two of us. He travels a lot and we see him only a day or two a week.

Last month, when I turned fifteen, I persuaded my parents to start letting me ride the bus to the art museum alone. I arrive in the morning and leave just before closing time. I make the journey every other Saturday. Sometimes I talk a friend into coming with me, but usually I go alone. My friends are boys, *teenage* boys, who are more focused on sports (and girls) than art. Which is fine, I don't mind going alone. I'm independent by nature.

I don't know what it is about the art museum that I love so much. I'm not artistic myself, not really, but I've always been drawn to art, paintings especially. It's not like I'm an art aficionado or anything. I don't know that much about art. I just know what I like or what I think is pretty. I don't draw or paint, that's not where my talent lies. I prefer to play the piano. I wouldn't say I'm particularly gifted in that department either, but I have a spot soft for Beethoven and I've been playing as long as I can remember.

Sometimes I sit on a bench, like I am right now, in front of one of my favorite paintings, and I allow myself to get lost in it. I get lost in the feeling, the possibility, and the beauty. And sometimes I write, like I am right now. Sometimes I write poetry. Sometimes I write fiction. Today I write a journal entry of sorts. I have a collection of them, that I guess for all intents and purposes is a journal or diary. I call it *Memoires* (that's memories in French). Pretentious?

315

Maybe. I just love the language. Sometimes the entries are about feelings, or events, but mostly they are collections of dreams. I have a very vivid imagination. And the most beautiful boy meets me there ... in my dreams ... almost every night.

The room is filling up with people and I feel the urge to move on to the next space. The inspiration has been sucked dry by the invasion of the masses. I gather my notebooks and put them in my bag, which is overflowing. I'm temporarily distracted by the amount of stuff I'm trying to put in my bag. Why do I have so much stuff?

I sling the bag over my shoulder and delicately snake my way through the crowd. I'm almost to the hallway when I risk a second look in my bag—just a quick inventory to make sure I didn't leave my favorite pen behind on the bench.

Just as I'm about to look up and get my bearings to find the exit leading to the hallway, it happens. I step forward too quickly, and my foot snags the side of some innocent by-stander's shoe. It's too late to avoid the fall, but I try to execute it with as much grace as I can muster. I fall to the right, as the foot I've just assaulted is on the left. I land splayed out, face down, in the open hallway. My bag skids across the floor and stops against the wall on the other side. I'm not hurt but the humiliation is absolutely painful. For a moment, I rest my face on the backs of my hands, which have broken the worst of my fall.

It all happens in slow motion. I raise my head and sneak a peek through my hair that is shielding me from the person to whom I owe an apology.

I see black Converse shoes. They're worn through in places, but they're clean and neat. God, I love Converse. Guys look really hot in them.

I sweep my hair aside and smile weakly, my eyes running from the shoes, to the dark jeans (they fit well, that's two points to the assaulted), to the faded T-shirt fit snugly over a thin, lean, muscular build, and then the instant before I see his face, his hand is extended down blocking my view. He's trying to help me up. With the flames of embarrassment rising in my cheeks, I accept his hand. It's strong and firm, but gentle at the same time. He pulls me slowly to a standing position, where I can get a better look at him. He's tall and skinny; just *right* skinny. I *love* just right skinny. I look up at him and he smiles. The smile lights up his beautiful gray eyes.

My breath catches in my throat. It's the boy from my dreams. I would know him anywhere. I exhale slowly and a smile melts through my lips, across my cheeks, and settles deep inside my heart.

His smile turns mischievous.

I love it when he does that.

"Hi, my name's Veronica."

"Hi, I'm Dimitri." His voice is quiet, but confident.

Life is sometimes ... memorable, wet (and beautiful), a racing heart, like a dream, tingly and covered with goose bumps, gentlemanly, sexy, imperfect, consumed with guilt, bruised and broken, over-thought, destined, an epiphany, mind-blowing, dead, whatever your heart tells you, incessant, finding something to live for, just a series of goodbyes, auspicious, enduring, just right, your past and your future, ceremonious, burning, a waiting game, a gift, looking back, just life ... and death ... *never-ending*.

Acknowledgments

Achieving dreams is hard work. It requires tireless dedication, luck, and an amazing support system—in equal parts. That being said, I would like to thank, from the bottom of my heart, the following:

My editor, Monica Parpal: who blessed me with her intelligence, talent, honesty, and kindness. She is a rock star! Without her, *All of It* would not have reached publication.

My first readers: Brandon, Mom, Marg, Barb, Robin, Debbie, Anne, and Liz. Your encouragement and support made all the difference. You helped make my dream a reality.

My parents: who always told me that anything is possible. They've cheered me on through every stage of my life. I still enjoy making them proud.

Creativity requires constant inspiration. For me inspiration comes in many forms: people, books, nature, and art. Personally, my writing process requires music. Constantly. Lots and lots of music. So, to anyone out there creating and sharing your music with the world—I thank you. Music provokes thought. Music evokes emotion. Music makes everything better ...

And last, but not least, thank you to my husband, Brandon (my Dimitri), and our son, Phoenix: my two favorite people on the entire planet. I love you. (Love isn't a big enough word).

Thank you, thank you, thank you.

About the author ...

Kim Holden lives in Denver, Colorado with her husband, Brandon, and their son, Phoenix.

Let's be friends.
We'll hang out.
It'll be fun.
Visit me here:
www.kimholdenbooks.com
www.facebook.com/kimholdenauthor

Also by Kim Holden:
Bright Side
Gus (coming 2015)

Made in the USA
Lexington, KY
16 January 2015